KERRY BARNES, born in 1964, grew up on a council estate in South East London. Pushed by her parents to become a doctor, she entered the world of science and became a microbiologist. After studying law and pharmaceuticals, her career turned to medicine. Having dyslexia didn't deter her from her passion for writing, she began when her daughter was born thirty years ago. Once her children had grown up she moved to the Kent coast and now writes full time.

Also by Kerry Barnes

Deceit
The Rules
The Choice

The Hunted

KERRY BARNES

ONE PLACE. MANY STORIES

HQ
An imprint of HarperCollins*Publishers* Ltd
1 London Bridge Street
London SE1 9GF

This paperback edition 2019

1

First published in Great Britain by
HQ, an imprint of HarperCollins*Publishers* Ltd 2019

A catalogue record for this book is available from the British Library.

ISBN: 978-0-00-831784-3

Printed and bound in Great Britain by
CPI Group (UK) Ltd, Croydon CR0 4YY

Bear, my shadow, my best buddy.
Gone but forever in my heart.

Prologue

A lamp cast its soft glow onto a round table positioned in the middle of the room. The closed, heavy red drapes gave the room a daunting – almost eerie – feel, as if the assembled group was about to engage in a séance.

Dread twisted around Ronnie's stomach. For a moment, he didn't want to speak, so afraid his words would come out as just a mere squeak, and that he would look less than a worthy man. The eyes that glared back at him were narrow and beady, silently interrogating him, or perhaps posed to intimidate. Either way, he was now in the lion's den, entirely at their mercy.

Was his fiancée really worth it? Her beautiful face and long shapely legs popped into his head – yes, she definitely was. So, he had either to prove his worth or be fucked off by her brother and his close allies. Until now, he hadn't quite grasped the power of these collective Jewish men. Sensing the intense atmosphere that pervaded the room, he knew they were more than just un-assuming businessmen.

He presumed this first meeting would be a case of proving

himself. After all, he was going to marry their queen, their worshipped sister. Now, he surmised that this meeting wasn't all about giving him the rundown on how to treat his wife-to-be. It was more than that – something much more profound, almost cultlike.

The way in which they sat side by side with their hands clasped on the table symbolizing an unspoken bond between them, did it mean more than honour among family? After all, the two men who were scrutinizing him weren't brothers by blood, they were brothers in a different sense. He suspected that they were united by a pledge.

Ronnie could feel that they were going to initiate him into something – whatever it was, he would soon find out.

The silence, which was perhaps a mere few seconds, seemed to linger. They were sussing him out, trying to read his thoughts.

He almost jumped when the taller of the two men, his future brother-in-law, spoke. 'I understand you are a man who wants to earn money . . .' He paused and glared, waiting for affirmation by a nod or a yes.

Ronnie twisted his head slightly, questioning their statement.

'We have a common enemy,' the speaker continued.

Ronnie raised his brow and waited, hoping he would get to the point.

'Arthur Regan!' He hissed the name through gritted teeth.

Ronnie's eyes widened. Yes, it was true: he and his brother Frank hated the Regan crew; in fact, they loathed them with a passion.

Arthur Regan was only nineteen and had already taken charge of all the knocked-off gear that entered Bermondsey. His little empire was strong-handed and growing fast. They may be just out of nappies, but they were taking over the manor and earning good money.

The business that had once been run by the Harman family had now been taken from under his nose just because the Regans had more muscle, and, worse, more front. The dealers, the robbers, and the pretty women were all being drawn in by Arthur's success.

So what was he left with? Fuck all, that's what.

He nodded and remained silent.

'You are aware, I trust, that when you marry my sister, you and your brother become an integral part of our family? With that comes accountability!'

Ronnie frowned. 'Of course, but what's that got to do with Arthur Regan?' With the menacing expression staring back at him, he wondered if he should have been a little less direct.

Ronnie watched in fascination as both men looked at each other and silently rolled up their sleeves to show a mark on their right wrist.

Still oblivious, Ronnie shrugged. Again, he wondered if his body language was really doing him any favours. 'Sorry. Am I missing something?'

'You have a reason to take out the Regans' firm. Although it may be very different from ours, it amounts to the same thing. We want Arthur Regan and his men hunted down for the scum they are. His home, his business, his family, and his fucking name will be ripped away, piece by fucking piece. That bastard and his followers shouldn't be walking the streets, making money, or even breathing the same air as us. So, if you want to marry my sister and enter our family, you must agree to be on our side, no matter what it takes to ensure their pathetic lives and those of their children are tortured and tormented until they are living like worms under a rock!'

A million thoughts tumbled over themselves as Ronnie tried to digest what the Jew was saying. Then, once again, his words were direct. 'What have they done to you?'

'Those cunts killed my brother, my beloved sister's twin.' The tall Jewish man looked to his left at the man seated beside him. 'And they killed his brother too.'

Ronnie glanced at the shorter man. A sudden shiver ran

through his body, and for a second, he thought he was staring at the devil himself. Portrayed in those dark, expressionless eyes and lopsided grin was a cruel streak.

Leaning back in his chair, Ronnie grinned. This was it. He didn't have to consider pledging himself to this pact, cult, or whatever the fuck it was. He was in. The Jews had money and a tight, nasty firm, and he had the prize bride. He had a gripe with the Regans, and so what better way to take over the manor than to do so with the help of a bunch of wealthy psycho Jews? Even better, he would take back what he believed was rightfully his.

He gazed down once more at the strange marks on their wrists and was startled by a rustling sound from across the room. He could just make out a brooding figure in the shadows. Something in his hand gleamed from the soft light of the lamp. In a sudden rush of panic, Ronnie's forehead formed beads of sweat and his mouth became as dry as a horse's salt lick. As the daunting man approached the table, the side lamp shone a light on the tool he had in his hand. Ronnie's heart rate levelled as soon as he realized it was only a tattoo gun.

PART ONE

Chapter 1

Kent, 2002

The summer evening was drawing to a close. Mike could just soak up the last of the pink shimmer in the sky before he would have to face the cold, hard-faced bitch he called his wife. As he stepped out of his Porsche and felt his feet crunch under the newly laid gravel drive, he sucked in the warm air and braced himself.

Sacha, the housekeeper, opened the door before he had a chance to put the key in the lock. Her sweet round face was loaded with anxiety. It made Mike bite down on his lip and flare his nostrils. 'Go on, love, tell me. What the fuck has she been up to now?'

Sacha lowered her gaze and shook her head. 'Sorry, Mr Regan, but I just can't do it anymore. I am handing in my notice . . . I can't, I just can't.' Her voice cracked, as she tried to hold back the tears. Mike held out his big meaty arms for his housekeeper to fall into. He'd known she wouldn't stay in the job for much longer. Sacha was too sweet and inoffensive. Dealing with Jackie was just too much for her.

He held her tight and stroked her long black hair. 'Come on, love. Don't get yaself upset. It's okay. I understand.'

She gently pulled away. 'I'm so worried about little Ricky, he is so . . . well, affected. Yes, maybe that's the word. I will come back tomorrow, Mr Regan, to take him to school, but after that, I have to leave. She's too . . .' Sacha looked into Mike's compassionate grey eyes and gave a smile loaded with sorrow. 'She's just hard work.'

Mike heard the cab driving up towards the house. He nodded and winked for her to go. He would deal with the aftermath.

As Sacha bustled herself into the taxi, she looked back to see Mike disappear inside the house of misery. Gutted she had to leave, she knew, nevertheless, that Jackie was becoming utterly out of control. The last straw was when she took a slap from her, for ushering little Ricky away before Jackie could say another cruel thing to him. Sacha would have loved to have swapped places with Jackie. Mike was perfect in her eyes, a Gerard Butler lookalike, rich and generous too. However, he was also faithful to his wife.

Mike stepped inside, gently closing the door, hoping that Jackie was crashed out somewhere. The house was quiet, so he crept up the curved staircase and walked along the corridor and into Ricky's room. He gulped back the lump that had lodged in his throat. There, asleep, still hugging a pillow, was his little six-year-old son. The curtains were drawn, and his night light was just bright enough to show that his face was still moist from crying. There, among the child's dreams, he witnessed another sob. Mike's heart ached for his son – his sweet little chubby boy, with the biggest eyes, button nose, and wayward floppy fringe. He wanted to pull him into his arms and hug him tight, but he didn't want to wake him. Quietly, he closed the door and walked back down the stairs and into the lounge. His shoulders relaxed when he realized he was alone. Loosening his tie, he went to the bar and poured a brandy, slowly allowing the bitter bite to warm the back

8

of his throat. He held the bottle in his hand and rolled his eyes. Thank God she didn't like brandy, or his vintage collection would be consumed by now. Jackie was content with a litre of vodka each day and didn't care if it was called Grey Goose or Mother Goose, as long as it got her pissed.

Mike took his weighty crystal tumbler, with a double shot of brandy, out through the French doors and onto the patio, where the garden lights automatically came on and flooded the pool area.

With Sacha handing in her notice, and the concerning call he'd received earlier regarding his arms import, he really needed to think about what to do, now that both work and home were a mess. He shuddered and gulped back the drink. If it was true, and his deal had been intercepted by the government agents, he was looking at going down for a long time. *Christ, what would happen to Ricky?* He had to keep his head straight. First thing tomorrow, he would call a meeting at which only his trusted men would be present. He stared as far as his eyes could see and surveyed the walled perimeter. For a second, he thought he saw something glimmer, and his heart stopped beating. *I am getting fucking paranoid now.* He had to get some sleep; the last few days had been intense, and he needed a clear head for the morning.

As he went back into the house and upstairs, the inebriated snoring from their bedroom made him pass by silently, hoping his wife wouldn't wake up. The last room on the left, the blue room, was cool and inviting. He removed his clothes and slid between the sheets, allowing the fresh cotton to engulf him. Just as he was about to drift off, a loud bang woke him and rattled his nerves. There she was in the doorway.

'Where have you been, ya fucking wanker!' spat Jackie, full of piss and vinegar.

Mike sat up and rolled his eyes; she was off on one again. For a second, he stared and wondered why the fuck he was still with her. Half dressed in a designer blouse and just her knickers, she looked like a streetwalker. Her hair was a mess with knotted extensions and her oversized, collagen-filled lips were twisted in an ugly fashion to match her tight, beady eyes. Botox, boob jobs and a fake tan had done her no favours. She was only twenty-six and could have passed for eighteen a couple of years ago. Why she'd had to have all that shit done was beyond him. He didn't recognize her anymore, but that wasn't the issue. It was her wild personality that had truly changed beyond recognition.

'Well, where 'ave ya been?' she demanded, standing there swaying with her hands on her hips. Even the sleep hadn't sobered her up.

'Fuck off, Jackie, and leave me alone, will ya!'

'You don't know what it's like for me to be stuck in this place all fucking day with that brat whining!'

Mike felt his blood rushing through his veins. If she'd been a man, he would have leaped from the bed and smashed her head straight through the window. He clenched his fists and flared his nostrils.

'Leave it, Jackie, and go back to bed,' he said calmly.

Jackie wanted a row; she needed to vent her anger, but he wasn't having any of it.

'Oh, that's it, Mike. You just bury ya fucking head in the sand . . . Look at ya. Think ya better than me, acting like I don't even fucking exist.' With her face screwed up, she egged him on, eager for a fight. Anything to get his attention – any attention.

'I'm warning you, Jackie. Go back to bed, or I'll forget you're a fucking woman.'

His deep raspy voice would have turned her on a few years ago but not anymore. She hated him – she hated everyone. Now she saw a change in his expression; it was a coldness that crept across his face. She hadn't seen him like that before and thought perhaps she'd pushed him too far, but the drink fuelled her on and she lashed back again. 'Oh yeah, fucking hardman. Well, you lay a fucking finger on me and you just watch. You'll be seeing that kid of yours from behind bars, and only if I fucking say so. I have so much on you, Mike, that you'll go down for a long time.'

That was the last straw. The thought that she could grass, and even worse have control over their son, incensed him, taking him to a pitch that would see the red mist come down. In one fluid movement, he leaped from the bed and lunged towards her, grabbing her by the hair and throwing her to the floor.

Her cheek caught the corner of the bedside cabinet, causing her to let out a dramatic scream.

Sucking in a deep lungful of air, he slowly calmed down and glared at his wife, who was squirming around on the floor.

'You bastard!' she yelled with a wilful jeer.

He sighed with relief that he hadn't killed her. But when he clocked her malevolent expression, he wished he had. No woman had ever pushed him as far. Wife or not, no one would make threats concerning his son. Yet hitting her went against everything he stood for. Things would have to change.

He had only been with Jackie for seven years, having met her at his twenty-seventh birthday bash. She was stunning back then, a natural beauty. Her confidence was what had attracted him to her. The party was a big affair with friends and wannabe mates all trying to buddy up to him. He had money and a reputation, but he wasn't stupid; he kept only a handful of close friends who were his business colleagues.

Then Jackie arrived with his brother's girlfriend. Tall and slim, with blonde waves tumbling down her back and shrouded in assurance, she swanned over to him and gave him a birthday kiss. He remembered the sweet smell of some expensive perfume, and how he'd decided to engage in conversation. Little did he know that all the bull she plied him with that night was just to get that fucking great diamond on her finger. She was a wild spirit and had no intention of sticking to one man. Her subtle make-up and sweet expression were deliberately aimed at getting what she wanted. She wasn't sweet at all, but by the time he realized what she was all about, he was up the aisle saying 'I do' and little Ricky was on his way.

He should have listened to his head when he saw the subtle changes; after all, no one can hide their real persona for very long. Perhaps it was the age gap, for she never settled down, always wanting to party and get pissed. But he was firm and put a stop to her antics with frustrating consequences. So she turned to drinking indoors during the day.

She got to her feet and shot him an acid glare. 'You, Mike, will wish you'd never done that.' She wobbled away, back to their bedroom, leaving him wound up and needing another stiff drink.

As he made his way down the stairs, his phone vibrated in his trouser pocket. He checked his watch; it was 2.30 a.m.

It was Eric, his brother. 'What's up? It's fucking early doors, mate.'

'You best get back over to the lock-up. We've discovered something you might wanna see.'

Mike ran his big thick hands through his loose waves and then scratched his bristles.

'Okay, mate. Give me half an hour.'

He didn't ask what. He didn't like to talk too much on the phone, just in case. He dashed back up the stairs two at a time and retrieved his shirt from the back of the chair in the spare room. Jackie was quiet, her mumbling and cursing having died off, so he assumed she'd gone back to sleep. Outside was deathly quiet. There wasn't even a sign of a breeze. So, when he clicked the key fob to his Porsche, the sound of the locks releasing, although expected, still made him jump. He was tired, the lack of sleep taking its toll on his nerves. As he drove towards the entrance, the gates automatically opened. Deciding to have one last look in the rear-view mirror, he gave a sigh of relief. Apart from the outside lights, the house was in total darkness.

Good, she was still asleep.

His lock-up was in the middle of West Kingsdown in Kent, cleverly hidden in a place called Knatts Valley.

Centuries ago, the area had been divided up into plots of land for smallholdings. Over the years, the residents had turned the dwellings into large houses with stables or workshops, and some even had log cabins for holiday retreats. Through the middle ran a narrow lane, hardly wide enough for two cars, so if any police vehicles travelled along it, the residents, most of whom lived on the wrong side of the law, would be instantly notified. The lane was dark and just up ahead was the turning onto his land. From the front it looked like two large log cabins, and behind was a workshop cleverly disguised as an average-looking garage. Smaller cabins surrounded it, and so for anyone passing through, it would appear as a holiday let. However, it was a carefully secured place of business that only a very select few knew about.

He turned off his headlights and parked behind the first log cabin and slowly crept towards the side door of the workshop. He had a gun in his hand, in case this was a set-up. But then he saw Eric appear and look around. Eric spotted Mike and waved his hand, beckoning him to come in.

From the outside, the lock-up looked small, but once inside, the space seemed to open up. In fact, it was large enough to house twelve cars, a small office, and a kitchenette. The building was lined with steel shutters inside and almost impossible to break into.

There in the middle of the room, under a spotlight, bound and gagged, was Travis, their new recruit. Surrounding him were overwhelmingly daunting men. Willie Ritz – tall, lanky, mean, and hard-faced; Ted Stafford or Staffie for short – who looked as though he was made of plasticine, with a bobbly nose and oversized biceps, and Lou Baker – who looked a little like Johnny Depp – greeted Mike with a nod. Then they looked at Eric to announce the news.

Mike put his gun back inside the belt of his trousers and kept his eyes on Travis. In a firm and controlled voice, he said, 'So, Eric, what's all this about?'

Eric was livelier than Mike, but being only ten months apart, they could have passed for twins when they were younger. Mike, the eldest, commanded more respect and his cool demeanour earned it. Whilst this six-foot-seven giant, weighing around twenty-five stone, was an intimidating sight, it was the intensity of his eyes that could strike terror into anyone who was brazen enough to front him out. Eric, though, didn't have the same presence about him, being slightly shorter and with a body that had once been muscular but had now turned to fat. Even his voice lacked authority, and when he spoke, he did so in a less measured way, often allowing his mouth to run away with him.

History was repeating itself. Like their parents, who had created the Regans' firm, Mike and his friends were also inseparable. As close as brothers, they worked together, played together, and more importantly trusted each other. Their criminal activities had earned them enough to move away from Bermondsey and they now lived in the cleaner surrounds of Kent.

By the time the boys reached adulthood, they were notorious. Living the straight road, paying taxes, and working for a boss just didn't appeal, not when they saw how their parents could earn a banker's annual salary from a single overnight job. So it stood to reason that they would all follow in their fathers' footsteps – and what better teachers than parents? Like being an apprentice, they learned the art of safecracking, ballistics, reading architectural drawings, and negotiating. As for understanding the tools of the trade for crafting their work, they were masters at extracting information and handing out punishment.

It was a rule that they had each other's backs, come what may, like their fathers before them. They wouldn't trust anyone outside the firm, especially once they were taking on bigger money-making crimes, like the import and export of firearms. Inexplicably, however, their activities had somehow come to the attention of the authorities.

'I think I'm right in assuming you've found the grass then, Eric?'

Eric gave his brother a cocky smirk and a nod. 'Oh, Mikey, my dear bruvver, I've found a lot more than that.'

Mike was intrigued. 'Oh yeah, and what's that then, Eric?'

'Well, ya see, we were under the assumption that there was a little spy in the camp, an informant for the Ol' Bill. But we were wrong, Mikey. See, Travis 'ere, ain't working for the Filth . . .' He kicked Travis's chair. 'Are ya, Travis?'

Mike inclined his head and stepped closer. 'Oh, is that so?'

The others were holding their breath, waiting to see if on this occasion Mike would lose the plot and rip Travis limb from limb. But they should really have known that was unlikely, given his track record. Mike was a strategic thinker, rarely losing his cool. He had twin gifts. Whilst there were not many men who could take Mike on one-on-one, he also had an innate craftiness about him. It had eased them out of trouble on many occasions, enhancing their firm's credibility.

Even his father and so-called uncles saw him as a force to be reckoned with. He'd always been the same. As a ten-year-old, he seemed to have more balls than the others and was lethal with his fists or any weapon at hand.

Nevertheless, their new venture took them into the realm of possible breaches of national security – it was Mike and his firm's biggest challenge to date – and their major concern was MI5 becoming nosy.

Their latest worrying matter was one of their more secure lock-ups in London getting turned over by the police. The cars were ready to be stripped and refitted, with all the gun parts carefully concealed in every orifice inside the car panels, before they were shipped to Ireland. But, two days ago, the police had surrounded the lock-up and turned the place over.

So there had to be a snitch. Luckily for Mike, though, his own inside man, DI Evans, had tipped them off. Mike was livid because that little tip-off had cost him more than the poxy guns were worth. Nevertheless, it had saved him from serving a big lump inside. But there was still a problem. There was a grass. And it wouldn't be the Irish buyers because they had no idea where the lock-ups were. And in any case, why would they want to sell the Regan firm down the river? It was a complete head-scratcher.

'So, who are ya working for, then, if it ain't the Filth?' asked Mike, in a menacing tone that would put the wind up any grown man.

Travis knew he was small fry in comparison to the men surrounding him. Right now, he was shitting himself. He knew it was over: there was no mercy showing on Mike's face. Those icy, emotionless grey eyes made his bowels move of their own accord.

It was true. Mike did have a look that was like death calling, a deadpan steely expression that unnerved many a man.

Staffie, the shortest of the five men, at five foot seven, with no neck, and a goofy, childlike grin, stepped forward holding a torque wrench. ''Ere, Mikey, ya don't wanna get ya hands all messy, now do ya, mate?'

Mike put his hand up. 'Hang on a minute. Before I smash the granny out of this geezer, I wanna know all the facts.'

Staffie nodded, chuckled, and then placed the wrench back on the tool rack.

'Take that gag outta his mouth. I think he wants to talk.'

Travis's eyes glistened as he nervously clocked the blowtorch that was resting on the long wooden bench. Terrifying thoughts pierced his mind. Jesus! A childhood memory of catching his arm over the steaming kettle reminded him of the pain, but he knew that would be nothing in comparison to a naked flame. He swooned and felt the warm liquid run down his leg. Totally consumed by fear, his muscles became flaccid and his bowels relaxed. He wasn't cut out for this work and stupidly he hadn't looked beyond the actuality of getting caught. However, now he was facing the consequences head-on.

Willie Ritz, the big meathead with the scar that ran from his forehead down to his chin, cut the gag from Travis using his diver's knife, his favourite tool. None of the firm ever understood why it was still his weapon of choice, even after an older gang of thugs had taken it from him in a street brawl and run that evil-looking jagged blade down his face. But Willie still turned that knife around in his hand and even kissed the blade. As tall as Mike, but with less meat on his bones, Willie liked to snort cocaine, especially if any violence was to be had. It raised his level of anger and sent him screwy and a little unpredictable. Whenever Willie's eyes were like saucers, and glared a piercing blue colour, Mike knew his friend had gone over the top, and so he would remove the supply that Willie kept in a pouch shoved down the front of his trousers. Only Mike could get away with it – no one else would dare.

With trepidation, Travis took a few deep breaths and stared wide-eyed, waiting for the inevitable.

'I think you'd better tell me what you've been up to, and, more importantly, who the fuck for.' Mike didn't shout or even raise his voice.

Travis looked at Eric and then back at Mike. 'No, listen, please, ya got me all wrong. I, er . . . I was just taking pictures for meself, no one else, I swear.' He knew it sounded stupid. Really, he had no excuse.

Mike looked at his brother. 'Well, Eric, this prick ain't playing ball, so you'd best tell me what happened.'

'Gladly. We all thought that the Ol' Bill were tipped off, yeah, and I dunno, I just had this sneaky suspicion that it was this little weasel, and so I followed the rat to his house. But, see, Mikey, Travis, 'ere, ain't too clever. He left his phone right there on the dashboard of his car with the doors unlocked. So, I thought I'd just have a little butcher's, ya know, to see if the little fucker had any numbers that I would recognize. Well, fuck me, lo and behold, on the screen was a photo of the London lock-up, and so, after 'aving a mooch through the other pics, I found what I can only describe as incriminating evidence. So, I ran in through his back door and there he was in the kitchen, taking his boots off. The shit-licker only had one of our guns tucked inside his fucking Timberlands.'

Mike looked back at Travis, who, in turn, looked as though he was going to pass out. 'So, how do you know he ain't working for the Filth, Eric? 'Cos I'm guessing you ain't completely sure on that score.'

Eric smiled confidently. 'I ripped the shirt off his back and he wasn't wired. I tied him up, and the boys and me ransacked his pad. There was no sign of the Ol' Bill being involved. So, we shoved him into the boot and brought him back here.'

Mike shook his head. 'Eric, Eric, you have a lot to learn. I dunno, I still think he's an informant, but I'll let Travis tell me the facts.' He turned back to Travis with a sneer. 'You will, won't ya, Travis? You'll be only too pleased to tell me bruvver 'ere exactly who you are working for, eh?'

Willie sniggered. He knew exactly how Mike worked and braced himself for claret flowing everywhere when Mike set to work on their captive.

Travis watched through eyes of terror as Mike removed his own shoes, his shirt and then his trousers. 'Hold me clobber, Eric. I've just had them dry-cleaned, and, well, I don't want them stained, do I?'

Like a boxer ready for the ring, Mike stood in just his under-wear. His legs were as thick as tree trunks and his chest was as wide as a standard doorframe.

'Staffie, hand me a screwdriver. It's only fitting, since this prick wants to screw me to the fucking wall.'

Travis let out a high-pitched scream like a girl. Then he began to wriggle and writhe about as if he'd been electrocuted. Mike looked at the others and laughed. 'Fuck me, I ain't even touched the knobhead.'

'No, no, all right, I'll tell ya. Please don't hurt me, pleeaasse,' he begged. The tears were streaming down his face and snot was bubbling from his nose.

'Getting covered in claret, it's pretty disgusting, don't ya think?'

Travis nodded furiously. 'Please, Mike. I'll tell ya everything ya want to know. Just don't torture me.'

'Torture? Who said anything about torture? No, Travis, it's called negotiation. Or do I mean interrogation? Well, let's hear it, then. Who's paying you?' He tilted his head to the side and gave a sarcastic grin.

Gulping back the fear, Travis thought about the firm he was just about to grass up. Either way, he was a dead man. If only he hadn't dated the sister. But how could he not? She was such a good fuck he couldn't get inside her knickers quickly enough. And then he'd had to prove himself worthy of her affections. Really, though, it was her brothers he needed to impress. He was sucked in; before he knew it, they had him planted in among the Regans' firm. He wasn't cut out for all this hard-core bollocks.

He stared at Mike's lifeless eyes, took another gulp of air, and said, 'Harry Harman.' Then he lowered his head and waited for the backlash.

Mike looked at each man with a deep furrowed frown, searching for some explanation. They either shrugged or curled down their lips. No one had a clue who this Harry Harman was.

'Mikey, do you want the screwdriver or the mallet? What's ya flavour?' asked Staffie, now eager to see the carnage.

With his eyes blinking away the sweat, Travis peered up and winced. 'Look, Mike, I don't know much, but I'll tell you everything. Just . . . please, don't use a tool.'

In an instant, Mike snatched the screwdriver from Staffie and plunged it into Travis's left kneecap. No one saw it coming, not even Travis. The pain was slow at first, until it reached every nerve in his leg and forced a demonic scream to leave his mouth. Lathered in sweat and writhing, he couldn't clutch his wound because his hands were tied to the chair. Mike waited for the blood-curdling cries to die down before he handed back the bloodied screwdriver.

'Mike, please, please don't torture me. I'll tell you everything, I swear . . .' His cries tailed off, as his head flopped down from the unbearable pain.

'And, Travis, me old son, I am a man of my word. Ya see, that weren't torture, that was a dig. Now then, when you get yaself composed and stop the blubbering, I'm ready to listen.'

Eric started to laugh but was instantly silenced. 'Shut it, Eric. This is no laughing matter, and you, ya silly git, took this rat on the payroll.' He shot his brother a deadly glare and bit his lip.

Eric was on the point of defending his actions. Being chastised in front of the men was a piss-take. Furthermore, he wanted to be seen as an equal in command. Ideally, he would have loved to have been the main man, but Mike took that position. He always had – at school, at work, and at home. But it was worse when it came to women. Eric's mind wandered, as it often did, to the one woman he'd wanted more than anyone – except Mike had got in there first. He was furious that when he'd expressed an interest in the woman, his brother had then dated her himself. Mike insisted he had already been seeing her, but Eric never believed that for a minute. However, he had the last laugh when she left the country, and Mike ended up with Jackie the tramp instead of his one true love.

'So, Travis, from the beginning, what the fuck are the Harmans doing nosing around my business?'

Travis tried desperately to put up with the pain and concentrate before Mike stabbed his other knee. The Harmans had sworn they had his back. Come what may, he wouldn't get hurt and when the business came their way, he would have a hefty cut of it. All he had to do was to find out where the lock-ups were, who their supplier was, and to record the evidence. The rest was up to them. Now, he wished he'd never agreed to any of it. It was no secret as to who he was doing over or how hard these men were.

The history of the Regans went back decades. The old man, Arthur, ran the firm with an iron fist. With his crew, they controlled the streets of Bermondsey.

Mike and Eric were Arthur's pride and joy. He brought them up to be a pair of chips off the old block, and they were – to the extent that they were even more fierce and reckless. Learning everything they knew from their father and his contemporaries, so they wouldn't have to learn their criminal trade within the walls of Wormwood Scrubs, it was almost an early baptism, except it began when they were aged thirteen and twelve respectively.

Travis often drank in the local haunts frequented by Eric and Mike. For years, he was just there mooching in the background, dealing a bit of cocaine and weed or selling knocked-off merchandise. It was Eric who had taken him on board, totally unaware that he was colluding with the Harmans. Yet Eric wasn't as sharp as Mike, and had royally fucked up this time, by not doing his homework on Travis.

'So, tell me then, Travis, because I ain't got all night, see. Are you gonna be the problem or the solution? It's your choice.'

'Harry Harman wanted me to take pictures of your lock-ups and stuff.'

Mike's blank expression spoke volumes. Travis had to put more meat on the bones to satisfy Mike's hunger for information.

'I was seeing their kid sister, Paris. I swear, I didn't want to get involved, but they . . . Oh my God, they're gonna fucking kill me . . .'

'No, they ain't, Travis, because—'

No sooner had Eric opened his mouth than Mike spat, 'Shut it! Eric, I do the talking, if ya don't mind.'

21

Eric took a step back and bowed his head to hide his clenched teeth. It was outrageous. Mike was really getting in his face now.

'Sorry about that, Travis. You were saying?'

'I didn't want to work for them, but they saw it as payback for seeing Paris. They said I owed them for taking liberties, and the only way to pay them back was to take poxy photos . . . That's all I know, I swear.'

Mike held his hand up for Travis to stop talking. He paced the floor and then spun around. 'Staffie, give me that screwdriver.'

In a sudden panic, Travis screamed, 'Please! No! They know all your lock-ups and how you're transporting the guns.' His breathing was fast, and he was tripping over his words. They left his mouth like a pisshead on the run with his pants down.

Mike twirled the screwdriver around with his huge fingers. 'You missed out the part about our supplier, Travis.'

Travis shook his head. 'No, they don't know, Mike. I swear, because I don't even know.' His round puppy-dog eyes looked over at Eric, urging him to say something.

'Is that right, Eric?' demanded Mike.

Eric snapped out of his sulk and mulled over the past events, trying to work out if there was any way that Travis would have known. He thought he'd been careful. But, had he been careful enough, though, by Mike's exacting standards?

'Yes, Mike. That's right.'

Mike wasn't a man to take unnecessary risks. 'What I wanna know is this: what the fuck are they intending to do with that information, Travis? Oh, and don't leave anything out. I want to know every last detail or . . . Well, let's just say I can replace those fucking guns with your body parts.'

Travis eagerly nodded. 'Oh, please. Come on, Mike. I don't know. They wouldn't tell me, would they?'

Mike held his hands up. 'Tell me this, then. Did the Harmans grass my lock-ups to the Filth?'

Travis nodded. 'Yes. They want you outta the picture, by any means, even if it means grassing. I swear, if I knew then what I know now, I would never have got involved.'

'Get the man a drink, Eric. It's gonna be a long night. Travis, I want everything you have on these Harmans.'

Chapter 2

Jackie was nursing a bruised cheek and drowning her sorrows with another large glass of vodka, disguised with orange juice.

Cooking up another storm, she eagerly waited for Mike to get up from his bed and get on his hands and knees to apologize and offer to send her off on a shopping spree with a fat wad of banknotes. Besides, as she saw it, he owed her big time. Little did she know that Mike wasn't even in the house.

Fifteen minutes later, as she was about to pour another drink, he appeared in the kitchen, looking washed out.

'Oh, been on a bender, 'ave ya? Well, you best 'ave a fucking big bunch of flowers 'cos this shiner is not going away anytime soon. And if you think I'm gonna say I walked into a wall, you're very much mistaken!'

Mike was exhausted, his mind now riddled with worry. Getting an earbashing from Jackie was the last thing he needed.

'Jackie, just shut it!'

She jumped down from the kitchen bar stool and stood with her hands on her hips. 'Shut it? Fucking shut it? Have you looked at my face? Well, 'ave ya?' she screamed like a woman possessed.

Mike lowered his head. At that precise moment, he wished it was Jackie sitting on the chair with a screwdriver through her eye.

'Don't you dare walk away from me!' she screamed, chasing him across the marble floor. 'You ain't getting away with it. I swear, Mike, you're gonna pay.'

In a fit of rage, Mike spun around, grabbed his wife around the throat and squeezed, watching her eyes widen in fear. She struggled to remove his grip and could feel her throat closing up. Unable to breathe, she really believed she was going to die. Then he let go and she collapsed on the floor, retching and gasping.

'One more word from your vile mouth and I'll fucking annihilate you. Now, I'm going to my bed and you're going to leave me in bloody peace, 'cos, Jackie, I've had enough of ya.' His face was red and angry, and saliva had formed at the corners of his mouth.

She knew she'd lost this fight. As he walked away, she grabbed the bottle of vodka with shaky hands and poured it down her throat. Then she slammed the bottle down hard on the worktop. 'Cunt!' she said to herself.

Yet, deep down, she knew he wasn't that bad – well, not to her and their son. There was many a woman who would give their right arm to be married to Mike Regan, living in a fuck-off mansion, with diamonds in the drawer and furs in the wardrobe. However, all she wanted – ever wanted – was his attention. She craved it. Life should be about her. She felt she'd earned it, coming from nothing.

So motherhood was a complete fuck-up. She missed the nights out in the clubs, being treated like royalty just because she was Mike's bird. She only stopped taking the pill because she thought he was getting a wandering eye. Really, she didn't want kids, end of. Pregnancy would ruin her very sexy body. Yet as soon as her son was born, she saw the end of the flash socializing and all the attention that had been focused on her.

Mike had taken a new stance on life. At last, he was settling down. The trips to their villa in Spain were spent building sandcastles and going out on their boat; he was totally absorbed in their son. The neglect, as she saw it, turned to resentment, and so she began to despise the boy. He looked at her with either sorrow or hatred, but either expression grated on her. Those sweet words that Mike had said to her before the birth were now reserved for their son, and if the truth be known, she was jealous and did everything to draw her husband's interest back to her.

It started with the boob job because she caught him looking at a woman with bigger tits than hers. Then she turned her attention to her lips because she assumed he liked that sort of thing. However, all the trips to the beauty salon for Botox and fillers made not one iota of difference: he only had eyes for his boy. When the parties at their home became tame, she tried to liven them up by making cocktails and encouraging the men to drink. But when she downed a few herself, that just infuriated Mike, and so he put a stop to those too.

So now she saw herself drowning in a humdrum way of life. And her wild behaviour became a major source of friction between Mike and herself. His sharp digs irritated her. 'How fucking old are ya?' he would say, or 'Grow the fuck up and be a mother. You ain't on Jeremy fucking Kyle.'

If only he knew how much she wanted out of this prison called adulthood. It was purgatory for a young hot-blooded woman like her, who craved sex and a heady lifestyle. For Christ's sake, she was only fucking twenty-six.

Just as she was about to reach for another hidden bottle of vodka, the doorbell rang. Without looking through the spyhole, she opened the door. It was Tracey, Eric's girlfriend.

'Cor, Jackie, the state of ya face. What's 'appened?' asked Tracey, following Jackie into the kitchen. Plonking her new Gucci bag on the floor, Tracey clambered up onto the bar stool, preparing herself for the gossip.

'That bastard up there, clumped me one last night.' She tried to force a tear; at least she could expect some sympathy from her sister-in-law-to-be.

Tracey looked as made up and fake as Jackie. Perhaps more

so. She'd also undergone the boob job, hair extensions and lip fillers. And yet, unlike Mike, Eric preferred his birds tanned and toned. She flicked her long bleached mane over her shoulder, placed her hands on the granite worktop, showing off her fake fingernails, and gazed down with pride at the tiny crystals she'd recently had glued on. 'So, what's 'appened then, Jack?'

Jackie poured them both a drink and sniffed back the fake tear. 'I dunno, Trace. He ain't the same. I reckon he's got another bird. Ya know what it's like. Fucking give 'em a kid and then they 'ave ya tied down and go off looking for a fresh bit of skirt.'

Tracey sipped the bitter vodka and poured more orange juice to dilute the rough taste. 'Oh, I dunno, Jackie. Mike ain't like that. He's probably got a lot on his mind.'

Jackie gave her an evil glare. 'And how the fuck would you know, Tracey?'

She was annoyed that her so-called friend was now sticking up for the enemy, as she saw him.

'Oh, come on, Jackie. We all know what his line of work is! Perhaps he's having a bit of bother.'

With a screwed-up face, Jackie spat back, 'Who cares about his business! Look at me bleedin' face. I didn't do that meself, did I?'

Tracey raised her eyebrow as if to say, 'Who knows?'

'What? D'ya think I'm lying, then?'

'Wind ya neck in, Jack. We all know you like a drink. I've seen you so outta ya nut, you've fallen all over the show.'

Jackie shot her jaw forward in anger. 'Don't come it, Tracey. I know your game. Ya come in 'ere all done up, with ya tits hanging out and half ya arse showing. Hoping I wasn't in, were ya?'

Tracey slammed the glass down, nearly shattering it. 'Now, you listen, Jackie. I didn't come 'ere to bloody row, and I don't like what you're saying. But I'll not be surprised if he does go else-where. I mean, look at the state of ya. And, Jackie, you're hardly Mother Teresa. He ain't blind, love.'

Those words were like a red rag to a bull. Jackie launched herself off the bar stool, and on her way to taking Tracey down, she managed to snatch a clump of her hair, pulling her heavily to the floor. Tracey yelped like an injured dog. She had hit her knee hard and was in absolute agony. Her friend's shrieks of pain brought Jackie back to reality. But before she had a chance to say she was sorry, Tracey pushed her away. Grabbing her bag and hobbling towards the door in her noisy stiletto shoes, she shot Jackie an evil glare.

'Fucking bad move, bitch,' she growled.

The door slammed shut and the silence left a buzzing in Jackie's ear. 'Cunt,' she mumbled to herself once more. She'd done it again, and this time she'd pissed off Tracey, her sidekick. She stared at the clump of hair on the floor and felt sick. Yet more disturbing was the threatening tone in Tracey's voice. Holding the bottle of vodka over the sink, she attempted to pour the last of the evil liquid away, but her hands shook so violently, she just couldn't do it. Instead, she poured it neat down her throat and swanned out to the garden to soak up the sun.

* * *

By the time Mike had got up from his bed, it was four o'clock in the afternoon. He pulled back the curtains and looked at his wife sprawled out on a sunlounger in the hot sun. He shook his head and thought about Ricky. He would be home from school any minute and would have to face a drunken mother with no cupcakes and sweet words, just drivel and sarcasm. Once he was showered and had climbed into his tracksuit, he went downstairs.

He found Ricky in the lounge, still in his uniform, and Sacha sitting there, looking all forlorn.

'Dad!' screeched Ricky, as he leaped from the floor and ran into his father's arms. Sacha gave him a half-smile and stood up to make her exit.

'I'm sorry, Mike. You know I love Ricky, don't you?'

Mike held his son, stroking his back, as his son nestled into his neck. 'I know, Sacha. Don't worry, I'll sort something. You've been good to me and Ricky and I won't forget it. 'Ere, take this.' He pulled a wad of fifties from his tracksuit bottoms. 'Take yaself on holiday.'

Sacha looked at him open-mouthed. 'I can't take all that.'

Mike's eyes softened.

'Babe, call it compensation.'

'Thank you, Mike.'

He winked and nodded. 'Don't worry, Sach. I'll take care of Ricky. That heartless sket won't be left alone with him, not if I can help it.' He put Ricky back on the floor and patted his backside. 'Go on, Ricky. You get on with your homework.'

He headed to the kitchen with Sacha on his heels. 'I'm gonna put her in a rehab place, and if she refuses, then she can fuck off. I ain't messing around anymore. She might be my wife, but Ricky is my son, and he comes first. It's a mighty shame she doesn't see it that way. Anyway, you get yourself off home and don't be worrying.'

Sacha stared out into the garden and noticed Jackie burning up from the sun. 'Er, do you think you should get her in? Christ, she looks like a beetroot.'

Mike chuckled. 'Nah, let her fry. It'll give her something else to whine about. Jesus, she's one ugly mare. Ya know, she was a good-looking kid a few years ago, but now look at her. She'd give Jackie Stallone a run for her money.'

Sacha laughed. 'Oh, Mike, come on. She don't look that bad. She's fashionably attractive.'

Mike looked away. 'Not my thing, I'm afraid.'

Sacha felt awkward: she had her wages and there was no reason to stay. Mike smiled sweetly and showed her to the door.

* * *

29

After playing hide-and-seek, Mike took his son off to a select restaurant just down the road from his huge Kent pad. The staff almost stood to attention and quickly tripped over themselves to have him seated and his food served. A few customers smiled and nodded out of respect. Just as their food arrived, one of his phones rang. It was Jackie, screaming obscenities, and in among all the shouting and bitching, she never once asked if Ricky was with him. With one swift movement, he dropped the phone into the jug of water and laughed.

Ricky, with a straw in his mouth, sucking on a smoothie, looked up and smiled. 'Was that Mummy?'

Mike would have denied it, but he'd gone past pretending Jackie was kind at heart. Even as young as Ricky was, he knew she wasn't a good mother.

Shortly afterwards, his other phone – his business one – rang. It was Eric. 'All right, Mike. All done and delivered.'

Mike smiled. *That will teach the dirty fuckers.*

* * *

It wasn't until early the next morning that the phone rang again. This time, he didn't smile; instead, he flared his nostrils and took a deep breath. 'Are you fucking sure, Eric? How do you know it was the Harmans?'

Eric was pacing the floor. Maybe they'd gone too far this time; after all, they knew very little about the firm.

'Mikey, what are we gonna do? Staffie loved that dog. I mean who does that, kills a dog, eh?'

Mike chewed the inside of his mouth. 'Eric, it ain't about the bleedin' dog, you fucking muppet, it's a statement. They're throwing down the gauntlet after what we did to Travis.'

Eric felt uneasy. The description of the dog's dismembered body was horrific, but then, so was Travis by the time they'd finished with him. Mike had used Travis's own phone to take the photos

30

of the aftermath and returned it to the man's car. He'd then texted Harry Harman from Travis's phone saying, *photo evidence in my car*. After he removed his prints from the phone, he left.

'I don't fucking like it, Mikey. I mean, what's next, and, more to the point, who's next?'

Mike was livid. 'Now, you listen to me, ya great pussy. Get a grip. I'll smash the fucking life out of each and every one of those cunts, if they so much as hurt a hair on anyone's head. Call a meeting at mine. We need to make a plan. I ain't taking this lying down.'

Eric felt sick. 'All right. See you in an hour.'

* * *

Ricky was up early and trying to put his school uniform on, while Jackie was still in bed. The sight of his little boy engulfed in innocence, with his hair sticking up and his shoes on the wrong feet, melted Mike's heart. Then he had a sudden sickening thought and shuddered. 'You ain't going to school today, buddy. You're going on a trip with Mummy.'

Ricky looked up and smiled. 'Are you coming, Daddy?'

Mike picked him up and hugged him. 'Not right away, my boy. In a few days, I'll join you.'

The sweet smile adorning Ricky's face drooped, and Mike almost sensed the fear. But, right now, his son was safer with Jackie than . . . he shuddered to think.

'Jack, get ya arse down 'ere, now!' he screamed up the stairs.

Jackie had gone to bed with a splitting headache and her face red raw from the sun. She could hear him shouting and tried to focus, but it was all a blur. She felt an uncomfortable throbbing covering her chest and her cheeks, and the banging in her head was relentless; it was a reminder that she'd fallen asleep in the garden. She sat upright and winced with the various pains. Then, she heard him call her again.

'All right, I'm coming!' she screamed back. She wasn't in the mood to drive Ricky to school. For one thing, she looked an absolute mess, and for another, all she wanted was to go back to sleep. After grabbing her satin robe from the end of the bed, she wrapped it around herself and slowly descended the stairs. With every step, she felt dizzy and had to hold the banister to stop herself from being sick on the spot.

Mike was staring at her in disgust. 'Fucking state of you. Jesus, you look like someone's dug you up from a grave.'

'Bollocks, Mike.' She gave him a death glare. 'What's all the screaming about, anyway?'

'Listen, Jackie, and I mean *fucking listen*.' He was narrow-eyed and deadly serious.

Jackie stopped in her tracks. 'What's going on?'

'Get ya bags packed. You and Ricky are off to Spain. I want you to go to the airport and wait for the next flight. And tell no one where you're going.'

She rubbed her eyes and tried to straighten her hair. 'What's going on?' she asked again.

Mike didn't have time to discuss business – not that he would anyway – but, now, time was of the essence. He needed his son out of the country.

'Jackie, for once in your life, shut the fuck up, get the bags packed, and just go, will ya? I'll join you when I can.'

'Well, you'll have to give me a few hours. I need to go to the hairdressers and the—'

Before she could finish, he aggressively snatched her arm and pulled her close. 'You'll get those bags packed and be ready to get on the road in fifteen minutes!'

She knew then she couldn't push him any further. Something serious was going down.

'All right. Get off me. 'Ave you booked a flight?' Her pitch was high and sarcastic.

Mike let go of her and snarled, 'You're one useless bitch. Just go to the airport and book the next flight, and if there ain't any today, then stay in a hotel until there is one! You've got the credit cards. Now, use your poxy pea-sized brain and get your arse into gear.' His deep voice, his spiteful tone, and the urgency of the situation were enough to clear her head in an instant. Without another word, she left the room and headed upstairs.

Unbelievably, Jackie was out of the house with their bags in record time. But he was disappointed by how roughly she bundled Ricky into the back of her white Range Rover. Her shoving Ricky the way she did raised his anger. He wanted to drag her by her extensions and ram her face into the wall. But he couldn't get caught up in yet another domestic; he needed his son away from here and soon. The thought of speaking to any woman like that, let alone hitting them, was just not part of his make-up. He always treated women with decency and respect and never in his life had he raised his hands to one – until the day before yesterday with Jackie. But there was no love left between them. The only reason he kept her around was because she was Ricky's mother, or she would have been gone years ago.

* * *

A black Mercedes pulled up on the drive and out crawled Eric, looking the worse for wear; his designer stubble was hardly Calvin Klein, more scarecrow, and his wide light-blue eyes looked dark and sunken. Mike spotted right away that his brother was sweating from fear, a thin layer of greasy mist cladding his face. He had aged overnight.

'Jesus, Mikey, that poor dog. Those Harmans are absolute animals!' he said, as he paced the floor, running his hands through his hair.

'Eric, listen. I won't let no fucker lay a hand on you. Now, calm down.'

Eric looked up through his long dark lashes, and for a second,

Mike felt sorry for him. 'I've sent Ricky to Spain with Jackie, to keep them out of the way. Now, what about your Tracey? Maybe she should join them?'

'You must be joking. Jackie only nearly scalped my bird, all 'cos she thought Tracey had her eye on you. No disrespect, Mikey, but Jackie was out of order.'

Mike put his arm around Eric's shoulders. 'Listen, it's gonna be all right. And I know what ya mean about Jackie. She's a cunt. Trouble is though, Eric, right now, she's my cunt, and I still have to look out for her. Mark my words, though. Once this shit is over, if she doesn't buck up her ideas, she's gone for good.'

Eric's ears pricked up. 'What? Are ya gonna dump her?'

'Yeah. She's pushed me to backhanding her, and that ain't me.' He sighed heavily. 'I don't love her. In fact, I fucking detest her. I should never have got with her and just waited for . . . Oh, never mind. I've got my boy to think about now.'

They headed to the bar in the lounge and waited for the others to arrive.

Eric thought about his brother's words and wondered if he was contemplating going back to his ex-girlfriend. He'd heard through the grapevine that she was in London. He'd been tempted to make a play for her himself, but this latest row between his brother and Jackie might have put paid to that pipedream. If Mike split with Jackie and knew his ex was back in London, he would no doubt go sniffing around.

'Mikey, I think I want to jack it in. I wanna settle down, have a family, and start me own business.'

Mike chuckled. 'Eric, you are a fucking bellend sometimes. What ya gonna do? You ain't even got a swimming certificate let alone a GCSE.'

Eric looked his brother over and felt that nagging sense of envy that seemed constantly to eat away at him. Being classed as second best to Mike was not how he saw his future.

'Anyway, Eric, we have more serious matters at hand than

career advice. 'Ave ya told Farver to stay in Florida? I want him outta the way an' all. This is a war we are walking into, and I don't know the level of their army . . . yet.'

Eric felt his stomach churn. 'Yes. Dad's staying another few weeks. Do you think they'll do us over, one by one?'

The brandy hit the back of Mike's throat and he swallowed twice. 'No! I didn't string up Travis's cat, did I? I fucking strung *him* up. They wouldn't have the guts to open up Staffie. Nah, they cowardly butchered his dog instead. Who the hell do they think they are, eh? The fucking Mafia?'

Within a few minutes, Lou and Willie arrived. Like Eric, they were unsettled. Staffie was the last to arrive and he was freaked out. Mike poured them all a drink, and they headed for the dining room where they used to play poker, until Jackie managed to ruin that too, with all her mad, drunken outbursts.

They sat around the table and Mike looked from one to the other; his sidekicks, they were. It was how it was from when they were born. His father, Arthur Regan, used to run the firm. Willie Ritz's old man, Charlie, and Staffie's father, Teddy, were the muscle in the crew. Then there was Lou Baker's father, Big Lou, who was the brainy one. They were Bermondsey boys with a serious reputation and an eye for a good heist or for pavement work. Robbing the security vans, they ran the manor.

'I don't like it, Mikey,' said Lou, always the voice of reason. 'It's not knowing enough about the Harmans that sits uneasily with me.' His tone was softer than the others and slightly more refined. In fact, Lou looked the odd man out. With his passion for sharp suits and his blow-dried hair sitting neatly behind his ears, he was always immaculately turned out – and more like their lawyer than a villain.

Mike nodded. 'Well, lads, that's our first job. I want every single fucker in South East London interrogated. I want everyone knowing that the Harmans are grasses. I'm gonna make damned sure that no other cunt will wanna work with them – that is, if they are attempting to take over the firms in our manor. These cowardly bastards will regret trying to bring me down, that's for sure.'

Willie was almost chewing his lips off, his last toot of cocaine having left him agitated, as per usual. 'I wanna know why they saw fit to grass our operation up to the Filth, and why us? I mean, we've got no beef with them. We don't even know 'em!'

Mike snarled. 'Well, I'll get to the bottom of it, even if it means ripping a few heads off along the way!'

Staffie jumped to his feet. He was raging. 'Well, I swear to God, if I get my hands on any of those Harman brothers, I'll gut them like a piece of fish. I fucking loved that dog. 'Orrible, evil lowlifes they are!' After a few deep breaths, he sat back down.

Mike poured him another brandy. ''Ere, Staffie. Drink this, mate, and calm yaself down.'

Mike looked at Staffie. He couldn't remember a time when the man was young or had hair; he was always the big bruiser with a thick forehead and hands like bricks.

'Right, get on ya phones now and call around. I want to know everything there is to know about these bastards.'

Chapter 3

Harry Harman entered his mother's kitchen with a face like a smacked arse. Doris was in her pinafore, not that this was unusual. Making a sandwich, she turned to her eldest son. Briefly looking him up and down, with no hint of an expression, she carried on slicing the cheese.

'Where's the ol' man?' His deep voice was gruff from too many fags and he had another distinguishing characteristic – a fat neck to match his overlarge head. A spiteful-looking man, he glared with hate most of the time. Those cold eyes never softened, even when he watched his mother with her crooked fingers, riven with arthritis, pouring tea into her dainty bone china teacup. She was almost fifty-seven and yet the boys still had her running around after them, cooking and ironing their shirts. They had moved out years before, with huge drums of their own, yet they would still bring their washing home, treating her as though she was their slave.

'I don't know, son. Shall I give him a message?'

Harry tutted. 'Nah, I need to find him, like fucking now!'

Doris stopped buttering the bread and wiped her hands on her apron. 'Son, he's probably up to no good with that old tom up on the Sandycroft Estate, as well you know an' all. So, I would be grateful if you didn't come in 'ere and raise your voice at me,' she said calmly, before she picked up the knife again and carried on buttering the bread.

Harry was seriously irritated. He knew his father was off somewhere having it away with the next tart who would put it out for him for a few drinks, but he felt somewhat guilty; he should have been more polite to his mother. Doris had a knack for winding him up with her righteous ways. She moaned constantly about their father and for good reason: he shagged everything in sight, and when he wasn't doing that, he spent all their money on drink.

Whilst she could at least thank her lucky stars that her husband never belted her one, her mother always said she'd married beneath herself. And as the years rolled by, she wished things had been different. Hindsight was a wonderful thing but if only she'd never said 'I do' at the time. Trying as hard as she had, she'd been unable to change him or her sons for that matter. All three were a chip off their father's block. And all of them had two things in common – a total lack of class and not a single brain cell between them.

Frank Harman wasn't the best-looking man in South East London, but he was okay – although he viewed himself as a Paul Newman double. If he was, Doris never saw it, and now he resembled the wrestler Big Daddy. Still, she'd made her bed and she had to damn well lie in it.

With three boys and a girl in the family, they sadly took on their father's looks and build, with the possible exception of Scottie, who was the better looking of the bunch. Paris wasn't too much of a looker without make-up and certainly never had her mother's sweet face.

Trying to keep up her posh voice and sophisticated ways only earned Doris the reputation for being a snob, and so, as the years dragged by, she became resigned to being put down at every turn by her insufferable children and humiliated by her villainous husband. Even her daughter had an air of arrogance about her, goaded on by the three boys. Their little princess, they called her. Doris wasn't so blinded by her antics as the boys were, though. She was a class-A tart and was always causing unnecessary bother. Flashing her new tits and a five-hundred-pound pout, she was a spoiled little madam.

If only she could be proud of at least one of her four children, but the truth was she was ashamed of them. Totally. Frank was to blame. He brought them up to do whatever it took to earn a few bob, and there was nothing legitimate in it either. He laughed at their naughty antics, and so it was no surprise that they were all off the rails before they even reached primary school.

'Where's Paris?' Harry asked, trying to moderate his angry tone.

Doris shrugged her shoulders. 'How would I know? I haven't seen her in a week. She's probably staying over with that new fella of hers . . . Travis, I think his name is.'

Harry knew that wasn't the case. He shuddered inside, remembering the picture of Travis in pieces. It wasn't the bruises that turned his stomach but the fact that it was obvious he'd been gruesomely tortured. The photo on the phone had served as an ominous warning.

As thick-skinned as he was to violence and life itself, he felt uneasy. Looking back at his brother Vinnie's feeble attempt at revenge made him want to crucify him. Gutting the dog was pathetic and instantly sent out the wrong message. He should have carved up Stafford, not the mutt: now that would have been a real warning not to mess with the Harmans.

'I've made some fairy cakes. Would you like one?' asked Doris, with a fake smile.

Harry thought he could see a trace of sarcasm on his mother's sweet face, but, on reflection, he assumed he was just on edge and angry. 'No, I need to get hold of Farver and Paris.'

Doris took her cup and plain cheese sandwich over to the

kitchen table and sat herself down. Harry watched her, and for the first time in his life, he noticed how lonely and pitiful she looked as she ate her boring lunch at the Formica tabletop in her plain dress and pinny. The vision of Travis and then this image of innocence, his mother, oblivious to her son's antics – he knew he wouldn't be able to bear it if the Regans hurt her. She wasn't like them. 'Muvver, can you go and stay with your sister for a while?'

Holding the china teacup in her hand, Doris looked up at her son and just stared.

Harry was uneasy. 'It's just safer for the moment, Muvver.' He softened his words.

'Have you forgotten, Harry, my sister passed away six months ago? You were all invited to the funeral . . . but I guess you were too busy to go.'

Harry swallowed hard. He did remember her mentioning something, and yet he'd forgotten about it. He'd been too busy at the time – although he wouldn't have gone anyway. He hardly knew his aunt. 'Well, have ya got a friend you can stay with?' His guilt now turned to annoyance.

'No, son, I don't have any friends because your father put a stop to having any of those! Anyway, why do I need to get away? What trouble are you in now?' Her tone was bitter.

'Never you mind, Muvver. Just do yourself a favour and get away for a bit.'

'No, Harry.'

With a deep furrowed frown, Harry glared. 'Listen, Muvver, I ain't fucking about. Ya need to get away from the house—' Before he could finish, Doris jumped up from the table.

'No, Harry! *You* listen to me for once in your life. I'm sick to the back teeth of being bullied . . . yes, bullied, by all of you. As for that useless father of yours, I've been pushed around by him for far too long, and I will not take it from you too. So, take note, sunshine, I'm not going anywhere. This is my home and not yours, so if anyone is leaving it's you, Harry. Christ Almighty, I've had years of hiding from the aftermath of your troubles or dodging the police. Well, no more!' She sat back down and took another sip of tea.

Harry sighed in frustration. Of course, she was right. For the first time in his life, he looked at her for who she really was – a downtrodden, washed-out woman. He pulled a chair out and sat opposite. 'Muvver, I've a flat down the coast. It's nothing too fancy, but it's okay. Why don't I take you there for a short holiday?' His voice was almost sweet; it was so unlike his usual gruff tone.

Doris gave him a wry grin. 'Harry, please stop taking my aloofness as stupidity. I'm fully aware of what you're up to. Since when did you do charm? If you think offering a trip down to the seaside is doing me a favour, you're very much mistaken. I know the truth and so do you. Like all of you, if I was to get hurt due to your antics, then none of you would be able to live with yourselves because you would be eaten up with guilt!' she said, with a raised voice.

'Muvver!'

'No, Harry, just shut up, please! A holiday down the coast? I never even knew you had a holiday home. I haven't been to the coast in over twenty damned years. You only want me to go now because it suits you. Me, invited to have a break? It's ridiculous.'

These words, coming from the mouth of this mild-mannered lady, stunned Harry. And the look in her eyes told him she was not going to put up with him pushing her around. The speed at which he jumped up from the table caused the chair to topple over. Before she'd a chance to say another word, he left, slamming the door behind him.

The cold, stark reality of the present situation made Doris tearful. Her dear sister's departure from this life was such a travesty. Doris deeply missed their weekly chats on the phone and the odd weekend trip up to Bath. It shouldn't be this way; she should have been able to sit and share a pot of tea with her own daughter and chat, but Paris was just like the others – all out for herself. Staring down at the china teacup, she heard nothing but the quiet humming sound of the fridge, her only company. It was a stark contrast to when her kids had lived at home; the constant loud noise had been unbearable. They never spoke – they always shouted.

Just as she stood up to wash up the cup and plate, the back door burst open and in stormed Paris. Usually, Doris would greet her, offering lunch or a drink, but not today. Today, she wanted nothing more than to be alone and pretend she'd never had a family.

'All right, Muvver?' she said, as she plonked an oversized bag on the table. 'I've got a few bits that need to be hand-washed. Put the kettle on. I'm fucking parched.'

Doris ignored her and continued with the washing up.

Paris rifled through her Louis Vuitton tote bag looking for her phone, still annoyed that Travis hadn't returned her calls. In among the make-up, hairbrushes and hairspray, she finally felt the rhinestone-covered phone case and retrieved it from her bag, only to find the battery had died. 'Oh, for fuck's sake,' she cursed, and dived in again to find the charger. After plugging it in, she returned to her seat and looked over at her mother. 'Did ya make the tea?'

Doris untied her pinafore and turned to face her daughter. 'No, Paris, I didn't. If you want a cup, then make it yourself.'

Paris's heavily made-up face produced a frown that even the Botox couldn't freeze. 'What the fuck's up with you?'

'I've had your brother in here demanding I move out for a while, I've had your stinking father take my last tenner from my purse yesterday, and now you, expecting your washing done and tea made. Well, you can all go and bugger off. I'm sick of all of you.'

Her caustic words made Paris gasp. She'd never heard her

mother speak with such hostility to her, nor wear that look of spiteful anger. It just wasn't in her nature.

Doris glared with tight lips, feeling her blood boiling. Her once sweet little girl was now nothing but a tart. Everything about her was fake, with her ever-changing bleached hair extensions, her oversized lips, and the thick black eyelash extensions, all of which made her look like a transvestite ready for a Las Vegas show. The skintight dress and fake tan would, Doris thought, be fine for the nightclub, but it was midday. Her look was more suitable for streetwalking around King's Cross, where she would probably make a fortune selling her arse. In fact, Doris wondered if the figure-hugging dress did Paris any favours, particularly as it was bright green and the lumps and bumps made her look like a caterpillar. Still, what did she know about fashion? On balance, the boys seemed to go for her, and she wasn't short of a fella. Perhaps it was the prodigious fake tits, mused Doris, that distracted anyone from thinking that she looked like a pig in lipstick.

Paris ignored the outburst and asked, 'Who wanted you to leave?'

Doris gave a dramatic sigh. 'Harry did.'

Paris guessed there was trouble. There was no way Harry would want their mother out of the house unless something bad was about to happen. Before she'd a chance to say another word, her phone sprang into action, bleeping with a string of messages. Leaping from her chair, she snatched her mobile, and with hands shaking from a hangover, she scrolled down the long list of messages and swallowed hard. She hastily dialled Harry's number and waited for him to answer, anxiously tapping her foot.

'Harry, what the fuck's going on? Muvver's got the raving hump, and I've had thirty missed calls.'

Harry told her he was on his way back and would pick her up in five minutes to take her to their seaside flat.

Now uneasy, Paris waited quietly in the kitchen. It was the

panic in her brother's voice that troubled her. Her brothers were never nervous: they were always self-assured, as if nothing ever fazed them. She was proud to be their little sister. It gave her a reputation and allowed her into places where drinks would be bought for her. She was spoiled, and she knew it. With a whinge, a whine, and a sulky pout, she would get the latest bag, shoes or even a car.

Annoyed, she called him back.

'Harry, why 'ave I got to go to the flat, for fuck's sake? Travis 'as promised me a long weekend in some foreign country. He reckons it's a surprise. Harry? Harry?' She looked at the phone and realized Harry had ended the call.

'Muvver, what's going on? I've got Harry telling me he's on his way, but now he's put the poxy phone down, and you ain't even gonna make me a brew!'

Doris stood in the doorway between the kitchen and the hall and sighed; her daughter was such a petulant, rude and insensitive little cow. She hadn't even looked up to acknowledge her mother; she merely applied a layer of lip gloss.

'Paris, you can wait for Harry outside.'

With her lip gloss in one hand and a small round mirror in the other, Paris froze and slowly flicked her eyes to see her mother looking deadly serious.

'You what?'

'I said you can wait outside for your brother and also take that washing with you. I'll not be your skivvy, ever again. And that goes for your brothers as well. Are we clear?' Each word was precise.

Paris frowned. 'What's wrong with you? I mean, 'ave ya started the menopause or something?'

Doris shook her head and walked away, mumbling under her breath, 'I started it years ago.'

Ignoring her mother, Paris began adding another layer of lip gloss. Suddenly, Harry came flying into the kitchen as if he had a rocket up his arse. 'Right, where's Muvver? I need her to come with me. You! Get ya gear. We have to go.'

He watched Paris still fussing over herself. Clearly frustrated, he once again shouted at his mother.

'Muvver! Come here! You have to leave wiv me, right now.'

Paris suddenly jumped up from her seat. 'What's going on, Harry?'

'Nothing. Just get yaself into gear and wait in the car.'

He looked down the hallway. 'Muvver, will you hurry up!'

There was silence. Beads of sweat were now running down his nose and he hastily pulled a handkerchief from his pocket and ran it over his wet face. 'Muvver!' he screamed again.

'Oh for God's sake,' he growled, as he marched along the hallway.

Doris casually appeared from the living room, looking right through Harry as if he wasn't even there. She'd been about to go upstairs when that irritating son of hers had started up again.

'Muvver, what's wrong with you? Can't you hear me? I ain't messing about. You have to come with me.'

Unexpectedly, Doris stopped, turned and glared, with contempt smeared across her face.

'Harry, take your precious sister and get out of my house. And, listen well! Before you upset my neighbours with your bellowing, close your big mouth, turn on your heels, and just go. I'm not going with you, so please leave, before . . .' She sighed. 'Oh, never mind. Just get out!'

Harry was looking at a stranger: this wasn't his mother. There was nothing he could do except physically throw her over his shoulder, and he wasn't about to do that.

Doris was about to shout, 'And don't slam the door', but it was too late. The back door banged shut, and she was left with a ringing sound in her ears and a tightening in her chest.

Harry almost pushed Paris with all her bags into his Mercedes. 'Hurry up, Paris. We need to get out of 'ere.'

With her brother panicking the way he was, and almost manhandling her, Paris sensed this situation was more serious than she'd previously thought. Usually, she would have been gobbing off, but, for the first time in her life, she remained quiet and allowed Harry to get himself settled and on the road before she opened her mouth. He didn't pull away gently either; he left rubber on the tarmac. Never would Harry drive like that, not in his precious top-of-the-range car.

'Harry, what's happened?' She kept her voice low-key.

'Well, princess, I hate to tell ya, babe, but your fella won't be taking you away for the weekend. He's dead.'

After being forcibly pushed into the back, Paris was leaning forward, gripping the corners of the two front seats. 'What?'

Her voice was so loud, it seemed to vibrate in his ear.

'Sit back and get ya seatbelt on.'

In a sudden daze, Paris sat back and fastened the belt. 'What happened? Who the hell killed him?'

'Did I say anyone killed him?' He knew that question was unfair. This mess wasn't his little sister's fault.

'Well, bruv, we wouldn't be flying up fucking Wrotham Hill like Lewis Hamilton if he died of natural causes, would we?'

He looked in the rear-view mirror. 'Sis, you don't seem upset. I thought you liked Travis?'

She squirmed in her seat. 'Well, yeah, 'course I did, but I weren't gonna marry him or have his babies. He was all right, sweet, really . . . Anyway, what's 'appened?'

'He was working for me, an inside job, but the silly bastard got sussed out and . . .' He paused, waiting for a reaction.

'So I ain't going away this weekend then? Fuck it. I was looking forward to that.'

Harry flicked his eyes to the rear-view mirror again. 'You're a heartless cow.'

She rolled her eyes. 'Well, I was taught by the best, Harry.'

The thought circled in his mind: she wasn't wrong. They had

pressured her when she was a kid not to show weakness and indoctrinated her in the belief that only wimps cry, and everyone is out for themselves.

He remembered when she was only thirteen, and all the girls in her class were invited to a party except her. She'd fallen out with this young girl called Amberley Fitzgerald. He shuddered when he thought about it; perhaps, on that occasion, his family had gone too far.

Amberley had made it quite clear that she wouldn't be friends with Paris because Paris had taken her boyfriend away. Amberley lived in a big house in Wilderness Avenue in Chislehurst. Her parents were bankers, and so she always had the latest clothes that outshone any other girl, plus she had a pretty face with long dark curly hair. She had it all. All the girls wanted to be friends with her, and so when they went against his sister, it was a racing certainty that all hell would break loose, no matter what.

When Paris came home in tears and told them that she'd been victimized and bullied, Harry and Vinnie went mental. They told her to stop crying and stand up for herself; no one must ever bully her, and, more to the point, get away with it. There was no such thing as having a friend; everyone has their own agenda in life. The only people in the world you could depend on were family. 'Tears are for weaklings,' Harry told her. In response, she wiped her cheeks with a tissue.

The very next day, outside the school grounds, backed by her brothers, Paris stood ready for the fight of her life. Her fingers loaded with cheap rings, she launched an attack the minute Amberley appeared. With no sense of control, Paris punched the girl relentlessly, gruesomely tearing shreds from the girl's face. Harry and Vinnie watched with pride as their little sister showed her worth, rucking as violently as any lad. The fight was eventually broken up by the head teacher, who was given a fierce verbal attack by Harry. All the way home they patted her back, showering her with praise.

Harry remembered his father's words when they arrived home: 'Now then, you start showing people who's the fucking boss. That little larruping will give a warning to all those silly little girls that no one messes with a Harman.'

* * *

In the rear-view mirror Harry witnessed the same expression as the day she'd sniffed back those tears and fallen into a world of callousness. Since then, she hadn't changed; she still had that sneering look to this day. Nothing ever fazed her. It was as if he and their father had ripped out her soul and left a void. Still, he loved his sister; she was loyal to them, regardless.

'So, tell me, Harry, what's going on? You look like you're shitting a brick.'

'Travis was tortured, the poor bastard . . .' He swallowed hard as he recalled the images of Travis on that chair with his eye scooped out and with his flesh ripped from his cheek; he could only guess it had been done with a claw hammer. 'I need to get you away, princess, because the bastards that killed Travis will be coming for us.'

Paris gasped, 'Oh my God, Harry. It's the Regans!' Her mouth remained open, digesting his silent acknowledgement. 'Are you fucking nuts? Seriously? Why would you get involved? This ain't our vendetta.' She paused, waiting for an answer, but then she noticed her brother's shifty eyes in the mirror and knew that he hadn't done it for the family honour.

It was always about the money with her family. Planning and scheming to ruin the Regan family was a continual source of conversation, from father to sons, like some hereditary disease.

His silence irritated her. 'I just hope it was worth it, Harry, because the Regans are legendary. And you may have kept me out of the business, but I ain't blind or deaf. And our flaming uncle and our ol' man should have cut their losses years ago.' She huffed. 'What I don't get is, if they have killed Travis, why are they coming for us, now they've had their pound of flesh?'

With a sharp intake of breath, Harry shook his head. 'All right! Paris, leave it, will you? Just let me think!'

The realization hit Paris like a horse's hoof in the teeth. 'Leave it, Harry? How can I? I'm mixed up in it now. I just don't get why they're after us now though, if they've already killed Travis . . .' Her jaw tightened. 'Harry, what else have you done?'

With her words ringing in his ears, he snapped. 'For fuck's sake, Paris, Vinnie has murdered Ted Stafford's dog and thrown its butchered body back in the garden. Now shut up and let me think.'

'Why would he do that?' she softened her voice.

'Because, Paris, he has shit for brains, he's taken too many drugs, and he thought that stupid stunt would have our ol' man singing his praises.'

They drove in silence for twenty minutes, both contemplating the reality of the situation.

For a moment, Paris felt sorry for her brother. They were close, and she looked up to him; yet, as much as she acted the needy little sister, she wasn't as oblivious to what her family's firm did as she made out. The years of brainwashing and inciting hatred towards the Regans hadn't worked on her, but obviously it had done the trick on Harry. Time would tell if the family would have their backs, now the shit had hit the fan. Or would they be hung out to dry?

Harry flicked his narrow eyes back to the mirror. 'I'm sorry, Paris, but I promise you this much. I will get it sorted out. But for the moment, we need to get down to the coast. I've left a message for Farver to fetch Muvver and bring her down an' all. I dunno what's got into the dopey cow, walking around like a fart in a trance. Was it me or did you notice her behaving strangely?'

'Yeah, she told me to take me washing and practically told me to fuck off. Menopause, I suspect. So what's gonna 'appen now? I can't stay in that poxy flat. I'll get cabin fever.'

Harry didn't answer, his mind now back on the photos of Travis. He took a few deep breaths to steady his nerves.

Chapter 4

On the way to Gatwick Airport, Jackie fumed. *Who the fuck did Mike think he was, demanding that she go to Spain?* She gritted her teeth and put her foot down, using the horn at the motorist veering in front of her. Why should she do as he said? He had no right. It wasn't as if he really cared about her. Maybe he wanted to move someone else in for a while? Could it even be his perfect ex?

Jackie went over in her head the number of times he'd looked her up and down with that expression of despair. Or perhaps it was disgust? She knew deep down she would always be compared to that woman who had fucked off and abandoned him. She would always be second best. Well, not anymore. She had her own plan. *Fuck you, Mike Regan.*

Ignoring the turning to Gatwick, she carried on along the M25. Ricky moaned. He needed the toilet, and in a flash, she told him to shut his mouth, which he promptly did. He didn't want another slap from her. She pulled down the sun visor and gawped in the mirror at her sore red skin and bruised face. Her anger climbed a pitch. *You just wait and see, Mike. I'll have the last fucking laugh.*

'Sit still, ya little shit!' she hollered, as she spotted Ricky squirming.

'Mummy, I need to pee.'

'Hold it in. You ain't a baby,' she snapped at him. Her sudden plan made her jittery. It was now or never, and Mike had just given her the final shove to put her future dream into action.

Ricky tried hard not to pee, but the rush out of the door this morning hadn't allowed for a trip to the toilet, and now he was frightened. Beads of sweat gathered along his hairline, as he struggled not to wet himself. Then, he couldn't hold it in any longer, and along with the torrent of wee, came a stream of tears. His mother would slap him. At least he was safe until she stopped the car. She was concentrating on the road ahead and didn't hear the tinkling sound. A small pool gathered in the hollows of the leather seat, and slowly, not making too much noise, he removed his tracksuit top to mop up the mess. Keeping one eye on his mother, he quickly slid the top under the front seat, praying that his trousers would dry out soon.

As young as he was, little Ricky was no idiot. He had his mother sussed, and he knew that how she treated him wasn't right. He loved his grandparents and Sacha, and adored his father, but he despised his mother. At six years old, he was fully aware of the spite she held for him. With an observant eye, he realized that they were now not off to Spain because he knew the drill: the parking, the airport customs procedures, the flight, and then the drive to the villa. They were on the motorway, passing signs and areas that he didn't recognize and heading in the opposite direction from Kent. Then he spotted the sign for the M11; he had no idea what that meant.

* * *

Mike poured Staffie another drink. He could see that the vile act carried out on Staffie's dog was ripping him in half. 'Listen, Staff. Do yaself a favour and get the dog outta your 'ead. I know you loved him, but you need to get yaself together, so that we can seek justified retribution.'

Staffie looked up at the huge man and knew he was talking sense. Besides, Mike was the one man he wouldn't argue with for two reasons: he was the hardest guy he knew, and he also respected him.

'You will 'ave your chance to avenge ya dog's death, but we need to round up this little Harman crew before they cause more mayhem. Got it?'

Staffie nodded and gave a smile that bared his uneven teeth, giving him a childish, goofy appearance. Many a fool regarded Staffie as being a bit simple, just because of his expression, and many regretted it. As much as he looked like a bulldog himself, he had a charm that was unmatchable.

'Good lad,' said Mike, as he patted Staffie on the shoulder. 'Right, I want you all to find out as much as you can. I'm gonna pay Izzy Ezra the Jew a visit. That man knows everyone and everything. Besides all that, the bloke needs to know who's been poking their nose into his little arrangement.'

Eric took a sharp intake of breath. 'Ya ain't going alone are ya, Mikey?'

With a cocky wink, Mike replied, 'Izzy is a ruthless Jew, but, bruv, he has no grief with me. However, Harry Harman, that little grass, will most certainly be in his bad books. Izzy set up our arms racket with the Lanigans. All he asked for was a cut in return, along with no fuck-ups. But now, he'll see the Harmans as trying to ruin his reputation. That man won't sit back and take it, not all the while he has a skullcap to pray with.'

Within an hour, Mike was parked up behind the old jeweller's place just off the Old Kent Road, well away from Izzy's manor in Tottenham. The shop was just a front; the main business was conducted at the rear of the building. Mike stepped out of his car. He made sure his jacket covered the belt that held his handgun and knocked three times at the back door. He paused and knocked another two times, following the code that Izzy insisted upon.

Slowly, the door opened, and there, taking up the doorframe, was Quasimodo, whose real name was Norman. He acquired his nickname due to his size and an ugly, twisted face that only a blind grandmother could love.

'All right, Quasi?'

There was no response, apart from a flick of his head to indicate that Mike could go in.

Passing the stacked tatty boxes and a rancid toilet without a door, Mike grinned to himself. He never failed to be amazed that after all the shit and smell from the entrance, there could be such a huge transformation. They went through the secure heavy metal door that led into Izzy's so-called office. Row upon row of books, housed on highly polished mahogany shelves, surrounded an enormous solid wood antique desk. But the central feature was a Persian rug. Anyone who entered had to remove their shoes before stepping onto it. Mike followed the rule, and with one eye on Izzy, he flicked off his footwear and walked towards the desk. Izzy hadn't even looked up; he was sitting on a high-backed mahogany chair and staring at a piece of jewellery through an eyepiece. Still ignoring him, he waved his hand for Mike to take a seat.

'Seventeenth century, this piece. The scag heads around these parts have no idea of the value of what they steal for me.'

He removed the eyepiece from his face and gently placed it on the desk along with the brooch. Clasping his hands together, he leaned back. 'I was wondering when you were going to visit me. Let me see. It's been three days, seven hours, and thirty-six minutes since the establishment turned over your lock-up.' His voice sounded relaxed; Mike knew, though, that it was just the calm before the storm.

'Yes, Izzy, and it's been forty-eight hours since I discovered the fucking culprit who grassed me.'

54

Izzy, a middle-aged man with piercing black eyes and thick white hair, in the classic slicked-back style to match his long beard, slowly nodded. 'You know, Mike, people swear when they have no other word to use. Anyway, I'm assuming you wanted to establish the facts before you showed up at my door?'

Mike sat as cool as a cucumber, not even blinking, his eyes firmly fixed on Izzy's face, although he knew only too well that Izzy was more than capable of pulling out a shooter and blowing him through the walls into the greengrocer's next door.

'No, Izzy, I came because I wanted to pick your brains, not 'cos I owe you or anyone an explanation. You had a business deal with me. Five grand to pair me up with a buyer for my guns, that's all the deal was. You got your money, and I got the name of the buyers. That, Izzy, is where our business was concluded.'

Izzy slapped his hands on the desk and stood up. Mike looked him over. He was dressed in a suit, complete with waistcoat and collarless shirt. A gold watch hung from his waistcoat pocket and three heavy gold chains swung from his neck. A distorted smirk revealed his gold back teeth as he glared at Mike.

'You, Mike, are forgetting a very important fact. I have a reputation and that means more to me than money.'

Mike laughed out loud. 'Never, Izzy. I don't believe it.'

'You and everybody else think I'm all about money, but you're wrong. My family and my honour mean far more. So, listen to me.' He walked around the desk and lowered himself to sit on the corner as he leaned close to Mike's face. 'You give me the names of the grasses, and I'll make sure they don't see their next bowl of porridge. The Lanigans want more than ammunition. That's just small fry. I'm in negotiations for bigger wares, and that, dear boy, is why you need to keep me well and truly in the loop. Now, I want names!'

Mike shook his head. 'Nah, Izzy. Let me deal with it because it's just got fucking personal. The little firm that grassed me up also killed Staffie's dog. I assume that was a warning.'

Izzy rose from the desk and pulled a cigar from his top pocket and lit the end, puffing away with his back to Mike. 'A dog, you say? And a warning? A warning for what?'

Mike realized it sounded stupid, but, nevertheless, like Izzy's honour, it meant a lot to him. But it wasn't so much about the dog – that was bad enough – it was the upset it had caused his friend.

Just as Mike was about to explain, the side door opened and in breezed Zara Ezra, Izzy's daughter. In her early thirties, this tall, slender woman had a swan-like neck accentuated by a wavy multi-toned bob. To Mike, she was the epitome of class and grace with an unforgiving, deadly sting in her tail. Her copper, cat-like eyes slowly blinked when she noticed Mike, yet her face remained inscrutable, with not even a trace of a gentle smile. Totally ignoring Mike, she went over to Izzy, pecked him on the cheek and pulled a wad of banknotes from one of the desk drawers.

Mike noticed how Izzy's face had lit up when she'd walked into the room.

'Is it all here?'

'Yes, my darling.'

'Good. I'll be back at teatime. Before you say anything, I have Joshua with me.'

Mike watched her every graceful step as she left the room.

'Nice-looking woman. Is she—'

He never got the rest of the words out of his mouth. Izzy slammed his hands down on the desk. 'Yes! My fucking daughter.'

Mike couldn't restrain himself from a slight smirk. He'd definitely got under Izzy's skin.

'I didn't think you swore. Besides, Izzy, I was only gonna pass a compliment.'

Izzy glared with his beady eyes. 'Anyway, were we talking about a war over a dog?'

Mike nodded heavily. 'Yep, over a bleedin' dog. But you and I both know that it's a statement. So, Izzy, it seems that a little firm run by three brothers, Harry, Vinnie and Scottie, have taken serious liberties, and although we sent them a clear message via their informant, they saw fit to brutalize Staffie's dog. And in my world, if not in yours, Izzy, that goes against the grain.'

Shaking his head, Izzy smirked. 'You lot are nuts. Okay, you do what you need to do, but if these Harmans are not found and dealt with in the next forty-eight hours, I'll take over, and you, Mike, will be owing me . . . Harmans, you say?'

Mike watched as Izzy's fingers, which displayed a variety of rings of all shapes and styles, wiggled as if he were about to play the piano.

'I didn't, but you knew it was the Harmans all along, didn't ya, Izzy?'

Izzy gave a slow, deliberate nod. 'Yes, I just wondered how long it would take you to work that out, Mike. I'm a shrewd man. I watch and listen. I backed off and allowed you to deal with the situation. But I was testing you to see how long it would take you to be upfront and inform me of the issues. You passed that test.' He waved his hand dismissively. 'Now, you have forty-eight hours, or you will be working for me.'

Mike huffed. 'Well, that ain't gonna happen – ever!'

Izzy leered. 'Our deal was that if you messed this little arrangement up, then you would be on my firm under *my* control. Remember, Mike, you are a man of your word. I hope your sidekicks are preparing to be answerable to me.'

Mike got up to leave. He bit his tongue before he said something he would regret because there was no way he would be working for Izzy the Jew – not while he had a pair of balls.

Izzy grinned to himself as he watched Mike leave. He was fully aware of the clout Mike had. He wanted him on his firm, as head honcho if need be, since Mike was gaining a reputation faster than Durex sales during the Aids scare.

Once outside, Mike clocked the tall figure, leaning with her back arched against a newly built brick wall. She was drawing on a long black cigarette holder. For a second, Mike saw her as a flapper girl from the 1920s. Bonnie and Clyde sprang to mind. He stopped and pulled a packet of cigarettes from his inside pocket and flicked open the lid to his engraved silver lighter. Before he put it back into his pocket, he looked at the etched image of his son. He made a mental note to call and make sure Jackie and Ricky had reached Spain safely.

'Have you upset Daddy, by any chance, Mikey?' Her words were cold and oozed confidence. He stepped closer and noticed her milky white skin had just a hint of pink, especially on her bare shoulders.

'You need sunscreen in this weather, Zara.'

She looked his way, ignoring his comment, and then she turned to blow smoke in his direction, her eyes narrowing in displeasure.

'How are you?' he asked, with a smirk across his face.

She pushed herself away from the wall. 'I'm fine, Mikey. Why shouldn't I be?'

Removing the cigarette butt from the holder, she threw it to the ground and placed her open-toe shoe over the top, stubbing it out.

She started to walk away, acting as if she had no interest in him, but he knew she rarely smoked and had been waiting for him – maybe just to see if there was still a little spark between them.

'So, you're back then?'

She shot him a look of anger. 'I have been for a while. How's Julie . . . Joanne, or whatever her name is?'

'You mean Jackie? She's a pain in the arse, a nightmare . . . but, hey-ho, life's a bitch, and I certainly married one.'

She searched his eyes for any sign that he still had that sexual hunger for her, knowing she could never read him. 'Well, you made your bed, Mikey. Your circus, your monkey.'

He sighed and looked her up and down. 'Yep, Zara, you got

that right.' There was an awkward silence for a few seconds. She assumed he still had feelings, or he would have waved and said goodbye – not stood there, looking her over.

'Well, Mikey, you bred with her.'

Mike had to bite his tongue. That comment was crass and in fact quite vile. His son was his world, and so the words stuck in his throat.

She clocked his stern expression. 'Don't look so offended, Mikey. It's true. You married her and had a kid, so she must mean something.' Zara took a step closer with a sneer plastered across her face. 'Unless, that is, Mikey, she is just an exceptionally good fuck.'

In an instant, he grabbed the back of her hair and pulled her face an inch from his. 'Nah, Zara. You were that.' And then he planted his lips on hers. Even though she struggled, he held her there, until he felt her relax and then he let her go.

She wiped her mouth with the back of her hand. 'You bastard!'

Trying to steady his breathing, he shook his head and walked away. He had to make his head rule his heart – once bitten, twice shy. As much as he felt the surge of excitement and rush of lust, she was still the woman who'd left *him*. Unable to look back, afraid of his own feelings, he marched on ahead. He shouldn't have kissed her either, but he wanted to demonstrate his power. Seven years ago, he would never have grabbed her like that – ever.

Zara watched him, her mind all over the place. She was seething, but as soon as he was out of sight, she calmed down and then smiled. There was an upside to this latest encounter: he still wanted her. But would he still, if he knew how much had changed?

* * *

By the time Mike returned home and called a meeting, the lads had done their homework on the Harman family and located the address where each family member lived.

'How'd it go with Izzy?' enquired Eric.

Mike raised his brow. 'As expected, he wants the Harmans dealt with as much as we do.' Not wanting to concern the lads, he deliberately left out the threat Izzy had made.

'Was he on his own?' asked Eric, trying to sound nonchalant but failing miserably.

Mike stiffened and turned to face his brother. 'Do you mean was Zara there?'

Eric shrugged. 'No, not really. I meant anyone.'

'Yes, Eric, I saw Zara.'

Dying to know what went on, Eric had to bite his lip; he couldn't appear too eager.

Unexpectedly, Mike snapped at him. 'You fucking knew she was back, didn't ya?'

Eric felt his face flush red. He looked at the others who had now almost frozen to the spot in disbelief.

'Well, yeah, I did hear that a while ago, but what does it matter? You're with Jackie and have Ricky. She's . . .'

The uncomfortable atmosphere spurred Lou to quickly change the subject. 'Listen up. Harry, Vinnie and Scottie Harman's pads have all been checked over. It seems they've gone into hiding. The only place not accounted for is their ol' man's.'

Mike sensed that the Zara discussion should be kept separate from the business at hand. He shot Eric a disparaging glare before calling for action.

'Right, then. Eric and Willie, you come with me. Get a tool and put on a first-class bastard attitude because we're paying the Harman family's home a visit.'

Eric looked away to ensure that his brother couldn't see the darkened scowl on his face. He wasn't capable of keeping a steely fixed expression like Mike could. In fact, if he was honest, he knew they weren't cut from the same cloth. And being riled up because Mike met up with Zara was taking his focus away from the job in hand.

Staffie jumped up. 'I wanna come, 'cos I have a fucking monkey wrench with the name Harman carved on it.'

Mike shook his head. 'No! Sorry, mate, but your temper will be a liability.' He held up his hands. 'Trust me, Staffie. You'll get a chance to leave ya mark, so be patient. You stop 'ere with Lou.'

With red-rimmed eyes and a sulky pout, Staffie slumped back into his armchair and gulped back the last of his drink. 'Yeah, well, if you weren't such a lump, Mike Regan, I'd tell you to go and fuck yaself.'

Mike grinned and gently tapped Staffie's face. 'Yeah, and if I didn't love ya so much, I'd clump ya for that comment.'

'I want my time with them, though, Mikey. Don't you kill 'em before I leave my mark.'

'Staffie, I'm a man of my word. You go and find that monkey wrench.' He winked and nodded for Willie and Eric to follow him.

Within the hour, Mike was in Lee Green, driving slowly along the road to Frank Harman's place. He looked at the house numbers and then clocked all the cars in the street, knowing that Harry and his two brothers all drove black Mercedes with private number plates. Yet this street had no flash cars parked with two wheels over the kerb.

'Looks like the Harmans are not at home, boys.'

'What does their ol' man drive?' asked Mike.

Eric looked at Willie and shrugged his shoulders. 'Dunno. I only got the details of Harry, Vinnie and Scottie. I didn't think about the ol' man.'

Mike sighed. He loved his brother, but there were times when he was really irritated by him. Why his brother could be so lax when he should have his mind on the task ahead was beyond him. He thought that perhaps Eric was distracted by the stupid notion that he could surreptitiously go after Zara.

Eric had once had his eye on her years ago, but it was made

clear to him that Zara wasn't interested. In fact, her exact words were, 'I find him a bit creepy.'

'So, Eric, now we won't know what we're potentially walking into.' He didn't raise his voice; he'd made his point.

The pained look on Eric's face said it all: once again, he felt inferior.

Easing his car into a space just three doors down, Mike paused and looked up to see if the street had any cameras. Then he craned his neck to address both Eric and Willie who were seated in the back.

'When we go in, I want quiet. No shouting. These neighbours are too close. I want you to act like the fucking SAS, got it? I want whoever is inside that house shitting hot bricks with a shooter in their face, and then I want them away from here, back to the lock-up.'

Willie lit up a cigarette.

'Put that fucking thing out. I've just had me motor valeted! Jesus!' yelled Mike.

After looking up and down the road, he stepped out of the car, followed by the others, and confidently marched up to the house. He nodded for Willie to accompany him and whispered to Eric to stay out of sight of the window, but to stand by the front door, in case anyone tried to escape.

Mike and Willie hurried up the side of the house and into the rear garden where they noticed the back door was ajar. In a flash, Mike pulled his gun from his belt and pushed the door open. As he walked into the kitchen, he detected the sweet smell of cakes being baked. Then he strained to listen, putting his finger over his lips, indicating to Willie not to make a sound. Slowly, Mike crept along the hallway and opened the front door, flicking his head for Eric to enter.

Once they were all in the hallway, Eric gripped his gun and poked his head into the living room, only to find the television on and no one there – as if the house had suddenly been vacated.

He strained his ears again, listening; he could have heard a pin drop. That was until, suddenly, they heard the toilet flush. He held his gun, pointing it to the staircase, awaiting the appearance of a Harman. There was silence for a few minutes until the toilet flushed again. Motionless, they waited. Again, the toilet flushed. Mike nodded and raised his brow for Eric to go and investigate. Gingerly, Eric climbed the stairs and listened at the bathroom door, the only one that was shut; once again, the toilet flushed and made him jump. He rapped hard on the door and waited.

'I told you, Harry, I'm not leaving this house,' came a woman's voice from the other side of the door. 'Now, please, leave me alone, and if you want to use the toilet, then do so downstairs and do not invade my privacy.'

Mike took the stairs two at a time and knocked himself. Again, the person called out. 'Harry, I'm busy. Leave me in peace. I'm not going to repeat myself, so go, and don't bother to come back.'

Mike looked at Eric and whispered, 'Let's go.'

They headed back down the stairs and gathered in the kitchen. 'Well, I can only conclude that the Harmans have made a practical realization that the best move is to run, 'cos they know the bogeyman and his posse are after them. Wanting to get their mum away tells me they know there's gonna be bloodshed, and they've a good idea of what we're all about,' stated Mike.

Now that Eric knew there were no men in the house, he felt brave. 'Let's kick that door in and drag her out. It'll give them something to be shitting themselves about.' Just as he was about to head towards the hallway, Mike's hand grabbed him by the scruff of the neck and fiercely yanked him back.

'What the fuck!' shrieked Eric.

Willie looked away. He knew Eric had cocked up again, just by the look of anger in Mike's eyes.

'What the hell are you *doing*? Jesus! Eric, since when do we hurt dear ol' mums? You are one stupid dickhead.'

Red-faced and boiling, Eric glared at Mike. 'And since when did they abide by the rules, fucking killing Staffie's dog, eh?'

'Keep ya bloody voice down. I don't want the ol' girl 'aving a bleedin' heart attack. Now, we're gonna wait 'cos she's expecting her boy back. From what she said, it's my guess that they've upped and gone, but they'll return for her.' He pointed his finger up at the ceiling. 'I mean, think about it. If they believe we're on the rampage, they ain't gonna leave her behind, are they?'

Still sulking, Eric replied, 'Who knows, Mikey? You seem to know probably more than they do. So tell me, then, if they left her behind, why would they come back for her?' he asked, with a knowing smirk on his face. He wasn't going to let his brother walk all over him.

'Well, think about it. If I asked our mum to do something and she refused, I'd get you to go in and ask, wouldn't I, or the other way around?'

Eric was seething; this was getting so personal now. He knew exactly what Mike was getting at. Their mother, Gloria, would do anything Mike asked of her, but she always questioned him, since he was the son who messed up all the time. 'Why can't you think more like your brother?' she would say. And Arthur, their father, was even worse with his comments. One of his favourite pieces of advice was, 'Take a leaf out of Mikey's book, and you won't go wrong there.'

Thinking of his mother, he wondered why she had to be so patronizing towards him. When she rubbed his arm or hugged him, she always gave him that sympathetic expression followed by, 'Something will come along for you, just you see.' She used that saying for everything: girlfriends, a good lucky earner, or even a bargain motor. But her advice never worked because Mike seemed to have all the luck.

Willie could feel the tension building and decided to intervene. 'I'm gonna wait in the living room to see if any of the brothers pull up.'

Mike stared at Eric. 'You go with him. I'll wait in the kitchen, in case they come in through the back door.'

Eric was still smarting. 'Why are you doing that? We'll see them if they pull up, won't we?' His tone was airing on sarcasm.

'Eric, look at the fucking garden.' He pointed out of the kitchen window. 'That rear fence has a gate. They could easily come in from the road the other side, yeah?'

Once again, Eric realized he'd been caught out. Another thing Mike was good at was casing a joint. If he hadn't been a criminal, he would have made a good detective. Just as Eric walked off in a huff, Mrs Harman appeared, standing there in the hallway. Mike quickly held his hands up, showing he was harmless.

Doris had heard all the commotion downstairs and was about to give the person she thought was Harry a piece of her mind. At that moment, she was drying her hands on her pinny and not taking her eyes off the big man.

'It's okay, love. Me name's Mike. I'm not going to hurt you, I promise.' He edged forward as if he was trying to calm a rabid dog. Yet Doris seemed unperturbed.

'Excuse me, but my cakes need taking out of the oven.'

Willie appeared. Having been so intent on keeping a lookout, he hadn't heard her come down the stairs or past the living room.

Although this tall man with a deep scar down his face, twisting an ugly jagged knife in his hand, would probably frighten the life out of most people, his presence left her unruffled.

'Put that away,' Mike ordered. Willie instantly shoved it in his belt.

Doris calmly turned back to face Mike. 'I need to get to the oven.'

Mike was almost taking up the doorframe. 'Oh, sorry, love,' he said, as he stepped aside.

Doris waddled past, picked up the oven gloves from the small square table in the middle of the kitchen, and opened the oven door, where she removed two trays of fairy cakes.

Meanwhile, the three men looked at each other in confusion. Their mothers would have been screaming blue murder. Unhurriedly, she placed the trays on the table and closed the oven door.

Rarely did anything faze Mike, but, on this occasion, Mrs Harman had completely wrong-footed him. 'Shall I put the kettle on, Mrs Harman?'

Eric just shook his head in disbelief.

'Well, how funny is that. I can only assume that you've come to take some sort of revenge on one or more of my sons, but there you are, offering to make tea.' She made a huffing sound. 'Not even they do that. Well, yes, I suppose I would like a tea, thank you.'

Mike pulled out a chair for her to take a seat, and then he turned to fill the kettle. Willie leaned against the doorframe. 'Sorry, missus. I didn't mean to give you a fright.'

Eric was rolling his eyes. 'I'm gonna wait in the car.'

Mike nodded.

'So my sons have upset you, I take it?'

'I'm afraid they have. But, listen, I won't take it out on you.'

Mrs Harman reminded him of his own mother. They were roughly the same age, although his own mum was always dressed in the latest fashionable clothes. She wore jewellery and never left the bedroom without a coat of pink lipstick.

This lady, though, couldn't be more different, with her flat grey hair, a thick waist, swollen ankles, and her old-fashioned twinset-and-pearls look. And the sad, tired expression, no doubt from years of being worn down, certainly accentuated the difference.

The kettle boiled, and Mike spotted the teapot and one china teacup and saucer; the scene reminded him of sitting in his grandmother's kitchen. 'Tea should only be drunk from a china teacup, or porcelain if ya can afford it,' she would say. He remembered her dainty cup with the floral pattern and the chip on the side. He also recalled the day he presented her with a whole tea set that he had nicked from Allders. Her eyes lit up and she hugged him. 'Aw, little Mikey. Now I can have all me mates over for tea.' She always called him little Mikey, even when he was six feet tall. He poured the tea just how his grandmother liked it and presented it to Mrs Harman.

'There ya go, love.'

Doris looked at the colour of the liquid and smiled. 'Lovely, that. It's just how I like it.' She gracefully picked up the drink and sipped it. As she gently placed the cup down, she sighed. 'So, may I ask what the boys have done now? I'm assuming it's bad.' She huffed again. 'But then, it always is with my lot.'

'You've no need to be involved. It's just business. I'm sure they know the rules.'

'The rules? No, they don't know the rules, love, I can assure you of that. Um . . . do you make your own mum a cuppa, then?'

Mike gave her a sympathetic smile. 'Of course I do. Why do you ask?'

Doris's eyes clouded over. 'Does she do your washing?'

Mike frowned. 'Of course not.' Then it dawned on him; she was comparing him to her own sons. 'I look after my mum. I take her for dinner every Sunday, if I can, and I wouldn't have my dear ol' mum lift a finger.'

'Yeah, well, see, that's where my boys don't know the rules. In fact, if I'm brutally honest, they're all shits, even my daughter. All out for herself, she is. You'd think I'd have had at least one good egg among 'em, but, no, they all take after their father, and he's a real horrible bastard.'

Mike pulled out a chair and sat opposite; he sensed she needed to get her annoyance off her chest. 'Do they give you a hard time, then?'

She took another sip of tea. 'Hard time? Ha, that's an understatement. D'ya know, Harry told me to go and stay with me sister up in Bath. Obviously, he was expecting trouble. I wanted to hit him with the saucepan. My dear sister has been dead for six months. My only ally, my Tilda, and that fat git didn't even remember she'd passed away. They're selfish, my lot. They come in this very kitchen with their bags of washing, their tans glowing from their holidays abroad, and then they slap down their shitty clothes for me to scrub. And as for Scottie, I know he has money, and yet he still goes through my purse and nicks me pension. That ain't right, is it? You wouldn't do that, would you?'

Mike had a sudden thought.

'Don't they offer to take you on holiday? I always make sure my mum has a good two-week break away somewhere nice.'

'Ha, my kids have never even offered to take me for a Sunday lunch somewhere nice, let alone a bleedin' holiday. I ain't been away since I went to Bath with me sister, what, four years ago now.'

'That's not fair, is it?' He softened his gruff voice.

'Life ain't fair, love. I should know,' she replied, taking another sip of her tea. She looked up at him. 'D'ya treat ya mum on her birthday an' all?'

Mike smiled. 'Yeah, I do, every year. I drive my mum to a place called Rye. It's beautiful, with cobbled streets and views as far as the eye can see. She loves the little tea shops, the antique shops, and the fish and chip shop. She stays in my seventeenth-century cottage and just enjoys soaking up the atmosphere.'

Doris was staring off into space. 'Ahh, it does sound wonderful. She must be so proud of you.'

'Well, I tell ya what. Why don't you go and pack a little suitcase and I'll treat you to a nice stay in the very same cottage? Call it a birthday treat, seeing that your own boys haven't seen fit to spoil ya.'

She blinked and came out of her daydream. 'What? Oh, no, I couldn't possibly. Besides, I don't even know you, and, well, I was just having a moan, really. 'Ark at me, chatting away, and you being all nice, an' all. Suppose you're really 'ere to bash me boys? Anyway, what have they done now?'

Mike sighed. He wanted to get the dear old lady away from the potential scene of a bloodbath. 'Yes, Mrs Harman, I'll probably give 'em a clump, but, really, I just want a word. They did something unforgivable, I'm afraid. In fact, it was very cruel.'

Doris nodded, genially. 'Sounds like them.' She stared at Mike and frowned, as her head slowly tilted to the side. 'Are you by any chance related to Arthur Regan?'

Mike sat up straight. 'Why?'

Her eyes seemed to drift off again. Maybe it was her escape to another time or another place. 'You just remind me so much of him, that's all. Now, he really was a gentleman, but he was a rogue, all the same.'

'Knew him well, did you?'

Unexpectedly, the tears in Doris's eyes welled up. 'Yes, I did. He was the love of my life, he was, before Frank came on the scene. Oh, 'ark at me. Never mind. It's all in the past.'

His mind now all over the place, Mike felt his heart beating fast. Could this woman, the mother of his arch-enemy, have once had a thing with his father? He was dying to know.

'Was this Arthur married then?'

She smiled and blinked away the tears. 'Oh no. We were very young. Never mind. Anyway, enough of all this. I don't think any of my sons will come back. They're too concerned with saving their own arses. I know you're probably wondering why I'm not running around frantic, like, or trying to escape to call them, but the truth is, I really don't care. I really and truly don't care what happens to them. They were never my children. They were Frank's – well, theoretically. I think I was just an oven to cook his evil seeds. There, I've said it, now. Look, I'm off to the church. You can stay and wait, but I bet they won't show their faces.'

Mike grabbed her hand. 'Listen, Mrs Harman. Please. You

deserve better. You'll love Rye.' He winked and tapped her hand. 'Go on, pack a bag, and let me spoil you.'

'Oh, I dunno.'

She was tugging at his heartstrings, and Mike wanted her away from the potentially violent situation more than ever. 'The truth is, Mrs Harman, yes, I am related to Arthur. I'm his son.'

Her eyes widened, as she stared. 'I just knew it. You're the spit out of his mouth. Oh my God. It's like looking at him years ago.' She pulled off the tea towel that covered the cakes and wiped away her tears. 'He was a cheeky bugger in his younger years, but he had such a kind heart. I can see you are so like him.'

After blowing her nose, she rose from the table. 'Well, what have I got to lose? Give me a minute, and I'll take you up on that offer.'

She looked around at the plain boring kitchen that she'd scrubbed clean every day just for something to do. With a sudden spring in her step, she hurried up the stairs and busied herself, throwing all of her best clothes into a small 1950s suitcase.

Willie chuckled. 'What the fuck was all that about, Mike?'

Mike took one of the cakes and bit into it. It tasted very bitter. Popping open the bin, he spat the mouthful into it.

'Willie, we're gonna wreak carnage on the Harmans, and I want her away from 'ere. The poor cow. But I have another plan up my sleeve. I'll tell ya later.'

He helped himself to a glass of water, swirling it around his mouth before spitting it down the sink. 'Jesus, she might be a sweet ol' girl, but she can't fucking bake.'

He covered the remains of the cakes with the tea towel and waited for Mrs Harman to return. Entering the kitchen with her face flushed and her suitcase in her hand, she reminded him of Mary Poppins. It was her overcoat, hat and brolly. His heart went out to her.

'Right, let's get you that nice holiday break.' He held open the back door and followed her along the side of the house. 'Now, you wait here, while I fetch the car.'

Doris looked up and down the road, eager to get away from the drab street. All the years she had lived there and not one neighbour had ever nodded or said 'Hello'. They always ducked their heads down, afraid of her mouthy kids.

What a life she'd led, what with Frank and his philandering and aggressive ways, and then her demanding sons and her selfish daughter. She sighed. How she would have loved a son like Arthur's boy. She could have had that life too, if it hadn't been for Frank worming his way into her affections and then almost raping her. Whilst some memories are best forgotten, she knew that that one never would be, even though it was such a long time ago now.

Chapter 5

Mike tapped on the car window, making Eric jump. 'Listen, change of plan, we're going to take Mrs Harman to Rye.'

Lowering the window, Eric screwed up his face. 'What the fuck for?'

Mike was getting irritated with his brother. He expected Eric to be one step ahead and not have to explain everything. 'Look. There's gonna be a fucking war. Firstly, I want Mrs Harman out of the picture, and, secondly, with her on the missing list, it may well drag the Harmans out of their hiding hole. Got me?' He tapped Eric's face.

'It's a long way, Mikey. Have we got time for all of this?'

'Eric, you move over. I'm gonna drive you and Willie back to the house, and then I'll take Mrs Harman down to Rye.'

'I think, Mikey, you're best at home putting the plans in place. I'll take her down to Rye.'

Mike sensed his brother was getting anxious about the violent battle they were planning to have, and he rolled his eyes. 'No, Eric. Your moody face is pissing me off, and I don't want her feeling uncomfortable, so just do as I say. Now, move over. I'm driving. Willie, you help her in the back and keep her sweet.'

Eric did as he was told, still with the strops. Mike turned the car around and parked directly outside the Harmans' house. When Mrs Harman came into view, Willie jumped out, opened the door, and bowed. 'Your carriage awaits.'

Doris smiled and hurried inside. She took one last look at the house that she'd grown to detest and made herself comfortable, whilst Willie took her suitcase and placed it in the boot.

'All set, Mrs Harman?' asked Mike, looking in his rear-view mirror.

'Please, love, call me Doris.'

'Okay, Doris. Now, I'm just gonna drop off these two, and we'll be on our way.'

Once Mike had left Willie and Eric back at his house, Doris joined him in the front, and they headed to Rye. He thought about his own mum. She would never in a million years have sided with the enemy. What had those boys of Doris's done to her that was so awful? He could only guess she'd been bullied. The house itself spoke volumes: the tired old kitchen that hadn't been updated since the seventies; the woodchip wallpaper painted time and time again; even the kettle was a bargain-basement one. He would never have let his mum live like that. No, not while he had a penny would his mother live like a pauper.

* * *

Harry had stopped sweating by the time he reached Broadstairs. Paris was asleep, her head tilted to the side and her open mouth dribbling. He was pleased she'd dozed off; he needed to get his thoughts together. He glanced at his phone in the holder and felt anxious. Vinnie was supposed to contact Scottie and make sure his father had got their mother out of the house. Impatiently, he pressed redial, the last call he'd made to his father's phone. It rang four times and then went over to voicemail. Paris stirred

73

before settling down against the sumptuous leather interior. He then tried Vinnie's number; luckily, within two rings, it was answered.

'Harry, what the fuck's happening? I ain't heard a word from any of ya. What's going on?'

Vinnie, a year younger than Harry, was more laid-back. He walked and talked more slowly than Harry. 'I can't find Farver. He ain't at the old slag's house, and he ain't in the boozer either. Scottie's on the missing list. So, I'm now on me way to Muvver's.'

Harry bashed the steering wheel. 'For fuck's sake, what's the matter with 'em all? Christ, when I get hold of Scottie, I'm gonna wring his scrawny neck. I left a message for him to call me.'

There was a pause before Vinnie muttered, 'Ya don't think the Regans have got him, do ya?'

Sweat again trickled down Harry's nose and he was breathing quite deeply. 'Nah . . . I dunno. Look, Vinnie, check Muvver's okay, will ya? Do whatever it takes to get her outta that house and then try and find Scottie. Call me and let me know what's going on . . . Oh, and watch yaself. The Regans may have someone plotted up.'

The phone went dead, and Harry took another deep breath. The vision of Travis popped back into his head, and he shuddered. He just hoped to God they hadn't captured his youngest brother. He would never forgive Vinnie if they had.

* * *

It wasn't until Vinnie pulled up outside his mother's home that he began to have sinister thoughts and dread filled his veins. What he'd done to Staffie's dog was wrong, and Harry had nearly throttled him when he'd heard. However, Vinnie had believed at the time that it was a smart move. Spotting the dog in the garden, an idea had popped into his head; he would show the Regans what the Harmans were capable of. Reality then kicked him in the teeth when Harry pointed out that if any of the Regans found him, they would no doubt do the same to him as he'd done to the dog.

He stared at his parents' home and bit down on his bottom lip, drawing blood. Up until now, all he knew about the Regans was what his family had told him. Every member of the Regan firm had a price on their heads – a hefty sum payable to any member of the Harmans who brought a Regan – or anyone else from their firm – to their knees. At the secret family gathering, it was rammed home to them that the Regans and their firm were the enemy.

Vinnie had wanted to impress his uncle and to be the number one son in his father's eyes. So, high on cocaine, he'd seized the opportunity to make his mark. Now he wished he hadn't. After all, he couldn't put the genie back in the bottle. He bit his lip again. This time he winced and shook his head. Every nerve in his body seemed to be on edge. He decided to drive up and down the street to see if there were any unusual cars in the area. Confident there were none, he parked down the road away from the house and hurried back.

As he entered the front garden, his hand gripped the Stanley knife inside his bomber jacket – his old faithful tool and one that he'd used many times to leave a mark on the offending opponent. On high alert, he snuck around to the rear garden and noticed the back door was open.

Without going inside, he scanned the kitchen and clocked the tray of cakes on the side, the smell of baking still lingering. He assumed his mother was still at home, and so he relaxed his shoulders and stepped inside. There was an eerie silence. Entering the kitchen, he suddenly stopped. His nerves spiked his senses, and he heard the faint tick-tock of a clock. Then, as he listened, he realized it wasn't a clock but a dripping tap from upstairs.

'Muvver!' he called out. There was no answer. He called her again and waited. In nervous frustration, he screamed, 'Doris.'

He often called her Doris – or more cruelly 'Boris'. Assuming she was ignoring him, as she often did, he marched along the hallway and sharply poked his head into the living room, before he stomped up the stairs. 'For fuck's sake, Muvver, are you bleedin' deaf or what? Answer me, will ya!'

There was silence except for the sound of the dripping tap; it was now really grating on his pricked nerves. In a flash of anger, instead of politely knocking at the bathroom door, he aggressively pushed it open.

Shit! A sudden gasp left his mouth, and he quickly stumbled back as if an invisible hand had pushed him.

'Oh my God!' he shouted.

His head was spinning, his stomach automatically heaved, and vomit shot through his mouth and nose. He choked and tried to take deep breaths, but it was impossible. The puke rose again, without giving him a chance to breathe. As he fell to his knees, his hands caked in yellow sick, he heaved again. His mind became so overloaded with images of what he'd just seen that he couldn't stay in this house of horrors any longer. Yet still, he couldn't breathe; his legs were now unable to move and his whole body felt an intense tingling sensation like an electric shock. He blinked furiously and shook his head, trying to pull himself together.

There, lying in the bath, with the tap still dripping, lay the mutilated remains of his father. His eyes still wide open, his mouth gaping in a twisted shape; it was an abomination. Large chunks of flesh had been hideously removed. His ears and his nose were missing, and strips of skin lay floating in the shallow pool of water that was not quite red, but obviously filled with blood. His eyes couldn't take it all in at first. He wondered if he was dreaming or whether this must be a sick joke. For, there, lying neatly on the white cistern was not just the offending weapon – the family's carving knife – but his father's finger with the wedding ring still attached, the blood from which was trickling down the side of the cistern, forming a tiny pool on the toilet seat.

The walls around him darkened. Knowing he was going to faint, he tried desperately to hold it together. He kneeled on the floor, away from the grim scene behind him, as he sucked in an enormous lungful of air. He tried to steady himself, but before he'd even reached the top of the stairs, the light-headed feeling got the better of him. Down he tumbled, crashing his forehead against the wall, and there he lay on the bottom tread of the staircase.

Stunned and dazed, he remained motionless; for a split second, he thought all of this had been a bad dream. That was until he heard the tap dripping again and he knew it was for real. Still in a blind panic, and with a lump on his forehead now swelling to the size of a golf ball, he managed to get to his feet and run.

He left the house, knowing that he would never return. Eventually, he reached his car and almost ripped the door handle off trying to get inside. As he drove away like a man possessed, he tried to process the events he'd just witnessed and plan what to do next. His first thought was to phone Harry.

As soon as Harry took the call, he heard the terror in Vinnie's voice.

'Jesus, Harry, I've just left Muvver's . . . Oh my God, Harry.'

'Slow down, Vinnie. What's happened?' Harry heard his brother's harsh breathing and held his own breath.

'It's Farver! Fuck me, he's dead. He's fucking dead. They've killed him. Jesus, Harry, they've fucking cut him up. In the bath, for Christ's sake. Blood's everywhere . . . It's disgusting . . .'

Paris stirred, snorted, and fell back to sleep.

'Are you there, Harry?' He sounded desperate to keep his older brother on the line.

'Yes, Vinnie. Christ . . . they fucking killed our ol' man? I swear to God, I'll have every single one of 'em.'

'Harry, what shall I do?'

Harry was in shock, but then sudden anger surged inside him, working its way up to his head. He felt as though he was ready to explode.

'You, Vinnie, you can do what the fuck you like. This is all your fault! I knew they wouldn't let killing the fucking mutt go, and now look what's happened. You are one useless prick!'

Ignoring Harry's accusation, Vinnie begged for help. 'Please, Harry, tell me what to do. They're gonna come for me. I just know it.'

It was the final straw. This shit-for-brains brother of his had acted recklessly without his say-so, and now Harry hated the pathetic sound of his brother's voice. 'Where's Scottie?' he growled through clenched teeth.

'I dunno. I came straight over to Muvver's, like you said, and I ain't heard from Scottie. Harry—'

Harry had had enough of his brother. 'Just find fucking Scottie. Then, once you've got him, call me. *Don't* fucking call me unless you have anything useful to tell me.'

Harry wiped the gathered beads of sweat before they ran into his eyes and stung him.

He was so focused on what had happened to his father, he hadn't even contemplated his mother's safety. He looked in his rear-view mirror and wondered how he was going to break the news to his sister. She loved her father more than anyone. He just hoped she would stay asleep until they reached Broadstairs.

* * *

Doris felt content soaking up the country views. Mike reminded her so much of Arthur that she felt at ease in his company. If he was only half the man Arthur was, then he was all right in her book. There were so many 'if onlys' in her life. The biggest regret was not waiting for Arthur when he went to prison. She'd received a message from Teddy Stafford senior that Arthur didn't want any visitors or letters. She should have known, back then, that Arthur didn't want her traipsing up to a grotty prison. Unaware that Frank had set him up, and was worming his way into her life, she succumbed to his affections. He got her drunk, had his way, and she was left walking up the aisle with her first-born due in six months.

She remembered seeing Mike as a baby. Arthur had met a woman, married her within the year, and they'd had their first child within eighteen months. There was no need for a newspaper in Bermondsey – the news travelled even faster than the new Eurostar service into London.

She recalled seeing Gloria proudly pushing her son around in a beautiful pram. Doris had been dragging her two sons to the shops, both with wilful minds of their own. Gloria looked like she'd stepped out of a magazine. She was wearing a red swing coat, with her hair immaculately bobbed and she'd even put on false eyelashes. With a spring in her step and her head held high, she strolled by, much to the admiration of Doris. Despite the small age gap, she knew Gloria actually looked ten years younger.

Gripped by sadness, Doris knew that if it hadn't been for the lie Frank told her, she would have waited for Arthur. She loved him so much, and still did, even though he was married to Gloria. There were no hateful feelings towards her though; after all, she had done nothing wrong. They knew each other from the estate, but they weren't on such friendly terms that they would stand and have a chat. So, they would find themselves nodding politely when they encountered each other – which Gloria did as she passed Doris.

Doris remembered that day like it was yesterday because more shocking was what she noticed after the woman had walked by. Doris was admiring Gloria's new coat and the expensive shoes, and just imagining herself wearing them and parading her son around. Just as Gloria passed the pub, Frank, who was idling in the doorway, pint in hand, stepped out and blatantly flirted with her. Doris watched in horror as Gloria began to walk away but Frank grabbed her arm. Doris saw how difficult it was for the woman to shrug him off. She knew what Frank was like when he'd had a few pints inside him. He was a forceful, won't-take-no-for-an-answer man. She contemplated walking in the opposite direction to do the shopping, but she couldn't leave the woman like that.

'Frank!' she called out. He responded by letting the woman go and then strolled towards her, veering from side to side. She held her breath; she knew he was pissed and he wasn't nice when he was drunk. But then, he wasn't nice anyway.

'What d'ya fucking think you're doing, woman? You ain't no fucking fishwife, so don't act like one. No wife of mine shouts their ugly mouth off in the street.'

She hurried away before he got really nasty. She didn't want the boys to witness it – not that it would have made any difference to them. Each of them, like their father, didn't have a generous soul. All three were like peas in a pod: obnoxious, rude and unruly. After she'd been to the Co-op and collected her Green Shield stamp-book along with a loaf of bread and a bag of flour, she wandered back along the street towards the pub. But as she approached the building, she could see a couple of the locals gathered outside. A car was parked across the road. There he was: Arthur Regan. He almost towered over Frank. All she could hear was Frank hollering through stupid slurred speech. He was pathetic. Arthur, however, dressed impeccably in a black suit and with his hair neatly cut around his ears, said very little. With ease, he grabbed Frank around the throat with one hand and with the other he punched him square in the face, knocking him across the pavement and into the road. Two of the locals tried to pull Arthur back, but he flipped them aside like he was swatting flies.

'You ever even look at my wife, and I'll find you and put you through a mincer.'

Towering over Frank, red-faced and irate, he snatched a pint of beer from one of the onlookers and poured it over Frank's face. 'Now, you little creep-keep well away from me and mine.'

As he stepped over the man, Arthur suddenly looked over at Doris. Holding his hands up and with a resigned shrug, he mouthed 'Sorry.'

She could still picture him mouthing that word. She never did know if he was saying sorry for bashing her husband or apologizing for the life she was now living.

* * *

As they finally drove into the pretty, cobbled street, Doris gazed in wonder. The surroundings were as Mike had described – breathtaking. The row of cottages that nestled in among the stunning twelfth-century church gave the town its character, and the old-fashioned flowers – climbing roses and wisteria – which adorned the brick facades, enhanced the classic English feel of the place.

This would be her first real holiday ever. Her heart was beating fast like an excited child's. She could just relax and enjoy the fresh air and wander around and do whatever she wanted, instead of having to jump to her husband's demands or listen to her grown-up children with their foul mouths and brash ways.

Mike opened the boot and retrieved her suitcase. She watched him as he pushed the key in the lock and opened the door to allow her to go ahead. She gave him a smile that made her face come alive. It was then that he saw how pretty she'd once been, before being dragged down by her brood.

The inside of the cottage was much larger than she'd imagined. She stepped from the hallway entrance into a rustic lounge. As she looked around in fascination, she admired the huge open fireplace built in traditional brick, noting with approval the beams on the ceiling and the walls. A sumptuous three-piece suite laden with thick cream fleeces looked inviting. Doris could see herself sitting there in the evening with a cup of tea and her feet up.

Doris followed him to her bedroom, Mike carrying her suitcase. She went over to the window and had to stoop a little to properly view the cobbled street. She didn't see Mike watching her from the doorway. He noticed how the sunlight was resting on her soft, rosy face. She seemed so much at peace. Sighing silently, he left her and headed downstairs.

He grabbed a pen and paper from the kitchen worktop and quickly wrote down instructions for the cooker and the boiler. He pulled the keys from the drawer and placed them along with a wad of banknotes on the table. The last part of the note read: *Enjoy your holiday, treat yourself, and I will see you in two weeks.*

Quietly, he left before she had time to thank him.

* * *

Before he reached the M20, he dialled Jackie's number, expecting a different dial tone. He was surprised to hear the usual English one. The phone rang until it went over to voicemail. He tried again with the same result. His anger heightened.

'Jackie, call me right away when you get this message!'

He was annoyed she hadn't picked up the phone, and even angrier that it left him with a worrying thought. He remembered Jackie having the hump, but surely she would have followed his instructions? He cursed aloud. 'Fuck you, Jackie!'

He should never have married Jackie, and if it weren't for little Ricky, he would never have done so. Her cocky sneers and smart remarks riled him up, and now, by ignoring his calls, she was leaving him raging. He assumed she'd ignored him and gone to the hairdressers, or perhaps the tanning salon. At this very minute, she was probably rinsing the credit card on new clothes for Spain. He bit his lip.

He could still see his little boy's face before Jackie shoved him into the car; his eyes were almost begging Mike. He hated that look; it made him feel so guilty. He detested his wife's lack of compassion. She was one of those women who was obsessed with the material trappings of life – the complete opposite to Zara. A sense of guilt momentarily clouded him. In his heart, he knew his relationship with Jackie had been on the rebound.

Gripped by not knowing where his wife and son were, he wondered if the Harmans had followed them. His heart began to race, and he redialled the number. This time, it went straight over to voicemail. He figured she'd turned the damn phone off.

By the time he reached home, it was almost dark. The men were still gathered in his lounge, all except for Eric, who had left shortly after Mike's departure.

Looking flustered, Mike asked Lou to call the airlines to check if all the planes to Alicante that day were full, because if they weren't then his wife should definitely have been on one of them.

Staffie noticed Mike was looking anxious. This was a rarity; the only time he'd seen him with vulnerability strapped to his shoulders was when Ricky once had the measles and had been taken to the hospital.

'What's going on, Mikey?'

'Jackie's phone has a British dial tone – she ain't in Spain. What's worrying me is the poxy Harmans. If they followed her and have taken my son . . .' His face reddened as he clenched his hands behind his head.

'Fuck me, mate, that's a long shot. Think logically. Jackie may have missed the plane or fallen asleep in the hotel. But I don't think the Harmans are clever enough to kidnap your wife and Ricky.'

Mike took a deep breath. 'But if they have . . . I swear to God, I will mutilate each and every one of them. Where's Eric?'

Staffie looked at Willie. 'I dunno, mate. Eric said he'd things to do and left.'

'Things to fucking do? Like what?' shouted Mike, now almost apoplectic with rage.

Willie shook his head. 'He didn't say, but I think he had the hump.'

Mike was about to explode again when his phone rang. He looked at the number. It was Izzy. 'Hello.' He sounded abrupt.

'Mike, I'm just letting you know you now have twenty-four hours to have the Harmans' heads on sticks, or I will deal with them myself. The Irish firm aren't happy that their goods didn't arrive. I've had to pacify that situation on your behalf. So, twenty-four hours, and then you, my boy, will be working for me. Just a reminder.'

Mike wasn't in the mood to reel in his temper, nor to pay homage to the Izzys of this world. Accordingly, he snapped back. 'You fucking listen to me. Right now, Izzy, you can shove ya threats up your arse. I've more pressing things to deal with. I want the Harmans alive and kicking with answers.'

'Answers?'

'Yes, Izzy. So, before you go hunting them down and blowing their brains away, I need to question them regarding my son. Now, get off the phone because I ain't got time for this bullshit.' Red-faced with anger, he abruptly ended the call.

Willie and Staffie just stared wide-eyed, mouths open. They couldn't believe that Mike was so staggeringly reckless. No one, absolutely no one, got away with talking to Izzy like that – not if they wanted to live.

As old and small as Izzy was, his facade was merely a front; he gave the impression that he was just an inoffensive Jewish jeweller trying to make a few bob. But buying and selling hooky gear was only a little hobby of his. Really, he could give Mossad a run for their money. His primary business was with the Italians and the Colombians, as well as a few influential firms in Ireland.

Although half of the small firms in London, Manchester and Hull were under Izzy's umbrella, Mike had kept his own firm out of Izzy's organization. That had been the case until the Irish arms deal was arranged. Now, he wished he'd never got involved, nor even clapped eyes on Izzy. He knew full well that if he refused to honour his promise, then the guy had the power to take over his manor and even do away with him.

Without warning, Mike snatched the heavy cut-glass decanter from the sideboard and hurled it across the room. The sound of the glass hitting the wall and splintering in all directions stunned the men into silence.

'Calm down, Mikey, we'll find 'em,' said Willie.

Lou got off the phone and shook his head. 'Sorry, Mikey, but all the planes that took off today had available seats. None of them were fully booked. She could have got on at least three planes.'

* * *

Zara sat opposite her father, with a deadpan face. 'So, why do you want Mike Regan on your firm?'

Izzy peered up through his hooded eyebrows. 'I know, Zara, about you and him.'

Her flushed face was a dead giveaway. All those years she had tried to keep it a secret. Remaining quiet, she hoped her father would elaborate.

He gave her a sympathetic smile. 'I want him on the payroll . . . for security.'

She frowned. 'Security? You don't need that, do you?'

'No, I don't, but when you take over, Zara, you will. I know he would be the one man to take a bullet for you.'

Casting a questioning look, she asked, 'Why act like you never knew? Why let me carry on stealing secret moments with him?'

Izzy was about to answer her, but she threw her hands in the air. 'Oh, forget it. It doesn't matter anymore. He's married now and I . . .' She paused, the words trapped in her throat. 'I have a business to run.'

Izzy allowed a wide crooked smile to adorn his face. 'Yes, my child. But you will need Mike Regan, because I will not always be around. And some people have bigger grudges than others.'

* * *

Mike's phone rang; it was a number he recognized. He stared for a few seconds before he answered and wandered away from the men.

'Zara?'

'Yes, Mikey, it's me, with a message from Izzy. I hope you realize that you only have twenty-four hours, or he'll be on the case.' Her voice was unintentionally cold and made Mike want to laugh.

The once-sweet woman was now turning into a clone of her father. Unbeknown to Mike, the cold stares and the stern tone were gaining her a reputation in the underworld – she was Izzy's daughter all right.

'I told Izzy to leave off, and Zara, me little princess . . .' His words were sarcastic. 'You tell him, if he interferes and the Harmans go missing before I get a chance to find out what they have fucking done with my son, I'll rip his insides out with a rusty fucking claw hammer.'

There was silence. 'Mikey—'

He didn't give her a chance to get a word in. 'Zara, acting like some cool gangster doesn't suit your sweet arse. Leave this shit to the big boys, honey. And didn't you just hear me? These Harmans, they have my son. So now you can understand why I ain't afraid to wage war on whoever stands in my way. So, if you're the go-between, then tell Izzy that.'

A sudden feeling of hurt whipped through her, followed by annoyance. How dare he have a go at her? She was only trying to calm the situation between her father and Mike, but he had just made it clear how he felt about her. Feeling hurt and belittled, she retaliated.

'And, Mikey, having an unchartered temper doesn't suit your sweet arse either. I'm sorry about your son, but I would take Izzy's words seriously, if I were you.'

Mike was about to have another go when the phone went dead.

She was right: he did have a temper. And, deep down, he knew he wouldn't be able to control it, not while he believed the Harmans had his son.

He stormed back into the lounge. 'Right, call the men. I want them plotted outside all the homes of the Harman brothers. I want someone in the Three Palms, the Cedars Arms, and the Jolly Roger. I want all of fucking South East London hunting down these bastards.'

Willie, having snorted a line of charlie, stepped forward, his foot tapping and his eyes wide. 'I'll go and show me face in the Cedars. That's their main drinking hole. I can't stand the fucking landlord, the sly fucker. He may have the little scrotes hidden upstairs.'

Mike could see he was fired up; he was always the same. The cocaine was a great motivator, and Willie was lethal, once he'd had a toot. He could also be a touch too reckless at times, but Mike could always be relied upon to reel him back in if required. However, right now, Mike had no intention of reeling anyone in. *When needs must the devil drives*, he thought. He was going to do whatever it took to get his son, and if that meant hurting people in the process, then so be it. He was blinded by his need to find Ricky and couldn't give a shit how he did it.

'Mikey, 'ave ya checked Jackie's muvver's? Maybe she's gone there,' Staffie said. He could see Mike needed to focus on the positive.

The clock was ticking. He knew that the longer the Harmans had his boy, the more likely they were to kill him. But if they did have him, surely they would have sent a message by now, with some form of a deal? With his hands together and two forefingers resting on his lip, Mike broke out of his thoughts.

'She doesn't get on with Gilly.' He let out a deep sigh and sat down heavily on the sofa. 'I dunno. I can't think straight.'

Staffie knew he had to take charge. 'Willie, you go and round the boys up, check out the pubs, and go and visit that landlord. Call us if ya hear anything. Lou, call Eric and tell him to get his arse back 'ere.'

Mike felt sick. Every nerve at the back of his head was on end; it was like a numbing sensation he'd never experienced before. He wasn't in control, and he knew if he didn't get a grip soon, he would lose it.

'Mikey, where does Gilly live?'

Mike rubbed his face in deep contemplation. 'Just up the road, ten minutes away . . .' He stood up, towering over Staffie. 'I'll pay her a visit. If the Harmans don't have my boy, then it means that Jackie has just fucked off. Jesus, give me strength if she has. I'll throttle her, the bitch.'

* * *

Driving once more like a lunatic, Mike arrived outside Gilly's house. He stared for a while at the patchy old pebbledash walls, the overgrown lawn, and the cracked front window held together with gaffer tape. It wasn't until he'd married Jackie that he found out where she came from. She was too embarrassed to take him to her house, always keeping up the pretence that she was from a good home. Jackie's inferiority complex often proved to be her own undoing. With her nose in the air, she would look down on people – and take enormous pleasure in doing so.

He knocked on a door that had seen better days. A croaky voice called out, 'Who is it? I ain't properly dressed!'

'Gilly, it's me, Mikey. Open up, love.'

He heard her rattling a key in the lock and struggling to slide back two bolts, before, finally, she pulled the door ajar. Through the small crack, where he could see her beady eye, the smell hit him: the whole place reeked of dogs, fags and piss.

'Let me in, Gilly, please. I need a word.'

She undid the security chain and stepped aside, allowing her huge son-in-law to enter.

As he wandered from the passageway straight into the living room, she waddled in behind him, her worn-out features on a par with the equally antiquated Dralon sofa, onto which Mike slumped.

He looked her over and shook his head. Gilly was a state and a half. Her once-thick hair was thin and straggly; it was held away from her wrinkled face by two hair clips. A bright-green velour tracksuit with 'Juicy Couture' embroidered on the back was her attempt at looking trendy. But the colour didn't do anything for her muted complexion, and the loose material around the knees and backside made her look even thinner than she was. He wondered if she'd ever been attractive in her younger years. Stick-thin and gaunt, she looked who she was, a typical junkie.

'What's up, Mikey? Ya never visit . . .' She noticed his white face. 'Mikey, love?'

'Jackie and Ricky have gone missing.' It hurt him even to say those words. A lump idled in his throat.

'They ain't 'ere, Mikey . . . and what's she doing? If I know my Jackie, and if she did do the off, she wouldn't take the boy. She loves herself too much, that one. Bastard of a mother she is . . .' She realized she'd just spoken out of turn. But there was no love lost: she hated her daughter. Not that she always had; in fact, she'd absolutely doted on her until the day her daughter found herself a Saturday job and started spending money on doing herself up. That was the time she turned on her mother, starting with all the bitchy comments and ending with violence.

'Gilly, where would she go? Who are her friends?'

Gilly took a seat. Mike noticed how thin she'd become; her bony mottled red feet were like those of a chicken. He looked at her shaky hands and assumed she was back on the drugs.

'Friends? You gotta be bleedin' joking, ain't ya? Don't make me laugh. The girl only uses people. How you put up with her, I'll never know. Ya must have the patience of a saint. It's Ricky I feel sorry for.'

His jaw tightened; just hearing his son's name made him feel sick with worry.

'Look, Gilly, can't ya think of anyone she may have gone to?'

Looking up at the ceiling, Gilly tried to think if Jackie had mentioned anyone from the past, but the reality was Jackie never spoke to her. Not about anything personal, anyway. With her, it was all just snide remarks. 'Oh, Mikey, I wish I could help, but ya see, I can't. Jackie, she's such a sly one. She's too many secrets, that girl.'

Mike jolted. 'Like what?'

Gilly was still a little stoned. She realized she'd just said far too much. She knew a lot about Mike. He could be like a Rottweiler when it suited him. He certainly wouldn't rest until she told him.

'Well?'

Gilly felt uncomfortable. She rubbed the front of her thighs with her arthritis-crippled fingers. Mike suddenly noticed that the room still had the threadbare carpets, the peeling 1970s wallpaper, and the former cream-coloured suite – now a dirty grey – that he'd seen on his last visit a year ago. A frown etched its way across his forehead.

She watched him scan the room. Then, without a word, he jumped up from his seat and headed towards the hallway and directly into the kitchen.

He glared with scornful eyes at the original council kitchen, made of cheap melamine that over the years had bubbled and split. The worktops had no edging on them and were sharp at the corners, to say the least. The linoleum tiles were an odd assortment and partly missing. He then focused on the dripping tap and the build-up of limescale on the sink. Everything in the room was old and rotten. The space in the corner, where the dog bed had once been, had a dirty brown stain on the walls.

He spun around to face Gilly and realized that he hadn't noticed until now how she was holding herself up with a walking stick. His worn, worried face was all too much for Gilly. 'What is it Mikey?' she asked, her voice soft and now very much concerned. She hoped the look on his face was because he was worried about her. But she got that wrong.

'You fucking scag head! All the money I gave you to have this shithole done up, so when my Ricky comes to visit he wouldn't scratch his face on this disgusting worktop, or crawl around in the filth. I bet you just snorted the fucking lot.' He expected Gilly to look suitably contrite. Instead, and to his utter amazement, he was met with a look of sheer horror – and disbelief – on her face.

'What money?'

'The fucking money Jackie took off me to get this house cleaned up.'

Now it was Gilly's turn to frown. 'I saw no money, Mikey. As Gawd is my witness, I ain't 'ad a penny off neither of youse.'

Mike detected a slight gypsy tongue. 'You're a fucking liar! I bet you spent every tenner on drugs, didn't ya?'

Gilly felt her limbs trembling; she needed to sit down. Slowly, she trudged over to the small rickety table where she sat uncomfortably. Taking a few deep breaths, she looked him squarely in the eyes as she replied, 'I ain't taken drugs in over ten bleedin' years. I only smoke the smallest amount of weed for me pain. And I've never touched it when I've been babysitting little Ricky, love his heart. As for money, don't you think if I'd had any, I'd have tried to make me poxy, flea-ridden home 'alf decent?'

Mike sighed. This evening was getting worse by the minute.

'So, you mean to tell me that Jackie never gave you a penny for a new kitchen, a sofa, even carpets, and, let me think, a swing set for the garden?'

'Swing set? Are you 'aving a laugh, Mikey? No, she never gave me fuck all.' Gilly looked around and felt embarrassed by the state of the place. 'Mikey, look, I never was this untidy. I do try me best, but I can 'ardly move me fingers, and the quack reckons I need two new knees. I know it looks terrible, but I do try to take Ricky to the park when I babysit every week . . . Mikey, you will still let me see him, won't ya? I mean, I love that baby, I do. He's all I've got to look forward to.'

Mike closed his eyes and took a gulp of air, trying to clear his mind. 'What d'ya mean by "every week"? I thought it was once a month you babysat?' He looked at her now with some compassion, and his voice softened. He might have known Jackie would have kept the money. She was all about the bees and honey. He knew she would take far more than she needed, and what she spent it on, he didn't bother to ask – it would only end in another row.

Gilly sensed his calmer tone and looked up. 'Tuesdays, Thursdays and every other Saturday, when Jackie gets her hair and nails and stuff done. She brings him to me after school or drops him off on a Saturday morning. I thought you knew? I mean, I'd never hurt little Ricky. I try me best to play games and read with him if it's raining. I don't cook in that kitchen. I always buy in little ready-made meals and cakes, so you don't have ta worry.'

Mike was trying to keep his breathing shallow, but his huge chest was puffing in and out, raising his whole torso by a good five inches.

'Sorry, Gilly. Of course I know you babysit Ricky, but let me get this clear. Jackie drops him off to you every other Saturday for the day and also on a Tuesday and Thursday after school for a couple of hours? And she never paid or organized for your house to be done up? Is that right, Gilly?'

She nodded. 'Yes, and I don't take drugs, apart from a small puff on a joint afore I goes ta bed. It's just for me pain, like.'

With flared nostrils, Mike chewed the inside of his lip. 'Where does she really go? 'Cos you women know if someone's just had their hair and nails done. I'm guessing she's been pulling a fucking fast one.'

Gilly had nothing to lose; she had to be honest. 'Nah, Mikey, I don't think she's getting her hair done. See, that's what I mean. That gal 'as bleeding secrets. I dunno why, though. She has what we all want – a nice home, food on the table, and holidays abroad. I would've given my right arm ta 'ave that. Still . . .'

Mike once again noticed a twang in her accent. He'd never noticed it before. 'I thought you'd have preferred a caravan anyway, Gilly?'

She looked sharply up at him, wondering if he was being spiteful. 'No point in keeping up a pretence, living a lie, is there? Yeah, I'm a traveller. So's my Jackie, if the truth be told. But, fair enough, she wanted to ditch that life, and, sadly, she wanted me to pretend I was a gorger. She made me swear down that I never told you that truth. With her new look and her money, the selfish cow wanted me to keep quiet and not let on. I did say to her that you would love her either way, if ya really loved her. But she was incensed. She swore, if I ever told ya, it would be the last time I'd see little Ricky, and I couldn't bear that. Ya won't stop me though, Mikey, will ya? Little Ricky-boy loves me, I knows he does. I wouldn't bring him up in the gypsy way, I swear.'

He shook his head. 'Nah, 'course not, Gilly. You're his granny, gypsy or not. You love him, and yeah, he does love ya. In fact, he loves the bones of ya. Do you have any idea where she would have been going on these Saturdays, or any other time?'

Now feeling more comfortable in Mike's company, she at last let her tongue talk freely. 'She's a go-getter, Mikey, always 'as been, like, since a teenager. She has no morals, not like a woman should 'ave, if ya know what I mean?'

'A tart?'

She pursed her thin lips together. 'Yeah, Mikey, a real slapper. Sorry to say it, mate, and her being my gal an' all, but, well, she is what she is. There ain't no changing her.'

Mike pondered for a moment. 'Gilly, I told Jackie to take Ricky on the next plane to our villa in Spain. I've got a bit of business to attend to, and I wanted them away, so no harm could come to them, and she knew that. D'ya think she would have ignored me, even knowing how serious it was?'

Gilly scratched her forehead and shook her head. 'I wouldn't think so, Mikey, 'cos she'd do anything to save her own skin. Yeah, I believe she would've gone to Spain.'

She could see Mike visibly shrink, his great big lintel-like shoulders now slumped.

'She never went to Spain.'

Gilly put her hands to her mouth. 'Jesus, this business. It wouldn't lead to our little Ricky getting hurt, now, would it?'

Mike looked at the worry that suddenly cast a pall on Gilly's face. Her eyes were alive with fear.

'No, Gilly, 'course not.' He didn't really believe his own words, despite trying to put her mind at rest.

He took one more look around the tired kitchen. 'It's late, Gilly, so I'll be off. Call me, if you can think of anywhere she may have gone, just in case she decided to find a place of her own instead of jumping on a plane to Spain.'

She struggled to stand up. For the first time, Mike had a very clear picture of his mother-in-law and not the crap that Jackie had been telling him. 'Are you really in a lotta pain, Gilly?'

She gave a sad smile, showing her missing tooth. 'Yeah, but old age gets to us all.'

The sad thing about it all was that Gilly wasn't old at all. She was a woman in her early fifties who could have passed for seventy.

'Once all this business is sorted out, I'll come back and organize a bit of help. I'll get you a new kitchen and freshen this place up.

94

I'll pay for a cleaner as well. I can't have Ricky's granny living like this.'

Her bony fingers clutched his arm. 'You're a good lad, Mikey. Ya muvver must be proud. It's just a shame I can't say the same about Jackie. But for me little grandson, I can, and I will. He's a chip off the ol' block, a mini you, if ya don't mind me saying.'

He quickly pecked her on the cheek and was gone.

Chapter 6

Jackie woke up feeling groggy. A bottle of vodka and a line of charlie had kept her up until the small hours. Now she lay with the sun streaming in through the window of the tidy little house close to Ely, Cambridgeshire. She didn't move her banging head but looked up at the small ceiling chandelier and smiled. As her hands slid across the warm empty space beside her, the smell of bacon tantalizing her taste buds, she closed her eyes. This was it: a new life. It was a future plan, but, considering the circumstances, it was now or never.

The only issue that had put a spanner in the works was the little boy, who she couldn't stand. Her scheme hadn't included him. The bedside clock flashed 11 a.m. and she thought she detected a whimpering sound, but it may just have been the gentle breeze whistling through the partly opened window. She cringed when she realized it was her son calling her.

'Mummy, please can I come out now?'

After gritting her teeth, she sat upright. *Trust Ricky to spoil the mood, the whiny brat,* she thought.

Unsteady on her feet, she snatched the silk robe from the end of the chunky pine bedstead, slid her arms in, and wrapped it around her naked body. She unlocked the door and angrily yanked it open. Ricky stepped back when he saw the temper in her eyes and the vein on the side of her temple pulsating.

'What's the matter now, Ricky?'

He looked up and tried to smile, his face bruised from the hard slap she'd given him when she discovered he'd wet himself.

His punishment hadn't ended there. In a fit of temper, she'd dragged him by his arm and marched him through the strange house and up the stairs. Forcefully, she'd pushed him into a small room with a mattress on the floor and a new quilt without a cover. When she'd slammed the door shut, and he'd heard a key being turned, his heart sank – he was locked in. After quietly waiting, while looking out of the tiny window until the skies turned dark, he'd gingerly tapped on the door and asked her to let him out. He was so hungry and thirsty, but his pleas were ignored. His mother was too engrossed in this strange man's company. And he didn't like what he was hearing either. This man, Scottie, whoever he was, was saying rude things to his mum.

Now, he was desperate. 'Mummy, please can I have something to eat and drink? I'm hungry and I need the toilet again.'

She grabbed him by the shoulder, causing him to wince, and steered him into the bathroom. 'Right now, you, ya fucking baby, use that contraption there. It's called a toilet. Don't you dare go pissing on that mattress either, d'ya hear me? I want my new home to stay clean and fresh, not stinking of piss.'

Ricky gulped. *A new house?* No one had told him they were moving. Bursting to wee, he hurriedly tried his best, but, as he did, he experienced a terrible burning sensation that made his eyes water. 'Mummy, it burns,' he whispered, his face now screwed up in agony.

'Yeah, well, that's what happens when ya wet yaself. Now, go back to bed and I'll fetch your breakfast when I'm ready.'

He wanted to ask if he could go downstairs, but from the look in her eyes, he wondered if he was better off keeping his mouth shut. Yet he was so thirsty, that he had to ask. 'Please, Mummy, can I have a drink?'

Ignoring her son, she shoved him into the small room and locked the door behind him, intent on returning to the bathroom herself to have a wash, reapply her mascara, and spray on some expensive perfume. She slipped the silk gown just below her shoulders, pulled her hair to the side, and gazed at herself in the full-length mirror. Her pert tits sat high up, and her regular gym classes had toned her stomach muscles. The sunbed sessions had indeed given her an even tan, and she believed that her reflection showed a real sexy woman. 'Fuck you, Mike Regan,' she mumbled under her breath.

As she added another layer of mascara to her lashes, she heard footsteps coming up the stairs. Smiling to herself, she exaggerated flouncing her hips as she met Scottie at the top of the staircase. 'I take it we're having breakfast in bed,' she laughed, allowing the robe to slip entirely to the floor.

Scottie grinned, admiringly. 'Looks like it, babe.'

He followed her into the bedroom, watching her neat, tight arse. The thought of food had gone from his mind as he placed the tray on the bedside cabinet.

Jackie giggled like a kid and positioned herself in what she thought was a sexy position before Scottie ditched his jogging bottoms and climbed on top.

Just as things were getting interesting, Ricky called out, 'Mummy, please can I have a drink?' In a fit of annoyance, Jackie pushed Scottie off. Grabbing the tall glass of orange juice, she marched to the adjacent room, unlocked the door, thrust the juice in Ricky's hand, and slammed the door shut, turning the key. She hurried back and dived on top of Scottie. 'Where was I?'

Scottie grabbed her hips and lowered her down onto his manpiece. 'There, me little cowgirl.'

Jackie pulled her hair to the side again and moved up and

down, expressing her most seductive face, or so she thought. She ran her hands over his chest and through his long hair until he shot his load and they both relaxed. Jackie climbed off and lay on her back. 'This is the life, eh, Scottie?'

Scottie was leaning across the bed to retrieve the cigarette. He wasn't one for many words, unlike his two brothers who always had a lot to say. His mother would call him sly, whilst Scottie saw himself as the mysterious type, a real babe magnet.

He took a few drags on his fag, sat upright, and swigged the tall glass of orange. Jackie took the drink from him and had a swill herself. The bitter taste hit the back of her throat. 'Jesus, vodka for breakfast? Now, I could get used to this.'

She shared his cigarette and the drink, and then she peered at the limp, greasy bacon sandwiches. Her stomach rumbled. She needed some food to soak up the alcohol from the night before, yet the bacon didn't look at all crispy or inviting. She wasn't the best of cooks herself; she had Sacha for that – well, until Sacha had left. Still, she could learn to cook. Not wanting to piss Scottie off for his efforts, she leaned across him and picked up one of the sandwiches. Carefully, so as not to drip the fat onto his chest, she put it to her mouth. After the first mouthful she swallowed, the second bite became easier.

'Cor, this tastes lovely, Scottie. I feel spoilt.'

'Let's spend the day celebrating.' He grinned.

As her eyes followed him out of the room, Jackie wondered what he had in store. But to her dismay, he returned with a bottle of vodka under one arm, a carton of orange under the other, and a spare glass into which he had stuffed a bag of weed and fag papers. She'd hoped that he would at least have presented her with gifts, perhaps even a bunch of flowers. She thought back to Mike, when she'd moved into his house. He'd bought her presents – bottles of expensive perfume, a gold Rolex and huge bunches of red roses. She smiled sweetly as Scottie poured her a glass.

'Only the best.' He grinned, holding up the Grey Goose.

She leaned against the headboard and watched as he rolled a joint. Compared to Mike, Scottie wasn't so big. Then again, who was? But he did have possibilities. Whilst Mike was older and more serious, Scottie had a charming, cheeky smile, which was a definite turn-on, and he seemed more reckless. Little did she know that Scottie Harman was her husband's arch-enemy.

* * *

Mike rubbed his face and looked around the room. Staffie was still asleep on one of the sofas and Lou was snoring in the armchair. Willie was busily making a coffee in the kitchen. It must have been Eric letting himself in that woke up Mike.

Standing there clean-shaven, and wearing a freshly ironed shirt, Eric said, 'Any news, then?'

Mike shook his head to wake himself up. 'No. And where the fuck 'ave you been?'

Looking sheepish, Eric shifted from foot to foot. 'I went to check that Tracey's all right.'

'What? Couldn't ya just 'ave fucking phoned her?'

Eric rolled his eyes. 'Look, Mikey, I came to see if there's anything I can do. I ain't 'ere for a row.'

Now livid, Mike jumped up from the sofa and stood an inch from Eric's nose. 'See what you can do?' His voice was climbing up in pitch. 'Me boy's missing, the Harmans 'ave started a war, and you wondered what you can do to help?'

Eric stepped back.

'This, you bastard, is partly your fault, taking on Travis in the first place. You fucked off to give Tracey a good screwing, and now you swan in 'ere like you're gonna do me a favour. What is it with you, eh? Call yaself a brother? Staffie, Lou and Willie are more my blood than you are.'

Eric turned away, his face burning and his fingers icy. He knew, though, that Mike was right. He'd gone to see Tracey and had spent the night with her. Then he'd got himself cleaned up and returned to lend a hand. However, he wasn't happy that Mike was throwing it all in his face.

'I don't know what you expect me to do.' His voice was suddenly cocky, but he regretted the words the second they left his mouth.

Mike grabbed him by the throat and shook him. 'I expect you to act like a man, not go running off to ya bird, ya no-good twat.' He pushed Eric so hard that he fell backwards and hit the tall glass cabinet. In a sudden fit of rage, Eric launched himself to his feet and threw a punch that caught Mike clean on the chin. Although Staffie and Willie quickly tried to intervene, it was clearly too late. The damage had been done. This tension had been simmering for a while now and the stakes had risen considerably to the point that trust between the brothers had plummeted.

But both Staffie and Willie were astounded that Mike didn't even move. They'd heard the crack and seen the force, but Mike stood there defiantly.

Eric then realized that if Mike hit him back, he would be out for the count. The intense stand-off alarmed the men. Never before had any of them seen that look on Mike's face. It was wild and almost unearthly; the whites of his eyes seemed to darken and his brows narrowed. In a flash, Staffie grabbed Eric and pulled him away, whilst Willie stood in front of Mike and Lou tried to pull Mike's arms behind his back.

'Easy, Mikey, easy,' said Lou, trying to calm the monster inside Mike. Lou could feel the tension in his friend's arms, as if his muscles had turned to steel. He knew he would have to use every ounce of his considerable strength to hold Mike back. It would easily take more than the three of them to contain him.

Eric managed to get away, out of the room, before Mike let rip and annihilated him. He waited outside in the front garden, hoping that Mike would cool off. Never before had he punched his brother, not even in jest. Whatever possessed him this morning, he knew he would regret it. He felt stupid for having brought Travis into the firm. And the fact that Mike had made him feel second best – not wittingly, but, nevertheless, he had – also made him jealous. Mike was treating him like shit in front of the others and that wasn't fair. They should be equal partners in the business, so therefore he should have an equal say. Yet the men always looked to Mike to give the orders, as if he, Eric, was a nobody. Suffering for long enough, it was time to stand his ground and at least be listened to. *Maybe that clump would have Mike thinking twice*, he thought.

Little did he know that inside the house, Mike was in a trance, his anger at its peak. He was fearing for Ricky's safety, and so, family or not, he was in the mood to smash the life out of anyone.

Staffie tried to talk Mike round, but that intense stare made it like communicating with a brick wall. Lou let Mike go, and Willie stepped aside to make the big man a stiff drink. No sooner had the men relaxed their shoulders than Mike was off, storming past Staffie and out through the front door. Eric didn't even have time to get his thoughts together. Mike grabbed his shoulders, spun him around, and punched him with such brute force that Eric's feet lifted off the ground.

For five minutes, as Eric lay prone on the grass, Mike stared down, holding his breath. *Had he just killed Eric?* Then he took in a deep breath as his brother began to groan. He waited for him to regain consciousness before he let rip. 'You selfish cunt. My boy's out there being fucking tortured, for all we know, and you waltz in my house acting like a hardman and show violence to me?'

Eric held his hand up. 'No, Mikey. Leave off.'

Mike towered over him. 'Leave off? Fucking leave off? Are you 'aving a laugh? You pathetic excuse for a man. Do one, Eric!' He waved his hands dismissively. 'I don't need you. You're a flaming liability.'

Eric was groping around on all fours like a drunken crab, before he got to his feet to flee. His head was still spinning. He had never been knocked out cold before. The pain was slowly making its way up his jawline and was now pounding like a pneumatic drill in his temples. No doubt, Mike had broken his jaw.

As Eric tried to open his car door, Mike called after him. 'Don't you ever come back. You ain't my brother!'

Eric was so hurt and angered by his words that he recklessly said the unthinkable. 'Yeah, and Jackie's such a slut that Ricky probably ain't even your son.'

Luckily, he managed to get inside his car before Mike reached him. However, as he drove away, Mike managed to smash two panels with his feet. Eric's car looked as if it had been kicked by an elephant.

There was nothing Willie, Staffie or Lou could have done, even if they'd wanted to. Eric had just rubbed salt in the wound; by anyone's standards, he had crossed the line, big time.

Mike, white-faced and fuming, stormed back through the hallway and into the kitchen. He tried to pour himself a strong coffee, in one of the small fancy cups. Agitated that he couldn't get hold of the tiny handle, he launched it into the sink and pulled a mug from the cupboard. Staffie could see the pain etched on Mike's face, so he took over and made him a fresh coffee.

''Ere ya go, Mikey. Why don't you drink that? Have a shower and clear ya head. Then we can decide on our next move.'

Mike gulped back the coffee and nodded, too angry to speak. Staffie was right: he had to get his head straight.

Ten minutes later, Mike appeared in the living room, clean-shaven and dressed in a fresh red polo shirt and cargo shorts. It was his eyes that dominated his appearance. They were still smouldering with anger.

'So, Willie, what did the landlord at the Cedars say about the Harmans?'

Willie was twitching; he needed some real sleep. 'Well, the little gremlin had to tell the truth – me knife was ready to take his tongue out.' He chuckled. 'He was only too eager to help. He reckons that Vinnie has been in, asking about his father and Scottie. He told the landlord to call him if either one showed up.'

'So it seems to me that the Harmans are panicking. But nothing's been mentioned about Harry, so I'm guessing Vinnie knows where he is, but not that little shit of a brother, Scottie, nor their father,' reasoned Mike.

Willie nodded, in confirmation.

'And their houses are being watched, yeah?'

Willie nodded again. 'Yep, me little brother's plotted up outside Harry's gaff. Young Felix is outside Vinnie's and Bruno is watching Scottie's place. There's been no activity at all. They'll call right away if any of them show their faces. Listen, Mikey. If they do have Ricky, I mean a big *if*, I think we would have heard by now. They wouldn't hurt him. I reckon they'd just barter with him, for an end to it all. They've gone into hiding, so they're obviously shitting it. The landlord reckons Vinnie was really agitated when he turned up. He said he was sweating buckets and stuttering.'

Mike paced the floor. 'So, Vinnie didn't even say a word about his mother?'

Willie shook his head. 'Nope. He was just after finding Scottie and Frank.'

'Right, I want every known associate of the Harmans armed with a message. The family can have their mother back in return for my boy.'

Willie smiled, showing his jagged teeth. 'Okay, chief,' he replied. He loved to throw his weight around, and being the most tempestuous of the bunch, Mike knew that he would do a good job. Sending a clear message, done with a touch of recklessness, was a wise move, and Willie was perfect for the job.

The phone rang and Mike stared at the number, shaking his head. 'For fuck's sake.'

He answered, waiting for the sarcastic gruff tones from Izzy.

'Mike, you now have only twelve hours.'

Mike wanted to smash the phone to smithereens, but his head took over. He needed his phone.

'Izzy, tell me. Which bit of "they have my son" did you not hear? If you do away with the Harmans, then who's going to tell me where my boy is? Do you understand where I am coming from?' He pronounced every syllable with clarity.

'The Irish ain't messing around, Mike. They don't take too kindly to having their business put in jeopardy, and more importantly placed under MI5's nose. They want this cock-up resolved within twenty-four hours or they'll be gunning for you – and, worse, me. So, Mike, you find the Harmans first or I will, unless you agree to work for me – and then I'll have them tied up and ready for questioning within the hour. The problem is yours, Mike.'

'Oh, trust me, Izzy, it will be your problem.'

'Is that a threat, Mike?'

'No, Izzy, it's a promise!' This time, he cut him off before he spat another word.

* * *

Zara looked at her father and shook her head. 'Really, was that necessary? You have the means to hunt down the Harmans, so why don't we just drag them in and let Mikey . . . I mean Mike . . . find out where his son is?'

'Because, my sweet daughter, you use a man's emotional state to your advantage. He will most certainly crack and give in. I guarantee that within a few hours he will be begging to work for me because he will need my help.'

'Oh, come on, Dad. He could find the Harmans himself. It's

not that he needs your help. It's only because you're setting a time frame. And if he can't locate these Harmans, why are you so sure you can find them in less time?'

'Zara, I shouldn't have to spell this out to you.' He sighed and leaned forward. 'I have a hundred times the resources Mike Regan has. So, fishing out the Harmans is not a problem. You should know how it works. To get what you want, you must find your opponent's Achilles' heel. Mike's is his son. I want Mike working for me for many reasons, but, the point is, he will do as I say because when we arranged the deal, he shook hands and agreed to the terms. Mike is a man of his word. That I do know, Zara. He will do anything to get his son back. Now, I suggest you toughen up and not let your feelings cloud the logic.'

'I don't have feelings for him!' she suddenly snapped.

'Oh, you do, Zara. Trust me on that one.'

* * *

Mike paced the floor. His nostrils flared as dread settled in the pit of his stomach. 'I cannot believe that Izzy could be such a cunt. As for Zara, why would she even get involved?' He snatched at the half-drunk coffee. 'Jesus, it's a fucking mess!'

Staffie glared at Mike. 'I know you cared about Zara, but from what I've heard, she is a cow! I have to give it to Izzy. He's raised a mirror image of himself. She's dangerous, that one.'

Mike gave a sarcastic grin and puffed out his chest. 'She ain't that dangerous. She's a waif of a woman.'

Staffie raised his scarred eyebrow. 'Don't underestimate her. She set someone alight not so long ago. I mean, what sort of a woman does that?'

'A cowardly one. I bet she had her men hold the poor bloke down first, before she doused him.'

'Even so, Mikey, it takes a lot to carry out an act like that, and, apparently, she stood back and watched to make sure the fella was dead. Well, so rumour has it. He was some immigrant, by all accounts, who tried to do her over for ten grand.'

'A rumour, Staffie, that she gave legs to and let it run. Anyway, I couldn't give a shit. She doesn't worry me. Nothing does right now except getting my boy back in one piece.'

Chapter 7

Paris lay still, curled in a tight ball on the sofa. Harry and Vinnie were in a state of shock and breaking the news to their sister was the hardest thing they'd ever had to do. The whole of Broadstairs must have heard her screams. It was at that point they realized that, as cold and harsh as she was, she really loved her father.

Harry's piggy eyes appeared as slits from stress and tiredness. Vinnie had to snort another line of speed just to keep himself awake.

'Harry, you ain't listening to me. Scottie and Mum are missing. I can guarantee the Regans have got hold of them. Our mum . . . surely they wouldn't do the same to her as they did to Dad? I mean, I know I wasn't the perfect son . . .' He stared off into space and bit his lip before his tears welled up. 'But I can't imagine her being tortured, not like what they've done to Farver. Jesus, Harry, it was sick.' He put his head in his hands, the vision of his father still haunting him. 'I can't get over it, Harry. They're fucking mental. What if . . . ?'

Harry was sitting listening to his younger brother droning on and on, while he was getting more and more enraged, until, finally, he flew from the chair, gripped Vinnie by his shirt collar, and shook him. Through gritted teeth, he hissed, 'Shut the fuck up, will ya! Just shut up. It's your fault, Vinnie. Your stupid idea of slaughtering the dog caused all of this.'

Vinnie didn't fight back. Instead, he began blubbering, like a baby. 'I – I did – did – didn't mean it,' he stuttered.

Harry let him go and threw his hands in the air in total frustration. That was all he needed, for Vinnie's stutter to return. He'd spent so many years waiting for Vinnie to spit out his words that it had turned Harry from a patient teenager into an exasperated man. Then, overnight, Vinnie stopped. No one knew why – it just happened. And that was that – until now.

Not knowing which way to turn, Vinnie pulled his bag of speed from his pocket, and with trembling hands, he snorted a long line and got up to pace the floor.

Paris stirred and began whimpering like a child. Harry kneeled next to her and rubbed her back. 'It's all right, princess.'

Vinnie looked at his siblings and wondered what on earth they had got themselves into. Paris screaming like a banshee, Harry fussing over her like she was five, and then him, with that horrible vision that he just couldn't shake off. To top it all, their mother was missing, along with Scottie.

'What are we gonna do now, Harry? We can't just sit here and do fuck all. I have to know what's happened to Muvver and our Scottie.'

Harry stood up and stared at Vinnie, pacing the floor like a madman. 'We'll call the Regans. We'll ask 'em what's going on. Maybe they want to use them as some kinda trade-off.'

Vinnie stopped in his tracks. 'You what? Tell me. What do we have to barter with, eh?'

The lack of sleep was draining Harry's thoughts. He just couldn't get his brain into gear. 'Well, nothing. The only other option is to call the Ol' Bill. Besides, what the fuck are we gonna do with Dad's body, eh? Let's just call the police and let them track the Regans down and get them banged up. Then we can just fuck off, away from all the shit.' Rubbing his balding head, he made a frustrated screaming noise. 'I never wanted to get involved in all of this anyway. I wish I'd just got on with me own business and not listened to all the crap that poured out of Farver's mouth.'

Vinnie gasped. 'Aw, come on, Harry, you d-d-don't mean that. This is our family you're talking about, and, besides, Farver's dead now.'

'Exactly, so where did the set-up get us, eh? The ol' man's brown bread. As much as I respected him, he never fucking told us how dangerous that poxy Regan family actually were, did he? "Take 'em out, screw 'em to the wall, they're nothing," he said. "You'll have a whole army behind you," he said. Well, all the numbers I'm dialling are dead and we're fucking sitting ducks right now. Can't you see it, Vinnie? The fucking tables have turned and we're the ones being hunted.'

Vinnie felt sick and inhaled air through his nose. He hated hearing Harry's voice getting louder and louder. Just as he was about to protest, he realized that really they had no option. They weren't geared up to take on the Regans and had been stupid to think they ever could.

Maybe in the past they could have done so, when they'd bragged to their father for the pat on the back, for how up in the ranks they were. A few men on the payroll and money coming in was what Frank loved to hear. So he'd urged them on. He wanted to have his sons rule the manor, like he should have done – and would have done – but for Arthur Regan. However, his boys were a chip off the old block: just like Frank, there was no finesse, there were no rules, and there was no sense.

'What if—'

'Shut it, Vinnie. You lost the right to make any decision the minute you cocked up.'

Vinnie lowered his head and resigned himself to the fact that Harry would call the shots.

* * *

After another quick shag, Jackie climbed off Scottie and flopped on the bed. 'I'm gonna go to the shops and stock up. D'ya wanna come?'

Scottie lay flat on his back with a joint hanging from his lip. 'Nah, me and shops don't see eye to eye.'

She tapped his ribs. 'Ya mean the security guards and you don't see eye to eye?'

He laughed and choked on the smoke. 'Get us another bottle of vodka, will ya,' he said, slapping her bare backside as she hopped from the bed.

Out of the corner of her eye, she spotted Ricky's small suitcase. 'I'll just give Ricky his clothes. He might feel cold.'

Scottie ignored her; he had no time for kids, and this had certainly not been part of the plan. This was one big fuck-up. After a quick shower, Jackie pulled on her tight-fitting jeans and a loose blouse. She didn't bother with a bra; she didn't need one. Once she had topped up her make-up, she reappeared to find Scottie with his eyes closed.

She snatched the small case and went to unlock Ricky's door. He was curled in a ball on the mattress. She called his name, but he didn't open his eyes. Assuming he was tired, she left the case on the floor and locked the door.

'Scottie, I'll be back in a minute. D'ya want anything else?'

'Nah!' he called back.

Outside, the vast fields were alive with bright yellow mustard seed, gently swaying in the breeze. The sight was so dazzling that she lowered her sunglasses before she set off.

The nearest shop was five miles away. When she'd first bought the house, thanks to Mike's lack of oversight of his finances, she'd thought it would be romantic to live in the countryside; it gave her a small taste of her roots. She imagined having a couple of horses in the back garden, but as she drove along the winding road towards the small village, she felt out of her comfort zone. It was remote, perfect for a hideaway, but that was about it.

Passing the flat, open fields, she thought about her childhood. She'd always been surrounded by countryside and had lived in a caravan with her neighbours only a few feet away. She had nothing against the gypsy way of life and indeed thrived on it. However, there were strict rules, the most important being the no-sex-before-marriage rule.

She soon discovered that breaking the rules would be a life-changing mistake, and one she would never forget.

* * *

When she was fourteen, and almost ready to be wed, she did, in her culture, the unacceptable. She slept with Tiger Shaw, a well-known traveller who headed the moves and ruled the roost. He had it all: money, status, and the deepest blue eyes that shone in the sunlight and twinkled when the moon was out. Waves of messy thick black hair tumbled around his rugged, tanned face. She loved him with all her heart, and he loved her. However, he was married to Lyla, an unattractive woman who came from a long-established family of travellers. Tiger was betrothed before he could walk, and so the two families joined forces.

Appleby Horse Fair hosted the biggest travellers' meeting in the country. Gypsies travelled from far and wide to buy and sell horses. The event was coming to an end, and so a big feast was laid on around a huge fire.

Everyone was apparently too busy talking horses to notice Jackie nudging Tiger to follow her. It was the perfect distraction, and so they slipped away into a nearby orchard.

But they hadn't countered on Lyla, who kept an eye on her husband, despite pretending to be engrossed in conversation with the other women. She wasn't daft; her husband was a good-looking man and used his looks to get what he wanted. She wouldn't be surprised if he'd had many a little chavi with the gorger girls in the towns. She could accept that, but not one of her own kind doing the dirty. She crept behind them, far enough away so that they wouldn't see her, and then hid behind a wide tree trunk. She waited and watched, holding her breath.

Like two rampant rabbits, Tiger and Jackie stripped off their clothes and, brazenly, she lay down for him, her legs high in the air.

Lyla knew then they'd done it before. Quietly, she scurried back to the campsite, alerting two older women. With a torch and a broomstick, they followed Lyla through the orchard and crept up to the spot where Tiger was still banging away. The oldest woman, Peachy May, shone the torch at the naked couple. Tiger leaped from his position, and with the light shining directly into his eyes, he turned to run, snatching his trousers on the way. Lyla, in her temper, grabbed Jackie's clothes and stomped off, followed by the two disgusted elders.

Once the initial shock had worn off, Jackie chased after Lyla and tried to rip her clothes from Lyla's grip, but, instead, she got a flash backhander from Peachy May and was knocked off her feet. In a desperate attempt to retrieve her clothes and her dignity, she gave chase again, but, by this time, she'd reached the edge of the orchard and knew she had to stop running or everyone would see her.

It was too late.

Lyla shouted to the crowd and spun around, pointing the torch at Jackie, who tried to cover her private parts. The sea of gawping eyes was too much to handle, and she turned back to the orchard and ran, fervently praying that Tiger would come to her rescue. He never did. Making a statement, Lyla burned Jackie's clothes on the fire. By morning, Jackie was blue with cold. It was Gilly who found her.

She was disowned by her family, her friends, and the girls and lads she'd grown up with. Gilly had no choice but to leave or declare her daughter a whore. Of course, the men laughed off Tiger's antics, but Jackie was left blamed and shunned.

They moved to Kent and the council gave them a house. Jackie completely turned her life around. In protest, she ditched the clothes and the accent – in fact, anything related to the gypsy life – and manipulated her mother into doing the same.

* * *

The memories saddened Jackie because deep down she did love her roots, the fields, the freedom, and the company. Going all out to find a man with money was her only quest. She wondered instead if she should have put her energy into begging the family's forgiveness.

It was too late now, though. She had her life, her own pad, and her new man. Scottie was a breath of fresh air after being suffocated by Mike.

When she'd first met Mike, he was as everyone had said – tall, broad, handsome and rich. He was so polite that at first it was hard to accept. Mike wined and dined her, he took her to every party going, and as he was treated like royalty, so was she. Being Mike Regan's bird gave her carte blanche to say and do just as she liked.

However, when she mistook his friendliness for flirting with other women, she decided to even the playing field a little. In Jackie's mind, Mike had her where he wanted her, and nothing could stop him from wandering off to shag who the hell he liked. Her experience of men was that they were all cheaters, takers and heartless bastards, so why would Mike be any different? She had to make an official claim, so she stopped taking the pill, and, sure enough, within the month, she was expecting. She shuddered, remembering that day. If it hadn't been secretly planned, she would have gone off and had a termination because kids didn't figure in her life at all. The parties, the fun and the drinks were all free and regular. She never dreamed that her life would suddenly come full circle: no parties, no fun, and indeed no drinking.

The beautiful Porsche Boxster he'd bought her was replaced with a bog-standard Range Rover, and that just about summed up her life. At four months pregnant, she had walked up the aisle and said 'I do' and so what she thought would be his handcuffs turned out to be hers.

The stretch marks and sickness that Ricky caused her made her detest him before he was even born. The moment he had been delivered, she saw a look in Mike's eyes that she'd never seen before – it was love. He doted on his baby – no one else mattered. His boy was his world, and she was second best, although she did manage to get a boob job a few months later, after complaining so much about her saggy tits.

But the defining moment in her relationship with Mike happened when she managed to talk him into giving her a joint bank card, which she happily rinsed. Over a period of six years, she deviously siphoned enough money from one of Mike's bank accounts to buy herself the small house on the outskirts of Ely, ready for the day she would fuck off and live the life she deserved. She never expected it to be so soon, though. The bruised cheek was the final nail in the coffin – well, that was her excuse, regardless of the fact that she probably deserved it.

As she pulled up outside the small convenience store in the quaint village, she climbed out of the car and breathed in the fresh air. The late September sun warmed her bare shoulders. She thought about a long relaxing dip in the pool, but her new house didn't have one. However, that was next on the list; she still had a few grand in the bank from the money he'd given her to renovate her mother's house. After she'd filled a basket with vodka, juice, and food for lunch, she paid the assistant with cash and hurried back to her car.

* * *

Ricky blinked hard, trying to focus. He felt sick and woozy, the orange juice having left a funny taste, but he'd been so thirsty that he had to drink it. Trying to stand up again, he wobbled, but he needed to find the phone in his suitcase and call his dad. Standing was too much of a challenge, so he crawled his way to the case and unzipped it, being careful not to make any noise.

Flipping the lid open, he stared down at his clothes messily thrown in the case. He didn't know how to pack, but his mum had told him to, because she didn't have time. So he'd thrown whatever he could in the case and grabbed his favourite toys, his homework, and the phone his dad had given him some time ago. It was an old pay-as-you-go phone that his father had since upgraded.

His dad was always replacing his phones, so he'd asked if he could keep this one. One afternoon, they played pretending they were soldiers, using the mobiles. His father had set up the phone with only his number, and so when Ricky turned it on, there was just the one number he could dial. Their mission was to find the lost gem. They used the phones like walkie-talkies. Then, the following Christmas, his dad had bought him proper walkie-talkies and the game of soldiers became an ongoing pastime.

His little fingers grappled under the clothes until he felt the mobile, his heart now beating fast. A second later, he pressed the on button. The screen lit up, and he stared at the number, although his eyes were still blurred. He knew that the only name on the phone was his dad's. He pressed the dial button and waited.

* * *

Mike was pouring another coffee, or trying to, as his hands were continually shaking. He needed to think with a clear head. Just as he took a sip, his phone rang. He stared at the number and his heart jumped a beat.

Snatching the phone in angst, he almost cried in relief.

'Ricky?'

'Daddy . . . come . . . and . . . get . . . me . . . please.'

'Where are you? Who are you with?' Mike's heart was racing because his son was slurring his words.

'I . . . don't know, Dad. I'm in a room . . . the door's locked.'

'Is your mum with you?'

'No, Dad. She's gone.'

'Who's with you, Ricky?'

'Um, some man. His name's . . .'

'Ricky, Ricky, answer me, son.'

Mike then heard a voice.

'Who are ya talking to?' It was a man's voice with a deep tone.

Mike was willing his son on to say the man's name. 'Who is he, Ricky? Who is he?'

A muffled sound was followed by Ricky saying, 'Scottie, please let me talk to my dad.'

The phone went dead, and Mike's heart felt as though it had fallen from his chest and into his stomach. Staffie looked on silently as Mike tried desperately to call the number back.

Mike's whole body shook and Staffie managed to grab him before he collapsed to the floor. Never in his life had he ever seen Mike cry, but now the big man was on the floor with his hands clutching his head, sobbing. The sound was heartbreaking, his friend wailing like an injured wolf.

'Listen, Mikey, he's alive, he's all right. Mikey, come on, mate. Let's find a way to get him back.'

'Jesus, he sounded drugged or drunk. What are they doing to him!' cried Mike. 'Fucking Scottie Harman has my son, and I'll make sure that he suffers. I swear to God, I'll keep him alive for a month and torture the cunt every fucking day.'

The sound of his son's desperate voice had wound Mike up to the point where he would kill any man that stood in his way. 'Right, I'm gonna go and see Izzy. If that Jewish prick thinks he can find the Harmans, then he needs to do it now and bring them back to me.'

Staffie didn't like Mike's madness. 'Listen, don't go tearing in there like a nutter. He'll shoot your head off. Take a breather, get ya head clear, and use your non-violent negotiation skills. Trust me, Mikey. I'd never usually tell you how to handle your own business, but, on this occasion, mate, I'm stepping in. We all want Ricky back safe, so please, wait a bit until ya mouth is filled with the right words. And, Mikey, no threats or violence.'

Mike nodded, but although his mind was agreeing, his heart was telling him to go in and terrorize the fucker.

Just as Mike was getting his breath back and calming his emotions, there was a knock at the door. Staffie looked through the window to see Tracey standing there, tapping her foot on the step and puffing aggressively on a fag. He pulled open the door, and before he even had a chance to invite her in, she stormed past him and went straight into the kitchen where she was met by Mike, who was now on his feet, red-eyed.

'Mike, what happened? Eric looks in a right state.'

Mike just stood there, staring at the woman.

'What's it all about, Mike? What the hell's going on?'

Staffie sensed that this encounter wouldn't go well, just by the penetrating steely glare on Mike's face. Any second, he would give Tracey what for and it wouldn't be pretty.

Staffie grabbed Tracey's arm, but she tried to wriggle free. 'Get your hands off me!' she yelled.

Tightening his grip, he tried to remove her from the kitchen, but she was having none of it. 'I only came to find out what the problem is. I'm not here to have a go at you. We're family, right?' She tried to appeal to his better nature.

'No, we ain't,' Mike responded. 'Who the fuck are you, anyway? You're just his tart and my fucking business ain't nothing to do with you. Now get the fuck outta my house!'

Tracey shook herself free. Her voice changed in tone. 'You prick, Mike Regan. I can guarantee you'll be sorry, mark my words.'

That was the last straw. In a quick robust movement, Mike

snatched Tracey by her hair extensions and dragged her all the way to the front door and threw her outside. The strength of the man was like Goliath. Tracey went flying and landed on the rough gravel drive. Stunned, she got to her feet and looked down at her grazed knees.

'Big mistake, Regan – big mistake.'

Mike didn't answer, just stared at her.

Staffie pushed past Mike, hoping to get Tracey off the property before Mike lost it again. 'Tracey, you need to shut ya mouth and get out of here.'

Tracey's eyes were wide, and her mouth maintained its oval shape. 'I ain't standing for this.' She pointed to the bloodied graze on her knees. 'I know more than you realize, so trust me: you'll be sorry!'

While Mike walked back into the kitchen, away from the mouthy bitch, Staffie, absolutely livid, stepped outside. 'As much as I care for Eric, it doesn't look good, his gold-digging tart sticking her nose in, now does it, ya stupid tramp?'

Tracey tried to straighten her hair and noticed half the extensions were falling out in clumps. Her anger rose.

'I've a fucking mind to call the Ol' Bill for what you two have just done to me. How would you like that, eh?' she screamed.

Mike had just reached the kitchen door when he heard those penetrating words. He flew back and onto the drive, towering over Tracey.

'You even think about that and I swear to God, I'll turn your face into a punchbag. Now, fuck off and tell my brother he's crossed the line. That's if he knows you're fronting me out, 'cos it's my guess he doesn't even know that his little tart's 'ere, does he?'

Tracey was suddenly nervous. She'd probably made matters a whole lot worse, and when things calmed down, and Eric regained his place in the firm, she'd no doubt be exiled and that was something she'd never planned. Turning on her heel, she held her head up and tried to walk away, but the fall to the ground had not only hurt her knees but also snapped the heel off her shoe. She then felt a right idiot, limping away like a pissed tart crawling home from a nightclub. As she got into her car and checked her hair, she realized she actually looked like she'd been on the drink too.

'Fuck you, Mike Regan. You're gonna rot in hell – all the fucking lot of ya,' she seethed.

* * *

Mike washed his face and stared in the mirror. He didn't recognize the reflection that glared back – the spiteful, ugly, tight-lipped expression – but he didn't care. The only constant consideration was getting his boy back. Jackie crossed his mind, and he felt a twinge of guilt because he hadn't really given her a second thought. Ricky, in his slurred speech, had said she had gone. But there was something about his tone. It was as if he wasn't worried about his mother, or maybe it was just confusion. A black cloud descended like the dark side of his conscience. It was whispering into his ear, telling him to do anything, even if it went against the grain. He understood that probably meant working for Izzy. If that was the case, then so be it. He would work as a Redcoat at Butlins if it meant he could have his son back.

Leaving Staffie to hold the fort, he headed for the Old Kent Road. He had to face Izzy alone. Staffie had practically begged to go along, but he couldn't think straight with people around him. The drive to Izzy's would allow him to get his thoughts in order and think rationally about how he should handle the situation. However, as soon as he approached the jewellers, his level head became unhinged.

Quasi was outside as usual, and, as always, he held his hands up to stop Mike and give him a pat-down. However, Mike wasn't in the mood for formalities; in one swift movement, he pushed

Quasi aside and tore open the big steel door. Like the Minotaur, he stood in the entrance to the office, taking up the whole frame.

Izzy was quickly on his feet, pointing a gun straight at Mike's chest. Mike ignored the weapon and marched forward, not even bothering to take his shoes off.

Izzy's eyes glared at the audacity of the man. He would have shot anyone else clean through the chest. But the need to have Mike on his firm saved him.

Sitting back down, Izzy placed the gun on the desk. Quasi stood sheepishly, hanging his head. 'Sorry, Izzy, he . . .'

Izzy waved his hand dismissively, and as soon as Quasi was out of the room, he smiled. 'I need a replacement for that useless, ugly idiot.'

Mike didn't wait to be asked to take a seat; he just plonked himself down and launched into a speech. 'Now—'

'Brandy?' interrupted Izzy.

Mike frowned. 'Whatever.'

Izzy pulled the bottom filing cabinet drawer open and removed a tray with three decanters and two crystal glasses. Mike watched the strength of the man as he lifted the weighty tray with one hand and placed it on the desk. He poured two drinks, pushed one under Mike's nose, and delicately sipped his own.

'This is one of the oldest brandies. One bottle is worth nearly as much as a new Bentley.'

Maybe if it had been a social visit, he would have savoured the taste. He'd always had a liking for vintage brandies. He gulped the drink back, aware that Izzy was shaking his head at him.

'You have the same taste as me. Don't insult me, Mike.' He poured another one and stared. 'Enjoy it. Don't treat it with contempt.'

Mike took a deep breath, relaxed his tense shoulders, and sipped the golden-brown liquid.

Izzy watched, now impressed. 'There, see how much better it is? Mike, there are just some things in life that you can't ignore the benefits of, so what good does it do, eh? Now, you know that brandy is exquisite, but, in your madness, you decide to dismiss it. A brandy that has been sitting in its cask for so long, maturing and gaining substance and standing out from all the others, should be respected and savoured.'

Mike sipped it again, trying to work out what Izzy was getting at. He always talked in riddles, but today Mike didn't want to play cryptic crossword puzzles.

'Okay, Izzy, you want me to work for you, yeah?'

Izzy smiled. 'I can offer you more money than you can earn, so it's a good offer. Why would you want to fight me? I don't understand. Most men would grab the opportunity with both hands.'

Mike didn't return the smile. He was on a mission, and he fought to hold back the words that would otherwise tumble out of his mouth.

'Like you, Izzy, my reputation means more to me than money.'

There was a silent pause as Izzy contemplated what Mike said. 'You will have a reputation . . . my reputation.' He paused again. Mike noticed how Izzy's posture changed. He was less confident, and his expression took on the resigned look of an old man.

Mike leaned forward. 'What's this all about, Izzy? I mean, you can take on any amount of muscle, so why me?'

'I have built an empire. I've worked hard, been ruthless, and I've more money than I can spend. I'm ready to retire, but I will not let my good name retire. So, Zara is going to take over.'

Mike scoffed and leaned back in his chair. 'Zara?' His tone mocked.

Izzy didn't react; instead, he just nodded. 'Yes, Zara. Now listen, you two may think you pulled the wool over my eyes, but I know about you both. The other day when you sat in that leather armchair and acted as if you'd never met her before, it showed guile, but it didn't fool me, even though your acting skills were excellent. However, my sensory skills are better. I knew a long time ago, so don't underestimate me.'

Mike ignored the comment. 'Why not Ismail? He's your son.'

Izzy nodded with thin lips. 'Yes, he is, but he's weak, fragile and stupid. My only son is a beautiful boy who has his adorable mother's eyes and heart-shaped lips, but, sadly, he also has her only weakness – her soft nature. He was born to walk around aloof, painting those ridiculous works of art. I knew from when he was five that he was never going to take over my business. A scraped knee, a sore throat, and he would bawl like a baby.'

'And Ismail's okay with that, is he?' Mike laughed.

'No, of course not, but who is he to argue? I want my business to be run by a strong leader, and Ismail showed his true colours by throwing a hissy fit when I broke the news. Now, when I was a young man of Ismail's age, I went out alone. I didn't just wait for my father to hand everything to me on a plate. I set up my own business.' He held his palms up. 'I proved I needed no one and so my father handed his business to me, not my four elder brothers. Ismail has proved nothing. He just wants it all, and he will happily sit back and spend every penny with no clue how to invest it. And, as for using these,' he looked down at his palms, 'he has no idea what they are even for. My Zara was different, is different. Never have I seen her cry. As a child, I would watch Ismail in a jealous rage beat her, and she would curl in a ball and wait for him to finish his tantrum, and then, like a serpent, she'd uncurl and attack when he least expected it. She could have killed him if she'd wanted to, but I think in many ways my daughter liked to have an opponent to fight with, so she never hurt Ismail badly enough to stop him coming back for more. I saw the look in her eyes. She was laughing at him. My girl is smart, she watches and listens, and most of all, she's not afraid.' He sighed. 'But you already know that, don't you, Mike? You have already tasted her breath, felt her passion, and experienced her stone-cold heart.'

Mike didn't care what Izzy thought of him. They had tried to keep their past relationship a secret, but right now, his only concern was for his son, and he wouldn't waste his energy in thinking up a grand lie.

'She ain't as cold and ruthless as you think, Izzy.'

Izzy's eyes widened, and his jaw tightened. 'Are you audacious enough to tell me about my own daughter?' His hand hovered over the gun that lay on the desk.

Mike laughed, making Izzy jump. 'You seem to think you know her so well, yet you get uptight when I tell you otherwise. A bit controlling, wouldn't you say?'

'You are taking me for a fool, and I don't like it, Mike. I'm no clown, and if you think there's a man out there who can control Zara, then you are the fool, not me. Do you understand me?'

Mike shrugged his shoulders. 'Izzy, I ain't interested in Zara, and if you want her to take over your business, then so what? Why on earth should I care?'

'Because, Mike, I want you to work with her, watch over her, take care of her, and make sure she never comes to any harm. You, Mike, are the one man who is perfect for the job. I've watched you run your firm. You are strong and bright. I want that for my daughter – a man who will have her back. Although she doesn't need anyone, two forces are better than one. And, as I said before, you will earn more than you'll ever earn running your own business, mark my words. Any big deals to be had are pushed under my nose first. I take them or leave them, but that's always my choice. The leftovers . . .' he smirked, 'they get offered to the likes of you.'

Mike clocked the seriousness in the man's eyes. He knew Izzy well enough to understand that an offer like this one was made only with careful consideration; it certainly wasn't a spur-of-the-moment impulse. So it also meant he could barter. Izzy had laid his cards on the table and Mike would too. This was the only hope he felt he had of getting his son back.

'Look, Izzy. I've a proposal for you.'

'Go on. I'm listening.'

'I want the Harmans alive and gagged in my workshop. I want my son found unharmed and back in my safekeeping.'

Izzy shrugged his shoulders. 'Yes, but what's in it for me?'

'You will have me running your firm under your name.'

Pulling a cigar from his pocket, Izzy lit the end, contemplating Mike's response. After a prolonged pause, he said, 'I think you've misunderstood me, Mr Regan. I don't want you to take over. I want Zara to do that, but with you by her side. She calls the shots. You ensure her shots are activated. Do you get what I mean?'

Answering to Zara was never going to happen. End of. He could see her taking the piss out of him. 'She can call the shots within reason, but I ain't gonna be her skivvy or allow her to humiliate me.'

'Just as I thought. You two really did have a relationship. From your words, I can only deduce you left her heartbroken.'

'No, Izzy, I didn't leave her. The bitch left me because obviously she thought too much of her father to go against his wishes.'

Izzy gritted his teeth. No one called his daughter a bitch. Still, he wouldn't lose his rag, not while they were negotiating. He knew what Zara was, and it pleased him to think that she took no shit from anyone.

'A woman in this line of work needs to be cold-hearted and—'

Mike interrupted. 'No, Izzy. A woman is supposed to be nurturing and sweet. This isn't the life for a woman. It's not natural.'

'That, my son, is probably true, but, in my case, my children were born into the wrong bodies. Ismail is like a girl and Zara is like a man.'

Mike threw his hands in the air. 'Okay, whatever. But, right now, I need you to get my son back. I have covered every pub, club and whorehouse to find out where the Harmans are hiding, and I'm coming up against a brick wall. You're my last call. And, yes, I will work for you, if my son comes back to me in one piece.'

Out of the blue, Mike heard a ringtone. It was coming from

Izzy's top drawer. Even Izzy jumped before he retrieved the phone. From the corner of Mike's eye, he saw the side door close. For a second, he thought he was imagining it because that door had been closed when he'd entered Izzy's office. His eyes flicked back to Izzy.

Mike couldn't hear who was on the phone, but the look of concern on Izzy's face said it was serious. His eyes twitched, and as he spoke to the person on the other end, he kept looking over at Mike with an expression of alarm and . . . *was it disgust?* Mike wasn't sure. He then realized that the conversation was about him. He waited until Izzy had finished.

Mike was on the edge of his seat. 'Who was that?'

'The deal's off, Mike. You're on your own.' He stood up to dismiss him.

'Wait! Hold on. What the fuck was all that about?'

'You haven't been truthful with me, Mike, have you? That was my man from the Met, asking where you are.'

Mike cocked his head to the side. 'So, Izzy, you're an informant? Well, fuck me. I thought you had some respect.'

'I'm no informant. Nevertheless, let me explain something. I am who I am, and someone who is far higher up than you. So, if that means I have the chief of the Met turning a blind eye in return for a few scallies' names, then that, my son, is called business. And while we're on the subject of right and wrong, I thought, you, Mike, had morals. I thought your lot lived by some code – no hurting women, children, and old men – but it seems to me now that you don't.'

Mike screwed his face up. 'What the hell are you on about?'

'You killed the old Harman man and made a right pig's ear of it. You got a bit sloppy, leaving the man in his own bath of blood, with half his skin missing. I'm not sure I want to have you in my firm, and certainly not looking out for my daughter. I mean, who makes a mess like that? I thought you had more savvy.'

Mike was still digesting Izzy's words. 'What the hell are you talking about, Izzy?'

'The Filth have nicked your firm and are now looking for you. They've had a tip-off that you and your lot went into Harry's old mum and dad's home. Apparently, you brutally murdered the old man and left him half-mutilated in the bath, before you did away with the old girl. So, the deal's off. I told them I haven't seen you, so you'd best scarper because I ain't getting involved in a shoddy mess like that, Mike.'

Rubbing his face and shaking his head, Mike tried to comprehend what Izzy was saying. The idea that his firm had been nicked was one thing; mutilating the old geezer in the bath though?

'Hang on a fucking minute. I ain't touched the old man, and if I did, I certainly wouldn't leave him in his own bath, would I? Jesus, yeah, I am a man with some kinda moral values. That weren't me or mine, I can fucking assure you.'

Izzy watched Mike's face and was taken aback by the look of shock written all over it. 'Then who, eh, Mike?'

An intense frown lowered Mike's eyebrow as he stared into space. His mind was replaying the moment he'd arrived at the Harmans' home, and then, like a camera zooming in on the action, he recalled the constant flushing of the toilet. He shook his head and sighed. 'You wouldn't believe me if I told ya who I think it was.'

'Try me,' Izzy sardonically chuckled.

'Yeah, I did go to the Harmans' place. They weren't there, except for the old girl. She was up in the bathroom. I thought it was weird when she kept flushing the bog and banging on about her privacy, saying she was busy. I thought it was really strange at the time. The whole incident was off the wall. Even her reaction when she saw me in her kitchen, it was as if we were old mates. She didn't seem bothered at all. She was more interested in her fucking fairy cakes. Looking back, maybe when she said from the other side of that bathroom door that she was busy, she actually was.' He paused and crumpled his face in disgust. 'I bet she was trying to dispose of ol' Frank's body bit by bit down the toilet. Anyway, I assumed there'd be a nasty row if one of her sons walked in, so I took her away for a short holiday.'

Izzy laughed again. 'And what sort of man would do that, eh?'

Mike glared with contempt. 'A man who has fucking morals, that's who.'

A satisfied grin spread across Izzy's mouth. 'Yeah, it stands to reason. Why am I surprised? Ah well, you'd better make plans, 'cos no way are the police gonna let this go. From the description of the old man, they're going to pull out every boy in blue and have them on the hunt. So, for now, you'd best put yourself up somewhere.'

'But, Izzy, Scottie Harman has got my boy drugged and locked up in a room somewhere. I can't get nicked, not now, not until I know my boy's safe.'

'I'll tell you what. A snake I might be, but if you honour your promise to work for me, I'll help you get your boy back.'

Mike took a deep breath and let out a loud sigh. 'Deal, mate, but please make sure no harm comes to him, yeah?'

Izzy held out his hand and gripped Mike's tightly. 'Shame my Ismail isn't more like you. Take one of my old bangers, the blue Polo, and you can plot up in a flat in Lee Green.' He pulled open the second drawer in the cabinet and handed Mike a bunch of keys along with a phone.

* * *

As soon as Mike left, Zara appeared from the side door. 'I heard the conversation.' She smiled sweetly, just the way her father liked.

'He's all yours . . . as long as he doesn't get banged up. And remember, Zara, he works for you. He's not your plaything.'

Zara gave a sneering glance back. 'So, what's the next move?'

'We get his boy back.'

128

'And the wife?'

Izzy grinned. 'He never mentioned her.'

With a hopeful spring in her step, Zara was about to return to the accounts, when her father called out. 'Zara, I want you to be very careful. The Harmans must be very brave, very stupid, or have serious backing to take on Mike Regan and his firm. So that leaves me concerned. What are the Harmans really up to?'

She walked back and sat on the corner of the desk, like he often did. 'Do you know this family?'

With a tired look, he stared off in deep thought. 'Yes, I did, a very long time ago.' Suddenly, his eyes focused. 'Anyway, make sure someone has your back at all times.'

Hidden behind Zara's smile was a concern for her father. He seemed worried, which wasn't a part of his make-up.

Chapter 8

Jackie returned to the house. The sun was hot, and the bright yellow fields almost resembled a desert.

Once inside, the fresh air having given her respite, she dabbed her shiny face with a tissue. The house was nowhere near as grand as her home with Mike, but she had made every effort to replicate some of it.

She unpacked the shopping and called up to Scottie. There was no answer; she assumed he was stoned again. She poured herself a double vodka, added ice from the freezer, and topped it up with orange juice. She smiled to herself. All these months of adding the touches to her new home had paid off. The freezer was stocked, the furnishings were coming along a treat, and she still had money to add more.

She'd been smart, managing to hide her bank account from Mike. Every penny he gave her, even the wads of banknotes lying around, she helped herself and stashed them all away. In his trusting days, he'd allowed her to open a bank account for Ricky, but her name was down as the signatory if there was a need to make withdrawals before he reached eighteen. There was almost a hundred grand in his account. The Rolex and the diamonds were all sold and added to the pot. She had well and truly rinsed Mike for everything she could. As she saw it, the twelve hours of labour and the slithers of white stretch marks had earned her that money.

She ran up the stairs and then looked at the locked door. She paused; she'd forgotten to feed Ricky or take him to the toilet. She couldn't send him back home sick – Mike would kill her. Slowly, she turned the key in the lock, almost afraid of what she might find. But, there he was, sitting on the edge of the mattress. He was in a daydream, his huge eyes staring at her, and his tiny face looking so frightened. He didn't speak; he just waited to see what she had in store for him, but what she saw staring back at her were Mike's eyes judging her.

'D'ya need the toilet?'

He nodded and tried to get to his feet.

Jackie noticed how wobbly he was – he was wandering, almost incoherently – but she assumed he was faking it. 'Stand up properly, for fuck's sake.'

She steered him to the toilet and stepped back. He tried to pull his pants down, but he was clearly struggling. Impatiently, she ripped them down herself, nearly knocking him over.

'Ahh, for Christ's sake, Ricky. Hurry up, will you!'

As he started to pee, he cried out, 'Mummy, it hurts!'

She looked down at the toilet bowl and noticed he was urinating blood. She tutted. 'That's all I need.'

Ricky was too dazed to notice the claret; he just felt the pain and began whimpering.

She silently led him back into the bedroom, forced him onto the mattress, and hurried down to the kitchen. She poured cold water into a tall glass and rushed back up the stairs. Thrusting the glass under his nose, she demanded he drank it. She stood and waited until he swallowed every last drop. However, his little stomach couldn't handle so much, and in one movement, and to her utter horror and disgust, Ricky's bodily fluids ended up splattered all over her new beige carpet. Then it dawned on her that she'd given him orange mixed with the vodka. Her six-year-old was drunk. He flopped onto the makeshift bed, his face a sickly shade of grey. Jackie began to worry now. If her son had alcohol poisoning, Mike would kill her, for sure. She hurried into the bathroom and poured more water into the glass. Trying frantically to get him to drink, she called for Scottie to help, but, again, there was no answer.

'For fuck's sake, Scottie, come 'ere, will ya?'

She held Ricky's head and forced his mouth open, using the edge of the glass. 'Ricky, will you drink this? Come on, it'll make ya better.' But her tone was far from sweet.

Ricky murmured and tried to drink the cold water, but he gagged and was almost sick again. Following her own remedy for a hangover, she decided to leave him to sleep it off. Something made her look out of the landing window, and then it dawned on her that Scottie's car was missing. She hadn't noticed when she'd arrived home, too eager to get inside. In a flash, she hurried to the bedroom. Scottie was gone. There was no point in calling his phone because when he arrived at the house she'd surreptitiously removed it from his back pocket, turned it off, and hidden it under the bed. She wanted their new life to be free of the past. She looked around for his holdall but that had gone too. What had happened? One minute he was all over her and the next he'd done a runner. She went back to the spare room and kneeled down beside her son. His deathly white face and the beads of sweat across his brow would have had any mother calling for an ambulance, but not Jackie. She shook his arm.

'Ricky, wake up. Where's Scottie gone?' She thought that maybe he knew. Ricky just murmured. She shook him again, this time harder. 'For Christ's sake, wake up. Where did Scottie go? What did he say?'

With his mother's voice ringing loudly in his ears, Ricky tried to wake up. 'Daddy's coming.'

'What? Ricky, wake the fuck up. What did you say?' Her heart was pounding.

'Daddy phoned me. He's coming to get me.' Ricky was still semiconscious, and his words were ramblings, but Jackie didn't see it that way. The fear of Mike finding her screwed any notion that Ricky may have had the wrong end of the stick.

Jackie sat back on her haunches and stared at her son drifting off to sleep. He must have been mistaken, surely? Mike couldn't have phoned her, as her mobile was switched off. She frantically ripped Ricky's clothes from the suitcase to see if he had one of his own. Then she leaped up and flew into her bedroom, searching everywhere for a phone. There, in the middle of the unmade bed, was a small Nokia flip phone. Her heart was now in her mouth. Of course the brat would call his precious daddy, and Scottie wouldn't hang around. After all, Scottie Harman was shagging Mike Regan's wife. Mike would go ballistic. He may have turned a blind eye to the odd indiscretion; however, setting up home with someone was a whole different ballgame. She looked at the clock and knew that Ricky, if he'd had the chance, could have only called his father an hour ago. It would take Mike at least two hours to reach her, and so she had to leave, and pretty quickly too.

With no time to waste, she packed her bags, retrieved her bank cards, and loaded up the car. Ricky was still incoherent and looking sickly. She rolled him in the quilt and carried him to the car, heavily plonking him onto the back seat. Then, she hurried back, took one last look around the house, locked the windows and doors, and went to her car. Not knowing where she should go, she headed north, as far away from London as she could.

Eventually reaching the M6, she paused, to the annoyance of the driver behind her. *Ireland*, she thought. She could go back to her roots.

Leaving the gypsy community had been a big wrench for both her and her mother. Even though she'd committed a massive faux pas, she should have been able to count on support from her mother, who had once been a tough cookie, and who would have fought any woman to keep them there. And she also would have had her Uncle Seth fighting her corner. But, instead, she and her mother had suffered the inevitable slur of being ousted from the gypsy community. It had been a hellish deal at the time and incredibly embarrassing for Jackie – and her mother.

But she was sure that despite everything, the gypsy community would look after their own and keep her safe. And they were good at hiding people. She hoped she would be able to count on her Uncle Seth once more. Furthermore, she had enough money to secure a decent caravan, a new state-of-the-art wagon, and hoped this would help her to make amends with her family. With enough money, she could buy her way back in. Once they were on her side, she could live her life with protection.

She headed towards Liverpool to take the ferry over to Ireland. Ricky made a whimpering sound and Jackie felt her stomach turn. If he died, then Mike would use every man in his firm to track her down. She had to make sure he was okay. The next service station was just up ahead, so she pulled into the car park. Locking the car doors, she trotted to the food hall, and there, to her horror, on one of the big-screen TV sets, was her husband's face. She froze and listened to the newscaster. 'Yesterday, the brutal remains of Frank Harman were found at his home. The police are now looking for thirty-four-year-old Mike Regan in connection with the killing.'

Jackie's mind went into overdrive. Jesus! What if he's on the rampage? He would sure as hell be coming for her. Nothing would get in the way of him tracking down his precious son. She had to make sure that, if he did find them, Ricky was a picture of good health – or she'd end up like this Frank Harman fella.

Pulling away, her mind was now back on Scottie and she felt a lump in her throat. Alone with a kid, and now ditched by the new man she'd believed would make her happy, she really thought life was a bitch.

As she drove along the motorway heading for Liverpool, an

unexpected tear escaped her eye. What had she done? Perhaps Scottie was fun and sexy, and he'd treated her like the only woman alive in the hotel rooms, but did he love her? Was this dream life only in her mind? She'd started saving money for a house long before she'd met Scottie, so perhaps she'd seen something that was never there. She wiped her eyes before her mascara ran and left her looking like a panda. If Scottie truly loved her, then he wouldn't have scarpered, surely? Her breathing became rapid, a panic attack gripped her, and she felt her throat tightening. Reality struck: she had just given up everything, and for what? All she'd had was a regular shag with Scottie, and she didn't even know his surname. Months of sleeping with him, sharing a joint, and enjoying a few meals followed by a bottle of vodka, what had she been thinking? He'd never said he wanted a relationship that was anything more than a quickie every so often. She tried to recall if he'd ever told her he loved her. Perhaps he never had, and yet he'd created this new scenario whereby he would move into their new house and play happy families. She went over in her mind the conversation she'd had on the phone after she'd left the family home. He'd agreed to pack a bag and meet her at the address she'd given him. She tried to recall if either of them had actually said the words 'live together'.

It was a sad but sobering thought. Neither she nor Scottie had discussed this idea, nor, in fact, ever planned it. He'd arrived before her with his holdall and a few bottles of vodka. Not much was said after that, as they were too busy shagging. She tried to cast her mind back to what they'd ever talked about, and it was either about how awful Mike was being to her, or what he was up to. Why she always ended up talking about her husband was a mystery, but the fact was she did all the talking. Scottie never said much at all. However, that hadn't been the case initially. He'd spoken for fucking England when Tracey introduced them at the Cat's Whiskers nightclub. He was her old schoolmate – so she said. Jackie winced at the sudden realization that Tracey was

Chapter 9

Mike was surprised to find the flat very clean. It was minimalist as far as furniture was concerned, but the fridge and freezer were stocked with all the essential groceries. Set up much like a holiday let, except this was Lee Green; it was not the sort of place where you would take a holiday. After making a coffee, he sat down on a two-seater settee in the small lounge, where he tried to get his thoughts together to form a plan. Knowing that all the boys were down the nick was worrying, to say the least. He was on his own now and desperate to find his son.

As he sat there thinking things through, he heard a key turn in the lock and jumped to his feet, retrieving a gun from the back of his trousers.

He recognized the voice that called out. It was Zara. Mike put the gun back and glared as she walked into the room. She was dressed differently in a pair of jeans, a white shirt, and a thin black blazer. Her pointed features and cat-like eyes seemed to be enhanced by the black eyeliner. He had to admit she was a very striking woman, a far cry from the one he'd ended up with. Jackie looked like all her friends, a plastic nonentity.

Zara explored Mike's expression, looking for any signs of vulnerability. 'So, Mikey, Izzy tells me that we have a deal.'

Mike shrugged his shoulders. 'Whatever, Zara.' He really wasn't in the mood for her sarcastic words; he assumed they were designed to rub salt into the wound.

'I will keep up my end of the bargain, but you have to keep up yours,' she jeered.

'Yeah, yeah . . . Look, Zara, what are ya doing 'ere? Really?'

She eased herself gracefully into the only available armchair. Crossing her long slim legs, she leaned back and smiled. 'I *have* kept up my end of the bargain, Mikey.'

Mike stiffened. 'What? You have my son?'

She shook her head. 'No, but I do have Scottie Harman. He's bound, gagged and oven-ready.'

His eyes darted around her face, looking for a sign that she was telling the truth, but Zara was hard to read now. 'And my son?'

Again, she shook her head. 'One thing at a time. You said you wanted the Harmans alive. Well, I have one for you and he's ready and waiting. So, like I've just said, now that I've delivered what I promised, it's time for you to do likewise, Mikey.'

He nodded and bit his lip. 'So, where is he?'

'Exactly where you wanted him. At one of your lock-ups.'

With his head slightly tilted in a questioning glare, he asked, 'How do you know where my lock-ups are?'

She tapped the side of her nose. 'I know more than you give me credit for.'

'And me brother. Is he still down the nick?'

The slow sarcastic tone in her voice vanished. 'Yes. The Ol' Bill are keeping them all in. The police are still looking for you, but the workshop has already been gone over, so they won't be back there. And regarding Scottie, one of my men found him pulling up outside his own gaff, the bloody idiot. Anyway, we have him, so do you want to question him?' She laughed. 'Mikey-style?'

Her new softened voice warmed him. But he was fully aware

that she had another side to her. The new alter ego, the gangster look, wasn't appealing and it made his stomach churn.

'Yep, I fucking do. But, Zara, I don't want no ladies present.'

Slowly, she stood up, and a sickly grin spread across her face. 'No! I want to see my employee in action.' That alter ego. It was back in the room.

Mike didn't have time to argue; he wanted to tear the face off Scottie Harman.

'Let's go then,' he demanded.

Zara realized she'd have to pull his reins in if she was going to be his boss.

'Drink your coffee first.'

Remembering that she was the one who was making the decisions – or he wouldn't get anywhere – he obliged by downing the hot coffee in one gulp.

* * *

He even lay down in the back of her car at her request to avoid being spotted because, right now, he wanted nothing to stand in the way of finding out where Ricky was. But he did this under sufferance. His temper was rising, like a pressure cooker ready to blow.

At three o'clock in the morning, the air was still and sticky. In Kent, a storm was brewing, and, like Mike, it was ready to let rip. From the outside, the lock-up was in total darkness. As soon as Zara drove across the unmade road, Mike sat upright, and as the car came to a halt, he opened the door, taking long strides towards his victim. Each step heightened his rage. Thoughts of Scottie holding his son, even drugging him – as he assumed – and locking him in a room, was enough for Mike to rip Scottie's bollocks off. Zara was hot on his heels. She was eager to see Mike's response, but she also wanted to be in control. Their relationship was like a modern-day Scarlett O'Hara and Rhett Butler script.

Mike flung open the heavy metal door, and, in a flash, he flew at the man tied up and fastened to the chair. In a quick movement, he hit Scottie around the head, knocking him over.

Taking a deep breath, Mike stood back. Two men, similar in size to Mike, were positioned with their hands in front of them. They could have been bouncers outside a nightclub. They didn't move. Zara nodded for one of them to pull Scottie back to an upright position.

Like a roaring lion, Mike bellowed, 'Where's my son?'

Joshua, the taller of the two, who had olive skin and similar facial characteristics to Zara, removed Scottie's gag.

The sneer that crawled across Scottie's face infuriated Mike. Instead of playing it cool and using his controlled demeanour to intimidate his victim, Mike screamed so loud that his face flooded crimson and spittle flew from his mouth. Scottie could see the frustration and wanted to aggravate Mike even more. The line of cocaine he'd snorted just before he was dragged from his car was still strong in his system and gave him more courage than he would typically have had under the circumstances.

As if a light had just been switched on, Mike knew that clumping Scottie around the head would only end up with the man being out cold. He would, therefore, be no closer to finding his son. Stepping back, he relaxed his shoulders and took deep breaths to control his raging heart.

Mike sighed. 'Oh dear, Scottie. Acting cocky really won't get you far. And trust me, by the time I'm done with you, you *will* tell me everything. I suggest that, if you desire a pain-free execution, you'd better start talking.'

Mike looked at the two men, who stood like statues. He smiled. 'Lads, I think you might want to leave. What I'm about to do will put you off rare steak for a long time.'

They looked at Zara for the okay. She nodded, and the men left the building. Scottie instantly grasped the seriousness of what was about to happen. The rush of adrenaline almost wiped out the cocaine, and a cold shiver swept through his entire body, causing his knees to shake so much that his legs bobbed up and down. As if someone had thrown a bucket of water over him, sweat ran down his face, and his pale-blue shirt showed off dark stains under the arms, making a V-shape. A sickly shade of blue lined his lips, and as the blood drained from his face, his complexion became grey and waxy. Mike nodded slowly. He recognized that look, the uncontrollable fear in a man that sucks the soul from his body, like a plum withering to a prune.

With eyes like saucers, bulging and pulsating, Scottie was terrified. He was the Harman brother who could ingratiate himself into the company of girls, and who could charm anyone into giving him their last pound. However, he had always left the violence down to his two older brothers, simply living off their reputation. He'd never banked on coming face-to-face with Mike Regan under these horrific circumstances. He wanted to speak, but he couldn't take his eyes off Regan, or even open his mouth. It was as if his tongue had glued itself to his palate. Too terrified to use his best asset – his charisma – he continued to stare.

Mike could smell the fear in the room, well aware that silence was a chilling tool to use. Slowly, he walked over to a Snap-on toolbox. The only sound in the room was the grating of the drawer sliding open. Looking in it, his fingers drummed the edge of the drawer, deep in thought. He closed it and shook his head.

Scottie was craning his neck to see what instrument Regan was going to use. Yet there was nothing in the big man's hands. Another stream of sweat ran down his nose. As he watched Regan walk to an even larger Snap-on toolbox, which had deeper drawers, he saw him slide open the bottom one and pull out a nail gun. Scottie's heart beat so fast he thought he would pass out, but at least that would be a respite from the pounding fear that consumed him.

Mike turned to Zara. 'This is going to be messy, and I'm

assuming that your white shirt is not a cheap number. If you stand there, it won't be white for long.'

On high sensory alert, Mike recognized that Zara's smile was forced and cemented into a disturbed expression. He was right.

'Think of it as probation. I want to see what you're capable of before I decide if you're the right man for the job.' Although harsh, her words were still laced with a tense edge to them.

'Don't blame me when the nightmares keep waking you up.'

Those words irritated Zara. She didn't want to be treated like a lady, but as a resilient woman. There was a difference. Surely Mike had the intelligence to see that? She was too far up the ladder to be disrespected. Her father had seen fit to hand over responsibility bit by bit because he knew she was up for the job. She had proved her worth when she discovered that the big chain of Italian restaurants owned by Izzy were using the pizza delivery service to peddle drugs. Instead of having the individuals wasted to prove a point, she demanded a cut in their illegitimate earnings, and found a more suitable cocaine supplier who earned herself and the Italians far more money.

'I'm not like your silly slapper of a wife, you know, and I think you need to have that thought at the forefront of your mind.'

A high-pitched chuckle left his mouth. Holding the gun, he pointed it at Zara. 'You're leaving yourself wide open, Zara. I could nail you to the wall, and that, my darling, makes you as silly as my so-called slapper of a wife. But the only thing on my mind right now is grilling this cunt!' His eyes suddenly narrowed, and a cruel smile inched its way across his stern, cold face as he turned to face Scottie.

Now with his back to her, Zara seethed. This wasn't how it was supposed to be. He should at least show her respect.

'I know you, Mikey. Torturing that piece of shit there' – she pointed to Scottie – 'is one thing. But you wouldn't have the guts, the heart, or any reason to lay a finger on me.'

For a second, the tension was almost palpable. It was like an invisible magnet, drawing the two of them towards it. Then, Mike broke the magnetic force with another high-pitched laugh.

He spun round to face her. 'That may have been very true . . . *but*, everything has changed since my son went missing!' He screamed at her with such ferocity that the veins almost popped out of his neck, making his eyes bloodshot.

A shadow of doom was cast over her face and she felt sick. Perhaps that kiss Mike had planted on her lips the other day really was a mark of disrespect, and he truly had no feelings for her. She stepped back, gawping at his crazy eyes. One of them had to give in, and she knew that it wasn't going to be him. Quickly, she decided to redeem the situation herself.

'In case you've forgotten, we're on the same side.' As the words left her mouth, she realized she sounded softer than she wanted to. Yet, miraculously, it had the desired effect. Mike's shoulders immediately relaxed, and he turned away to face Scottie.

The pause in the proceedings allowed Scottie to unstick his tongue.

'What do you want from me?' His tone was childlike; it was a far cry from the confident charm for which he was known.

'Where's my son?' Mike didn't scream or shout; he had to keep controlled and treat Scottie as he'd done Travis. But it was hard to keep up the pretence because he wanted to kill him with his bare hands. However, a torturous tool usually loosened the tongue.

Holding the nail gun to Scottie's shoulder, Mike glared.

'All right, all right, please don't fire it. I'll tell you.'

Mike pressed the tool harder into Scottie's shoulder.

'He's with Jackie. I left them at the house. I didn't hurt him, I swear.'

Mike was about to pull the trigger when those words registered. He tilted his head to the side and lowered his weapon. Then, he dipped his eyebrows in confusion. 'You what?'

Scottie's eyes flicked from Zara to Mike. 'She came on to me. I swear, there was nothing in it.'

'Are you shagging my wife?'

Zara was now in her element. Scottie Harman shagging the silly tart of a wife – she couldn't have made it up. 'See, Mikey, you married a no-good slut of a woman.' Instantly, Zara knew she sounded contemptuous, but it was too late to take back what she'd just said.

For a second, Mike felt he was being mocked, and he tried to assess the situation. Having Zara in the background laughing at him increased his anger to a higher level.

With a quick movement, he turned to Zara and fervently spat, 'You need to grow up!'

In a fit of fury, he raised the nail gun and fired it into each of Scottie's shoulders, and then into his right kneecap. 'You fucking liar! You locked my boy up and drugged him!'

Scottie was gasping for air. The pain was so intense that he could hardly breathe. 'No!' he squealed. 'Please, I'm begging you. Please, I never drugged him. I didn't lock him up. Jackie did!'

'Liar!' shouted Mike, just before he fired another nail. This time it flew into Scottie's arm, missing the bone and shooting out the other side.

'Argghh, please, please, no! I'll tell you the truth. Please!'

Mike took a deep breath and once again he lowered the tool. Walking over to the corner of the room where a water machine stood, he grabbed one of the plastic cups, placed it underneath the tap, and filled it with ice-cold water. Two gulps and it was gone. He wiped his mouth with the back of his hand and then poured another. This time, he allowed the water to coat the nape of his thick neck.

He suddenly spun to face Zara. 'And don't you ever have a dig at me about my wife again!'

Still coming to terms with the gruesome sight and the blood-curdling screams, Zara didn't really listen to Mike. She'd never expected him to be so calm and calculated. What she was witnessing was probably the most dangerous man in the South East. His recklessness appeared so undisciplined that it was sending unnerving signals through her brain. This was a side to Mike that seven years ago she'd heard stories about and yet couldn't have imagined. To her, he was a sweet, gentle giant with charm and tenderness who could have her in the sack within five minutes.

Mixed emotions gripped her. Mike had just spoken down to her like she was working for him, or, worse, behaving like some naive kid. But she was supposed to be in charge. Realistically, though, how could she be? She was witnessing a man who would scare the shit out of the Devil himself.

Maybe, she thought, *this was her father's way of testing her, to see if she could dominate a man like Mike.* Still, she had to have the last say.

'Well, Mikey, I'm concerned that you made the decision to marry a woman like that. Also, she should have been completely under your supervision. If you can't control your wife, then maybe Izzy was wrong about you.'

With his back to her, Mike acted as if she wasn't there. His complete dismissal vexed Zara into silence.

'So, Scottie, you'd better start talking. Leave anything out, and I'll know. I have a gift: I can smell a bullshitter five miles away,' smirked Mike.

Scottie fervently nodded, knowing that Regan was serious. The deranged look in his eyes wasn't the expression of a kidder.

'I swear, I didn't know she was your wife. I didn't even know she was married . . .'

Mike retrieved the nail gun and this time placed it over Scottie's eye. He wasn't going to fire it. Scottie would then be dead, and he wouldn't have the answers he was looking for. Zara winced and swallowed hard. Scottie was so petrified, he didn't realize that the force of the compression would push the nail straight through his brain.

'Okay, please, I did know who she was. I just wanted information. We wanted to know how you were getting the guns over to Ireland and where you were buying them from. Oh, come on, Regan. You would have done the same. It's just business,' he pleaded.

Mike just stared at him in silence.

'She was all over me, I swear. She had a mad idea that me and her could shack up together, but I never had any intentions. It just went too far.'

He looked for any reaction from Regan but was met with a blank, unreadable expression. However, it was enough to know that the pain he was suffering was very likely to become a whole lot worse. In fact, he was beginning to feel so light-headed, he thought he would pass out at any moment. Taking a deep breath, he tried to look Regan squarely in the eye.

'I never hurt your boy. I swear on me farver's life. I wouldn't hurt a kid.'

Mike smiled, showing a neat line of white teeth. 'There's no point in swearing on your farver's life. He's dead.'

Scottie blinked as the sweat dripped into his eyes and stung them. 'Dead?'

'Yep, skinned alive and flushed down the bog.'

Scottie felt a wave of temporary anger that subsided as soon as another surge of pain engulfed him.

'So why did my six-year-old son sound like he was on drugs, eh?'

'It was Jackie, I swear. It was her. She told me to meet her at her house. She shut her kid in—'

'My kid?' yelled Mike, pressing the gun harder into Scottie's eye socket.

'Yeah, okay. Jackie gave him vodka and orange. I don't know why she did it. I promise, I never even spoke to the boy except to ask him who was on the phone.'

'Where did you meet my wife?'

'Cat's Whiskers nightclub, a hen do. Her mate . . .' He stumbled over his words, in part because of his injuries, but he was trying to keep his mind focused to prevent giving too much away. 'Her mate told me she would be there.'

Mike's face dropped. He felt oddly cold.

'Who the fuck is her mate?'

'I, er . . . she's just an old slapper.' His voice was a whimper.

'Where's my son now?'

'I dunno. At that house still, I expect. It's near Ely. The address is in me sat nav. I promise, I left when she was at the shop. I just grabbed me stuff and went . . .' His words trailed off as his face paled over. Then, he fainted.

Mike's deep sigh sounded like a growl.

Zara was staring at the blood dripping from the gruesome puncture wounds. She pictured Jesus on the cross, in the film *The Passion of the Christ*. For some reason, it wasn't the sight of Scottie being tortured that turned her stomach, but Mike's steely disposition.

He turned and nodded and made another demand of her. She didn't argue this time but slipped outside the workshop and spoke with the two men waiting outside. She asked one of them to return to Scottie's car and call her with any addresses stored in the sat nav.

The skies outside were now dark and menacing, the storm was about to break, and as soon as she slipped back into the workshop, the thunder made her jump. Yet Mike didn't even flinch, pre-occupied with prising out of Scottie everything he needed to know. He glared as Scottie came to.

'Whose house is it?'

Scottie frowned. 'Hers, I assume.'

Mike kicked the chair, causing Scottie to yelp like a dog. 'I swear that's what she told me. It was her house. She owned it. She wanted a new life.'

Mike glared. 'What, with you, ya fucking ugly weasel?'

Scottie eyed up the gun and thought better of saying any more. If he was going to survive, he needed to box clever. Little did he know, Regan was going to kill him anyway.

'Why did she give my son alcohol?'

Scottie wanted to say it was an accident and that she never knew the drink had vodka in it. However, he needed to turn Regan's aggression onto Jackie – to be seen as the innocent one – well, at least regarding her son.

'Jackie wanted him drunk to keep him quiet. I told her it was wrong. I wanted to get him out of that room and to the hospital, but she wouldn't have it. She said she would keep him locked up and quiet.' He waited for a sympathetic reaction – or at least an even-handed one.

But you can't kid a kidder. Mike turned on him and kicked the chair so hard that the leg snapped. Scottie came crashing down, landing on the injured knee. He screamed out in pain.

'It's all very convenient, wouldn't you say, a little yarn like that, eh, Scottie? How long did it take you to think that one up? You and your dippy brothers think you can take me for a fucking fool, do ya? Ya grassed us up to the Ol' Bill to have us nicked, so you could then 'ave me outta the way, allowing you to run around like sneaky rats looking into my business. Then that failed, and so ya brainwashed divvy Travis into taking pictures of my set-up, and ya didn't think we would suss ya. Then, to top it all, in the cunt stunt trade, ya went and gutted me pal's dog. You Harmans are a tent short of a full-blown fucking circus. Ya grassed, ya went against the rules, and now ya think by blaming my wife that somehow lets you off the hook.' He tapped his foot, looking down at Scottie who was squirming in pain. His body was still held to the chair by the rope tied around his middle.

'By not stopping Jackie from harming my boy, as I see it, Scottie, you are as fucking guilty as that bitch. Yet, I'm wondering why I should believe you. How the hell do I know you haven't done away with the pair of them? It would be right up your street, wouldn't it, Scottie, since you and your brothers have been brought up the wrong way? There are rules and you've just broken every one of them.'

Scottie felt shooting pains all over him. There was an intense burning feeling as if every nerve was alight. The cocaine must have cleared from his body, allowing the terrible agony to take a real hold. His eyes red-rimmed and full like a frightened child, he tried to look up at Regan.

'No, please, you have to believe me. I haven't touched her or your son. I swear, as soon as your boy said he was talking to you, I knew then I was in trouble. I expected you to be on your way. I wasn't gonna hang around. I never wanted all this aggro. It was me dad and . . . they were the ones, not me.'

Mike raised his eyebrow and protruded his lower jaw. 'You have squealer embedded in your arteries, don't ya?' He stepped away and laughed aloud. 'Easy to blame ya ol' man since he's now flushed down the khazi. Right: if you hate Harry and Vinnie so much, you'll want to see them punished, won't ya?' Mike, in his anger, overlooked the fact that Scottie stumbled over his words when he grassed his father. Those were two names that nearly tripped off his tongue.

Scottie felt his stomach contents climb his throat and rush out through his mouth and nose.

Zara looked away; she couldn't bear seeing people being sick around her. She slid the door open and crept outside, taking in great gulps of air, until she steadied her unsettled stomach. Moments later, she returned.

Mike waited for an answer from Scottie.

'What do you want from me?' cried Scottie.

'I wanna know where they are, and if they have my son. And until he's back home safe and sound, I will spend every day turning you bit by bit into mushy peas, starting with your fucking eyeballs.'

The current pain he was in was enough to know that Regan wasn't

149

bluffing, but he couldn't grass, not on Harry and Vinnie. They would string him up. He briefly pondered over his options, but the pain was making him sick; he couldn't get his head straight, and all he could concentrate on was how he could get out of this mess.

'The address is in my sat nav. I promise you, Jackie has him.'

'Well, Scottie, we'll see about that because you're gonna be here until I've checked out this so-called address near Ely.'

Scottie was well aware of how long it would take to go to Jackie's house and back. He wasn't sure if he could hold out.

Zara's phone interrupted his thoughts. 'I've got the address, Mikey. I can call in a mate who lives that way.'

Mike spun around and snatched the phone from her, staring at the text message of the unfamiliar address.

Zara was still slightly queasy and didn't have the energy to pull Mike up on this latest slight to her authority.

'Call ya mate!' he demanded.

The tables had now turned. Zara was answering to him. This wasn't supposed to happen. She dialled one of her associates who was plotted up just outside Cambridge. It was a landlord of a pub that Izzy had set up as a stopgap for arms coming down from Scotland. The arrangements made, she slid it into her pocket. With her head tilted to the side, Mike noticed how tired and drawn her face looked.

Blood leaked continuously from the wound in Scottie's shoulders, and pooled around his face that was now pressed against the floor. His energy was drained, and he couldn't hold his head up.

Mike was like a tiger pacing its cage, waiting for the call, praying that his son was safe. Half an hour seemed like an eternity to everyone.

Zara's ringtone made her jump; it didn't affect Mike, though, who stood rooted to the floor in anticipation. He couldn't hear the voice on the other end of the phone, but he watched Zara's reaction to the caller. She shook her head.

Sympathy spread across her face as she told him, 'No one's there. My contact had to break in at the back. All he found was a kid's suitcase in a small room.'

Mike's temper took over his senses. He ripped open the top drawer of a metal toolbox and retrieved an axe. With both hands, he held it above his head and was about to bring the lethal implement down and break Scottie's head in half when Zara grabbed his arm, and, somehow, using all her strength, she pulled him away. Even Mike was shocked by the power inside her thin arms.

'Wait. I've an idea.'

Mike lowered the axe, his chest heaving.

'Tell him to call his brothers. Weed them out. If they have Ricky, then he's our only hope of finding them right now.'

For a moment, Mike was back in time seven years ago, with the sweet woman who smiled coyly and showed him so much affection. She tried to smile now, but inside and unbeknown to him she was hurting. Yet he was heartened by the way she'd said the word 'our'.

Taking the phone from her, he looked at Scottie who had his eyes squeezed tightly shut. 'What's Harry's number?'

Opening his eyes, Scottie tried to recall it, but the pain was dulling his senses. A swift kick, though, soon made him think faster. 'No more, please. I'll tell ya.'

Mike had his finger to the ready as Scottie reeled off the digits.

'Ask him where he is and tell him to meet you at the Portobello in one hour.'

Scottie nodded. As Mike pulled the chair onto its three legs, he held the phone to Scottie's ear. It rang twice before Harry answered. Mike was close enough to hear the call.

Scottie nervously stared at Regan. 'Harry, where are you?'

Harry was obviously raging. 'Where the fuck are *you*, more like? Jesus, Scottie, I thought the fucking Regans had murdered you. Muvver's gone missing, and the bastards have killed Farver.'

Scottie's eyes widened. 'Where are ya, Harry? Can you meet me at the Portobello pub?'

'You what? No, I fucking can't. Get yaself down to Broadstairs now, you stupid cunt.'

Scottie stared at Regan waiting for a clue as to what to say next. Mike mouthed the words 'Where is he?'

'Whereabouts in Broadstairs, Harry?'

There was silence for a second. It then dawned on Mike that Broadstairs was either their hideout or their holiday home. It would seem strange, therefore, for Scottie to ask Harry for the address.

'Are you all right, Scottie?'

Quickly, Scottie replied, 'No. Harry, they've got me. They're gonna fucking kill me.'

Mike ripped the phone away and held it to his own ear. 'That's right, Harry. So, if ya want ya brother alive, then you give me back my son.'

'You bastard! Ya killed me ol' man, ya sicko. Now you wanna kill me brother? If you touch him, Regan, I will destroy you . . .' Harry was so blinded by fear, and concern for his brother and his mother, that he didn't twig right away what Mike meant when he'd said, 'give me back my son'.

'Trust me, Harry, when I fucking get hold of you, you'll know the real meaning of destroy because I'll shred you like pulled pork. Now, where's me boy?'

Stupidly, Harry still didn't think to deny that he had Ricky. Not thinking on his feet, he launched into attack mode.

'I will hunt you down, Regan, every last one of your family, and I'll wipe you all off the face of this earth. You will be sleeping with one eye open, you no-good stinking fucking cunt. You went below the belt, Regan, killing me farver the way you did. Now, where's me muvver?' he bellowed down the phone.

'I want me boy, and you can have ya muvver.'

'An eye for an eye!' replied Harry, who apparently didn't quite grasp the meaning of the quote. He thought it meant a straight swap.

'You bastard. If you dare to touch my kid!' screamed Mike, as he looked at Scottie and stuck his finger in his shoulder wound, making him yell out in pain. 'Did ya hear that, Harry? I will continue torturing your brother until I have my boy back and in one piece.'

With his mind all over the place, Harry was hard-pressed to think of a way to save his brother. Scottie had clearly been up to no good. He was so sly that, unlike his brother Vinnie, he held his cards close to his chest. Although Scottie loved their father, there was a closer bond between him and his uncle Ronnie, Frank's brother, who'd always said that Scottie was the son he never had. He was right. Ronnie was clever and crafty with no morals – a master at the art of using people for his own ends. Scottie was just the same.

Then, it dawned on him. Perhaps his brother was on his own mission and had done away with Mike's son. He wouldn't put it past him. He recalled Scottie telling him that he had his own plan to take down the Regan firm. However, at the time, Harry had thought that his brother was too busy to sit and listen to theirs and had used the excuse to go off and screw his bird – the one he'd kept a secret.

Harry's thoughts darkened at what he assumed his brother had done, raising his anger and trepidation. Vinnie had killed the dog, and now that Scottie had kidnapped the kid or worse, both brothers' actions had led to severe consequences, with the brutal murder of his father and possibly his mother. Christ, had his brothers no fucking sense at all? Next, it would be him on the block.

'Jesus. How the hell can I give you back someone I don't bloody have? Ask my prat of a brother, 'cos I sure as hell have no fucking idea what you're on about. I—'

'Okay, I'll leave my axe to do the questioning!' interrupted

Mike before he cut the connection and raised the sharpened tool above his head.

'No!' screamed Scottie.

'Harry said you know where my son is!'

Scottie was mortified. His brother had just signed his death warrant – but he would get his revenge. 'No, Harry has him. I had nothing to do with it. I don't even know where Harry took him. I swear, if I knew, don't ya think I would tell ya? Come on, Mr Regan, please! I swear to God, I don't have him. I wouldn't hurt a kid – ever!'

His pleading words meant nothing to Mike. Zara wasn't quick enough to stop him. The axe came down and completely removed Scottie's face and the front part of his brain. He died instantly, but his body still shook and twitched. With blood all over his face and up his arms, Mike stood there, frozen by the realization that he'd acted irrationally, by allowing his temper to control his actions – with devastating consequences. He should have waited until he was 100 per cent sure of the facts.

Zara wanted to vomit there and then but could only bend over and dry-heave. She felt Mike's meaty arm rub her back.

'Go outside, Zara, and get some fresh air. I need to get this place cleaned up.' His voice was softer, more caring. Even in among the blood and mess – in what was an almost surreal situation – she wanted to feel his hand on her for just that little bit longer.

There was no more playing about who was in charge; it was not a battle of wits anymore. It was raw emotion, and no one could argue with that.

'Joshua can help.' Her voice was croaky from heaving.

'No, darling, this is my mess. Besides, I don't know him.'

He sounded resigned, or perhaps just exhausted. She took the bloodied axe, twisting it around in her hands.

'Well, I trust him. And he'll be cleaning up my mess too. There. It has my DNA on it.' She threw the axe to the floor.

Chapter 10

As the sun came up the next morning, Mike slowly opened his eyes and felt the warm, smooth skin beside him. Zara was still asleep. Gently, he sat up, not wanting to wake her. She looked peaceful, her dark hair and olive skin so striking against the pure white linen sheets. He stared for a while, admiring her delicate bone structure and the gold chain that held a tiny ring, which was gathered in the pocket of her collarbone. He watched as it moved up and down with the gentle waves of her breathing. He followed the contours of her body and gazed at the peaks and troughs of her hips and her long thighs. There was not a blemish, except for a few fine slivers of silver stretch marks just below her navel. Everything about Zara was natural, and with hardly any make-up, she was still a very attractive woman.

Rubbing his hands through his hair, he got up from the bed and crept from the room to make a coffee to liven himself up. His thoughts turned to Jackie. He wondered if Scottie had told the truth; however, there was the frightening doubt that screamed at him: *what if he hadn't?* He couldn't imagine any sane mother plying their child with booze. If she hadn't taken Ricky away, and their disappearance had anything to do with the Harmans, then what the hell were they playing at? He just couldn't fathom why they weren't screaming for a deal. A fair swap. What could be more important than Harry's mother and his brother's life? He was usually a reasonable man; nevertheless, right now, Mike didn't care, and no one and nothing would stand in the way of getting his son back.

Just as the kettle boiled, he sensed her presence in the room. 'Mikey, about last night . . .'

With his back to her, he replied, 'Don't worry. It won't happen again.'

Grateful that he had his back to her, so he couldn't witness her hurt expression as she quickly blinked away the tears, she said, 'I know, Mikey, I get it. You were tensed up and I was just a sexual release for you.'

Her tone was anything but harsh. Mike turned to see Zara with her arms folded to cover her breasts, that would otherwise have been visible through her long, thin T-shirt. Her tousled hair and rosy cheeks stirred that old attraction, and Mike looked away from her.

Their affair had been a long time ago, and too much had gone under the bridge to even think about resurrecting anything now. Yet he was fighting the urge to take her back to the bedroom for another full-on session, on a bed that had been virtually destroyed by their animal-like lust in mauling each other's bodies last night. Seven years. Seven years away from each other hadn't killed their former passion. Far from it: the ripped clothes, the bite marks, the scratches from sharp nails, the taste of each other's skin – they were testament to that.

An unexpected feeling of guilt plagued him. His son was missing, yet he was being drawn into another sexual encounter at the initiative of Zara. He instantly changed the subject.

'It was a bit over the top yesterday. It was something you shouldn't have been a part of,' he said, in a low tone.

Still hurt, she raised her eyebrow. 'You're forgetting, Mikey, I'm your boss.'

156

Not perturbed by her comment, he tapped her on the nose. 'Would you like a coffee?'

She knew then that the boss thing wasn't going to work. 'Yes, please, er . . . Mikey, I need to ask you something.'

He turned away and pulled out one of the white cups and poured a black coffee from the percolator – he remembered Zara didn't take milk. Then he placed the cups on the small kitchen table. As Zara took a seat, Mike pulled out the chair opposite. He sipped his coffee and then nodded. 'What is it, Zara?'

Nursing her cup, she leaned forward with her elbows on the table. 'Frank Harman.'

'What about him?'

'I saw what you did to Scottie. Did you kill Frank and cut him up like the police are saying?'

He could have taken exception to a question like that, but he felt more drained and concerned with Ricky being missing than worrying about Zara making disparaging insinuations.

'No, Zara, of course not. Look, love, this has all got so outta hand. Your father's involvement is ridiculous, and I made a mistake in going to him for help. Now you're immersed in it, and I understand that you wanna take over ya ol' man's business, but, Zara, there are other ways. Watching a man getting tortured proves nothing. It doesn't make someone tough. It can, though, brand a person a monster and distort the overall picture.'

He placed his cup down and clasped his hands together. 'What you saw me do is the dark side of my line of work, and I know it has made you question who I am. And now I look at you, Zara. You are a good person but you're continually trying to prove your worth to your father. It's not who you are, babe. And me killing an old man is not who I am either.'

Like Mike, Zara would also have flared up at those words, but something between them both had changed. The bitterness had subsided.

'Sorry, Mikey. I should have known that.'

He smiled. For a second, she thought she saw the former twinkle in his eyes that she remembered so well.

Without thinking, she said, 'Did you ever really love me, Mikey?' As soon as those words left her mouth, she wished she'd never said them. It was such a long time ago and so much had changed – for both of them.

'Yes, babe, I did, but you just fucked off out of the blue and left me wondering what the hell I did wrong. Anyway, you obviously got on with your life, but so did I.'

She wanted to tell him the truth about why she'd gone, but she just couldn't. Her fingers toyed with the chain around her neck, and she swallowed the emotion that felt as though it would strangle her. However, Mike noticed her tender expression.

'Zara, I only married Jackie because she was expecting Ricky. I wouldn't have otherwise. I liked her. She was fun and sweet, but I never loved her, not like I loved you. But she was expecting my son, and so I had no choice. I got wed and now . . .' He paused and sighed. 'Now Ricky is out there somewhere. I pray to God he's not hurt or worse.'

She realized this wasn't the time or place to talk about herself. Mike was too distraught about his son, and she knew exactly how that felt.

'Now, first things first, we need to get the Ol' Bill off your back. You said to Izzy that you believe Mrs Harman killed her ol' man.'

'I can't be 100 per cent sure. Anyway, I took her down to me holiday pad in Rye, to get her outta the way. She's a real sweet ol' girl, she is, and if she did kill Frank, I can't blame her.'

Zara nearly spat out her coffee. 'Sweet? She tried to flush her ol' man down the loo and you call her sweet?' She laughed, a wholesome laugh, and for the first time in years, Mike's spirits lifted when he saw the real Zara.

Their laughter was cut short, however, when her phone rang. It was Izzy.

'Zara, are you with Mike?' he asked.

'Yes. Why?'

'The DI has been on the phone. He seems to think we know of Mike's whereabouts. Someone has definitely been talking. Anyway, he had some interesting news about Frank Harman's murder. It appears that he died of arsenic poisoning. They found cakes in that house laced with enough poison to bring down a fucking elephant. So, unless Mike is into baking cakes, then the old girl is the likely suspect. Interestingly, they reckon they found remnants of a cake in the bin. It looks like someone had a bite and spat it out. Lucky for them, or it would have killed them. That wouldn't have been Mike by any chance, would it?'

Mike was leaning in to hear the call. He smiled and nodded.

'Dad, it *was* Mike.'

She handed Mike the phone.

'Izzy, have they let the boys go or are they still down the nick?'

'They're out. And the Harmans, I take it, are still walking the streets?'

Mike chuckled. 'Not all of them.' His voice turned sour. 'And, Izzy, you need to keep up your end of the bargain. My son is still missing.'

There was a silent pause before Izzy coughed. 'Mike, bitterness is a dangerous emotion. It can turn people. It can stop them from seeing the wood for the trees.'

'Izzy, stop with the fucking philosophical lectures, will ya? I'm not at fucking school.'

'Zara gave me the low-down on what happened yesterday, and your temper may well be misplaced. You want someone to pay for your boy's disappearance, and yet you're not facing facts. This wife of yours is the likely culprit, so, for the time being, concentrate on saving your own skin, or, I warn you now, you'll be inside serving a great lump.'

The message was exactly the sobering wake-up call that Mike

needed. He handed the phone back and rolled his eyes. 'So, you're still determined to have me under your control, Zara, eh? Running to Daddy and telling tales?'

She shook her head, her eyes pleading. 'No, Mikey, it's not like that. When you were asleep, my dad called me and asked what was going on. I couldn't ignore him. He can tell if I'm lying. How the hell can he help if he doesn't know the facts? Yeah, look, initially, when you and Izzy made a deal I was . . .' She stopped and took a deep breath. 'I was pleased. I had been angry for years that you got married and your life was hunky fucking dory, when I had nothing. To have you answering to me, it seemed like payback. The truth is, Izzy does want you in the firm. I'm taking over, and, in fact, Mikey, I've already been running a big part of it. I ain't the simple girl you once knew.'

Mike's mind switched off. He was pleased that they'd both adjusted to one another again; but, as much as he liked Zara, he wasn't interested in renewing their former relationship. His priority now was his son, and so the most pressing concern was to have a plan in place to find him. Time was passing by, and he was not going to spend all day hanging around.

'Look, I'm going to Rye. I need to talk with Mrs Harman, the poor cow.'

Mike's dismissiveness left Zara feeling empty. 'Um . . . what shall I do?'

'Go and talk to Izzy, because now your clock is ticking. Izzy made a deal and he's not making good on his promise. I want my boy and the rest of the Harmans found.'

She looked down at the dregs in her coffee cup and held in the sigh that wanted to leave her lips. The reality was that last night didn't mean as much to Mike as it did to her. But it had felt as though it did – at the time.

* * *

160

The rain had left the roads flooded and Mike was frustrated with driving an old banger. The windscreen wipers squeaked as they flicked back and forth, and that was grating on him. As he hit the A21, the traffic slowed down.

Crawling along in the single lane gave Mike time to calm his overactive mind. Which was fine until a troubling thought came out of nowhere. How did the Harmans know about the arms deal in the first place? The only people who knew about it were Izzy, the Irish buyers, and, of course, his own men. So at least one of them had informed the police. As much as he disliked Izzy, he knew in a strange way he could trust him. He thought about Jackie shagging Scottie and then hearing him say that Frank and Harry had it in for him. None of it made any sense. What the hell did they want?

He couldn't get his head around it all. First, he needed to persuade Doris to own up to her husband's murder. He felt guilty about it because she was just a sweet lady who probably lived a cruel life at the hands of her own family. He wouldn't tell her what he'd done to her youngest son, though. It would break her heart, and she might inform the police.

As he drove up the hill towards the cottage, he tried to prepare mentally for how he would break the news to Doris that she would have to go to the cop shop with him. Mike parked the car directly outside and climbed out. Maybe being older she felt the cold because strangely all the windows were closed. He jangled the keys in his pocket and thought it better to knock than to let himself in.

With no response, he decided to go in and wait for her. He suspected she was out shopping or had gone out to eat. After closing the door behind him, he called out, 'Hello? Mrs Harman?'

Satisfied that he was alone, he wandered past the living room and straight into the kitchen. He noticed a china teacup and saucer lying on the draining board; it wasn't one belonging to the cottage and he smiled. She must have treated herself in one of the antique or vintage shops; Rye was full of them.

He put the kettle on and wandered into the lounge to open a window and let out the slight odour in the warm stale air. He had to stoop to enter the lounge.

Just as he was about to stroll towards the window, he noticed an opened photo album, letters, and a note, all spread across the large steamer trunk coffee table. Then his eyes were drawn to Doris, who was sitting in the chair sound asleep. He didn't want to startle her, so he stepped back. But as he kept his eyes on her, a strange feeling came over him. She looked odd. Her lips were a shade of purple and her waxy skin was a creamy colour. *Shit!* She wasn't asleep, she was dead.

'For fuck's sake, that's all I flaming well need,' he said aloud. For a few seconds, he studied her carefully to check that she really was dead, but it was obvious; her chest was perfectly still. Then guilt swept through him. He was initially annoyed because his only ticket out of jail was if Doris made a statement to the effect that she'd killed her husband – if she actually did do it. Now she was dead. The poor woman hadn't even died in her own home.

His eyes fell back to the photo album and the note, and then he saw the empty prescription medication bottles. There was such a mixture, but among them were sleeping tablets, so he assumed they had knocked her out before she died. He didn't want to touch the paper, but he felt the urge to read the message, assuming the album had been left open at a poignant moment in Doris's life. He looked more closely. There were little handwritten comments inside the cellophane that held the photos in place. He kneeled down and studied them closely. The first photo was of Doris on her wedding day. She was not the typical glowing, blushing bride, that was for sure. In fact, she appeared sullen with her high cheeks thin and tight and her eyes looking at the floor. Frank Harman, with a cocky grin on his face, looked a flash bastard with his thumbs up as if he'd won a bet. The note beside it read: *The day when I said until death do us part, well, it couldn't have come quickly enough for me. You lived for too long. I had to end it.*

Mike reread the note. Bingo! This was the confession he needed to get the police off his back, but his sudden elation was dampened when he glanced back at Doris. 'You poor cow.'

Then he looked at the next photo. It was of her again, this time holding a baby. However, what should have been a picture of a proud mother looking adoringly at her precious bundle was a shell of a woman – she was thin, pale, and almost grieving. The note read: *Harry, you were my first-born devil, like your father. If you read this, then you will know how much I wanted to be free of you.*

The third photo was of her and the four children, each one of them with sneering smiles. There was nothing cute about them.

In the next photo, Frank had a pint in his hand. Alongside him was another man. They were so much alike, they could have been twins. It put him in mind of the Kray twins, albeit an uglier version. The other man, obviously Frank's brother, had a girl on his lap. She was a pretty little blonde child, approximately the same age as Doris's youngest son, Scottie. They were on a beach, probably Margate, and yet, once again, Doris seemed so miserable. He suddenly felt a lump in his throat. His mind turned to his mum and their family photos; she always had a beaming smile on her face.

The note next to it read: *I was never a part of this family, I was just a breeding machine for your father. You all used me and abused me, your father most of all. So, if you hate me for taking his life, then so be it. You never loved me anyway, not even you, Paris.*

Unexpectedly, Mike felt a wet tear trickle down his cheek. He rarely cried and hastily brushed it away. Why Doris was getting to him, he didn't know, but he felt a deep sadness; it was because he was glimpsing into someone's past and witnessing how life had dealt her such a raw and cruel hand.

The fifth picture was a black-and-white one of her and his own father, Arthur. He stared as if he was looking at a photo of himself. That had to be the most moving picture of all. The difference in Doris – looking so young, beautiful and happy – was amazing. Her smile went from ear-to-ear, showing off her glowing complexion, and the shine in her eyes was like the moonlight on a summer's evening.

'What did you do to her, Frank, you fucking bully?' It was a strange feeling. She meant nothing to him, and yet she represented so much. She'd obviously loved his father, and yet she'd ended up with Frank, who, from the photos and the notes, had clearly made her life a misery. He read the letter next to the picture.

You, Arthur, were my one true love, and I know how much they detested you. They tried so many times to bring you down, but you were too wise to be fooled by them. I have written down some names and dates, and I hope it will all make sense to you. I only wish I could have done more.

Mike read the words again. *Who were they?* Mike wondered. He guessed she meant her husband, but who else did she mean? He flipped the page and studied the other photos. Another one showed Frank, his brother, and two other men, all roughly the same age, dressed in dark suits and grinning into the camera; they weren't broad, beaming smiles, only sly smirks. He peered closer and then he saw something else. Just in view over Frank's belt was the handle of a gun. Carefully scanning the picture again, he spotted a bat just behind the trouser leg of one of the other suited men. Slightly out of view was another man; just his shoulders, an arm, and a leg could be seen. The arm had a white long-sleeved shirt, rolled up. As Mike leaned closer, he could just about make out a tattooed number along the right wrist. And when he studied the photo again as a whole, he noticed that each of the men was hiding something away from the camera. It was amazing how a photo could tell a thousand words. He wondered who had taken the picture. Would it have been Doris? Surely not. Or maybe she was telling a story.

This was odd. He turned the page and his eyes were drawn to newspaper clippings. One contained the murder of Kenneth

Keller. Mike knew that name. Kenny had worked with his father, and as young as Mike had been back then, he remembered him well. Because whoever had killed Kenneth had broken the rules by shooting him in the back.

Below that clipping was another photo of Frank's brother dressed in a suit. His expression suggested a real touch of arrogance; it was a face you would love to punch. This album really was showing the past. Following on was another newspaper clipping, dated 1995 – it was the murder of Monty Stafford, old Teddy Stafford's brother.

Mike felt uneasy. He had loved Monty; he'd been so much like Staffie in looks and character. Monty supposedly hanged himself; to this day, Mike's father and his uncles never believed it for a minute. Much like Staffie, he was built like a brick shithouse and was a tough man with a tough mind. He called suicide victims cowards. So, he definitely wasn't the type to hang himself. Old Ted, Staffie's father, had been beside himself with grief, and it was only with the comfort of the others, like Arthur, that he got through it. There below the clipping was the man from the previous photo, the one with the bat.

Mike shuddered.

As he carried on going through the album, he realized that Doris had indeed told the story. In effect, it was a war between the Harmans and his father's firm. Yet the difference was the Harmans were slippery cowards – not straight-up men who fought for the manor like honourable gentlemen. He cringed at the sneakiness of them. In the past, his father had mentioned that he always believed there was someone lingering in the background, who knew far more than they should have. Yet he had never been able to discover who had passed on information, resulting in two of his deals being intercepted by the police. There were also a few odd incidents, where he and his firm had been jumped whilst unarmed.

As he turned the next page, he gasped aloud and almost jumped to his feet. There in her wedding dress and standing next to Frank Harman's brother with a cocky smile was the probable culprit. This was the very same woman who'd come for Sunday tea, who'd taken him to school, and who'd helped their mother with family parties. She was their home help. She was the fucking fly on the wall.

'Shit me! Carmella, you bitch!'

Doris Harman had indeed set out to tell a story and what a story it was. All those years, his father was fighting with a firm that didn't play fair. He couldn't understand though, why now, after all this time, the Harmans were rearing their ugly heads. He'd had no previous issues with the family; in fact, until recently, he'd had no idea who they were. What did they have against him and his father?

Mike glanced over at the four letters. One was addressed to the police commissioner, one was to a lawyer, one was to his father, and the last one was to himself. He stood up, holding the letter addressed to him, and again he eyed the woman in the chair.

He soon realized quite how much detail she'd put into planning all this. Her hair was all curled, she had a tiny amount of blusher on her otherwise white cheeks, and she was wearing an evening dress, a long blue satin gown with tiny sequins around the neck. On her wrist was a charm bracelet, and he recognized that it was the same one she was wearing in the photo with his father. Then he looked at her hands. The wedding ring had left an indent and was missing. He glanced back at the coffee table and there it was on a handkerchief.

He walked over to the sofa and sat down, pulled the letter from the envelope, and began to read.

Dear Mike,

I am sorry for using your beautiful cottage to take my life. I intended to end it today because September 29th was the day I met your father. I loved him very much. I hope if you find me, I haven't left a mess. Please would you ensure the other letters go to the intended? It's strange because it seems that you are the only person I can trust. Maybe it's because I trusted your father and you remind me so much of him.

I wish you every happiness in your life.
Doris

Mike felt another tear working its way down his face. The last few days had been very draining. Now finding a woman so heartbroken that she'd ended her own life was driving him to behave entirely out of character. But first, he now had to weigh up the pros and cons. Contacting the Filth was a no-no in his line of work. Nevertheless, it might be the quickest way for him to establish his innocence once the police had done their homework. And it seemed the best solution to clear his name quickly, so he could focus on searching for his son. The downside was that the search for his son would be delayed by a good two days.

Emotions were running high in his head. Instead of seriously thinking things through, he picked up the phone and made the worst decision of his life – he called the police. However, before they arrived, he took photos of the letters and the album and hid the camera under the floorboards. If that evidence went missing, at least he had proof.

With a warrant out for his arrest for the gruesome murder of Frank Harman, the police arrived in droves, with flak jackets, guns and dogs. As he opened the door, a firearm was aimed at his chest. Slowly, he stepped forward, with his hands above his head. He expected no less. Two officers grabbed him and threw him over the bonnet of a police car and cuffed him. Radio conversations could be heard, the cottage was taped off, and a black van arrived containing the forensic team. He remained silent with his face pushed against the metal of the police car bonnet. He didn't struggle either; there was no point in risking being hurt or shot.

The officers surrounding him parted like the Red Sea for Moses, to make way for the detective. Mike didn't recognize him because he was from the Sussex Police. He knew they would go over the top – probably see him as a serial killer.

The detective inspector was a scruffy, short individual, with a few strands of unruly hair blowing in the breeze. He had an unkempt grey beard and bushy black eyebrows. His pale-blue shirt was tight against his beer belly and his black slacks were shiny from being ironed rather than dry-cleaned.

'Mr Regan?'

The officer pulled him upright from the car to face the DI.

'Yes. That's me.'

'I am Detective Inspector Hornsby.'

Mike nodded but remained expressionless.

'Do you know we have a warrant out for your arrest?' His voice didn't match his appearance. Mike expected him to have a squeaky, slimy voice, not a deep, commanding tone.

Mike shook his head. 'Nope.'

'Right, from what the Met DI tells me, you'll know the drill. So, Michael Regan, you are under arrest for the murder of Frank Harman. Anything you say can and may be used in evidence against you . . .'

Once Hornsby read him his rights, Mike smirked. 'Sorry, but my name isn't Michael Regan.'

Hornsby raised an eyebrow and looked back down at his notes. 'I just asked you if you were Michael Regan and you nodded.'

'No, you didn't. You asked me if I was Mr Regan, which I am, but I am not Michael. My name is Mike.'

Hornsby flared his nostrils and waved his hand. 'Same bloody thing.'

'No, actually, it's not. My name is Mike, not Michael. It never has been and never will be. Now, you want to get this right, Detective Inspector. No slip-ups. I want to get down to the station, get this shit cleared up, and leave.'

With a loud chuckle and a shake of his head, he scoffed. 'Oh, dear me, you're a right one, mate. You, *Mike* Regan, won't be going anywhere.'

With no emotion on his face and his shoulders back, Mike gave a slow nod. 'Okay, Detective Inspector, then let's get this over with, shall we?'

Hornsby glared with narrowed eyes. That was usually his line; and yet he thought it would be prudent not to argue the point. This titan of a man was cold and calculating.

'Oh, before we go, there are letters inside from Mrs Harman. One is addressed to the police commissioner and one to her lawyer, and then one is mine and there is one for my father. I trust you will see to it that they end up in the right hands?'

Hornsby frowned. 'What are you insinuating?'

Mike smiled. 'That question right there suggests you have a sinister mind. What I'm *suggesting*, Detective Inspector, is that you would ensure those letters are rightfully given to the names on the envelopes.'

Hornsby felt his face flush. He huffed and turned away to give his team orders to clear the area and allow forensics access. One of the officers opened the car door, and before he even had a chance to push Mike's head down to get in, Mike beat him to it.

With one officer in the back seat and two in the front, they pulled away, tailing another police car. The DI followed in the car behind. The radio beeped, and Mike could hear Hornsby saying, 'We have to take the suspect to Maidstone. It looks like they already have a team on the case.'

Mike hoped that Detective Inspector Evans was up for leading the investigation; he would have this mess turned around in record time, allowing Mike to be back out and home. Evans had taken a good few quid from the Regans. Even though he was an arrogant bastard, he was greedy and never gave the force a second thought if he was going to collect a decent wedge to line his deep pockets.

As soon as they arrived at the police station, Mike was steered through into the back, to the custody suite. Having been pulled in numerous times, he knew it well. However, he had kept his nose clean as far as they were concerned. His firm was tight and his business even tighter; at least it had been, until the Harmans had made themselves busy.

The custody sergeant noted the contents of Regan's pockets, wrote down a few details, and then an officer led him into a cell, minus his shoes and belt.

Unlike many people entering a police cell, Mike was not nervous, angry or frustrated; he was calm and went with the flow. Just as he lay on the cold blue plastic-coated mattress, the door opened.

'Regan, you can make your phone call.'

Mike jumped up, turned his back to have the cuffs replaced, and followed the custody sergeant out to the phone. He reeled off the number that he'd memorized. The sergeant dialled it and then held the phone to Mike's ear. No way were the handcuffs coming off. If Mike wanted to kick off, they knew it would take four burly officers and a stun gun to bring him down.

'Zara, it's me. Call Brandon and tell him I'm at Maidstone nick. Mrs Harman's topped herself. Call me brother, tell him what's happened and . . .' He looked at Grant, the custody sergeant, who was clearly trying to eavesdrop, and glared for him to move away. Grant shoved the phone under Mike's chin so that he could clench it in place. The officer then stepped back. Comfortable that he was not having a three-way conversation, Mike went on, 'Tell Izzy to get me back what's mine.'

'Mikey, listen, I er, I mean, I care . . .'

'I know, Zara, so please do as I ask.'

'Yeah, sure.'

Mike lifted his chin, released the grip of the phone, and allowed it to tumble down and almost bounce off the floor. As Grant grabbed the receiver, he sneered at Mike and nodded to another officer to escort him back to his cell.

Once he'd nervously uncuffed Mike, the officer locked the door and returned to the main custody desk. 'Fuck having a row with that big fella. If he did what they reckon he did, he's one dangerous psycho.'

Grant rolled his eyes. 'Too much TV, if you ask me. Mike Regan has been pulled in here more times than I've had hot dinners, and not for killing oldies either. I know his type. He's ruthless, yes, but only with his own kind.'

Just as Grant was about to launch into the history of the villains from Bermondsey, the door swung open and in walked Connor Rollinson, a new detective. It was the first time that Grant had laid eyes on the man. The description his colleagues had given him wasn't far off. With a slight build, around five foot eight, he was dressed like a gangster and had a grin that would irritate a blind man.

'So, where's Regan?' There was no hint of civility coming from the man's mouth, just a hostile tone to his voice and an evil glint in his lively eyes. He stood with his hands on his hips, his mousy hair slicked back, and sporting a neat goatee. No one would ever have guessed that this cocky shit of a young man would be leading this serious crime investigation. Grant was laughing inside. The new DI may have met his match.

'Take Regan down to the interview room and then bring along a couple of teas, will you?'

Grant carefully moved his fringe away from his eyes. 'Cake and biscuits with that?'

Rollinson was about to walk away but stopped dead in his tracks and spun around, a cheeky, childish giggle leaving his mouth. 'Yeah, why not.'

'Prick,' muttered Grant, under his breath.

Mike was taken to the interview room and left alone with just his thoughts and the hope that DI Evans would make an appearance. As the door opened, in walked Rollinson, who arrogantly slapped his interview notes on the table, removed his leather jacket and pulled out a chair. Then he eyed Mike.

Mike didn't even twitch a muscle on his face. He stared and waited.

'So, Mr Regan, this is how it's gonna work. I will ask the questions. You answer them. We write a statement. Job done.'

Mike remained silent, thinking what a lemon this DI looked and sounded.

'So, for the recording, please state your name and date of birth.'

Mike didn't answer; instead, he tilted his head to the side and looked at Rollinson as if he was an idiot.

'Oh, I see. So, you are going to express your rights by a no comment?'

Mike laughed. 'No. I'm waiting for my brief. So, until he's present, there'll be no interview.'

'I get it, Mr Regan, so let's go off the record. You and I can have a little chat.'

'On or off the record, there will be no conversation until my lawyer is present. And if I know Brandon, he'll already be at the station, so don't waste your time or mine.'

Rollinson stood up so fast the chair flipped over. He stormed from the room but returned within five minutes, with Brandon Miles on his heels. The detective's eyes burned into Regan's and his jaw tightened; he was in charge and he wasn't going to have the likes of this man – some hotshot who'd managed to escape the law on more than one occasion – get one over on him.

Miles was in his mid-forties, a tall and smartly dressed man. His father was good friends with Mike's, and although they had chosen different paths in life, they both came from the same background. Miles winked and shook hands with Mike. He then turned abruptly to face Rollinson. 'I need a meeting with my client . . . alone.'

Rollinson left, slamming the door behind him – again.

'What the fuck is going on, Mike? I've not had a wink of sleep. They've kept the lads in for hours. They just got out this morning and now you're inside.'

'Fucking 'ell, Brandon, it's a long story, mate.'

Miles nodded. 'Well, I charge by the hour, so take as long as you like.'

'Listen. They have letters and an album that belonged to Mrs Harman, er . . . Doris.'

Miles opened his briefcase and pulled out a letter. 'Don't worry. Mrs Harman sent me a letter. It arrived at my office this morning. I guess she didn't leave anything to chance. It says she killed the old man. I can prove she wrote it too because I am acting as her lawyer, so I have her signature. Fucking mental, eh? She knew my dad and yours. She made a will a few years ago, leaving her half of the house to the Cats' Protection League.'

'What am I doing in here, then?' asked Mike.

'Give me a chance. When I received the call that you were here, I was in my office reading this letter.'

'So, what now?'

'I'll get the DI in and present him with the evidence. It's not a get-out-of-jail-free card, and they may want to make further investigations. But I think they know he was poisoned. Something about fairy cakes.'

Mike's eyes widened. 'Fuck me, Brandon, I nearly ate one of 'em. I thought it tasted so rank, I spat it in the bin.'

'Yep, I know. They found it and did a DNA test.'

'Well, I wouldn't bloody poison meself, would I?'

'You know how it works, Mike. They have to gather enough evidence to go to the CPS, and they can't fuck this up. The man was found in a right state. Sit tight, and within forty-eight hours, we'll have you out of here.'

Without warning, Rollinson burst into the room.

Miles jumped up. 'Our meeting isn't over.'

'Well, it's lucky you're here because, Mike Regan, you are now being charged with the murder of Scottie Harman. Where were you yesterday afternoon?'

Miles's mouth opened, and he slowly turned to face Mike.

Rollinson had a conceited grin plastered across his face, watching Mike's shoulders slowly slump. His face drained and his eyes clouded over.

Miles gaped in horror at Mike visibly crumbling. Never before had he seen him look so vulnerable. The big powerful man with confidence oozing from every inch of his body suddenly shrank like a deflated balloon. Miles knew then they had his client banged to rights.

Numb from the waist up, Mike couldn't take it in. No way could they pin that on him. Not unless someone had grassed. His lips tingled from shock, and his mouth felt as though he was sucking a piece of chalk. *This couldn't be happening, surely?*

'Scottie Harman was found this morning in an old oil pit two miles from your premises. Traces of his blood were found on the floor of the lock-up. Harry Harman claimed he received a phone call stating you were holding his brother, and that you'd threatened to kill him.'

Mike realized it was over. Someone who knew him well must have given the police that information. Only a handful of his closest men knew about the pit. He didn't know what felt worse – the thought of being nicked for murder, or the notion that one of his closest friends or family had sold him down the river. He was now in an unthinkable position. How would he find his son, and who could he trust to help him?

PART TWO

Chapter 11

2003, a year later

Jackie was sipping a glass of vodka and staring across the field when Cora Smith rapped on the door. 'Jax, me boy's got a good bit o' gear. Juicy Couture. Velour. Your size.'

'Come in, Cora. The door's open.'

Cora was in her mid-thirties, a stick-thin woman, with black dyed hair and an orange fake tan. She was wearing cut-off jeans and a bright-green crop top, which showed her stretch marks, each one from a new pregnancy, six in all.

She was up the aisle at the age of fifteen and had produced her first son just before her sixteenth birthday. Married to Seth's son, Tatum, Jackie's second cousin, Cora knew no different. It was the gypsy way to be wed at such a young age and conceive as soon as the wedding night.

Tatum wasn't such a lousy husband. He provided a good caravan and put food on the table, but when he went out partying, Cora had to stay at home and care for her ever-growing family. Seeing her father and her uncles doing the same, she accepted it as just a way of life.

When Jackie had arrived back at the site, with a new state-of-the-art caravan, car, and cash in her back pocket, she was accepted but kept at arm's length. She'd lived the gorger life, and her son wasn't a pure gypsy. She told them that her husband was a grass, a no-good man, who didn't provide for her or the boy. Everything she had, she emphasized, had been from her own efforts. At first, they were sceptical, but as she followed tradition and kept herself out of their business, they started to bring her into the fold.

Tatum had his eye on Ricky; he clocked how quickly the kid could move. They called him the Quiet One, and as the months rolled on, he was given the name Mouse.

'So, what's he got?' Her accent was back, but unlike the others, she spoke more slowly. Cora, however, spoke so fast she could have been on speed.

'This is all tasty gear. I've all the colours, a score each.' Her face was eager and alive, as she chewed on gum which made her huge gold loop earrings dance. She frowned as she looked around Jackie's caravan. ''Ere, whatever's the matter with ya? My Tatum would muller me if I let me van get as dirty as this, girl. Ya wanna get the duster out and a bit o' Dettol. It smells really shitty.'

'My van, my mess, not your fucking business, Cora.'

Cora knew she had to reel her neck in. She could see the pound signs dwindling away if she upset Jackie.

'Yeah, ya right, girl. Anyway, d'ya wanna give the tracksuits a go?'

Jackie sipped her drink and nodded. 'Bring 'em 'ere then, Cora.'

Cora was looking uncomfortable. 'Er, Tat don't want them leaving the van. Any chance ya could come over and—'

'Listen. If Tatum wants to sell 'em, tell him to bring 'em to me.'

Cora sensed there was something going on between her husband and Jackie, but she was far too naive to realize the truth. 'I'll tell 'im, Jax. Ya got any baccy? I'm clean out.'

Jackie stood up from the table and opened a kitchen drawer

filled to the brim with cigarettes. Cora gawped at the amount. 'Cheers,' she said, as Jackie handed her a packet.

She wanted to get in with Jackie because Jackie always seemed to do all right for herself. For a start, she was never without money, and her van was full of top gear, including all the latest gadgets. It was different inside her own trailer. Hers was in an older style, with plain sofas and a small oven, in which she had to cook two lots of food for her brood. Tatum merely slapped her one when she complained about the time it took. 'Be grateful you ain't cooking outside on the fire!' he shouted at her.

Even Jackie's tea towels had Chanel embroidered on them. Her glass table and leather dining chairs were stunning. And her sofas were chunky, plush, and finished in cream leather. Cora couldn't understand why Jackie wasn't polishing every day. She would have been if she'd had a van like hers. Although Cora was jealous, she never said so because Jackie's wealth meant status and the gypsies were treating her as if she had clout.

'Shall I put the kettle on, Jax?'

Jackie nodded. 'If ya must, girl.'

Too thick-skinned to get the hint that she was a pest, Cora flicked the switch on the stainless-steel kettle and started rabbiting away while Jackie stared out of the window sipping her vodka.

'Where's my boy?'

With a cup in her hand, Cora slid herself onto the seat opposite Jackie. 'He's out with Tat and me two eldest lads.'

A questioning look on Jackie's face made Cora chew the inside of her lip.

'You tell your two eldest that whatever they earn from my boy is to be split four ways. Me, Ricky, and them.'

Cora flicked her long fringe out of her eyes and laughed. 'Jax, they're just out and about, a bit o' scrap metal. Ya know, nuffin big—'

Jackie slammed her hand down on the table. 'Don't you fucking mug me off, Cora. Ya think me boy don't speak? Well, he speaks to *me*. I know they have him climbing through windows.'

She didn't actually know that at all. Nevertheless, she knew how the gypsies worked on the site. Her boy was too small and weak to be scrap metalling. He was ideal for climbing into people's houses and opening the front door to let the bigger lads in, though.

Tatum had a dog called Sheriff that he'd trained as a lookout when he went robbing. However, only a few weeks ago the dog had died, and so Jackie knew full well Tatum would be engaging another lookout. Ergo, he had his eye on her boy. Ricky didn't speak to her and hadn't done since the day she'd arrived at the site, but she warned him that if he ever opened his mouth to anyone, then his dear old daddy would be locked away and he would never see him again. For some reason that fear had been embedded in Ricky's brain. Apart from a nod or a shake of his head, not another word left his mouth. In many ways, it did her a huge favour because however much bullshit she spouted, Ricky would never confirm or deny it.

Cora gave a nervous laugh. 'The boys are only out having a bit o' fun. They're teaching your boy a trade. Scrap metal earns a decent enough wage. It's cushty. My boys—'

'Teaching me boy a trade they might be, but it ain't in scrap metal. It's burgling.'

Cora's eyes scanned Jackie's, looking for a sign she was going to laugh it off, but there was an unmistakable look of spite.

'Burgling? No way.'

Jackie suddenly grabbed Cora's hair and pulled her close. 'Liar! You go back to your ol' man and tell him from me, if he's making money outta my boy, then I want my fucking share.' She let go of Cora's hair and pushed her away.

With a look of shock and anger, Cora jumped up. 'Touch me again, Jax, and I swear on me muvver's eyesight, you'll be sorry. My Tatum will roast yer alive.'

Jackie let out a sarcastic chuckle. 'And what makes you think he ain't already?' She glared at Cora, watching her ready to explode with anger.

Her crimson face highlighted her bright-green eyes, and the veins in her neck were ready to pop out. Now, incandescent with rage, she shouted, 'You skanky, dirty fecking whore. My Tatum wouldn't touch you with a cattle prod. You're old and washed up, Jackie, an 'as-been, and a fecking—'

She didn't finish the sentence. Jackie leaped from her chair and smashed the glass tumbler into the side of Cora's face, knocking her into the wall. Luckily for Cora, the glass didn't break, or she wouldn't have escaped with just a bruised cheek. But it was enough for her to scarper. When fuelled by the booze, Jackie was a complete nutcase. She had a name for herself, and yet Cora thought she would never turn on her. Little did she know that Jackie would turn on anyone: she never gave a shit, as long as she got what she wanted.

By the evening, Jackie had slept off the drink and was up, showered, and dressed in a pink satin Chanel bathrobe. It was one of her best sellers. She'd made a grand selling boxes of the items to the hairdressers and beauty salons – in fact, she couldn't unload them fast enough. Naturally, she kept one for herself. Tatum never let his wife have any of the knocked-off gear he got, so Cora was left with an old pink bathrobe that had probably belonged to her mother and had definitely seen better days.

A loud rap at the door made her jump; she knew exactly who it was. She'd already watched the truck arrive and seen Tatum and his sons climb down from the cab. They were laughing and punching each other on the arm. Tatum ruffled Tyrone's head; it had clearly been a successful day. Then she saw him pull Ricky from the back of the truck and drop him to his feet. There was no hair ruffling or a pat on the back. Tatum simply headed towards his caravan with his sons in tow, while Ricky wandered off to the edge of the woods where he sat on a log. This he did every evening, like some strange ritual.

Jackie intuitively knew that within ten minutes Tatum would be over with something to say. No doubt Cora would be milking her bruised cheek for all its worth. Jackie licked her lips at the thought of what would happen next. That was the thing. She thrived on attention, and having been bored out of her mind all day, she needed a pick-me-up. She didn't have to wait long. Opening the door with a winning smile, she said, 'Whinging about her fucking face, was she?'

Tatum, a slim but toned man, who grinned like Brad Pitt and winked like George Clooney, was the best-looking man on the site, and he knew it. It wasn't hard. Most of the men were butt-ugly. A few years younger than Jackie, he was still quite mature. The men his age gave him respect because he could turn a shilling into a pound and could handle himself. Jackie was sexually attracted to him, but that was all. She wasn't a lovesick teenager waiting to share a few stolen moments – she could take him or leave him. Her secret trysts with Tatum were purely to kill the boredom and to satisfy her insatiable sexual appetite.

He stormed through the caravan, slamming the door shut behind him. 'Don't fecking push me, girl. I don't give a flying feck that yer hit me missus. But telling her I gave you a roasting is wicked.'

Jackie was on cloud nine. The stupid man was putty in her hands. Raising her neatly plucked eyebrows, she grinned. 'But ya did, though, didn't ya, Tat? If I remember rightly, it was a real good horny wet shag. And, Tat, ya loved every fucking moan and groan. Your large pulsating cock between my legs was like being on a spit roast, Tat, eh?' Her eyes and her slow words had him fired up. Her pert nipples poking through her satin gown were begging to be sucked.

'You whore, Jackie.'

Gotcha, she thought wickedly. 'I don't see you paying me.' She smirked, as she slowly pulled the satin belt from her waist, allowing him to see what she had on offer. He was stunned into silence as she slowly parted her legs and ran her hands down past her navel and into her fanny. Slowly withdrawing her finger, she sucked it and smiled up at him seductively.

What had been a mild erection thirty seconds ago was now full-on. Intending to give Jackie the warning of the century, his animal instinct and urge now took over. Unbuckling his belt, he forced her onto the table where he pulled her legs apart and gripped her breasts hard. He couldn't wait: he needed to be inside her before he shot his load.

Lifting her legs in the air, she offered it to him on a plate. He was harder and faster than usual, his emotions mixing anger with pleasure, and as much as she moaned in ecstasy, he banged her harder. 'Take that, you fucking whore, Jackie, and that.' He banged her so hard it actually hurt. *So, he thinks he's going to get one over on me, does he, the thick fucker,* she thought. She debated whether to stop him. But the desire for sex was as strong as his. 'Harder, baby, harder.'

Digging his fingers into her legs, he suddenly spun her over. The speed and strength of the man almost winded her. Struggling to break loose was futile. Now having her where he wanted her, he grabbed her hair and entered again, but this time, he didn't hold back and rode her like a wild horse. He pulled her head so far back she could hardly breathe, and then, before he came, he pulled away and shoved his cock into her anus. She felt beaten, humiliated and assaulted.

Slowly letting go of her hair, he pulled away and did up his trousers. Jackie was slumped over the table, gasping for breath. After slapping a fifty-pound note on the side, he left without another word. He'd made his point. Jackie was getting too big for her boots, calling the shots on the site, ruling the women, and now thinking she could lord it over him. He wasn't having any of it. The fact was, he knew she had sussed him out regarding her son: Ricky was a good little earner. A skinny runt, he would do exactly as he was told and not answer back, unlike his own boys who had runaway gobs on them. But he wasn't about to share what he stole with the likes of Jackie – who had no man to call upon as backup.

* * *

He returned to his own van where Cora was still holding a cold tea towel to her face. 'What she say, Tat?'

Tatum grinned. 'Not a lot. I told her to keep her lying tongue to herself. I ain't 'aving some two-bit slag upset my wife.' He kissed her on the forehead and lifted the lid to see what meal his wife had made for him.

'Your favourite, Tat. Chicken stew. Only the best bits o' kanni an' all.'

'Good girl.' He smiled.

'Tat, what's that wrapped around ya wrist?' She could see a coil of black hair, and it wasn't her own.

Tatum looked down and saw the remnants of hair extensions he had ripped from Jackie's head. 'I ain't 'aving a fucking hedge mumper and shit-stirrer on this site, so I gave her a little reminder of what I'd do if she tried it again.' He quickly uncoiled the hair and let it drop into the bin.

Cora giggled, assuming he'd given Jackie a slap.

* * *

Slipping her arms into her silk gown and clicking her head from side to side, Jackie walked over to the kitchen cabinet and pulled out a new bottle of Grey Goose, poured a generous helping into a glass and drank it neat. She shuddered and had another gulp, hoping it would relieve her discomfort. As the alcohol took a grip and she felt her muscles relax, she gazed out of the window and across the field to the edge of the wood. Ricky was sitting on the log, gazing up at the sky.

She did wonder if he was the full ticket.

Chapter 12

Wormwood Scrubs Prison stood like a medieval tower. Arthur shuddered as he thought of his son spending twelve years inside. He gripped his wife's hand as they waited in the queue. The shock of the sentence had not only aged him, but it had taken two stone off his wife. Ricky was still missing and now their son was locked away. The stress had well and truly taken its toll.

As soon as they were seated in the visiting room, Gloria pulled out a handkerchief and blew her nose. Tears lay heavily in her eyes. She struggled to smile when she saw him walk through the door; her tall, heavily built son was a shadow of his former self. Gaunt and pale, there was absolutely no life in his eyes. If she could have swapped places, she would have done so in a heartbeat.

He bent over and kissed her on the cheek and nodded to his father. 'It's good to see you, but I don't want you coming up here. I'm fine. To be honest, I'll find it easier if you ain't traipsing up here to this shithole.'

Gloria sniffed again and clutched her son's hand. 'Now, you listen to me, Mikey Regan. If I want to walk all the bleedin' way 'ere to see my boy, then I will. Now, no more talk of stopping our visits.'

He shook his head. 'Mum, I've got a life sentence. Twelve poxy years – okay, so I've already served a year on remand. Thing is, I can easily serve my time, but it kills me to think of you coming here. You're me mum. You don't belong in here among the fucking scum of the earth.'

He shot a look at two junkies; one of them was passing a packet of heroin to the skinny, scabby prisoner seated opposite. He watched as the man tried to surreptitiously shove it up his backside.

'It ain't right, Mum. You carry on writing 'cos I look forward to your letters, but, please, stay at home.'

Arthur looked over at the tuckshop. ''Ere, Glor, go and fetch us some teas, will ya, babe?'

Gloria wiped her sodden cheeks and nodded. She guessed her husband wanted a private word. Mike's eyes followed his mother as she ambled off to the canteen area, dressed smartly in an emerald green suit and a floral scarf.

'Don't bring her again, Dad. This ain't no place for her.'

Arthur rolled his eyes. 'I can't stop her, son. She's ya mother.'

'Any news, Dad, on Ricky?'

Arthur shook his head. 'I'm sorry, son. We've phoned every school in the Home Counties and we've heard nothing. Ya mother's called every damn beauty shop and hairdressers, trying to find Jackie – nothing. As for the Harmans, they may be under police protection. No one knows where they are. We keep hitting brick walls. I won't give up, son, I promise.'

'And what about Eric?'

There was a pause. Mike noticed his father's expression as he shuffled uncomfortably.

'Dad?'

'He's jacked it all in, son. He reckons there are too many firms out there wanting to take over. He's gone to Spain to make a new life.'

'You what? Fucking hell, what's going on? I've got fucking

orders to fill. What happened to me shipments? Did he sort them for me?'

Arthur's eyes appeared to sink back into his head. 'No, son. Me and the boys have. I secured a set-up down the coast. It's pretty safe. The place is in total darkness during the evening. The council won't pay for the lights. It was a former ice-cream parlour, but it's secure enough as a lock-up. Young Staffie and Willie Ritz are overseeing that lot. I got a buyer from up north, and Lou's doing the delivery. I've had to buy a new truck to keep the Filth off his back.'

Mike could see the young man in the older body, just by the way his eyes came alive when he spoke about work.

'Lou's taking a chance though, Dad. Fuck me, if he got caught, he'd serve a longer stretch than me.'

'I know, but they're determined to keep the business going. They want it still up and running by the time you get out. And I need you to keep a lid on your temper. I've heard you're spending weeks down the block. It'll only damage ya chances of parole.'

Mike felt bad. His father was right; it only took the slightest little upset, and he was flying into uncontrollable rages.

'Eric hasn't been to see me. It's been a year now.'

'He says he can't bear to see you in prison. He just can't do it.'

Mike felt his head getting hot, as he tried to hold down his fury. He took a few deep breaths. 'Please tell me you don't believe that?'

Not knowing where to look, Arthur just smiled and then sighed. 'I dunno, son. He seems so spooked these days. I think it's not having his big brother around. He ain't like you, Mikey. Eric was always in your shadow, trying to imitate you. He wanted so much to be like you, but he never could be, and the truth is, he never will be.'

Mike's bubbling temper curbed. 'Is he still with that Tracey?'

Arthur smiled. 'No, she scarpered, apparently, after you flung her onto your drive. No one's seen her since. Good job as well. Ya mother couldn't stand her, and you know what mothers are like. No woman is good enough for their son. Ya know what's strange, though? Ya mother heard that she'd taken a right beating, and I'm not sure if the rumour was true because women love to gossip in the hairdressers, but she was seen with Frank's daughter and both were beaten half to death.'

'What? Who by? We never even knew where the Harmans were hiding out.'

'I don't think it had anything to do with us. Apparently, it was a woman on her own who beat them with a metal cosh. Whoever she was, she had some power behind her. She smashed the life out of them. Yet, it's all hearsay and probably not even true. Besides, what kinda woman walks around with a metal cosh?' sniggered Arthur.

'A woman with an axe to grind, that's who,' replied Mike, his thoughts drifting to Zara.

Gloria toddled back with a tray of goodies. 'Bleedin' 'ell, they were slow. Anyway, there ya go, babe. There are a few chocolate bars ta keep ya strength up.'

She eased herself onto the cold plastic chair and passed Mike a cup of tea. 'Did ya tell Mikey about the letter from poor ol' Doris?'

Arthur shook his head. 'Leave it, Glor . . .'

'She was a sweet woman, ya know. I always felt sorry for her. That ol' man of hers was a right nasty bloke.'

'I guessed that, Mum, from the photo album.'

'Yeah, well, he tried to grab me once. A right creep, he was, but luckily, Doris called out to him, and I managed to escape. She told ya farver in the letter about all the things her ol' man did.'

Arthur nudged her. 'It's in the past, Glor. Leave it there.'

Now irritated, Gloria decided to continue, regardless. 'He had ya farver beaten up. It took four blokes to bring him down. The coward couldn't do it himself. Apparently, she saved up a lump of money from her little sewing job, but that bastard found it and used it to pay the men to do over ya dad. He then—'

'Glor, stop it. It doesn't matter now. The fella's dead.' His voice was now raised to a pitch that made Gloria sit back.

'Okay. Anyway, Frank Harman groomed his boys into taking over your business. Doris heard everything. I did feel sorry for her, bringing up those 'orrible brats of hers.' She suddenly laughed. 'Do you ever remember that time? You must have been six years old, and I took you and Eric to the park. Little angels you two were, and there you were playing on a swing, minding ya own business, when a kid came over, a couple of years older than you, and dragged you off.'

Mike couldn't recall it; it was too long ago. 'No.'

'Well, he did. He hauled you to the ground. I was cross because you had new clothes on and you were covered in grass mowings. Still, you got up and cleaned yaself down. I had a picnic laid out, as did a few of the mums, it was such a nice day. Then, all of a sudden, the boy tried to do the same to Eric. By the time I got to my feet to stop him, you had this heavily built bruiser on the grass and it wasn't a little roll-around scrap either. You were punching him hard in the face. I mean really hard. I tried to pull you off, but you were a strong lad. I looked over to see whose kid it was and the only woman sitting alone was Doris. She didn't move. I pulled you and Eric away and watched this lad stagger back to his mother, kick over the plate of sandwiches, and spit in her face. I knew then she was living a life of hell. Then I brushed you two down and felt pride like never before. You, Mikey, said sorry for messing up ya clothes and then put ya arms around my neck and hugged me. Doris was watching, and I could see the sadness in her eyes. What a shame, eh?'

Mike was thinking about his own son – how Ricky often flung his arms around his neck and told him how much he loved him. Tears began to show.

'Listen, it's killing me being stuck in here and not out there finding my son. Please promise me, you'll do everything to find him? I'll even sell the house to pay for it.'

Gloria reached across and held Mike's hands. 'Now, you listen to me. Your farver and I are doing all we can.' She looked at Arthur who nodded for her to carry on.

'We've got a private investigator on the case. Ya dad's put up a reward among the firms for his safe return and for the address of Harry Harman.'

Mike relaxed his shoulders with a sigh of relief.

'I know, love. You're used to being in control, but ya hands are tied. Me and ya dad's ain't, though, so we're doing everything we can. Remember, babe, we love him too. He's the apple of my eye, like 'aving you all over again. So, until the bleedin' day I'm pushing up daisies, I will always search for my little sunshine.'

As the visit came to an end, Gloria pulled out her handkerchief and wiped away the tears. Arthur, as tall and broad as Mike, hugged him tightly and whispered, 'I will avenge whoever has Ricky. I swear to God, I'm gonna kill 'em, even if it's Jackie, unless ya muvver gets there first.'

Mike patted his dad's back. 'I know, Dad.'

Chapter 13

Staffie dragged the net over the pool, collecting a few stranded leaves and debris from the jet washing. It was the least he could do for Mike. Every weekend for the last year, he'd checked the house, the water pipes, the heating system, and anything that could break down and cause a problem.

The boys still met there every Thursday and discussed business. It was Wednesday, and Staffie was choked up. It was Ricky's birthday; he would be seven years old today. If Mike was at home, there would have been balloons, fireworks, and everything that would make a boy's birthday special. He could only imagine what Mike was going through alone in a cell, thinking about his boy out there somewhere, or, worse, dead.

Life had changed a lot since Mike went away. Staffie's phone rang. He dropped the net and scrutinized the number.

'Hello, who's this?' There was no warmth in his tone.

'Staffie?'

The woman's voice sounded firm, and he thought he recognized it.

'Yeah, who is this?'

'Staffie, I need a meeting, PDQ. Can you meet me somewhere? Bring Willie Ritz and Lou Baker. I think you'll all want to hear this.'

'Sorry, love, but who the fuck are ya?'

'It's Zara.'

Staffie stiffened, feeling a cold chill wash over him. 'What d'ya want?'

'Relax, Staffie. This ain't any funny business, I can assure you, but I think I have what you want.'

'Um, yeah . . . I'll meet you in two hours at The Plough Inn in Eynsford,' replied Staffie, now nervously intrigued.

She could detect the concern in his faltering voice. 'No funny business, Staffie, I promise. I'm a woman of my word.'

With trembling hands, Staffie phoned Willie. 'Listen. I've just had a call from that Zara, Izzy's daughter. She wants a meeting today at The Plough Inn, in two hours. Call Lou, bring a tool, and tell him to do the same. I don't like the sound of it.'

Willie turned his diver's knife over in his hands. 'Any idea what it's about, bruv?'

'She reckons she has something we want.'

'Okay, well, best we meet her, then. I'll pick up Lou and see ya there.'

As Staffie went to turn on the alarm, he saw the little red leather football belonging to Ricky. He had a sudden thought and prayed that the 'something' she had was Mike's son. His heart began to race, and he had to calm himself down and not get too excited, but he longed for that to be true. He loved Ricky as if he were his own son. His boy was now nine years old, and although he didn't live with the mother, he did get to see little Arty every so often, which was usually if his mother wanted a break.

Staffie finished tidying up, locked and alarmed Mike's home, and left. The Plough Inn was only a short drive away, but he could murder a pint and so he headed there early. Again, he phoned Willie. 'I'm here and having a beer, if ya wanna join me.'

'On our way, mate,' replied Willie, who was fired up and raring to go.

Staffie sensed that Willie had snorted a line of cocaine because he often spoke faster when he had.

He walked to the bar and looked around; the place was almost empty. On a hot day, most of the passers-by would take their drinks and sit on the riverbank. It was warm enough, but because it was a weekday, there was hardly a soul in sight. The barman served him, and he took his pint over to the table by the window. From here, he had a clear view of the car park and the main door. He couldn't really remember what Zara looked like as he'd only met her once before when she was having a meal with Mike, but that was years ago.

After ten minutes or so, Willie came bounding in, followed by Lou. They waved over to him and bought themselves a beer before heading his way.

Willie was lively. 'So, mate, what d'ya reckon she wants?'

Sitting quietly, Lou looked a touch uneasy. 'I don't like it because somewhere behind this meet will be Izzy.'

Staffie chewed the inside of his mouth. 'I'm not sure about that. She gave me her word that there would be no funny business.'

Lou still didn't look convinced. 'Mike's away, Ricky's missing, and the Harmans are running around out there scot-free. The truth is, to this day, we still don't know who grassed Mike for Scottie's murder.' He shivered. 'It gives me the bleedin' heebie-jeebies.'

Staffie nodded. 'Yeah, mate, I know, but what if she does have Ricky?'

Willie nearly choked on his beer. 'D'ya reckon?'

Staffie shrugged his shoulders. 'She said she thought she had something we want. Come on, lads. Look, for all we know, she may have Ricky. Jesus, I said it out loud.' He held up his empty pint glass.

Lou sighed. 'It did cross my mind, but she would have said so on the dog and bone, surely?'

194

Willie had finished his beer in record time. Still fidgety, he jumped up. 'Same again, lads?'

They nodded, downing their last dregs.

Just as Willie was carefully balancing a tray with their pints, Staffie heard two cars pull into the gravel car park. He quickly glanced out of the Georgian-style window and glared. The first vehicle, an Audi TT, slotted into a space, shortly followed by a black Range Rover that parked next to it, blocking the view of the Audi. Willie placed the tray on the table and leaned across Staffie to see for himself. The second car had three men inside, and as they climbed out, Lou rolled his eyes. 'Are you fucking kidding me? I thought she said there wouldn't be any funny business?'

Staffie felt hot under the collar and wondered if the bitch had lied. They continued to watch as she came into view; they saw a slender woman, dressed in black leather jeans, a tailored white shirt, and a black leather jacket. Her hair was dead straight and pulled back in a classy-looking ponytail. She confidently walked across to the front entrance and the three men who had arrived in the second car followed her. They were tall and heavy men, obviously her henchmen. Instinctively, Willie gripped the handle of his diver's knife while Lou felt for his gun tucked in his belt.

As Zara entered the pub, she scanned the bar and then clocked Staffie. To his surprise, she waved like an old friend would. Then she motioned with her hand, offering to buy them drinks. Willie stared in disbelief, Lou frowned, and Staffie, feeling the tension, got up to greet her politely, leaving his two sidekicks miffed.

In her long black high-heeled boots, she was roughly the same height as Staffie. Flipping her sunglasses just above her forehead, she held out her hand for Staffie to shake. 'Glad you could come. Before we talk, would you like a drink? I'm having a shandy.'

Staffie wasn't sure what to make of her. She looked sophisticated, and with her three gorillas standing behind her, she appeared to be pretty dangerous.

Once they were all armed with a drink and sitting at the table, Lou wasted no time and cut to the chase. 'So, Zara, what's this all about? Mikey's inside, our business with the Irish is over, so—'

She quickly intervened. 'No, Lou. That business hasn't finished. That's exactly the point.'

Willie tried to hear if there was a tone of sarcasm, but the gentle, open smile on her face still had him flummoxed.

She scanned the room to ensure no one else was within earshot. 'The Harmans.'

Staffie felt the hairs on the back of his neck stand up. Just the sound of their name made him angry. 'What about them?'

She looked at her three minders who sat at the next table. 'We have them.'

Staffie nearly knocked the drinks over as he shot forward. 'You fucking what? This is no game, lady.'

'It's taken a year to hunt them down, but in the end, we found them in their underground hideout. I made a promise to Mike – well, my father made a promise to Mike, and since I've taken over, I've honoured it. We did vow to get Ricky home safe, but that I haven't been able to do. His wife has vanished off the face of the earth, so I hate to say it, but the Harmans may have done away with her and Ricky. Anyway, if you want the truth – and I'm sure you've ways of getting it – the Harmans are all yours.'

Staffie, Lou and Willie were dumbstruck. It was such a lot to take in, but the look on her face gave them no real cause to worry.

'Where are they?'

She leaned forward. 'They are tied up for the moment, in one of my lock-ups.'

'Who?' asked Lou, coldly.

'Harry, Vinnie, and that silly bitch of a sister, Paris. I nearly had her once before, but she can fight like a bleedin' feral cat, and her mate, the dizzy blonde, Tracey, was nearly as bad. Some chef was outside having a fag in the back alley. He called the Filth and so me and the lads had to scarper. I lost track of her then. I didn't mention it to Mike because after that they went into hiding big time.'

Willie laughed. 'So, it was you then, that gave 'em a good bashing?'

Zara joined in with the laugh. 'Well, not me exactly, more me metal bat, Maggie. She did all the work.'

Willie laughed again. 'She?'

'Yep, Maggie's my iron maiden. I named her after Maggie Thatcher. Strong woman, she was.'

Even Lou had to chuckle at that, his tense shoulders and tight neck now more relaxed. 'Blimey, you're a cool cookie. But I gotta say, girl, ya don't look the type.'

She raised a well-defined eyebrow. 'No, you would never think that, would ya? Skinny minny me has a black belt in four martial arts, can fire a gun and hit the bull's-eye twenty times in a row, and throw me nunchaku without knocking myself out.'

Willie was really warming to her. 'Gawd, if you can fling a nunchaku without clouting yaself, then you go up in my books. Those things are lethal. I tried it once and gave meself concussion.'

Lou nearly spat his drink out. 'Nope, Willie, you've always been a bit dopey.'

The discussion returned to the more serious matters at hand. 'So, Staffie, I don't know how you wanna play this, but, if I remember rightly, Mike said that one of them killed your dog and you want retribution, so that's why I'm here. Mike's inside, and I think it would be disrespectful if the Harmans were just permanently removed without you having your revenge, and, besides, you may want a few questions answered.'

Staffie looked at Lou and then at Willie. Both grinned and then nodded to Staffie. There seemed to be an unspoken language between them as if they could read each other's minds. Growing up together and remaining close after all these years gave them

197

that gift. A twitch of an eye, a particular smile – each meant different things.

'Yeah, I think we need to have a word. Is the place equipped and secure, with no possibility of a comeback?'

'Clean as a surgeon's scalpel.' Her words were enunciated so slowly and coldly that they lent a hint of psychopath to her.

Lou could picture Mike saying that. A thought popped into his head. Whether it was the two beers that upped his confidence or the don't-give-a-shit mood he was in, he blurted out, 'Do you still have a thing for Mikey?'

She twirled the small ring that hung on a chain around her neck and paused before answering, looking at each man in turn. 'I've risked my neck hunting down the Harmans to find out where Mike's son is. So I guess that answers your question.'

She stopped and looked at her own men. 'Could you wait for me in the car? I'll be out in a minute.'

Without a murmur or a quizzical look, Joshua got up first and held out his hand to shake Staffie's, who stood up and returned the polite gesture. Once they were out of sight, Zara continued. 'Izzy is dying. He wanted Mike to be on the firm for my sake. My dad felt I needed a bloke who he could trust and who would look after me. I don't need Mike for that, though, as you can see. I have my own men. Joshua is a cousin, and he's like a shadow. The other two, I've known since I was five years old, so I have my security, and they get paid well. You three and Mike are all tight. Well, so are we.' She paused and looked down at her drink. 'The truth is, I love Mike, and I can't handle seeing the big man shrinking. He's so distraught because he's eaten up with pain, not knowing where his son is. One way or another, we need to ease that pain. So, lads, in short, there you have it.'

Staffie was stunned that Izzy's daughter was so open. Lou, who was always more circumspect with people he didn't know, had now reversed his opinion of her and was eager to believe everything she said. A woman like Zara, laying her emotions on the line, was a message that she was on their side.

'Do you really believe that the Harmans had anything to do with Ricky's disappearance? Or, like Mikey told us on a visit, do you think that Scottie was having an affair with Jackie, and he left her at the house that we now know she once owned? I mean, she must have planned to leave Mikey because she was siphoning his money away and ploughing it into that property,' pressed Lou.

Zara sighed. 'I was there when he killed Scottie. I couldn't stop him in time, or I would have. I think Mike lost the plot. His anger was affecting his judgement, and he didn't question that bloke enough to get the truth. It did make sense what Scottie claimed, but, on the other hand, it could have been a carefully planned manoeuvre. Leaving the string of doubt blowing in the wind is eating Mike up. The only way we're going to know the truth is by questioning the Harmans Mikey's way. I've had my people searching for Jackie for a year now, but not a single trail has popped up, and I'm talking about the best of the best for that job, so all we have are the Harmans.'

Willie rubbed his hands together. 'Well, let's get going.'

Lou grabbed his arm. 'What about Eric? Shouldn't we . . .?'

Willie glared back with a cold look in his eyes, while Staffie looked to the floor.

Zara clocked the unease. 'Mike said he's fucked off to Spain. Eric couldn't handle it anymore. Me, I think differently.' She hoped the men would air their views too, but instead they kept quiet.

* * *

By nightfall, Staffie, Willie and Lou were parked up at the back of an address given to them by Zara. This was unlike their lock-up; a whole different ballgame. It was an aeroplane hangar with two other large buildings. The surrounding fields, awash with

199

poppies and meadow flowers, went on for miles, with no other buildings in sight. Zara's Audi and two other vehicles were parked up in front of the hangar. Staffie zipped up his short leather jacket and pulled on his gloves. Willie was seated in the back and Lou was in the front, smoking a roll-up.

'Why do you smoke that shit?' asked Staffie.

'Saves money and it helps me cut down, 'cos I can't normally be bothered to roll them,' replied Lou.

Willie laughed. 'Nah, ya tight bastard, ya always nicked my Bensons. Wanna line of charlie?'

Staffie grunted. 'Cut out the cocaine. I don't want you letting rip. Remember, we need information, not an excuse for re-arranging their limbs.'

Willie kissed his diver's knife. 'She ain't been in use for some time now.'

'Willie, stop snorting that shit. Ya look deranged, mate,' said Staffie, staring at him through the rear-view mirror.'

With an ugly grin, Willie winked. 'I am deranged.'

Lou rolled his eyes. ''Ere we fucking go. Willie, keep a lid on it. You can use ya weird boggle eyes to freak 'em out, but hold off with the tools.'

'If I cut off a finger or two, it may speed up the answers.' He was joking, but this wasn't the time for playing around.

'If anyone's gonna cut up the enemy, it's fucking me, after what they did to me dog.'

Willie looked at Lou as if to say, 'Here we go again.' They knew that even after a year, Staffie wasn't going to forgive the Harmans for what they'd done to his beloved dog. With a quick movement, Staffie was out of the car, and as he opened the back door for Willie, he held out his hand.

'Ya want a line of gear, Staff?'

Staffie shook his head. 'No, ya divvy, I want ya knife.'

Willie looked Staffie over and narrowed his eyes. 'Oh, I dunno. Ya might cut yaself.'

'Fuck off, Willie. Just give me it. I wanna gut them, like they did to my dog.'

Lou got out of the car, not at all happy with the way the conversation was going. 'Now, listen to me . . . ' He paused and sucked on the soggy end of his roll-up, before throwing it on the floor. 'Forget the issue with the dog, yeah? We need to find out about Ricky. So, put the poxy notion of what they did to ya mutt outta ya head.' His voice was firm and commanded attention. As a rule, Lou was the quiet one and only spoke when he had something relevant to say.

Staffie lowered his eyes and mumbled under his breath. 'I still wanna cut 'em.'

Zara was waiting outside. She had returned to her home and changed into a casual T-shirt and blue designer jeans, but, even so, she still had a sophisticated sleekness about her. With her shoulders back and her chin up, she gave them a mischievous look like the cat that got the cream.

'All right?' she asked, looking at Willie, who by now had the effects of the cocaine written all over his face. He looked scarily deranged.

Staffie sniggered. 'Ugly fucker, ain't he?'

A soft smile crept across her face. Noncommittally, she smiled. 'Perfect for the job.'

'Yeah, I guess ya wouldn't wanna bump into him in a dark alley,' laughed Staffie.

Lou joined in. 'Dark alley? Any bleedin' alley, more like!'

Willie laughed along. He was used to being the butt of the ugly jokes.

'Nice place, Zara,' said Staffie, as he glanced around the immaculate hangar. It was vast with three sides and an open front. A light aircraft stood there, gleaming under the lights like a showpiece. The walls were lined with large tool racks and air and fuel pumps. Again, everything was spotlessly clean.

'One of Izzy's hobbies.'

'What, flying?' asked Lou, surprised. He couldn't imagine a man like Izzy with his headphones on, doing a loop the loop.

'No. He collects vintage planes and has them restored and then he watches me fly them.'

Willie's eyes were on stalks. *What can't this bitch do*, he wondered? 'What, you're a pilot?'

'Yep, among other things. I've been flying since I was ten. Izzy let me go up with his own pilot so many times that I learned to fly. I loved the feeling so much that one day, when my dad was looking over another plane, I got into the light aircraft that I was used to and took off.' She laughed. 'Dad nearly had a heart attack, and when I brought the plane down, I was grounded for a month – in the true sense of the word.'

The three men saw another side to Zara; it was apparent she really was reckless. Maybe the rumours they'd heard about her weren't an exaggeration. They had clearly underestimated her.

The pressing matter at hand was addressed by Lou. 'So, where are the prisoners, then?' He looked around and couldn't see where she might have locked them up.

'Follow me,' she replied, as she spun round and walked towards what looked like a blank white wall. She then pulled a hand-held device from her pocket and pressed the button. A section of the wall began to slide across, revealing a hidden entrance.

'Impressive,' said Willie.

She allowed enough of an opening for the four of them to walk through. Inside, the rear of the hangar was a fairly big area, a third the size of the front. A metal bar attached to the rear wall held the parachutes for skydiving. And there, also tied to the wall bar, were the remaining Harman clan.

Harry looked the worse for wear. With dried blood on his nose and a purple bruise under his eye, he had obviously taken a beating. He had either been stripped on capture or he'd only been in his boxers when they'd found him. The plastic ties held him up with his arms pinned out either side of him in a crucifixion pose.

The ties were so tight his hands had turned purple. His eyes were full of fear, yet he couldn't speak, the duct tape doing its job. Vinnie was handcuffed in the same fashion, dressed in jeans and a T-shirt, with sweat marks under the arms. His eyes were wide as he stared in terror. Harry and Vinnie were big men, but, unlike Mike, who was all muscle, their bodies had turned to fat. Harry looked particularly gross, with rolls of it forming around his navel.

Also standing with her hands cuffed to the wall bar was Paris, who hadn't come along for the ride, that was for sure. Her tights were ripped, her mascara had run, and her nose was bruised, but she was stoic in defeat, and, amazingly, she emanated defiance. With her upright stance, and still in her stilettos, she looked what she was – one feisty little bitch. Staffie was eyeing them with satisfaction, very pleased that they'd had their comeuppance. Suddenly, Paris started yanking the handcuffs, trying to speak, but it was a futile effort. The tape made it impossible.

Willie was itching to get stuck in and he walked over to them. 'I think this tart wants ta talk, don't ya?' As he went to remove her tape, she gave him short shrift: with a swift kick between the legs, he doubled over in agony.

Paris's euphoria was short-lived, though. Zara took one step closer, lifted her leg, and gave a swift fly kick, catching Paris in the chest. She was struck with such force that it almost knocked her out. She struggled to breathe because she could only suck air in through her nose.

'Didn't you learn anything from your last beating?'

Zara was so composed and in control, Staffie wondered what she needed them for.

'One of you is gonna live,' said Lou, out of the blue, which took everyone by surprise.

There was stunned silence; even the Harmans looked eager to listen, each one fervently hoping it would be them. Willie was still hopping around in agony, holding his balls and wanting to puke. He looked over at the young girl with anger. If looks could kill . . .

Lou felt the need to intervene; he could see Willie was very close to losing the plot. Ripping the tape from Paris's mouth, he watched her gasp as if she had been held underwater. But despite her discomfort, it was clear from the way she curled her top lip and gave him that daggers-drawn look, she wasn't going to kowtow to her captors.

'Fuck you!' she snapped, once she'd got her breath.

Zara let out a loud laugh. 'No, darling. I really think it's you who's fucked.'

With a last-ditch attempt at antagonizing her captors, Paris sucked the saliva from inside her mouth and spat at Zara. 'Cut these plastic ties, you bitch, and then we'll 'ave a real fight. Just me and you. Or are ya too chicken?'

Incensed at the disgusting phlegm now on her clean T-shirt, Zara moved so fast that not even Willie could stop her. She pulled a knife from her boot and sliced the ties from the younger woman's wrists. Before Paris could even grab Zara's hair, Zara had her arm up the girl's back, almost dislocating her shoulder, propelling her away from the wall.

The others watched in surprise, especially Lou, who couldn't see the point in Zara getting her hands dirty. However, her face showed an anger that probably needed to be satisfied.

Paris was screaming obscenities while Zara circled her. Lou wondered if Zara was getting a real kick out of it or whether she was demonstrating to them how tough she was. His thoughts were cut short when Paris ran forward with her head down as if to ram Zara. But, in a controlled manner, Zara moved sideways, snatched the back of Paris's hair, and thrust her face into the wall. The sound of her nose making contact with concrete made Lou cringe. But Paris wasn't done. She turned, her eyes watering and her nose pissing blood, before bravely launching another attack.

Zara shook her head. 'Give up, Paris.' She laughed, mockingly. 'You fucking skinny piece of shit. I'll murder ya!'

Zara, who was standing in a composed martial arts stance, dared her on. Yet, as soon as Paris pulled her arm back to throw a punch, it was over. Like the wings of the humming bird, Zara's hands moved so fast. One open-handed crack went to the chin; the next to the throat was followed by a sideways kick to her knees. Paris was on the floor, unable to stand, focus or breathe.

Staffie and Willie were open-mouthed; they had seen fights, and plenty of them, but Zara took their breath away.

She turned to see their stunned expressions and casually smiled. 'Fine. She's had her fight, so can we get her tied back up and talking?' Pulling plastic ties from her back pocket, she slapped them in Staffie's hand. 'All yours.' She winked.

Staffie and Willie dragged Paris back to the wall bar. She was too out of it to realize what was happening. By the time she regained full consciousness, she was tied up and helpless. They waited a few moments for her to catch her breath. Then, like the character in the film *The Exorcist*, she was off again, spitting and hissing.

Of the three of them, Lou was the most refined, speaking with an intelligence and assertiveness that made him stand out from his friends. 'So, tell me, Paris. It seems to me that your brothers have dragged you along with their little scam. Travis, your under-handed boyfriend, tried to do us over, but I guess you know that. I mean, it stands to reason you were in on it.'

'Fuck off!' she yelled.

'So, I'll take that as a yes, then?'

Paris didn't like his cool tone. She would rather he was screaming blue murder. Shouting – well, she could handle that.

'Who gives a shit? Ya killed him anyway.'

'Well, I give a shit, Paris, because, sweetheart, I wouldn't want to hurt an innocent person. It's not in me nature, ya see.'

Staffie could see the cogs whirling around in her brain. Lou's astute mind and clever use of words was fucking with her head, as she weighed up what he was really telling her.

She, though, needed to be one step ahead. 'I didn't know he had anything to do with it.'

Willie's cocaine-infused brain was ready to wage war. He pulled his knife from his belt, and in a flash, he had it at her throat, 'Liar!' he screamed loudly in her ear. 'I'll cut ya fucking tongue out, if ya don't start telling the truth.' With that, he jumped past her, and with a fluid movement, he sliced the jagged knife down Vinnie's arm, ripping straight through his shirt and into his muscle, which flapped open like a slab of liver.

The muffled scream had an immediate effect on Paris. No longer brash and cocky, she looked aghast, first at Willie and then over at her brother's horrific wound. Glancing back at Lou, her eyes were begging him to help Vinnie. 'I didn't know, I swear it. I had no idea. I thought he was just running errands for Harry,' she cried out, choosing to ignore Harry who was pleading with his eyes for her to shut up.

'And I suppose you had nothing to do with Staffie's dog being hung, drawn and quartered, either?'

She frantically shook her head. 'No, no way. I didn't know. Really, I didn't know.'

'Which one of these bastards killed the dog, Paris? Was it Harry or Vinnie?' asked Lou, with brooding eyes that bore into her.

Paris was now trembling all over, to the extent that the others could actually see her legs shaking. 'I, er . . . I don't know.' She looked back at Vinnie's arm – torn open right down to the bone. His face was pale and clammy, and she could hear the heavy drops of blood as they splattered on the sheet of plastic under their feet.

Willie clocked her fear and tormented her further, cutting Vinnie's shirt from top to bottom and also leaving a thin scratch. Vinnie tried to pull his hands free, and a blood-curdling sound came from behind the tape. Paris was almost shitting bricks with fright at seeing her brother's glassy stare of horror. She couldn't grass on them, but maybe she had a chance to save her own skin, if she could keep her mouth shut long enough and not let her anger get in the way.

Unperturbed, Lou pulled a roll-up from behind his ear. He sparked up and took a deep drag. 'Who killed the dog, Paris?' he asked again.

Intent on stopping further bloodshed, Paris stupidly responded with, 'Oh my God. Stop all this. Please. I don't know.'

Incensed by the out-and-out lie, Willie flew back to Paris and pressed his blade against her mouth. She didn't move, petrified that just one deep breath would have her smiling like the Joker out of Batman.

'You lying whore!' screamed Willie.

Staffie could see that Willie needed winding in. 'Enough, Willie. I think she's got the message.'

Jerking his head like a marionette, Willie was a scary sight. But it was his eyes that terrified everyone. He looked what he was: a man in turmoil, totally unpredictable.

Realizing that Willie wasn't the full shilling, Staffie grabbed him by the arm and forcefully pulled him back.

'Ease off, tiger. You'll have your chance, if she doesn't talk.'

Harry and Vinnie had gone from frightened to petrified, and that was the biggest motivator for telling the truth. Paris observed their faces, and, sure enough, what she saw sickened her. It was at that point she knew: they would be singing like canaries if it wasn't for the duct tape. Their sweaty brows and bulging eyes were tell-tale signs. In contrast, her fear, unlike her brothers', had turned to anger; she could feel her temper rising and it gave her courage, something she had more of than Harry and Vinnie put together. Staffie had a hold of Willie's reins, and she assumed that his modus operandi was designed to scare the shit out of her. *Well, dream on*, she thought. In any case, they wouldn't really kill her, surely?

'So which one of your fucking fat brothers killed Staffie's dog, then?'

'Go fuck yaself,' she spat, her face suddenly smeared with indignation.

Staffie gripped Willie tighter, to stop him launching into a frenzied attack.

'Okay, Paris, I'll ask a question. Where's Ricky, Mike Regan's son?' intervened Staffie.

Paris had heard the rumours that the boy was missing, so she wasn't shocked by the question. However, Staffie and Lou expected her to be surprised and act like any innocent person would. Paris's anger, though, made her not only arrogant and brazen, but, more importantly, very foolish.

She laughed. 'Wouldn't you like to know.' She saw this as a game of snakes and ladders, where she was moving up and had control. Her eyes locked with Staffie's, daring him on.

Unexpectedly, Joshua came into the room and called out, 'The Filth are on their way.'

That's all we need, thought Staffie. 'Fuck! How do you know they're coming here?'

Joshua replied in a serious tone. 'I have a nifty police scanner, and they're on my radar. We have fifteen minutes before they get here.'

Whilst they looked at Zara for direction, Paris saw this as an opportune time to be plucked out of her nightmare. Naively, she thought she was going to be rescued. With the arrogance and confidence of youth, she blurted out, 'Ha, not so fucking cocky now, are ya? Well, you lot can rot inside with old Big Bollocks Mike Regan. You'll never know where we buried his kid.'

Feeling smug, she never in her wildest dreams thought that any of them would hurt her now, not while the police were on their way. Unfortunately, she hadn't done her homework on her female adversary. Zara would never carry out an act such as this, unless it was carefully orchestrated.

Harry and Vinnie were making as much noise as their gags would allow, in their desperate attempt to shut their sister up. Harry couldn't believe she could be so stupid.

But she was so confident that she carried on. 'You can tell Mike fucking Regan that his kid is out there in a field being eaten by the worms, and he'll never even have a fucking gravestone.' The fact that the men were all looking at each other in horror gave her the gumption to face them off.

But she never banked on Willie being coked up to the eyeballs and more reckless than her. He didn't consider the consequences – but then he never did, once he was high. With one quick movement, he pulled his arm back and rammed the diver's knife right through her mouth and straight out the other side of her neck. 'There ya go! That fucked ya Hollywood smile!'

Her body went rigid as the thick black blood bubbled like a dirty oil leak from her gaping, twisted mouth.

'What? Ya wanna say something? Oh, sorry, ya can't. Not sure a plastic surgeon could work his magic on your boat now, princess!' A sudden giggle was followed by a fully-fledged smile of pride.

Lou tutted aloud, clearly baffled by Willie's irrational state of mind. 'A bit OTT, Willie.'

Willie laughed again. 'Nah, not me, mate.' He turned back to soak in the carnage he had inflicted. 'Oops, Lou, you're right. I think she's dead.'

Harry and Vinnie both squirmed in horror. As Zara looked at them, her nose screwed up in disgust. Harry's faeces flowed like a dam bursting at its seams, spreading across the plastic sheeting to where she was standing. And it was clear that Vinnie was in no better shape. He was now choking so much on his vomit that he couldn't catch his breath. Puke shot out through his nose, but it became clogged up, and his eyes rolled to the back of his head. He died very quickly, leaving Harry the only one alive. A dark cloak of utter dread seemed to hang from his face. The gruesome sight ran like ice through his veins, and he felt the lights dimming as he passed out.

Zara sighed. 'Look, there's no point in carrying on with that bastard.' She nodded towards Harry, hanging like a scarecrow by his purple hands. 'Staffie, take Willie and Lou, drive around the back and across the grass field. There's a small track. Get on it, and ahead, you'll see a line of bushes with a small opening. You'll get ya car through, and then you'll be on the side road that takes you up to the main one. If you turn right, you'll end up in a village where there's a nice pub called the Red Bull. I'll meet you there in an hour.'

Staffie nodded and hurried towards the front of the hangar with Lou and Willie following. Leaving quickly, they tore across the field, and then they found the track, feeling every lump and bump. When they spotted the opening in the bushes that Zara described, they were out and off to the pub. Once they had their bearings, they slowed down and eased into the small pretty village. There, they were finally able to relax.

'Fuck me, that was so surreal. Did I dream that just happened?' said Staffie, still shaking.

Willie laughed. 'Well, I got blood on me knife, so, yep, that really 'appened. Staffie, have ya got a baby wipe?'

Staffie steered the car with one hand, whilst with the other, he opened the glove compartment. Inside were disinfectant wipes and he flipped them over his shoulder for Willie to get cleaned up.

Lou lit up another cigarette. 'So, the fuckers killed poor Ricky? What utter bastards. I just wished we hadn't had to leg it. I really wanted to kill that fat cunt with me bare hands, once I'd ripped his fucking fat arms and legs off.'

There was silence as the three men pondered what had happened. Staffie slowed down as they approached the pub car park. 'How the hell are we gonna break it to Mikey?'

No one answered, still lost in their own thoughts. Eventually, Staffie got out and took a deep breath; tears were ready to cascade down his face. Tough man or not, he didn't care: he was devastated. Lou wiped his nose and sniffed back his tears. Then, he too got out from the car, put his arm around Staffie, and whispered, 'I hope Zara ain't killed Harry, 'cos I wanna torture the cunt.'

Willie looked at his bag of cocaine and contemplated having another line, but how could he? With little Ricky dead, this was one moment in his life when he needed to stay compos mentis. Placing the small plastic bag of powder back into its pouch, he slowly got out of the car and joined Staffie and Lou. They stared across the field adjoining the pub.

'He loved that boy so much, it's gonna destroy Mike when he hears the news.' It was the most sober Willie had ever been.

'I just can't believe it. There was us thinking that Jackie had buggered off with him. Maybe it was just wishful thinking.'

'Yeah, she'd obviously planned to fuck off, but she would never have taken Ricky. She couldn't stand that kid. I used to watch her. She was so fake. She only said nice words when she knew we were within earshot.' The unpleasant recollection made Staffie clench his teeth.

'Nah, I reckon that Scottie got in with her. He fucking knew who she was, and then, once he coaxed her into leaving, he took the boy,' said Lou.

Staffie wiped his eyes. 'So where *is* Jackie then? That Zara told us she's used the best investigators to track her down. It's like Jackie's disappeared off the face of the fucking earth.'

Lou nodded. 'Maybe she got cold feet and was gonna go back to Mike, and the Harmans wouldn't have that, so they killed her an' all . . .' His words trailed off at the thought of never seeing the boy again.

They stood side by side as the sun began to go down behind the lush green hills. It would have been a beautiful sight but they were oblivious to their surroundings, their thoughts elsewhere. A chapter of their life was closing. Who knew what the future would hold for any of them.

After a good few minutes, the men sauntered over to the garden bench. Staffie wandered into the pub to buy a bottle of whisky. They needed a drink.

When Staffie returned with a bottle and four glasses, a car's headlights shone in their direction as it slowly crept upon them. Willie was facing the bright glare and couldn't make out if it was the Filth or just a random passer-by. The car turned into the car park, stopped beside their vehicle, and as the lights were turned off, they clocked it was Zara. She was alone this time.

She opened the car door, gracefully climbed out, and swanned over to them.

'A drink for me?' she asked, as she removed her driving gloves.

Shocked by how matter-of-fact she was, Lou got up from his seat with a quizzical look. 'What 'appened?' he asked, as he handed her a glass.

She knocked it back in one mouthful and gritted her back teeth. 'Cor, that's shit.'

They didn't laugh or say anything but waited anxiously for the news.

'It appears that among us is a grass. No one, as far as I'm aware, knew that I had the Harmans kept at the hangar, so did you guys mention it to anyone . . . like Eric, by any chance?'

Staffie's jaw clenched tight, and he raised a cynical eyebrow. 'No way. We, er . . .' He looked at her stony face, debating whether or not to air his thoughts.

But it was Lou who spoke up. 'Nah, Zara, we don't deal with Eric anymore. It's just us motley crew, and, of course, Mike. It must be someone on your side, love.'

He waited for Zara to spit out a few defending words, but he was pleasantly surprised, as they all were, when instead she took a seat and sighed. 'Maybe you're right, but I have no clue who would be so flaming well brave as to grass me up. Only a handful of people know about that hangar.'

'And Scottie? We didn't even know you had Scottie at the time.

Only you, Mikey, and your cousin Joshua did. So, I hate to say it, but I think the grass could be one of your own.'

With another sigh, she replied, 'But it wouldn't be my minders, Joshua, Lionel or Chard, that's for sure. I have far too much on them. Besides, they're top of the payroll. Joshua is closer to me than my own brother.'

Willie noticed Zara shivering from the cold night air. He took off his jacket and gently placed it around her shoulders. She smiled gratefully. 'It's a fucking nuisance. Lucky for me, there's a little area that only me and Izzy know about. Well, obviously, my men do now. It's a small underground acid pit. So, we got rid of the mess before the Old Bill searched the place. See, that's why I know there's a grass. That door I opened by remote control was specially built by Izzy. My dad loved to play James Bond. He was like a mole, what with building secret hideaways, some of them underground. He's a genius at architecture. No one would ever guess there's a secret room in the hangar unless they pulled out a tape measure. And even then, without the hand-held device, they'd need a bulldozer to break it down. Yet the police knew it was there. That is a real concern.'

They could tell by her weary expression that the thought of a grass from her side was preying heavily on her mind.

Staffie watched her expression as her shoulders gradually relaxed. She fascinated him. If he was honest, he was attracted to her. Like a chameleon, she could change her stance at the drop of a hat, from this stone-faced boss to a soft-hearted woman with an enchanting smile. But her vulnerability right now was the cold. She huddled inside Willie's oversized jacket, hunched up like a child as if she'd just stepped out of the sea with a towel wrapped around her.

'Why do you call your ol' man Izzy and not Dad?' he asked.

She smiled. 'When I was young, he told me never to call him Dad in public. He didn't want anyone knowing I was his daughter. Perhaps he was worried an enemy would kidnap me and hold me to ransom. Mad, eh? So whilst he spent a lot of time preparing me to take over his business, he never lost sight of the fact that I might need protecting. He even sent me away some time ago because things were getting too hot.'

Not one to mince his words, Willie said, 'Ya father must have a good idea who's grassed us. Izzy even knows what Satan's up to. I'm sure he has that cunt on speed dial.'

Zara wanted to laugh but her face melted into extreme sorrow. Her words came out as a whisper. 'I can't ask him now. As you know, he's dying. It's only a matter of days, unfortunately.'

'Oh shit. Sorry, love.'

Her smile hid her grieving pain. 'I would speak to him about it, but I want him to believe I have everything under control. He's signing all his possessions over to me. Everything. Not that I'm keeping quiet, though, in case he changes his mind and gives it all to Ismail – but I want him to pass away in peace with that crooked smile on his face.'

She stared off, visualizing her father with his cheeky, wonky grin, and it filled her heart with pain. She would be facing the loss of the second person that she'd ever loved with every ounce of her being.

Chapter 14

The heavy burgundy curtains blocked out most of the light. Even in the middle of the summer, the large room was dark – apart from the flickering flames from the open fire and the bedside lamp. Zara hated the room; it was so overpowering. The chunky ebony four-poster bed and oversized antique gilt-framed paintings dominated the room. Slowly, she approached the bed and looked down at the withered old man, a shadow of his former self. She wanted to laugh because he appeared so angelic, dressed in his white bedgown, with his snow-white wispy hair and trailing bedraggled beard in full view. Without his false teeth, his concaved mouth aged him by twenty years. Slowly, his eyes blinked and opened as a lukewarm smile crept across his milky face.

'Dad, it's me, Zara.'

He closed his eyes, too exhausted even to keep them open. Almost imperceptibly, he nodded, acknowledging her presence.

She noticed his hands trembling as he tried to point in the direction of the window. His wrist was still covered by an oversized gold Rolex watch that he never removed. Nervously, she turned to see a man in the shadows.

'Oh, fuck me, Ismail. You frightened me.' She softened her pitch. 'Have you been here long?' She went to embrace her brother, but he stepped away from the curtains, dismissing her gesture.

'All day, I find myself listening to the old bugger's mutterings of guilt.'

'Ismail!' she snapped. It was as though she was listening to another person. Her brother had never spoken so harshly before. He was always full of fairy farts and coloured pansies. He liked to think of himself as a philosopher and an artist – and a cut above everyone else.

They bore a resemblance in their physical stature. But from the neck up, he wasn't so attractive. He had a longer, oversized nose, a thinner-lipped smile, and his eyes were more amber than mahogany and they sat closer together, giving him a boss-eyed appearance.

Before storming across the room to leave, he spat, 'This is your job, playing nurse, not mine. You were his number one.'

She allowed him to close the door without giving him a good going-over, too washed out and worried to concern herself with her little brother's hissy fits. The only sound in the room now was the grandfather clock and Izzy's death rattle. It was a sure sign that he was on his final path from this world. She held his hand and felt him gently squeeze hers. Even the weakness in his grip felt like a hammer in her heart.

She was so proud of her father: his strength, his wisdom, his cunning. Even the villainous stories she'd heard about him, she guessed were watered down for her benefit.

Allowing the tears to run effortlessly down her already damp cheeks, she held his hand to her mouth and kissed it. The room was silent, the clock stopped ticking – which almost seemed stage-managed – and, as he took his last breath, she was suddenly overcome with emotion, as if he'd just walked from the room. She let out a heavy sigh. Gently laying his hand by his side, she got up to open the curtains.

* * *

216

Downstairs, with a folder in her hand, Zara sat in the study, another grand room with antiques and walnut bookcases. She looked at the phone and braced herself. She had to be strong to say the words 'Izzy has died'. She had to say them so many times before what she was actually saying to herself held any real meaning.

The postman distracted her thoughts and she went to collect the letters. There, on the top of the pile, was one from the prison. Eagerly, she ripped open the envelope and saw the visiting order from Mike. Her heart suddenly felt like a lead brick. She would have to break the news that his son was dead. In despair, she fell to her knees, hugging herself in uncontrollable sobs. Her heart was broken, but now she would have to break someone else's. *How cruel life can be.*

* * *

Ricky couldn't stand to be around his mother, especially if she was drunk or hung over. But his vision of his father was fading and he wanted to know if she had a photo. Try as he might, he couldn't form the words and instead stood there pleading with his watery eyes.

Angrily, she glared at him and couldn't have been more vicious. 'Don't you dare fucking look at me like that. You're too much like ya father, judging me with those evil eyes.'

She looked away and gulped a large mouthful of neat vodka. Cruelly, through slurred words and a hideous giggle, she spat, 'He's dead now, anyway.'

The words reverberated in his head. His father was dead, but there would be no funeral, no hugs, and no sentiments of compassion – just those four shocking words.

Every day when he sat on the log at the edge of the woods and looked up at the stars, he would pray that his father would come and rescue him. And every night he tried to remember his face, his voice even, but the memory was fading fast, and he wished he could have just one recollection and hold onto it, to help him to sleep at night. The song 'You Are My Sunshine' whirled around in his head. At one time there had been love, he was sure of it, but not now; his life was a cold and lonely existence, being pushed from pillar to post, shoved through windows, and clipped around the head by Tatum and his sons.

He was pulled from his reverie by Tatum's arrival at their caravan.

'Come on, boy. I ain't got all day!' he demanded, as he tugged Ricky by his faded old T-shirt over to his truck. 'What are yer waiting for? Get in the back!' Ricky placed one foot on the bumper and tried to pull himself up, but he slipped. He tried again before Tatum shouted at him and this time he managed it, but the sharp edge of the flatbed truck dug deep into his fingers and made them bleed. He curled them into a fist to stop them hurting and then he sat himself down, hoping that this time the drive wouldn't be too long. Yesterday's trip had rattled his bones, and by the time they'd reached their destination, he was aching all over and feeling sick. The sun beat down and burned his face and arms. Yet it was far less harsh than in the winter when it rained; he was often soaked to the skin and had to wait all day until he arrived home to warm up.

Thoughts of running away often wandered into his mind; however, he had no place to run to, as he couldn't even remember where he used to live. But then, what did it matter anymore? His father was dead. He never did come for him.

Tatum started the engine and bellowed for his boys to hurry up. Ricky watched as they hurried from their caravan, holding what looked like iced buns and bottles of cold lemonade. His mouth watered; he loved lemonade, but the only time he ever had any was if Mena brought it over. He noticed how Tatum joked with his sons by pretending to punch them on the arm.

The last punch he'd received had been a real one – from Jackie. He'd been in her way, as usual.

* * *

The hours of sorting out Izzy's accounts, planning a funeral and grieving the death of her father had left Zara exhausted. Ismail was as useless as a knitted condom, and she was beginning to resent him. He should have been her rock; instead, he was like a sponge, sucking up her energy by moaning, sulking and pouting. She always knew he had a mean streak, but never in her wildest dreams did she believe he could be so uncaring. She put it down to grief.

Staffie, however, had been a great support; as soon as she'd called him to let him know that Izzy was dead, he offered his condolences and his help.

Today was the day that both she and Staffie would be breaking the devastating news to Mike. Staffie offered to drive; the journey to the prison would be a small respite at this arduous time.

Deciding to dress down, she wore a loose-fitting plain blue dress and covered her arms with a white cotton cardigan. She didn't bother with any make-up, just a spray of Chanel No 5. If it had been a normal visit, she would have dolled herself up and probably been flirtatious, but not today.

The bottle of whisky she and the men had shared two nights ago in the rural pub garden had allowed them to bond. So, when Staffie arrived to pick her up, he hugged her, whispering his apologies regarding her father's death. It wasn't an awkward embrace but a heartfelt hug. She felt comfortable in his company. They had two things in common: each other's trust and their love for Mike.

The waiting room inside the Scrubs smelled damp and metallic. Each bang and clang of the metal doors being opened and closed was like a hammer tapping her brain.

As soon as her name was called, they rose to their feet and looked at each other. He gripped her hand. 'I'll tell him,' said Staffie, with sorrowful eyes.

Her tentative smile hid her real feelings of trepidation.

As they entered the visiting room, Zara spotted Mike right away, although he was a far cry from the man who had stood in the courtroom just over a year ago. His usual strapping square shoulders were rounded, his face was sullen and drawn, and there was no longer a spark in his pale grey eyes.

Staffie pulled out a chair for Zara to take a seat and he quickly sat down himself. Mike looked at them both in turn. It was then that Staffie could really see the soul had been sucked right out of the man. Staffie struggled to think of the right words to say. How the hell would there ever be an appropriate way to tell a man that his son was probably dead? He felt his throat constrict as if an invisible rope was strangling him, trapping the words that he tried to express.

'So, Staffie, how are things? Any news?' asked Mike, in a flat, uninterested tone, expecting the same answer – that there was no news, but his men were doing their best.

Staffie looked at Zara and then back at Mike. 'Yes, mate.'

Mike recognized that edge to Staffie's words and his heart fluttered. He sensed that what they were about to tell him was momentous. He urged Staffie to go on.

'Zara found the Harmans.'

Mike's eyes flicked to Zara, pleading her to tell him, his mouth dry in anticipation. Yet he knew by her expression that she felt uncomfortable being the messenger on this occasion. She couldn't look him in the eyes, her lips turned down at the edges, and she was blinking back the tears that were already cascading down her face. He began shaking his head. 'No, please, tell me . . .'

Staffie shook his head. 'I'm so sorry, mate. I really don't know what to say.'

There was silence and they waited for a reaction, both feeling the mix of emotions that would tear at Mike's heart and bring him to his knees.

His eyes were awash with fear. 'No, please, no. Tell me Ricky's alive. Please!'

Staffie reached across and grabbed his hand. 'Paris Harman said that they killed him, but . . . she may have been lying, Mikey. I'm not so sure she was telling the truth.'

'What exactly did she fucking say?'

Staffie lowered his eyes. 'I forget exactly, but the gist of it was that we can all rot inside and we'll never know where they buried Ricky—'

Before he could finish, Mike let out a howling sound.

The sudden gut-wrenching scream could be heard in each prison cell within Wormwood Scrubs. Every inmate, officer and visitor was haunted by the heartbreaking scream bellowing from Mike's mouth. The two officers overseeing the visiting room were startled, and, at first, they didn't know what to do. The newest member of the Scrubs was a young officer, Drew, who had trained in the army. He radioed over to Garrison, Mike's personal officer. Then he went over to the table and put his hand on Mike's shoulder. But, before he could say a word, Mike shrugged him away. 'Fuck off!'

The young officer was taken aback by the hateful glare and thought it best to remove his hand. Staffie waved the officer off, gesturing that he would deal with Mike.

Drew didn't argue; he decided it was safer to return to his post. Judging by the size of Mike, it would need four officers to restrain him if he kicked off.

Placing his hands over his face, Mike sobbed. His whole body writhed around, the pain so immense it was physically wounding him. The inmates and visitors were stunned. An old lady visiting her son began to cry; she had never in her life seen a grown man so distraught. Another woman jumped up and headed to the small tuck shop and ordered three sweet teas and hurried over, carefully balancing the tray. Zara smiled and took the teas, mouthing the words 'thank you'.

Mike was so inconsolable that Zara got up and put her arms around his shoulders and hugged him tight. He shook as the pain claimed every muscle in his body and tortured the very thread of his being.

'Why, why, why would they do that? He was a baby, a fucking baby. Oh my God!' he screamed in agonizing grief.

Staffie had tears streaming down his face, too choked up to speak. He knew it would crush Mike more than anything, but he just couldn't imagine how the big man would react. Staffie didn't know what was worse – hearing that Ricky was dead or seeing the torment on Mike's face.

Trying to calm Mike down, Staffie said, 'Mikey, come on, mate. She may have lied. Please!'

Abruptly, Mike stopped rocking and uncovered his face. There were no more tears. Instead, they were replaced with a deep-seated anger. His eyes were cold as he gave Staffie a hard stare. Through gritted teeth, he hissed, 'And did ya fucking brutalize 'em? Did ya fucking make 'em pay?'

Staffie was startled by the incensed expression and the tone in which those harsh words were delivered.

'Yes, we did, we, er . . .'

Returning to her seat, Zara stepped in. 'Mikey, we cut them up, rearranged their faces, and then set them alight.'

He looked back at Staffie, who slowly nodded in agreement.

Officer Garrison had an air about him, much like the taste of Marmite. You either loved or hated him. He was one of the longest-serving officers and had known Mike as a kid when he visited his own father in prison. Garrison was impatient, arrogant and fierce. Even at fifty-eight years of age, the inmates wouldn't provoke him. He didn't have time for the scallywags and two-bit druggies, but he did have time for Mike and men like him. He marched over to Mike's table and placed a heavy hand on the man's shoulder, gripping it tight.

'The legal visiting room's free. D'ya want a private visit, Mike?'

Too dazed to think straight, Mike shook his head. Garrison then kneeled down beside him. 'What's happened, son?'

All the modern rules and training didn't apply to the mature officer. He was of the old-school generation, and accordingly given respect.

Mike wiped the bubbling snot with the back of his hand and brushed his soaked cheeks. 'My son's dead.'

As if Garrison had been hit in the face, his head physically shot back. 'Jesus, I'm sorry. Look, why don't you come with me? Let's get you to the wing. Your visitors can come back tomorrow. I'll see to it that they have a VO on the door. Or, if you wish, you can use that private room. Whatever you want, Mike.'

Mike was so gripped by grief, he just nodded. 'I need to be alone.'

Zara and Staffie were on their feet as Garrison winked. 'I'll take care of him.'

Zara grabbed Mike's hand before he was led away. Slowly, he turned to face her and shook his head; he didn't want to embrace her or anyone. He had to be alone to grieve.

Staffie slid his arm around Zara's waist and guided her to the exit door. 'Let's leave him be. There's nothing we can say or do that'll help him now. But he's a strong man. He'll get over it.'

As she fingered the chain around her neck, Zara whispered, 'He'll never get over it. He'll simply learn to live with it because he has no choice. But get over it? No. Never.'

Those words crystallized in Staffie's mind. He then realized from her sad expression that she was speaking from bitter experience.

Garrison walked slowly by Mike's side, silently allowing the man to get to grips with the tragic news. He wasn't sure how he should handle it; having a man the size of Mike losing the plot would be like trying to pin down an angry bear. His best course of action was to take him back to his cell so he could be alone with his heartache.

Gregg the Smoke, a long-term friend of Arthur Regan's, was in the cell opposite. He was nicknamed The Smoke because he was a bomb expert – but one of the explosives he'd used to blow up a safe went wrong and blew up half of Streatham High Road. It was lucky it was in the middle of the night, when, back then, no one was around.

Mike often had a natter with Gregg and found the old man a good laugh with his tales of the past.

Today, though, there would be no jokes or banter. Mike sat heavily on his bed and looked up at the one photo he had of his son, his first school photo, with his tie skew-whiff and his thick mop of hair sticking up. Mike's eyes continued to stream as he looked at the little boy's huge smile, with deep dimples and round pools of innocence edged in thick black lashes.

In the doorway, rolling a cigarette, Gregg looked over at his friend. 'Beautiful, eh?'

Mike blinked away the tears and nodded.

'You looked like him, ya know. You were a bruiser of a boy, with big eyes that could charm a nun out of her knickers . . .' He edged his way in. 'Mikey, boy, it's gonna be hard, mate, no denying it, and me, well, I can't pretend I know how ya feel, 'cos I don't. I can't say anything that's gonna make it better, but I've seen what grief can do to a man in this fucking shithole.'

Mike leaned back and bashed his head against the wall. 'I ain't gonna top meself, Gregg, if that's what you're thinking. That's too easy. I'm gonna live, and it's gonna torture me, but it's what I want. If I hadn't been in my line of business, me boy would still be 'ere.'

Gregg lit up his cigarette and sat on the bed next to Mike. 'I didn't mean that, Mikey. I mean, it can make you so angry that you turn into someone you're not.'

'No disrespect, Gregg, but I don't give a fuck.'

Gregg patted his knee and left. He knew then that Mike would be that very angry man – and God help anyone who upset him because he was like a festering volcano ready to erupt. In fact, Gregg mused, he was very like Arthur in that respect. Mike was a controlled man, aware of his own size and strength. He wasn't one to throw his weight around. But, regrettably, that control had all gone now.

Chapter 15

As Zara waited in the mourners' room at the side of the synagogue, dressed in a black shift dress and an accompanying black hat and veil, she glared at her brother. 'When you washed Father down did you remove the band from his wrist?' she asked coldly, and with no expression on her face.

He was casually leaning against the wall. 'Of course I did. It's the custom to be buried in just a modest gown.'

'You know he wanted that band left on though, didn't you?'

He shrugged his shoulders. 'He was dead, so he couldn't speak.'

'You are cruel and stupid, Ismail.'

'Don't you dare call me stupid, Zara. You'll soon realize that I'm far from that.'

Zara rolled her eyes but didn't want the day spoiled by a needless argument. She stepped forward and tidied his collar and smoothed down his tie. 'There, that's better.' As she looked up and smiled, he returned a cheeky grin, just as he used to when she straightened him out.

Once the ceremony and the burial were over, she threw dirt onto the grave and allowed a tear to fall. According to custom, she remained with her head down, so she was unaware of who surrounded the graveyard.

As soon as the last handful of dirt was thrown, she lifted her head and was instantly alarmed. There stood Guy Segal. He was just a few feet away, tall and upright, with his long white beard, and his face swathed in sheer arrogance. Her heart rate shot up like a firework rocket and she felt the vibration from her teeth chattering.

His expression of hate turned to a sympathetic smile, with his head dipped to the side as if to say, 'You poor, poor, little girl.'

Yet she wasn't a little girl anymore. His evil glare and sarcastic tones wouldn't bother her again. She turned on her heel and walked towards her car. She needed to think. Why the hell was Guy Segal at her father's funeral? Her father had hated him. She got as far as three strides when a tight, bony-fingered grip stopped her in her tracks. She paused before spinning around. She knew it was him – she *knew* that grip.

'Wait, Zara . . . we have things to discuss!' His insistent voice would have had an effect on some people, but not her, not now.

She shrugged him off and stood squarely in defiance. 'No! Guy, we have nothing to discuss. You have some nerve coming here. My father would turn in his grave if he knew you were even in the country.'

Guy was in his early sixties although he looked much older. Glancing down at his shiny patent shoes, he shook his head and then looked back up. 'Zara, I have been back in the UK for a few years now. Your father and I may have had our little differences but he was still my brother.'

His slow and condescending tone raised her anger enough for her to lose her cool. 'Brother? He was no more your brother than the Pope is mine.'

His face turned bitter. 'He may not have been my brother through blood. But he was more than that. It is something perhaps you wouldn't understand.' He held up both hands. 'Anyway, Zara, your father wanted me to help you once he had left this world, so we need to sit down and discuss the future.'

The bare-faced audacity of the man was beyond her. With a deep frown and a curled lip, she coldly replied, 'My father would never have wanted you anywhere near me or my fucking business. He would rather a monkey's uncle be in charge than you!'

As she went to walk away, he grabbed her again. This time, he leaned into her ear and whispered, 'Yes, Zara, and now that's exactly who he has running his firm. He lost his mind. Perhaps his illness pushed him to make silly mistakes. But I know he wanted me by your side, to merge our firms and work as one. Regrettably, he was too mentally ill to realize it.'

Looking away, she clocked the confident smirk on her brother's face, and then she noticed a few other mourners smiling Guy's way. Men she'd never met. Unease gripped her by the throat.

'You're like a bunch of vultures! Look at you.' His supercilious smile wound her up even more, but she would have the last say. She was in charge now. 'You and your family firm ain't welcome here, so go back and crawl under the rock you came from. My business will be run by me. Keep away and . . .' She gave an exaggerated huff. 'Concern yourself with your own future because mine has absolutely fuck all to do with you.'

'You have a lot to learn, Zara. Two forces are better than one. Together—'

Suddenly, Zara let out an exaggerated laugh. 'Yeah, you're right there, Guy. So, when you have enough clout, money and respect, come and find me.'

She'd had quite enough of listening to Guy, so she stalked across to her brother.

'What the fuck's going on, Ismail?'

A slow smile crept its way across his face. 'What do you think, Zara?'

She didn't take too kindly to his sarcastic reply; with one swift movement, she angrily grabbed his arm and marched him out of earshot. He tried to brush her off, but she hissed in his ear.

'Fucking struggle, Ismail, and your arse-lickers will see you for the pussy you are.'

Not wanting to cause a scene, he relaxed his arm and followed her to the car.

'Now, I will fucking ask you again. What the hell's going on?'

'Dear sister, you may have the money and the business, but in our community – no, I mean mine – you simply don't have the respect.'

Her anger and frustration made her bite her lip and clench her fists. She wanted nothing more than to land a punch right on his long pointed nose.

'And why would that be, Ismail? Have you been spreading rumours?'

He grinned again, this time with a dry scoff. 'No, I don't need to. They are laughing at you. Izzy should have given the business to me, not to a woman. What you don't understand is that without respect, Zara, you have nothing, and I will stand over Father's grave and say "I told you so" when you lose it all.'

Just as she was about to lay into him, his expression changed.

'Look, Zara, you're my sister. I love you dearly, and I want you to succeed. I'm not interested in the business. Izzy left me enough to get on with my own work, my legitimate affairs. I have the support of the community, and the truth is, you don't, but so what? It doesn't matter in your line of work.' He chuckled. 'The truth is, I was jealous, but look at the turnout we had. They all respect me, so what the fuck does it matter? I'll be there for you, but, really, we live two very different lives.' His words seemed to hold some compassion, and Zara fell for them.

* * *

Willie, Staffie and Lou were all nursing serious hangovers. Willie was particularly wrecked since he'd been greedy with the cocaine and was suffering a major comedown to boot. They'd all crashed at Staffie's pad. Lou's wife told him not to grace the doorstep until he was sober, and Willie's wife was so used to his antics she didn't even bother to call him. Flashing the bacon into the hot frying pan, Staffie decided to wake them up with a hearty breakfast.

But before he'd even had a chance to sip his first cup of coffee, the phone rang. A glance at the number made him put his brain into gear quickly. It was Zara.

'Hello, Zara. How did the funeral go? All good?'

'Yes, er . . . sort of. Look, Staffie, can we meet up?'

'Yes, of course. When and where? Shall I bring the others?'

'Yes. Somewhere private, if ya don't mind.'

The sizzling sound was too loud for Staffie to hear Zara properly, so he walked into the living room, only to find Lou and Willie both half naked, scratching and yawning. He rolled his eyes and wandered into the games room, his pride and joy. 'Yeah, is everything all right?'

'I'm not sure, Staffie. Where can we meet?'

'D'ya wanna come to mine? I'll have the garage open, so you can drive right in, and I'll shut it behind you. No one will see your car then.'

'Text me your address and I'll come straight over.'

Once Staffie had sent her the details, he hurried back to the living room. 'Listen up, you two smelly bastards. Zara's on her way. She wants to talk. Something's bothering her.'

Willie stopped blowing his nose and sat up straight. 'Are you sure about this, Staffie? I mean, she's a bit of a fucking target. Izzy's dead. All those firms that owe him will fuck her off. The Italians will take the drug money for themselves. And, let's be honest, who has she really got behind her?'

Staffie took a deep breath. 'She honoured her fucking word when she gave us the Harmans, so we can't refuse to help her. So, Willie, she has us backing her. And, besides, Mike will go apeshit if we ignore her. Ya know what he's like.'

Lou was about to light the end of his joint when Staffie snapped at him. 'For fuck's sake, she's gonna be 'ere any minute. Get yaselves cleaned up and open the fucking window. It stinks in 'ere, like a sodding brewery. I've got spare toothbrushes upstairs, so sort out ya sour railings.'

'All right, Mrs fucking Doubtfire. Keep ya hair on.' Willie laughed.

Staffie plumped up a few cushions and hurried back to the bacon. Once he'd switched the gas off and placed the frying pan in the oven, he sprayed the room with air freshener and waited for Zara to arrive. Ten minutes later, Willie and Lou appeared, looking fresh and ready for the meeting.

Zara's Audi spun into the drive and straight into the garage. Staffie pressed the button to close the garage shutter, hurried into the kitchen, and opened the side door. Zara stepped out of her car looking fresh in her blue slacks, a white blouse, and a designer bag to match.

He held the door open for her to come in and offered her a coffee.

She smiled and said, 'Any bacon sarnies on the go? I'm starving.'

Staffie raised his eyebrow. 'I thought you didn't eat pork?'

Zara laughed. 'Bacon ain't pork, is it?'

As he retrieved the frying pan from the oven, he looked at the bacon burned to a crisp and laughed. 'Well, I don't think there's much pork left in these rashers.'

Staffie got to work making a pile of sandwiches while Zara made the coffee. They all gathered around the dining-room table and tucked in like old school buddies.

'I know you're all wondering what I'm doing here, but, the truth is, I feel safer with all of you. There's a traitor in my camp. Yesterday at the funeral, I was being watched. It was either that or I'm getting paranoid.' She looked at each of the men in turn. 'I've got a big deal going on. The Lanigans.' She stopped and waited for a reaction but there was none.

231

'When Izzy handed over the firearms deal to Mike, he did it to rebuild a relationship with this Irish firm, as he had bigger business on the table. Well, my dad left the details with me. He warned it was risky and dangerous if anything were to go wrong. The fact is, there's a load of money in it for us. I say "us" because I want you to come in with me.'

Staffie grinned, his eyes darting from Lou to Willie.

'What kind of work is it?' asked Lou, as he glanced over at his friends. They were as intrigued as he was by this development.

Zara's face lit up and she gave them a conspiratorial grin. 'Pharmaceutical drugs.'

Willie laughed. 'You can't be serious? Surely, there's more money in cocaine and methamphetamines than paracetamol?'

'Yes, there is, but I'm not talking about paracetamol. I'm looking at morphine and this new slimming tablet.'

Willie screwed his nose up. 'Surely that won't make a bundle on the black market?'

Again, she grinned as if she was holding onto a dark secret. 'Let me explain.' She held her hands up. 'I'm sorry, that sounded so patronizing, but the problem we have is that importing cocaine is risky, and the punishment if we were to get captured is harsh. This is an easy job, but it needs careful planning. Before I go on, are you in?'

Lou, with his lawyer-speak voice, said, 'It's not that simple, Zara. Firstly, what's in it for us? And secondly, who else is involved?'

'Okay, Lou, I will be open and honest with you from today. So, the Irish firm are paying me five million.' She paused and waited for the figures to fix in their mind.

Expecting them to be wide-eyed and excited, she was surprised when Lou just lowered his bottom lip and slowly nodded. 'Again, what do we get?'

'A fair and acceptable cut.' Her voice was firm and demanding. She was morphing into her father.

'What do you need us to do?' asked Lou, his hands clasped together.

'Izzy had information from his men, who he had plotted up inside the company, that one of their main filling plants, a bit like a factory, is closing down. They have a warehouse, but you can't just break into it, and if you did, you wouldn't be able to get a van inside, it's so secure. However, when they close, which is in three weeks, they'll be shipping the drugs to a drop-off point in Dartford, Kent, their old laboratory set-up. From there, it'll be moved to Hertfordshire and held in a secure building. We only have one go at this because the stopover move is all kept hush-hush. They think they can leave the drugs there overnight with just six security guards. Now, I would have hijacked the two trucks on the way to the temporary site, but these will have a police escort, all unmarked cars. Once the cargo arrives at the warehouse, though, it's left to these dopey guards to oversee. So, my friends, it's ours for the taking. I've got three refrigerated vans organized and we'll have two hours to load up and then move them to the hangar.'

'So, what's our part in all this?' asked Lou, swirling the remains of the coffee in his cup.

'The guards need to be kept quiet. And when I meet Mr Lanigan in Ireland, I want all three of you there. Izzy had his concerns. The Lanigans are ruthless bastards by all accounts, and so the handover could prove to be an issue. Izzy had this thought out a long time ago because the plan to close the site was in place well before Mike was arrested. Now he's in prison, I need trustworthy men onside . . .' Her words tailed off as she thought about Mike.

Staffie piped up, 'Well, since Mike can't help, we can, can't we lads?'

Willie was fidgeting. He needed some nicotine. 'Would you excuse me, Zara? I'm going outside for a fag.'

Zara frowned at Staffie. 'Can't we smoke inside?'

'What? Yes, of course, you can. Lou, fetch the ashtray, will ya?'

Willie felt more relaxed and disappeared, only to return with a bottle of brandy and four glasses.

''Ere we go, girl. Get ya laughing gear around that.' He chuckled, and then he turned to face Staffie. 'It's Staffie's best bottle. There's no use saving it, Staff, eh?'

Staffie glared, aware that Willie knew he wouldn't say no – not in front of Zara.

'I think we can do the handover. You won't even need to show your pretty face,' said Lou, who was too arrogant for Zara's liking.

'No, let me get something straight, Lou. No disrespect, but the Irish will need to see my face. They have to know who's behind it and who to fucking worry about.'

Without thinking, Lou butted in. 'Yeah, but you're a woman. They'll think they can walk all over you, whereas—' He'd no sooner got the words out of his mouth than she shut him down.

'Don't take my niceness in front of you to mean I am weak. I'm not. The last man who tried that, I caved his face in with a metal bat. What do you think a man can do that I can't, except fuck with a cock?' Her cold words hit home. Lou sat up straighter. She was right. Her sweet ways were who she may be, but there was another side to her, and he felt a cold shiver run up his spine.

'Lou, I want you guys there because I know you're good at your jobs. Ya take no shit, you're afraid of no one, and you'll have my back. Strong I might be, but if it means I'm fronting the Irish boss and his mob, then I need some hard-core blokes backing me. Don't get me wrong, Lou. I've got men, but I need more than that for this work. I want a force who can bulldoze a small army, if needed, and who know enough sneaky moves to be able to have my back. So, do we have a deal?'

'Deal,' said Willie, unexpectedly, followed by agreement from Staffie and Lou. They clinked glasses and began working out the finer details.

After two hours had passed and more bacon sandwiches and

expensive brandy had been consumed, Willie sighed. 'It's like old times, eh, except Mikey and Eric aren't here.'

Zara nodded. 'I'm just keeping Mikey's seat warm.'

Staffie felt choked up. 'Nah, Zara. When he's out, if we ain't too old by then, we'll pull up another chair.'

Tilting her head down and looking up through her eyelashes, she gave a sorrowful smile.

Willie being Willie, and with no decorum, asked, 'So what happened, then, Zara? Why did ya fuck off?'

Her eyes widened. She had offered to be open, but this question was so close to her heart, it was hard to spit the words out. 'I didn't fuck off. I was sent away for my own safety. Izzy wanted me out of the way to sort out some mess. Sadly, it was to do with me.'

'What did ya do?' asked Willie, eager to hear the details.

She shook her head. 'I was the only girl born into the Ezra family. We don't have arranged marriages, but, in my case, it was proposed that I would marry Benjamin Segal, to join the two families together. It was a silly pact my father and Guy Segal made when I was a baby. But I threw a spanner in the works and flatly refused. I was brought up to be tough and fight for what I wanted, and that certainly wasn't to marry some Jewish man with a ginger beard and rat-like eyes.'

Willie spat out his drink and laughed. 'Not a match for Mikey, then?'

'Yeah, and so I went to live in France for a while, with no contact with the UK. The feud ended, and the Segals returned to Israel. Apologies were accepted on both sides and that was the end of it. I hoped that once I returned to England, Mike would be waiting for me and he would understand, but he wasn't there for me, and he . . .' Her voice cracked. 'Anyway, *c'est la vie.*'

Lou mulled over her words. 'So, this Segal bloke and ya dad fought because you were seeing Mike when you should have been marrying this ginger prick, then?'

Zara raised her eyebrow. 'No! . . . Mike and I kept our relationship a secret. I suppose it was part of the excitement. But, no, it wasn't because it was Mike. It could have been any man. The fact was I stood my ground in our Jewish community, so I guess I was viewed as a rebel.'

Staffie was going over the conversation in his mind. He saw it as a genuine heartbreaking love story. He was aware of how Mike had adored the woman, secretly, before he had met Jackie; and he knew his friend was nursing a broken heart. But whereas many men would have crumbled, Mike hadn't. However, the experience had changed him. He became harder, more insular. But every cloud has a silver lining, and in Mike's case it was his boy. No one stood a chance of getting Mike's attention if Ricky was around. He doted on him; in fact, he worshipped the ground the boy walked on. Staffie could see why, though; Ricky was such a sweet kid, so who wouldn't have loved him?

Chapter 16

Three weeks later

The lookouts called Willie to inform him that the two trucks carrying the pharmaceuticals were on their way, along with the unmarked police escort. It confirmed that Zara's information had been correct.

Arnie Sheffield, the inside man on the job, was already stationed at the warehouse. Willie and Lou watched him as he entered the site.

'Cor, you would have thought this was just a disused factory. I'd never 'ave thought that in among those old buildings was a proper lock-up. Even the drug companies are sly ol' bastards,' marvelled Willie.

'Well, of course they are. They're crafty. I bet 'alf the drugs are placebos. They're the biggest money earners, after oil,' replied Lou, who was feeling rather proud of his knowledge.

'I wonder what used to go on inside those labs?'

Lou chuckled. 'Didn't ya muvver tell ya? That's where she got you from. You're one of the rejects, you ugly git.'

Willie gagged on his fizzy drink and the contents shot out of his nose. 'You cunt! Now look what you've made me do.'

Lou laughed along. 'See what I mean, ya mutant?'

Staffie got the all-clear to lead the vans to the pick-up point. In each van, drivers were armed with weapons and they had ropes to tie up the guards. So, once the heist was in place, they would have enough muscle to bring down the guards and load the cargo.

The trucks arrived and the gates were opened. Willie then sent an emoji of a smiley face to Zara's phone. As soon as the last police car left, Willie drove down the driveway and through an opening in the rusty old fence. What had once been a highly attractive entrance, with a huge water feature and grounds that would have won a Garden of the Year award, was now an overgrown mess. The place was blighted by old rusty signs, cracked concrete drive-ways, and buildings that were secured by metal shutters. The place would have been ideal for a ghost film. The warehouse was behind the first block, and it was hidden from the public. One security guard patrolled the site alone – not because there was anything of value left, but because it was dangerous for kids and ideal for criminals to hide all kinds of things.

Willie parked just out of view of the warehouse. He snorted a quick line of cocaine and leaped from the car. He was followed by Lou. They had studied the plans and knew they could get in through the loading bay at the back. Inside the warehouse was row upon row of shelving, similar to a DIY superstore. There was also a partitioned area kept at four degrees Celsius for all those medicines that needed to be stored in the fridge. On the right-hand side was another partitioned area – the office.

Their job was to creep in through the back, make their way to the front, and then press the button to open the main steel shutters.

Arnie had assured Zara that as soon as the trucks were inside, he would have the back door unlocked and would gather the security guards inside the office to give them a briefing. That would provide Willie and Lou with enough time to get in and open up the front.

All was going to plan, but just as they were creeping past the office, an old security guard stepped out of the toilet next to the button that opened the front. Willie froze, but Lou, with an air of officialdom, calmly approached the stunned man. 'I'm Dr Baker. I have to check the temperature of the cold store for our records.'

The guard studied Willie; the man couldn't have looked less like a professional, looking more like a patient from a mental hospital. Certainly, there was nothing about him that would indicate he was there in any official capacity.

'Er, sorry, do you have any ID or, er—' The guard was utterly taken aback and unsure whether or not to call the others or radio for help.

'Oh, yes, of course. Hold on a sec. I'll just collect it from my car.'

Willie kept quiet; he knew Lou had this under control. In his suit, and with his softer-looking face and an ability to speak in a more refined manner, Lou was used to passing himself off as an official when the need arose. Willie then guessed that Lou needed him to distract the guard, so he spoke up.

'Could you point me in the direction of the tacho readings?'

The older man then realized that they knew exactly what they were talking about and assumed they genuinely were officials from the labs.

'Yes, of course. You'll find them in that cabinet next to the door to the cold store.' He stepped forward, pointing in the direction, distracted enough for Lou to press the button. As soon as the shutters began to open, the guard spun around. 'Hey . . . what are you doing?'

Lou gave an exaggerated frown. 'Fetching my ID.'

'Er . . . no, you can't open that.'

Willie lunged forward, placed his hand over the guard's mouth, and dragged him into the toilet, where he pulled from his back pocket some self-locking plastic cable ties. The older man was not fit to fight or even to put up a decent struggle. He didn't resist as Willie gently forced him to the floor.

'Jesus, I'm too fucking old for this. Listen, son, don't cut me circulation off, there's a good lad.'

Willie wanted to laugh; this was too easy. 'Nah, mate, ya gonna keep schtum, yeah?'

The old boy looked pale and a little breathless. 'Get me puffer out, will ya, and give us a couple of squirts.'

Willie loosened the man's black tie and felt in his pockets for the inhaler. After placing it to the guard's mouth, he pressed twice and then popped it back into the man's jacket pocket.

'Good lad.'

As soon as Willie opened the toilet door, he saw Zara's men, along with Staffie and Lou, creeping their way towards the office. Arnie had been true to his word, keeping the guards inside for an impromptu briefing. The men working for Zara quickly burst into the office, and luckily for them the guards were all old has-beens who surrendered willingly – which was a good thing because some of Zara's men were a little slow on the uptake and didn't look like they were up to the job. Bound and gagged, the guards were left comfortable, with no need for any serious violence.

Then the work began. Before Willie helped to load the boxes, he checked on the old man and removed his gag. 'You all right, pop? D'ya need another puff?'

'No, I'm fine, boy. Christ, I don't get paid enough for this shit.'

Willie sighed and asked for his address.

The guard's eyes widened. 'Oh, leave off. There's no need to hurt me family, boy!'

Willie chuckled. 'I was gonna drop off a bit of dosh, that's all. For your trouble.'

The old man's eyes suddenly came alive and he instantly reeled off his address. 'Nice one, lad.'

Once the drugs were all loaded, they had enough time to get

away, before the next lot of guards took over and alerted the police.

As soon as they arrived at the hangar, Zara had the vans redressed with toyshop adverts made from vinyl sheeting plastered over their sides. The number plates were changed back to their originals. The set-up was complete. All she needed to do was to cross the border to Ireland and meet Lanigan's firm.

Staffie and Willie leaned against one van. The crates of drugs had been placed into large cardboard boxes that had stickers of plastic Wendy houses all over them. Willie watched as the last of the vinyl was sealed onto the vans.

Zara rubbed her hands together and she smiled with flushed cheeks. 'Nearly there, guys. Now for the last part.'

'Er . . . yeah, about that,' said Staffie, as he looked to see if any of her men were within earshot. 'Ya men, Zara. To be frank, love, they're as much use as a fucking chocolate teapot. If you need muscle for the handover, then these bunch of pricks ain't fit for the job, trust me.'

She looked at Willie, who nodded in agreement. 'I gotta say, though, Zara, both the detail and organization were shit-hot. Ya did good, girl, but ya firm are weak. Those guards weren't even ex-army. They were all old men. And that fuckwit over there,' – he pointed to the man who was slumped over, looking exhausted and sipping a mug of tea – 'he couldn't fight his way out of a paper bag. If we'd faced young, fit and feisty men, this heist would have been scuppered big time. We would all have been banged up.'

She sighed and gave a resigned nod. 'I know, but they were the best I had, since Izzy's main men seem to have all suddenly retired . . .'

Chewing her lip in thought, she wondered if Guy Segal had had anything to do with that. But none of her men had mentioned his name since the funeral. It was as if a ghost had passed through, attempting to put the wind up her. She shook the idea from her

241

mind. Besides, Guy wasn't rich; as far as she was aware, the only Jew with clout was her father. Guy was a nobody.

Willie openly pulled out his pouch and snorted a line of charlie. It had been a long night, and he needed a livener. 'Right, girl, if you need heavy-duty muscle, then we'll fucking find ya them. It'll cost ya, though.'

Her eyes lit up. 'I'll have to invest to grow my business. So you find me good men, and we can carve the business up, eighty-twenty.'

Lou stepped in. 'Seventy-thirty.'

She laughed. 'You fell for that, Lou. I would have gone higher on your side, but it's a deal.'

Willie pulled out his phone. 'I'll call the lads.'

Zara stared as he rounded up his men – Mike's men. It should have been Mike by her side. She shook her head in frustration – it was no time for being sentimental.

By the next evening, they had rolled off the ferry and were heading for Kilkenny. The meeting was arranged for three o'clock that afternoon at a remote guest house owned by the Lanigans. Willie jumped in Lou's Range Rover and Staffie drove Zara in her Mercedes; the Audi was way too small for the likes of any of Mike's men. The van drivers were all accompanied by Mike's old firm; they included Willie's and Staffie's younger brothers and two cousins – all built like brick shithouses.

Just as they approached the narrow lane that led to the meeting point, they stopped the vans, and some of the men climbed into the back, out of view. It was a prearranged precaution. In the eventuality of something going wrong, a driver would hoot his horn as a warning, and the men in the back would leap out, ready for combat.

Zara looked in the mirror and smoothed down her hair; she didn't want to look either tired or sleepy. This meeting was a big deal, and it was all going so well that it would set her up for serious business in the future. While Lou waited outside with a

242

clear view through the front windows of the guest house, Staffie and Willie accompanied Zara but not before Willie had snorted another line, ready to be fired up if there was any action to be had.

Zara felt pretty confident as she walked in to meet the main man. The first thing that struck her was that the décor of the guest house reminded her of *Alice in Wonderland*, with odd chairs and tables and china teacups and plates. With so much chintz and sugar for a meeting, it was very different from the meeting places she was used to, which these days seemed to be workshops, basements and warehouses. To the right sat three men, who were so chunky their suits looked ridiculously tight against their bulging biceps. She guessed right away they were Lanigan's backup. Then her eyes diverted to the left where two much older men were sitting at a table.

The first man was thickset, with white skin and a mop of jet-black hair with not a grey streak in it. He looked her up and down. He didn't smile or nod or even offer her a chair. His piercing blue eyes cast down to his watch, and then, slowly, he glared up at her. For a moment, she felt her heart rate increase. Behind that dark, intimidating expression was a soulless man. Keeping her breathing calm, she followed his eyes as they shifted towards Willie and Staffie.

The thickset man pointed to the chair, but she had other ideas. She needed to exert her authority, and so she remained standing and gave him a look of contempt.

The person sitting next to him was smaller, thinner, and had ginger hair peppered with wisps of white. He was roughly the same age. He needed putting in his place as well, so, with a flick of her head, she motioned for him to leave, to the amusement of the dark-haired man who she concluded must be Lanigan.

With the tension rising, Zara remained composed and reticent. She then nodded her head towards an area on the other side of the room for Willie and Staffie to sit down. They instantly moved as she indicated, signifying to Lanigan that she was in charge.

Willie didn't sit down; instead, he leaned against the wall and glared at the men sitting on the sofa. Staffie decided to sit on a high stool by the small bar area.

Lanigan nudged the man beside him to leave, and as soon as he was gone, Zara sat down. She was used to doing business, and it had never bothered her before, but her father's warning about this meeting had spooked her. She told herself to get a grip and not to be intimidated by Lanigan's fiendish eyes.

He leaned forward and whispered, 'I've a gun under the table that can blow your fecking fanny off, so just ta warn yer, that if yer think for one minute that you'll do me over, then think again.'

As he leaned back to face her, a slow smile crept across her face. 'And if ya think you can do me over, then, likewise, I have a gun under this table pointing right at your bollocks – or ya stomach, if it's hanging over them.' She hardly moved her lips when she hissed the words like a snake. 'So Mr Lanigan, now we have that matter cleared up, let's get down to business, shall we? Firstly, I'm not in the fucking habit of traipsing all the way to Ireland, but, on this occasion, out of politeness, I was prepared to meet with you here. Secondly, I am a businesswoman, and I conduct my business with trustworthy people like myself. And thirdly, if you ever threaten me again, I won't return the threat. I'll fucking blow your bollocks off.'

Lanigan smiled, showing his perfect set of teeth. But Zara didn't return the smile, knowing that if she did, a nervous giggle would leave her mouth. Right now, she had to keep her cool.

'Do you have the merchandise – all of it?'

She nodded and rose from her chair. As soon as she did, Willie pushed himself away from the wall and Staffie got up from the stool. Lanigan glared. 'So, you felt the need to have protection?' This time, his smile irritated her.

She replied casually, 'Like you, I'm not taking any chances.' She looked over at her two burly associates. Out of the corner of her eye, she sighted the ginger-haired man hovering at the doorway that led to the back of the house.

As soon as they stepped outside, Zara could see to her left a large blue Transit van hammering along the lane, and then, as she looked to the right, another one was about to block her and her men in.

Her heart was in her mouth – it was a bastard set-up! Now her own cars and vans, all lined up, were completely boxed in. She spun around to face Lanigan, who laughed in her face.

'You fecking stupid sly bitch, ya thought you could stab me in the back!'

No sooner had the Transit vans come to a halt than three men jumped out from each vehicle. Staffie went to pull Zara away towards her car, but he was too late to spot the danger. Lanigan grabbed her hair, and, at the same time, one of Lanigan's minders cracked Staffie on the side of the head with a metal cosh. The blow was hard enough to knock him off balance, breaking his back tooth and causing his mouth to fill with blood. In a fit of rage, he turned, steadied himself, snatched the cosh from his attacker, and proceeded to beat him about the head with it.

Zara's van driver sounded the horn. Instantly, her men leaped from the back of their vans and began tearing into Lanigan's mini army. Willie's brother, twice the size and twice as ugly, grabbed two of them and smashed their heads together.

Meanwhile, Lanigan was dragging Zara by her hair back towards the guest house. As he tried to grapple with the gun that was shoved down his belt, Zara had time to spin round and give him a karate kick in the solar plexus, causing him to hit a stone wall, loosening the rocks. Momentarily stunned by the impact, he didn't see what happened next. With one quick movement, Zara grabbed a heavy rock and smashed him in the face, knocking him out cold.

She turned and was amazed at what she saw. Staffie was beating the life out of the man who had struck him with the cosh, and

Willie was ploughing a hammer into another bloke's skull. Even Lou, the smallest of them, had managed to take a bat from a man much bigger than himself and was using the man's head as a baseball.

Quickly, Zara searched around for the ginger-haired man, the one she'd asked to leave the meeting. As the carnage continued, she opened the door to the guest house, and, to her surprise, there he was at the table. With a cup of tea in his hand, he looked up and smiled. 'Your father said you could handle business. I guess he was right, Zara.' He held out his hand. 'Davey Lanigan. I'm pleased to meet you. All the money is in the room at the back. You can count it, if you like. And I trust all the goods are as your father promised?'

Still catching her breath, she curled her lip in anger and slid her hand behind her belt. 'Oh, no, Mr Lanigan. You tried to have me fucked over.' She pulled out her gun and pointed it at the man's face. 'I was fair, decent and honest, but you, ya cunt, weren't. So you don't get the goods. But I will take payment, thank you very much.'

She heard the door open behind her but didn't dare to take her eyes away from the person she now believed to be Lanigan.

Willie and Staffie walked up behind her. 'Everything all right, boss?' asked Staffie, still spitting blood.

'Yeah, believe it or not. Meet the real Mr Lanigan. He's just offering us compensation. The money's in the back, lads.'

Staffie frowned, totally confused. 'What? But I thought that geezer out there was Mr Lanigan?'

'Nope. Apparently, this prick is.'

'That's fucking right!' spat the man.

Willie, who was making strides towards the back room, suddenly stopped dead in his tracks and spun around. 'Say that again?'

Lanigan looked down.

'I said, say it again, you cunt!'

Staffie was rattled by Willie's action. 'What's going on, Willie?'

'This ain't Lanigan. This guy's a fucking Londoner.'

He turned to Zara. 'Something stinks!'

As Willie stared, his brain was rapidly processing events and images from the past. *Of course! It was the man's hooded dark eyes.*

Without warning, he lunged forward and grabbed the ginger-haired man by the throat. 'Liar, ya cunt! I fucking know who you are. I know your rat-like face! It's haunted my dreams, you evil bastard.'

In a second, he tore at the man's jacket, ripping it from his shoulders, and then he pulled the shirt away to reveal a long uneven scar from the neck down past his shoulder. 'I remember cutting this fucker up, before I was done over by him and his mates. I don't forget a face, not one that left me with this mark.' He pointed to the scar that ran from his forehead down to his chin.

Staffie gasped. 'What the fuck? Who is he, Willie?'

Still gripping the man's neck, Willie slowly replied, 'Some shit of a man that needs a gang to fight for him.' He glared at him. 'Ain't that right?'

'Wait, Willie. Don't kill him yet. I wanna know who the fuck this cunt is. Staffie, go and find out if the man I've just bricked is the real Davey Lanigan. We need to know who this geezer is.'

Still holding the cosh, Staffie returned to the scene of the bloodbath. It resembled a film clip from *The Walking Dead* but on a smaller scale. Battered and bruised bodies, with chunks missing from their heads and faces, were crawling around moaning and crying.

Lou, out of breath, was leaning against the wall, still trying to make a roll-up.

'Lou! Organize the boys to get our vans out of here, will ya?'

Lou waved his hand in acknowledgement, too out of breath to talk.

Staffie looked down at the meathead who he'd battered with the cosh. His head was swollen black and blue and his hand was crushed, but he was alive and slowly coming out of his dazed state.

'Who's Davey Lanigan?' he hollered at him.

The battered man groaned. Still unsteady, he tried to get to his feet. Staffie grabbed his arm to stabilize him but he pulled away from Staffie's clutches and took three steps.

'My dad,' he croaked, before he slumped down next to his unconscious father.

'And who the fuck are you?' asked Staffie, determined to get the facts straight.

'Neil Lanigan.'

Staffie watched as Neil attempted to bring his father around. All he got were incoherent mumblings. Blood dribbled from his mouth and a wheezy sounded vibrated in his throat.

Neil looked up at Staffie. 'Please, help him.'

Staffie threw the cosh aside and leaned down to help Neil hoist his father to an upright position. He was a heavy lump, but, between the pair of them, they managed to drag him inside and onto the sofa.

'This is Davey Lanigan and his son Neil.'

'Get the men a drink. I want them talking!' instructed Zara coldly. Staffie marched to the small bar area where he found a bottle of Irish whisky and brought it over to the Lanigans.

Managing to drink some and dribbling the rest out, along with blood and fragments of teeth, Davey Lanigan opened his left eye and tried to focus. The right eye was completely closed.

'Who is that guy?' demanded Zara, as she pointed to the ginger-haired man.

A sudden scream made Zara and Staffie look over at Willie, who, by now, was as high as a kite on cocaine and carving a line down the ginger-haired man's face with his diver's knife.

Staffie rolled his eyes. Willie had turned into the monster again.

'Wait up, Willie. We need answers first.' It was like talking to the Hulk when he'd turned green.

As soon as Zara heard the vans starting up to drive away, she frowned at Staffie, her nerves clearly rattled.

He returned a smile by way of assurance. 'It's okay. Lou's organizing them. Lanigan's lot are all incapacitated. But we need to get the goods away from here, before we have any other visitors, 'cos something dodgy is going on.' He looked over at Willie, who was now angrier than he'd ever seen him.

They waited another few minutes for the ginger-haired man to recover his senses, and as soon as he was wholly focused, Zara asked him his name. He glared at her but didn't speak.

With a deep Irish accent and slurred speech, Neil Lanigan began to talk. 'He came to warn me father that you were setting us up and not to trust you or yer men.'

'Well, he fucking lied. Those vans had the gear, as promised. I am a woman of my word and your stupid father was hoodwinked. Who? I mean, who the hell is he?'

'His name is Harman. Ronnie Harman.'

Instantly, Staffie hollered, 'No! Willie! No!'

Zara's eyes widened as Willie held the diver's knife in the air, ready to plunge it into Ronnie's head.

* * *

Zara casually sat opposite Ronnie, as if she were about to have tea. She slid the gun down the back of her trousers and pulled out a packet of cigarettes.

'Now then, Ronnie Harman, how did you get the information that I had a deal with the Lanigans?'

She sparked up the end of her cigarette and blew the smoke into his face. It was a deliberate act. Ronnie's eyes were already stinging from the blood that oozed out of the deep cut to his forehead that Willie had given him.

The cocky expression had left Ronnie's face, and he appeared the old man he was. He huffed. 'It seems that when ya father departed this world, he may have left you the business, but he didn't leave you with the truth.'

Willie's knife was now an inch away from Ronnie's neck. 'Don't talk in fucking riddles. What truth? What are you on about?'

Zara could sense that Willie was a heartbeat away from slitting Harman's throat. 'Willie, wait! I want Ronnie to tell me everything he knows – starting with why his family felt the need to interfere in my father's business, why they grassed Mike to the Filth, and why they killed an innocent six-year-old boy.'

Harman's face turned slowly into a provocative sneer, and it had Zara raging. With her eyes filling up, and her anger boiling, she shot up from her seat. 'Ya know what? Fuck it! Take this disgusting turd outside and tie the bastard to a chair. I'm gonna look for marshmallows.' Totally incensed, she stormed off in search of petrol. Staffie and Willie had never seen her so angry.

With a high-pitched laugh, Willie dragged Ronnie outside by the throat whilst Staffie carried a chair. It suddenly hit Ronnie what she meant – *Christ, they're going to set me alight.*

Staffie noticed Lou and his brother, Felix, were still dragging the wounded men towards one of the blue Transit vans. Lou called over to Staffie. 'I'm gonna load them up in their own van and take 'em away.'

Staffie nodded. 'Nice one, Lou.' He looked over at Felix and grinned to himself. Whilst Lou was short and suave, Felix was his polar opposite – tall, well-built and clumsy, his immense muscles indicating considerable strength – akin to Colossus. He was dragging two men, one by each hand, leaving Lou straining to pull one dead weight.

Struggling and pleading, Ronnie was tied to the dainty pink chair. Zara returned with a can of petrol. She knew that being out here so far from anywhere, the place would have a fuel supply somewhere. The back of the house led to a garage, where, inside, there was a conspicuously large can of petrol.

The men stepped back and watched in horror as she poured the fuel over his head and then whacked him with the can. 'You scummy bastard. Now you'll fucking speak!'

With his face burning and his eyes streaming, he screamed like a girl. 'No! Please, I'm begging you!'

'Who's the grass, Ronnie? Who fucking told you about this job? Why are you out to get us?' She stepped back and took a few deep breaths to calm her anger. She had to get a grip. Holding her lighter and flicking it over in her hands, she noisily breathed in and out through her nose.

His eyes widened, and he struggled so much that the chair tipped over.

Staffie, however, pulled it back onto its four legs. His stomach was now churning; he had never seen anyone set alight before. As he looked at the expression on Zara's face, he realized that she really was bloody dangerous. Izzy was right to have let her take over.

The recognizable sound as she sparked the light made everyone hold their breath, except for Willie, whose fury often made him very excitable.

'Wait! Please, I'll tell you!' yelled Ronnie. He took a deep breath to give himself enough time to think. Whatever he told her, she was going to end his life. But, by giving a name, there was an outside chance he might save himself from being murdered in this horrific way. 'Please, if I tell you, will you just give me a bullet in the head?'

Slowly, she nodded, her face showing not even a twitch.

'It was your cousin Joshua.' He held his breath and prayed she wouldn't throw the lighter.

With her breath now intensifying at every heartbeat, she fought back the urge to set the man ablaze.

'You fucking liar! Joshua wouldn't grass me up. Not in a million years.'

Ronnie knew he needed to wear a poker face, just for a moment, to ensure that Zara would believe him. 'He did, though. He gave me the information because he has a debt to pay and he needed the money.'

'Fucking liar,' she screamed, as she flicked the lighter again. 'Joshua wouldn't do that to me!'

Ronnie knew her mind was ticking over; it was just a matter of time before she would consider her cousin as the culprit. 'He had a gambling problem.' *That should satisfy her*, he thought. Everyone knew Joshua liked to gamble.

Her mind went over and over what he'd just said, and her anger increased. It was feasible, she reasoned. Despite all the money she paid him, Joshua was always borrowing money to pay off his debts, but something was niggling her. The Harmans weren't a big enough outfit to pull this off, surely? And there was just him. All the Harmans, as far as she knew, were now dead, weren't they?

'And the kid? Why did your lot kill the kid?'

Ronnie Harman knew he couldn't come up with a plausible explanation – because he had no idea who she was talking about. His brother had been found murdered in the bath, and his niece and nephews were missing. There wasn't anything else he could tell her. At this pivotal moment, he hated his own family just as much as he hated Izzy and his cocky bitch of a daughter.

Why his brother Frank hadn't brought the boys up to be astute and to use their brains rather than their brawn was beyond him. Harry, especially, was a mouthy, egotistical knob, who had brainwashed Frank into believing he could take over the big firms. Ronnie should never have listened to Frank. However, Frank was so sucked in by Harry and Vinnie's web of big-bollocks bullshit that he genuinely believed his sons were up to the job.

As much as he detested Harry and Vinnie, he did have a soft spot for Scottie. So, he had carefully devised the plan with his favourite nephew to get in with Jackie and bleed her dry for information. Scottie, who had more respect for Ronnie than his own father, agreed. Yet, until his brutal murder, he hadn't managed to find out anything of real value.

As to what had happened to Jackie and her son, it was still a mystery. He never believed Scottie would have had the guts to kill them. However, he couldn't underestimate anyone, and certainly not Zara, after watching her in action. This classy woman could fight like an alley cat, and he grudgingly had to admit she'd led her men well. Nothing would surprise him now.

'Look, please listen. My nephews were reckless and stupid. What they did was nothing to do with me. I had no idea. I swear to God, I never knew, and I promise you, if I'd had an inkling, I would have stopped them. I'm not into killing kids. I was out to make money, that's all.'

'Nah, I'm not having that. You and your family are nothing but low-life chancers. There's no way you would have gone this far without someone backing your corner. Who are you working for?'

Ronnie's eyes widened; clearly, she wasn't stupid. Either he had to tell her the truth or impress her with his acting skills. He chose the latter.

'I might be a small outfit compared to Izzy's, but I have brains and knowledge. If you hadn't brought more muscle with you than I'd predicted, I'd have got away with a chunk of money, wouldn't I? So, Zara, you may look down on me as a nobody, but it didn't take a big firm to almost screw you over. So, there you have it.' He ended with his tone almost resigned, giving what he thought was a first-class performance.

Zara had to admit he was right; nevertheless, there was still something niggling at the back of her mind.

Ronnie's hopes of escaping with his life went out of the window when he saw Zara slowly flick over the lighter in her left hand. But then she gripped the gun in her right. He prayed she was right-handed.

True to her word, she lifted the gun and fired the bullet clean between his eyes. Willie and Staffie were aghast at the sheer precision, and Staffie was relieved in some ways that he wasn't witnessing a man on fire. Willie, however, slumped his shoulders; he would have quite enjoyed toasting marshmallows.

As Neil Lanigan held his father in his arms, Davey began to come around. The blow to the head had done damage, but it hadn't killed him. Zara walked over and called for Staffie to fetch some water to help the older man.

At that defining moment, Staffie saw Zara for who she was – a woman of steel, laced with fairness. She was like Uma Thurman's character in *Kill Bill*, in the way she exuded confidence and for her exploits in adversity. In that respect, she was the female version of Mike.

An hour later, Davey Lanigan was fully conscious and was sitting upright, sipping brandy. The blow to the head, although severe, was not life-threatening. Because he was blessed with having a hard skull, he only suffered a mild concussion. His whole demeanour changed; whether it was from the clump or the new-found respect, he was ready to listen to Zara.

Staffie and Willie stood by Zara's side as she stared at father and son.

'So, you took Ronnie Harman's word over my father's, then?'

Davey, still holding an ice pack to his face and wiping the blood from his broken nose, replied, 'Not lightly, though. He had all the details. For a man to be so well informed, I had to take it seriously.'

'What details did he share with you?'

He tried to take a deep breath, but it hurt, and he coughed. Zara had broken his ribs with her powerful kick. 'He said if you arrived at the meeting with those men' – he pointed to Willie and Staffie with a sneer – 'then you would have no intentions of a fair deal. You were going ta rob me blind with violence.'

'But you didn't even give me a chance to show you the cargo. It's all there. You were ready to attack from the get-go!' She twisted her head, waiting for an answer.

Davey swallowed hard and nodded. 'Harman informed me that the second you opened the back of the vans, we would be jumped.'

'And you took his word on that, yeah?'

He shook his head. 'No. He said that if the vans arrived wrapped in toyshop vinyl, then inside there wouldn't be any drugs – just brute force awaiting us.'

Her eyes widened. 'How the fuck did he know that my vans would be covered in toyshop advertising?'

Bowing his head, he replied, 'He said that you were working with another firm and using yer father's name to do business. Apparently, this firm are evil bastards who'll kill an old man in his bed ta get what they want.'

'You fucking fool, Lanigan. If this Ronnie Harman had successfully taken me out, then he would have done you over, eventually. This little plot was just to take me out of the picture, and I'm not so convinced he was on his own.' She sighed. 'Well, today, I have learned a lot, and I have you, Mr Lanigan, to thank for that, albeit it is a bit messy. The Harmans are a small firm.' She stopped and laughed. 'They *were* a small firm. I guess they're all dead now. I have to give it to them. They outsmarted you, Mr Lanigan, and nearly cost us our lives. It was a clever plot to turn us against each other, but this proves that I am not so easily taken over.'

Davey remained with his head bowed in shame. His small army and name had now been destroyed. If his head wasn't so sore, he would have bashed it against a brick wall.

'Oh, and by the way. Just so you know. It was the Regans who were supplying you with arms, until the Harmans grassed them up to the Filth, which put a temporary stop to operations.'

'The Regans?' He shook his head. 'Ya know, yer father never divulged the name of my supplier.' A frown crumpled up his otherwise swollen face. 'Zara, Ronnie must have known that, or he wouldn't have told me they were a dangerous bunch, ready to double-cross me.'

'Yep, and he nearly got away with it.'

'I'm not a man who says sorry easily, but I *am* sorry. You've taught me a valuable lesson too.'

Zara smirked. 'What's that? Don't believe everything you hear?'

A ghost of a smile crept over his face. 'No, never underestimate the strength of a woman. I think I may need the hospital.'

'Well, there's enough morphine in the back of the vans to put the whole of the British Army in a coma. So, what now, Mr Lanigan?'

'As I said, the money's in the back. It's all there. I guess the deal's off and you'll want the money for compensation?'

She smiled. 'No, I ain't taking the vans back. It's too risky. You can have the gear, but I want the money, three cars, and your son.'

His eyes suddenly opened wide. 'My son?'

She nodded. 'I'll let him go, once I'm back on home soil. He can take one of the cars back. Don't look so fucking worried, or I'll take that as you still don't trust me. And that, Mr Lanigan, would bother me.'

Neil sat by his father's side. Up until now, he'd kept quiet. 'It's okay. I will go with you. Er, the men. Where are they?'

Lou had returned right on cue, holding up two sets of keys. 'Sleeping it off in the back of one of the vans. But some do need to go to a hospital. That's if they survive long enough.'

Davey coughed. 'Fecking leave them there for a while, the useless bunch of clowns.' He raised his head and stared Zara in the eyes. 'I do trust you, because if I didn't, I would have offered to take my son's place.'

* * *

The trip back to England was a solemn affair with Zara and Staffie quietly contemplating the events of the past couple of days. Willie and Neil Lanigan went home in Lou's car and the others travelled back in three of Davey Lanigan's vehicles.

The silence was broken only when Staffie asked whether Joshua would have grassed.

'I've been thinking of how he could because right now Joshua is in Cuba with his wife and has been for the past three days. I should have held back from putting a bullet through Ronnie's head, until I realized that it couldn't have been Joshua. I can't imagine Josh ever doing that.'

'So who is the grass?'

'I dunno, Staffie, but I will fucking find out and God help 'em.'

As they drove through the green rolling hills, his mind was going over the incident, thinking how he and everyone else had underestimated Zara. Never had he met a woman who could fight as well as himself.

Chapter 17

Once they were home, Zara shared out the money and released Neil. He was warming to Mike's firm. Despite all the devastation the men had caused, they actually made him laugh. Zara, a woman of her word, ensured he was seen to at a hospital, that he was fed, and he was given sufficient money in his back pocket to fill the car with fuel to drive home. His departure was like saying goodbye to old buddies.

It seemed they had all been duped by an enemy who was almost equal to them both.

The situation had bothered Zara, and although she shrugged it off in front of the men, it still plagued her mind. She contacted Joshua who greeted her with a sunny, upbeat tone. He was merrily describing the Cuban hotel and the fun he was having, when she stopped him in his tracks.

'Joshua, where did you get the money to go to Cuba?'

Surprised at her cold tone, he replied, 'Are you okay, Zara? What's the matter?'

'Answer the question. How did you get the money?'

Without a hint of hesitation, he said, 'I know Uncle Izzy left me that money to get myself out of debt and to buy a house, but I didn't think he would mind if I had a holiday, I mean . . . Oh shit, you're pissed off with me 'cos I squandered it on a holiday. Yeah, I guess I shouldn't have. Look, Zara, I'm sorry. I will do good with the rest, I promise.'

Her heart sank. She had actually believed that scumbag over her own cousin, having forgotten that Izzy gave him a lump sum to sort himself out. The details were left in a letter for her.

'Sorry, Joshua, I'm just all over the place at the moment. No, you enjoy Cuba, and bring me back some of that Cuban rum.'

Joshua chuckled, relieved to hear a more vibrant tone in her voice. 'So, you're not angry with me?'

'No, Joshua, never.'

* * *

She pondered over what Izzy would have done. But he was a man of power, and although he'd handed it all over to her, she wondered if she really had the know-how to keep it going. Someone had grassed, and her father would have sussed it within an hour, but she was struggling and feeling vulnerable. Having Mike on board would have been the answer; he would know what to do at every turn. She pulled out the visiting order from her father's cabinet drawer and sighed. The last visit had been soul-destroying. She was still struggling to get Mike's distraught face out of her mind.

After a sleepless night alone in her father's ornate house, Zara woke up with a splitting headache. The rain was relentless as it hammered against the Georgian window. Sitting upright and looking around her childhood bedroom, her eyes filled with tears. The room held so many memories, but, unfortunately, not all of them were good. However, she did remember her mother's voice gently whispering to her as she lay with her head on the plump pillows, her teddy bears taking up more room than herself. Those moments and hundreds of others with her mother were such joyous ones. Then she pictured her father's sad eyes when he'd told her that her mother had passed away.

That was the night she'd been hurried from her bed and taken away to a safe place, where the alarm systems beeped and the big German shepherd dogs patrolled the perimeter. How strange that, when she had lain in Mike's bed years later, she'd felt even more secure.

As she slowly plodded down the wooden staircase in her bare feet, the silence was a reminder that she had no one.

Reading the newspaper, she noted that the headlines were dominated by an increase in drug-related crime; the news contained nothing that would lift her dismal mood. After a few sips of coffee, she got herself showered and dressed, ready for the visit. She washed and blow-dried her hair and coated her skin with a lotion, but she didn't feel it appropriate to wear make-up; after all, he hadn't officially said she was his girlfriend. With the exception of the last visit, the previous ones had been pleasant and probably just a distraction for him, but everything had changed now, since she had given him the news regarding his son.

She rushed to the car with a brolly keeping off the rain. Concerned that the storm would cause more traffic on the roads of London, she put her foot down and hurried towards the prison. Luckily, the downpour was temporary, but the unrelenting heat of the past few days had cooled. She found a seat and waited in the visiting room. Her thoughts went to Mike. She wondered how he would look, and if there would be a warmer reception than last time, or whether Mike would still be beleaguered with torment.

The visiting room was packed as always. Mike was the last to enter. She held her breath as the door opened. There he stood, scanning the room to find her. *No glimmer of a smile*, she thought. He looked stone-faced and cold-hearted as if the life had been sucked out of him. He raised his head and nodded as he approached. Zara gave an awkward smile and stood to greet him, but he didn't hold out his arms for an embrace; instead, he sat down and placed his elbows on the table.

'How are you doing, Mikey?'

He huffed at that question. 'How do you think, Zara?'

Ouch, that was cold, she thought. 'I know it must be so hard, but . . .'

His jaw clenched. 'Stop, Zara, just stop. I am sick of people telling me what I should do. There are no buts, Zara. It's hard. Full, fucking, stop.'

She was about to touch his arm, but she sensed there was no point. 'I . . . er . . . I wanted your advice, Mikey. I wondered if you could help me.'

He sighed and leaned back on the cold plastic chair. 'In case you haven't noticed, I'm in prison, and so I don't think giving advice will be any good to anyone. The truth is, Zara, I came out to tell you and anyone else who has a visiting order, I want to be left alone. Don't come up again.'

'Look, love, I know how you feel—'

She didn't have a chance to finish before he ripped into her.

'Don't you dare tell me you know how I feel. You have no bloody idea.'

Zara felt her temper rising; he wasn't the only one who had suffered, not by a long chalk. 'Yes, I bloody do!' she replied, equally stony-faced.

'Just do one, Zara, will ya. I don't want anyone up here visiting. Ya *don't* know how it feels, so shut it.'

Eugene, one of the officers, moved closer, and Mike clocked him out of the corner of his eye.

Zara got up from her seat and gave him a look that he'd never seen before. Her face cast such a dark sadness. He raised his brow, as if he was trying to comprehend something.

'The thing is, though, Mikey, I do. I know *exactly* how you feel.' Her words were so direct and honest that they seemed to hit him. He might as well have been struck a blow in the sternum.

Immediately, he realized she wasn't playing the patronizing do-gooder; she needed to tell him something important. He decided to give her a chance to get it off her chest.

In a flash, he was up from his seat and grabbing her wrist to pull her back. Eugene, not understanding the situation, then clutched Mike's arm. 'The visit's over. Let the lady go!'

Mike let go of Zara's wrist, and, like a gorilla, he shook off Eugene. 'Get the fuck away from me, you shitty little weasel.'

Eugene, a white-haired, light-skinned man, went almost faint from shock.

Zara then knew she had to calm the situation down before Mike was hauled off to solitary confinement. She held up her hand to the officer. 'It's okay. Please, I need to speak with him.'

Eugene didn't need telling twice; he was only too pleased to leave them to it.

She pulled out a chair and sat down, followed by Mike, who wouldn't take his eyes off hers.

'How do you know how I feel?' His tone softened and his shoulders lowered like a tyre being deflated.

She sniffed back the tears and tried to stop her bottom lip from quivering. As she was inclined to do under stress, her fingers caressed the ring that hung on the chain around her neck.

'He was six months old . . . he was so beautiful . . .' She stopped to wipe her tears. 'He had dark hair and the biggest grey eyes.'

As Mike's strong hands enclosed hers, she looked up to see his eyes heavy with tears.

'Oh, Zara, babe. I'm so sorry. I truly didn't know.'

She stared back and allowed her tears to tumble effortlessly. Then she tried to speak, but the sob was trapped in her throat. Mike rubbed her hands and wiped away her tears.

'I couldn't tell anyone. I was in hiding. Izzy sent me away for my own protection. I didn't even know I was pregnant before I left England.'

It didn't dawn on him at first, he was so immersed in her sorrow. 'Ahh, Zara, bless your heart. If only I'd known.'

He meant if only he had known that she'd lost a child, but she took it another way.

'I wanted to tell you, Mikey, I swear, but it was such a dangerous situation, and by the time things died down, it was too late. I thought, why should two of us suffer?'

Suddenly, he let go of her hand. His eyes narrowed with the surprise – yet another sucker punch inside two minutes – and he looked across the table in consternation. 'What? He was *my* baby?'

She realized then that he'd had no idea what she was talking about. 'I'm sorry, Mikey, I'm really sorry. I wanted to come back to England with our son and . . .' She looked down, wiping her wet cheeks.

So many emotions flooded his brain – shock, hurt, anger – but Zara's feelings took precedence. She was the one who was hurting. She had held her child – his child – and nurtured him. He may have lost two sons, but one of them he'd never even known about. He had the urge to know his baby's name.

'What did you call him?'

She looked up. 'Michael.'

Unexpectedly, and without permission, he got up from his seat and pulled her into his arms and gently caressed her hair. 'I'm so very sorry, babe.'

If it had been any other inmate, the two duty officers would have marched Regan off the visit for what he'd just done. Common sense prevailed, on this occasion, although it was a close-run thing.

Later, Mike would look back at this moment, seeing it as a turning point in his malaise. But, right now, something inside him released, and all that suppressed hurt and anger that he'd bottled up for so long simply vanished. As he pulled away to look into her eyes, his face looked completely different. He returned to the old Mike. 'What advice, babe? How can I help?'

She sat down and wiped her nose with the cuff of her sleeve before clearing her throat.

'I had a business deal with Davey Lanigan, and when I met

him face-to-face to do the swap . . .' She leaned closer and whispered, 'Ronnie Harman was there. The deal nearly went tits up, but, luckily, I had Staffie, Willie and Lou on board or I would have been toast.'

Mike puffed out his chest in anger. 'You *what*? Did you say *Harman*?'

She nodded. 'But, listen. Something strange is going on, Mikey, and I just can't work it out.'

'What the fuck was Harman doing there? I hope the boys ripped his fucking head off!'

She waved her hand impatiently because she needed him to listen. 'No, they didn't. I did. But, Mikey, something more important than the Harman thing is going on. Look, Izzy set up this deal with the Lanigans. I took over and all was going sweet. But it turned out Ronnie Harman had managed to convince Lanigan that if I turned up in vans covered in toyshop adverts, there'd be no merchandise inside, just heavy-duty muscle. Anyway, luckily for me, I did have a few heavies – actually your guys – because the Lanigans had two Transit vans on standby, full of their own men.'

'They didn't hurt you or me boys, did they?'

'No,' she laughed. 'No, not at all. The Irish firm got battered, though. Anyway, that's not the point. What I need to find out is how the fuck Ronnie Harman knew I had the vans covered in toyshop ads and men inside ready to fight.'

'Well, it's simple, babe. There's someone on your firm that's after bringing you down. Like you said, no one knew about the hangar, apart from your own family. Who else would have known about the Lanigan deal? It has to be an insider who was working with Ronnie Harman.' His face tightened and he banged his hand down on the table. 'Fuck me, I wish I was out of here. It's so frustrating.'

She sighed. 'Other things have been happening. Some of Izzy's men have retired. My supplier for the Italian restaurants has gone on the missing list. So, I feel like something is going down, and whatever it is, it's much bigger than the Harmans. Besides, they're all dead now.'

Mike chewed the inside of his lip. 'The man with the most clout in London was your ol' man, so there may be another firm testing the water, now he's off the scene. And, Zara, whoever it is, they've managed to get someone onto their side who's extremely close to you. Zara, think about it. Izzy was putting it out there that you would take over. He placed you on the front line, taking care of business, so the Italians and the Colombians would all know that you were the boss once he'd gone. That firearms deal was just a tester for me, wasn't it? He matched me up with the Lanigans for his own ends. He wanted to have me on your firm, to work with you, didn't he?'

She grinned. 'Well, yeah, he wanted to see how tough you were, and, I have to be honest, he pushed you to see if you'd be afraid of him. And, well, you proved that when you told him to fuck off . . .' Her face suddenly saddened. 'There were some things that my father hid from me. I think he would have told me more, but his illness took a grip sooner than he thought it would. He knew about us, Mikey, and about the baby. All that time, I thought I'd kept it a secret. I think that's why he wanted you by my side. Perhaps he assumed we had an unbreakable bond.' She looked up, hoping for a sign that Mike would admit it.

With a deep frown that almost covered his eyes, Mike said, 'Of course he knew about us. And I expect he knew you'd be faced with trouble. Perhaps he saw it brewing before he died. That's why he wanted me on board to help you, knowing I would. And if I wasn't in this shithole, I'd be there for you.'

'He was such a clever ol' git.' She smiled, thinking about how much her father really had looked out for her. 'I never could fool him.'

Holding her hand, he squeezed it and smiled.

The bell rang. Visiting was over. Mike leaned forward. 'The

Harmans must have been working for this bigger outfit, and it's my guess that this firm has men on the inside. Look, promise me you'll lie low for a while? I'll talk to the boys. At least we don't have the Harmans to worry about—'

'I'm not so sure. Although Frank and Ronnie are dead,' she interjected, 'I have a sense they were working for someone else. Izzy wasn't worried about the Harmans. He must have assumed they were all bumbling idiots and never realized that they may have been involved with someone more powerful – but who, I have no idea. It wouldn't be any of Izzy's men. I mean, my men haven't mentioned the name of another firm.' She suddenly paused and frowned. 'Unless . . .'

Mike gripped her hand tighter. 'Unless what, Zara?'

'Guy Segal. But . . . no, it can't be him. He's just a sly old fool and wouldn't dare take me on. He doesn't have the clout, the money, or the presence. Plus, he's got to be sixty-five years old now.'

Mike chuckled. 'That means fuck all. Me ol' man's not much younger and he's still as dangerous. But listen, stay low, go away for a bit. Fuck the business. It's not worth it, babe. You have enough money. Ya dad left you almost everything.' His eyes glowed with a gentle expression. 'You're worth so much to me, Zara, and I don't want you hurt. I know you're tough, but I can't lose you as well.'

Her heart skipped a beat; *Oh Christ*, he did still love her. That look in his eyes made her melt. He was the only man she'd ever loved. But she'd also made a promise to her father to keep the business going, so how could she let him down now?

As if Mike had read her mind, he went on, 'Izzy couldn't have predicted this, but I know he sent you away to protect you. And as your fella, I'm going to do the same. He wanted me to look out for you, and I'm telling you to go away for a bit. Go to the most unlikely place, where no one will think to find you. Ditch ya phone and speak to no one. I reckon someone's listening in on your calls or your conversations. Change your car. Tell your closest friends, family, whoever, that you're off on a short break to Spain, and then go somewhere else. Get a new phone and just send Staffie a smiley face, so we know you're okay, and leave the rest to me.'

The constant tightening in her chest had gone; she could breathe now. All the bricks had been lifted from her shoulders.

'Finish up your visits, please!' bellowed the officer at the desk.

There was an awkward moment when both Mike and Zara just gazed at each other.

'Mikey, I do still . . .'

'I know, babe, and I love you too. I always 'ave. So, do as I bleedin' well say and stay safe, yeah?'

She nodded and lowered her eyes.

The parting embrace was gentle yet firm, and he held her close and gently kissed her neck. 'If you meet someone special, then, that's fine, babe. Just promise me you won't do anything stupid. I can't bear to lose two people I've loved.'

'I'll wait for ya, Mikey, I promise. I never did love anyone else. It's always been you, and I guess it always will be.'

Chapter 18

The email arrived, confirming the purchase of a one-way flight to Spain. She printed it off and left it on the desk for anyone to see. After packing a small suitcase, she loaded the boot of the taxi and left in the dead of night to travel to Gatwick Airport. However, she had no intention of flying to Spain. As soon as the taxi pulled away from the terminal, she hurried over to the rental office and hired a car for a week. If she was seriously being watched, then whoever they were would check the taxi office to see where she'd gone. Driving to Liverpool, she prayed that they would lose her scent. After the set-up with the Lanigans, Ireland would be the last place she would go – in her enemy's eyes – surely?

The drive was tiring, but a few stops for coffee and a bit of time to refresh at one of the service stations had her bright-eyed when she knocked at Davey Lanigan's door.

Neil appeared. His bruises were still visible although his eye wasn't so swollen. 'Come in. Me father's in the lounge.'

She followed him through the double oak doors that led into a wide entrance hall. During the first meeting with Neil, she hadn't taken a good look at him, for obvious reasons. With deep-blue eyes and clear skin, he was attractive, but there was only one man on her mind – Mike. She gazed at the plush, elegant décor, complemented by an antique cabinet and a stunning display of fresh flowers.

Once inside the large lounge, where there was an inviting open fire and an enormous thick rug, providing a homely feel to the room, her eyes then focused on Davey, sitting on one of the four sofas.

She gave a sympathetic smile when she saw the black bruising down one side of his face. His eyes didn't hold that former evil look, which had oozed such confidence. She wondered if she really had knocked him sideways.

'Sit down, Zara,' he said, gesturing with his hand.

She hoped she hadn't jumped out of the frying pan into the fire. Yet, somehow, as she gracefully sat down, her instincts told her she should not feel threatened by Davey Lanigan.

A moment later, she heard the stomping of high heels from the hallway. She turned to face a middle-aged woman with red hair, pale skin, and a thunderous expression. She was wearing a black dress, which showed her middle-aged spread.

'You've got some nerve, girl!' she bellowed in a thick Irish accent.

Zara jumped to her feet, before the raging woman could tear into her.

'Tania, stop right there. You have no fecking business, interfering. Now, get the feck out!'

Tania, evidently his wife, screwed her face up and glared at Zara. 'The fecking state yer left me old man in, I've a good mind ta fecking smash you one meself.'

Zara suddenly laughed. 'Listen, lady, no disrespect, but it was a fair fight.'

Neil laughed along, and Davey had a massive grin on his face. 'It was dat all right.'

Tania huffed and scowled. 'Well, I don't fecking know. Women fighting like men. What's the world coming to? Well, I best offer yer a drink. A pint of lager, is it?'

Zara laughed again. 'No, thank you. A cup of tea would be lovely, though, and . . . er, please, don't spit in it.'

A peachy grin swept across Tania's face. 'You'll be lucky if I don't shit in it. No, okay, love. It seems that silly ol' bastard 'as forgiven yer, so I best do the same. One lump or two?'

'Oh no, it was only one lump, right across the face.'

Tania rolled her eyes. 'I meant sugar.'

With a wink, Zara replied, 'One, please.'

The ice had been broken and they were now set for business.

'So, Zara, let us be perfectly frank with each other,' said Davey, sitting upright. 'You and I were well and truly set up. However, Ronnie Harman had underestimated you.' He coughed. 'And so did I. But that's not the issue. The point is, now we both have a common enemy.'

She smiled. 'Oh yes, we do, and as I see it, really, I did you no wrong. I'm a woman of my word, and you know that now.'

He looked at his son and smiled. 'Yes, you are.'

'Davey, something is going on, and I don't think the past incidents are all down to the Harmans. They weren't strong enough to have that much front. I do believe there's a bigger man behind all of this, but the problem is, I have no idea who. The truth is that in the last few days my business has been slipping away from me.'

'Well, there lies the problem. No successful firm can survive when the fear has gone. Izzy is dead, God rest him, and you are left alone. I don't think Izzy ever underestimated you, but he may have miscalculated the loyalty and goodwill of his men.'

'I'm sure you're right because my men are backing off with no explanation.'

Davey sniffed the air. 'I'm not sure how we can help, apart from keeping you safe here, which I feel obliged to do. I at least owe Izzy and yourself that much.'

'Did you know my father well?'

Davey grinned and nodded. 'I think I knew as much about

Izzy as he knew about me. The thing is, Zara, your father's set-up was much like mine here in Ireland. We had mutual respect. I was straight with him and he was likewise. We couldn't really afford to feck each other over and we never trod on each other's toes. I really wouldn't have wanted to have upset the man. He was fecking dangerous.'

Zara chuckled. 'He said the same about you.'

'You see, Zara, it's all about persuading people to make the right choices. The carrot and the stick are powerful motivators, that they are.'

She nodded, listening to his words of wisdom.

'Okay then, Davey. I think we could work together because my father also made it known that you were a very serious mob and not to be crossed. Back in London, your reputation precedes you. That can only be good for business.'

Davey grinned. 'Yes, no doubt he did. And we have a genuine respect for your firm, Zara. Tell me then about your proposal, and I may have one for you.'

Her eyes lit up. Instantly, he saw the devil in them and waited for her cheeky expression to turn into words.

Their conversation was interrupted by Tania shuffling her way into the living room with a tray of refreshments. She looked at Zara and winked. 'Tea and one lump.'

Davey eased himself forward to look at the tea. 'Did you make me a coffee?'

Tania raised her eyebrow. 'Go make yer fecking own. All that shouting at me earlier, and now yer expect a drink? Bollocks.'

Zara didn't know whether to laugh or look away. She hadn't seen a couple like this before and wondered if they were happy or terribly miserable.

'What? Tan, make us a nice coffee, will yer?' his voice softened.

She grinned. 'There, look, yer silly ol' bastard. It's on the tray.'

She chuckled and left the room.

'You were saying, Davey?'

'Well, actually, I wasn't, but, anyway, you told me that this Mike Regan was the man who supplied me with the arms?'

Zara nodded and sat up straight, hoping this would lead to a deal.

'Can you make contact and get the deal back on for me?'

Zara now knew she had a business to barter with. 'Okay, I can get you a regular supply of arms, but I want your help in return.'

'Go on,' replied Davey.

She smiled and picked up her cup. 'First, I hope I can trust your wife,' she said, before she took a sip.

Neil laughed. 'It wouldn't have been spit, it would have been arsenic, if she'd had any doubts about yer.'

With a nod, she said, 'It's all about trust, eh?'

Once she placed the cup and saucer on the coaster by the side of her, she sat back, smoothed down her skirt, and took a deep breath. 'I need to stay in Ireland. I can't have anyone in England knowing where I am. I have all the business contacts and know the ins and outs with the drug dealers, the suppliers and the buyers. Restaurants are supplied by me, but lately they're pulling out. I want that business back, but I can't be seen to be doing it myself. They need to think that your firm is taking over. Do you think you can handle it?'

It was Davey's turn to chew it over. 'And I take it that in the process, you want to know who's behind the firm that's attempting to run you out of town?'

'Yes, that's about it . . . oh and trust. You have to trust me.'

'Well, Zara, you have my assurance that I trust you, so tomorrow we can go over the finer details, and if we both make good money, then it's got to be a win-win. And I think we can do more than take back your business for you. If we find whoever is trying to bring you down, they must have businesses of their own – or, if not, they have to be rich – so we will be taking over their assets as compensation.'

272

She sighed with relief and relaxed her shoulders. 'Is there a B&B near here?'

Neil jumped up and waved his hand. 'You can stay with us. The house has enough spare rooms, and mum's bark is worse than her bite. I think she likes to have a woman around instead of just men.'

Davey eased himself off the sofa and stretched his legs. He seemed to have aged since the fight and the bruise on his face made him look vulnerable. 'I think someone else will like your feminine company too.'

He shot Neil a look and smiled. Zara suddenly felt awkward. Neil was a looker, a muscle-bound hunk with gorgeous eyes, but her love was for Mike.

Tania overheard them and was in the doorway before they could say another word. 'If that bitch is staying, she can have the front room. It's aired, fresh and warm.'

Zara wanted to laugh again, but the thought of a comfortable bed suddenly made her feel very tired.

'Neil, fetch her things in.' Tania turned and looked Zara up and down. 'I'll show yer to your room.'

Immediately, Zara felt her world had just become somewhat bizarre.

The spare room was beautiful with soft lemon walls and pure white bed linen covered by a thick duvet.

Tania's tone became sweet and more mumsy. 'Now then, girl. Through that little door there is the en suite. If yer draw the curtains, you can get a few hours' sleep. Driving for hours has probably washed the life outta yer. If yer need anything, just scream for me. The others do.'

Zara tapped the short woman's shoulder. 'Thanks, Tania, and look, I never meant to cause such a mess to Davey's face.'

With a guttural giggle, Tania nearly lost her breath. 'Aw, no, Zara. He's always been that fecking ugly.'

Joining in with the laughter, Zara began to relax her guard and felt exceptionally secure in her surroundings. So much so, she forgot herself. 'Tania, I am okay here? I mean . . .'

Tania's eyes searched her face. 'Of course yer are.' She looked at the bedroom door and back to Zara. 'Between you and me, Davey said yer were a fair woman. My Neil came home in one piece and that's your doing. And sorry about earlier. I just thought yer would barge in my house like a bully, demanding all fecking sorts, but yer seem just normal, really.'

Zara had no idea what that meant, but she was going to take it as a compliment anyway. Hopefully, tomorrow, things would look up.

* * *

Ricky sighed when he saw how small the window was. He had grown so much in the last eighteen months that slithering through a tiny window was painful. More often than not, it left him with cuts and grazes. Tatum gave him a leg up and told him to hurry. No sooner was Ricky on his feet in the downstairs toilet than he heard a sound from outside the door. He froze, not knowing what to do next, but then he heard Tatum calling through the window. 'Get a move on, boy!'

Ricky faced the door and then looked back at the window. He listened again but there was silence. He quickly grabbed the handle and pulled it open to make a quick exit to the back door. But, as he did so, a deep growl was followed by a sudden chomp on his left leg. The growling sound was coming from a large dog that had pulled him to the ground and now had his leg firmly in its mouth. The situation didn't bode well for Ricky. The monster was shaking him around the hallway floor like a rag doll. Ricky couldn't even scream; the fear engulfed him, sending him into a panic. He tried to grip the dog's head to pull its huge jaws from his calf, but this only incensed the animal. Out of the corner of

274

his eye, he saw an umbrella leaning against the wall. He reached out and managed to clasp the handle; with all his strength, he hit the dog on the head, but to no effect. So terrified that it was going to rip his leg off, he held the umbrella like a spear and thrust it as hard as he could straight into its eye. Relief came when the dog yelped in pain and ran off up the stairs. Ricky could hardly catch his breath. The pain and the oozing blood, seeping through his torn trousers, fed his fear. With so much adrenaline now coursing through his body, he mustered the strength to get to his feet to open the back door, before collapsing on the doorstep. The rest was a blur; he could hear Tatum's voice somewhere in the background but it was hazy. Apart from the dog biting his leg, all he could recall was lying in the front seat of the truck while Tatum drove.

He woke up in a hospital bed. A doctor was talking but he could only see his lips moving. The bright lights against the white ceiling made him blink. Then he experienced the distinct taste of anaesthetic. A tube was slowly pulled from his throat, leaving it dry and sore.

The doctor, a slim, clean-looking man with pure white hair and flushed cheeks, gave him a generous smile. 'So, you are with us now? Do you know where you are?'

Ricky nodded. He remembered being in a hospital once before, when he'd tripped over a brick wall and needed stitches to his eye.

'Your father tells us you can't speak. Is that right?'

Ricky widened his eyes. *What? Had he heard the doctor correctly?*

'Can you speak?' asked the doctor again.

Ricky shook his head and tried to sit up. He had to see if his father was there. Maybe Jackie had got it wrong after all, and his dad had come for him, but any glimmer of hope was quickly dashed. Leaning against the wall was Tatum, with an over-the-top smile. Ricky then realized that Tatum had made out he was his father. A tear suddenly escaped, although he tried to brush it away.

The doctor turned to acknowledge Tatum. Ricky listened hard.

'Elijah will have to stay in for a few days, until we're satisfied that the wound is knitting together. We've tried to use the skin to seal the laceration, but it's very likely that it may not heal as we'd like it to. So, in my judgement, it would be best not to move him. He will be on antibiotics and taken to the ward. My team will keep a close eye on him.'

Ricky was in despair. Not only had Tatum effectively treated him as a nobody, but the man had also pretended he was his own son.

By the time he was on the main ward, Jackie arrived. He watched, cringing, as she stumbled into the room, knocking a steel trolley flying. The highly polished floor was slippery, and in her stilettos she struggled to balance as if she were on an ice-skating rink. Dressed in a denim miniskirt, a crop top, and her hair dyed the blackest it could be, Jackie plonked herself on the chair beside him. More pissed than normal, she slurred her words. 'I've a good mind ta sue the arse off the owner of the dog that bit ya foot.'

Her behaviour was enough to put anyone off drink for life. She looked and sounded so ridiculous that he closed his eyes and pretended to be asleep, but she went on and on just talking shit. Then she was quiet, and he heard another voice.

'I'm Dr Larkin, your son's surgeon. Elijah will need peace, quiet and rest, so it may be an idea if you pop back tomorrow, Mrs Menaces.' His words were short, sharp and commanded attention.

With his eyes still shut, Ricky could visualize her squirming.

'Oh, all right, if that's what you binks vest. I mean, I loves me boy, poor sod.' She was so drunk that she couldn't have strung a coherent sentence together if she'd tried.

The sound of her clip-clopping heels and the doctor saying,

'Oh, be careful, Mrs Menaces,' told him she was leaving. He opened his eyes to see the doctor standing in the doorway and staring down the corridor, watching in horror – or was it fascination? He glanced back at Ricky and gave him a pitiful smile.

PART THREE

Chapter 19

2009, six years later

Guy Segal stroked his long beard and scrutinized the accounts. There were papers strewn across his desk, leaving just enough room for a large computer, showing a spreadsheet of complicated calculations.

'It appears that you have made some enemies, Ismail. The Italians have turned their backs on us, and when one of my men went to collect the takings, he was met by another fucking Irishman, who claims that he's running the restaurant. Since when do the Irish make fucking pasta, eh? That's four pizza houses and two restaurants run by leprechauns. I can't lose any more business,' he stated, with a raspy tone to his voice.

Ismail bravely replied, 'In our line of work, what do you expect! It's dog eat dog. But I'm working on a deal with the Turks. Now, they don't mess about. Any Irish who step on their turf, trust me, they'll be butchered. The Turks are handy with a kebab knife.'

Guy slowly snarled. Ismail was pushing his luck.

'It's a shame, Ismail,' – he looked him up and down – 'that you do not resemble your father, for as much as he became my enemy, he was still a man to fear and respect. But you, Ismail, I am beginning to have less and less respect for. Maybe I was wrong about you.' His eyes were boring into Ismail. 'It's not the middlemen I'm concerned about, it's the supplier. Without the cocaine, you idiot, we have nothing.'

Ismail had worked out a deal with the Turks, for them to sell on cocaine from their takeaways. With a vast financial reward, the Turks had grabbed the arrangement with both hands. Yet Ismail hadn't considered the fact that he didn't have a current supplier. Marchant, who had supplied his father and who had been supplying Ismail, was now blanking him. Standing in the bright, sleek office, the complete opposite of his father's, he wondered if he'd taken on too much.

From as young as fifteen, he had been made aware that his sister was the one his father had chosen to take over the business. His big sister, the golden child, who could wrap Izzy around her little finger, was held in high esteem and paraded as a trophy. He felt she was rubbing his nose in his failings. He was a nobody, and as the years went by and Izzy's dismissal of him increased, he had begun to detest Zara and his father.

Naturally, he would go where he was respected and praised. The fact that his supporter was Guy Segal, his father's enemy, made the relationship even sweeter. At least Guy was honest with him and told him the truth about the feud between his father and the Segal family. Ismail felt empowered and had one thing over his sister, and that was the truth. His father may have hidden his tattoo, but the day he'd died was the day Ismail went and had his own one done, as a mark of respect for Guy, and as a dishonour to his father.

But now he felt uncomfortable with how Guy was grilling him; it was like Izzy all over again. Those black burning eyes full of disappointment made Ismail shiver. He had to be on top; he yearned for the pat on the back.

'Carlos can still supply us. The more the merrier. Let's face it, he can supply the Irish and us. And slowly I will have the Irish run out of London.' As the words tumbled from his mouth, he knew how absurd they sounded. As if Carlos, who was only a small-time supplier, would be capable of dealing with both him and them.

Guy's anger was climbing. 'I can't believe that you really are so stupid. You swan around like a fucking fairy, snorting half the poxy gear yaself. You think you have a deal with the Turks, you silly prick? They'll rob you blind, cut you up, and serve you like a fucking doner kebab.'

After throwing his hands in the air and banging them down on the desk, with such force that it sent some loose papers flying, Guy launched another verbal attack. 'You have no supplier, Ismail. Don't you get it? Christ, you told me you could sell ink to a squid, ice to an Inuit, but you can't even tie your own bloody shoelaces up.'

Stupidly, Ismail looked down at his feet.

'My God, Ismail, you really are pathetic. You still have no idea what's happened to your sister, and there you are, telling me that you have everything under control.'

Ismail attempted to speak but was shouted down. 'If my sister went missing, I would have the whole firm out finding her, but not you, Ismail. You sat back and tried to walk in her shoes, sorting business, and acting like you'd taken over from Izzy. And yes, Ismail, it should have been like taking candy from a baby, but even with her out of the way, you still couldn't get it right! All you had to do was let everyone believe that you had your sister's back and continue to run the business in the hope that she'd return. Yet, for some reason, you've fucked it all up.'

Ismail knew Guy was right. Before, it was simple: to be the eyes and ears for Guy. It was a doddle, placing bugs in Zara's car and in her handbag and listening behind closed doors. They would never dream that behind the paintbrush and canvas were those big ears of his, listening to everything. Zara wouldn't suspect her own brother.

If only Izzy hadn't treated him as if he were the poor relation, only humouring him when the need arose. Revenge was sweet in his mind.

After a honeymoon period, when Ismail could do no wrong, now it was different – almost like the relationship he'd had with his father. He didn't get the pat on the back for all the useful information he'd shared with Guy. In fact, he wasn't held in high esteem anymore because the fact was, his father was right. He didn't have the balls to front men or go in hard – he was a pathetic wimp. His vision of swanning around in a flash car, with men kissing his feet, and having the respect his father had enjoyed, was now going up in smoke.

He suddenly had the need to sit down. His legs felt wobbly and he experienced a tightening of his throat. Did Guy want to do away with him?

'Stop trying to get the business back. What you need to do is to find out who's behind this Irish firm and also find out what's happened to your sister. Everything is still in her name, and you, Ismail, need to get proof that's she's dead before you can take her assets. We need a serious cash flow, and since you have failed to keep the business going, you need to free up some of the money locked down in all those properties of hers.'

Ismail nodded, just to stop Guy from screaming at him.

'Now, fuck off, Ismail, and come back when you have good news!'

Ismail was only too eager to swing on his heels and leave. Guy had a tendency to make him need the toilet. As he hurried away, out of the office and along the corridor of the dry-cleaners, he was met by Guy's son. He couldn't stand Benjamin, with his narrow eyes and pale skin; he was ugly, both in looks and attitude.

The feeling was mutual. For a while, when Ismail had been treated like the golden boy, it had enraged Benjamin to the point where he couldn't bear to see his father singing Ismail's praises and treating him to gifts. Even a gold watch – a family heirloom that was worth a mint – was given to Ismail. It should have been handed down to him.

'Fucked up yet again, Ismail, did you?'

Benjamin stood with his shoulders almost touching the corridor walls. His cold grin, showing off his heavily chipped and stained teeth, turned Ismail's stomach. He couldn't put up with anything less than perfect when it came to a person's mouth.

'Well, well, Ismail, the runt. You can't get fuck all right. Father is gonna be so intrigued by what I have to tell him.'

Ismail wanted to shoot Benjamin, but, again, he didn't have the guts – or a gun for that matter, too afraid that it would be turned on himself. 'That's good, Benjamin. Maybe you will lighten his mood.' He didn't wait for a reply; instead, he shuffled past Benjamin and slithered away like the snake he was.

Dressed in his long grey coat, which could have covered a bear with room to spare, Benjamin strolled into his father's office. His beaming smile, marred by the lack of dentistry, didn't make Guy cringe. His son was a big, manly man, not groomed and polished like that tart Ismail.

'Ah, my boy, what news do you bring?' He knew his son's expression meant he had something up his sleeve.

'This Irish firm is run by Davey Lanigan.'

Guy shook his head and sighed. 'I thought you were going to tell me something I *didn't* know?'

Taking a seat, Benjamin laughed. 'Yep, but I bet you didn't know that the Lanigans are working with Willie Ritz and Teddy Stafford, did you?'

With a raised eyebrow, Guy leaned back on the chair, the cogs turning, as he tried to process this news.

'The Lanigans and Ritzes? But I assumed . . . I mean, after the set-up, I thought that they'd be arch-enemies. How did they do that? Their fucking head honcho, Mike Regan, is inside – just where we want him. Ritz and Stafford wouldn't have the brains to . . .' He paused and took a deep breath. 'What business is this, then?'

'Guns.'

Benjamin's smile was not reciprocated. His father's grave expression was a concern. 'I thought you'd be pleased. You've always said knowledge is power.'

Guy snapped out of his gaze. 'Yes, but so is a dangerous fucking army!'

He picked up his silver engraved pen and twirled it between his fingers. 'Are you sure that the Lanigans are working with them? Because I can't see it myself. I mean, I heard there was a nasty battle, and old man Lanigan came off worse.'

'Who told you that, Father?'

Guy waved his hand. 'One of the drivers. He's one of Izzy's weaker men, but I keep him on because he's useful. I had him almost paralytic, and he told me all he knew. However, what he didn't tell me was what must have gone on inside that guesthouse, after Ronnie was shot in the head. Fuck me, we have been so damned stupid.' He flung his hands in the air and his body deflated.

'What is it? What's going on?' asked Benjamin, uncomfortable with the resigned look on his father's face.

'We've taken too much for fucking granted. Jesus, how could I have overlooked that?'

'Father, what are you talking about?'

Guy flared his nostrils, and in one sudden fit of anger, he wiped clear the remaining papers from his desk, the sudden, explosive movement making Benjamin jump.

Guy stood up and then banged his fist on the desk. 'It's Zara, that fucking scheming cunt!'

'I'm lost. What are you talking about?'

Guy glared at his son. 'She's not fucking dead, you imbecile! The Lanigans haven't done away with her. No, they're fucking *working* with her. For fucking years she's been right under our bloody nose. Why didn't I realize? Only she would have known the deals, the suppliers, and my business. Izzy would have told her everything. Jesus, I just can't believe I assumed she'd been murdered. She's fucking playing us at our own game!'

Hesitantly, Benjamin spoke his innermost thought. 'You'll need to be careful. Don't tell anyone you've messed up—'

Guy tore into him. 'Me?' He poked himself in the chest. 'You should have been holding the reins by now. What are you, forty-one years old? And you're still tied to my belt. And why, I ask myself? It's because you, like fucking Ismail, are completely incompetent. Spoiled, you are. You're a lazy, spoiled bastard. Throwing your weight around, when you have four or five men behind you. I know you, Benjamin. You're a bully when it comes to the weak, and now you have the bare-faced gall to tell me not to admit I made a mistake . . . me . . . bloody me.' He looked for something to throw at his son, but apart from his computer everything was on his polished oak floor. Instead, he banged the desk again. Benjamin, afraid that his father would hurt him, or worse, have a heart attack, got up to leave the room.

'Don't you dare walk away!' screamed Guy. His face was red against his white hair and beard, his eyes glowed green, and the veins bulged from his temples. 'Sit back down! Now!'

Slowly, Benjamin resumed his seat but held his head down in shame.

'I trusted you, Benjamin, to run my business with the help of that prick Ismail, but look at you, the pair of you. Even with Izzy's men now on my side, you've still allowed his business to slip out of our hands. My God, your generation have no stamina. All you could ever provide are clowns, fit for a circus.'

Not wanting to lose face, Benjamin said, 'Look! Now we know she's behind all this, we're one step ahead. I'll have her hunted down and buried.'

Guy's eyes were now bulging with temper. 'You stupid, stupid arsehole!' he screamed. Looking at his son's downcast face and

287

his hands trembling on his lap, Guy took a long, deep breath. If he carried on like this, he would have a coronary. Accordingly, he moderated his tone, but only slightly. 'Hunt her down? Benjamin, you are not fit to wear your tattoo. You are no hunter, I'm afraid. You, my silly boy, are the fucking hunted, mark my words. Zara is far cleverer than you are. My God, you may bully your wife and any other women, but Zara is not some weak female who you can just take down. By Christ, Benjamin, she's slowly but surely built an empire, leaving us to think that we've taken a small piece of hers. It's not the Irish who have taken over the biggest deals, it's fucking her. And you think you can just take her out?'

'Well . . . yes, I mean, we know now. And I'd love to break her long scrawny neck, the evil bitch.'

Guy gave an exasperated laugh. 'Well, take note, Benjamin: Zara is certainly Izzy's daughter, and like him, she'll be one step ahead of you, as she has been for years. Also, know this. She hasn't just got the Irish, she has Regan's firm backing her. So, if you want to take her down, be warned. You'll need to have an army stronger than hers, and a brain far smarter.' He paused as he cast his eye at his son and finally shook his head. 'The only way, my boy, that you'll ever win, is to weaken the firm. Firstly, have Mike Regan's firm out of the way, locked up. You need to grass them up to the police. Then, you must deal with the Lanigans!'

Benjamin felt his heart go in his mouth. This went against the grain and demonstrated just how weak they really were. If their own way of taking over was to grass, rather than using fear and violence, then it clearly proved they were powerless. Still, without her mob backing her, she'd be exposed and on her own, ready for the taking, and he would be the one to show her how wrong she was to have laughed in his face. And whilst he was doing that, he would show his father that he was fit to wear that tattoo.

'Contact your cousin. She'll know what to do, since you're

clearly not capable of even wiping your own arse. She'll be more than eager to sort out Zara's and Regan's firms. After losing nearly all her family at their hands, I'm sure she'll relish getting stuck in. My sister would be turning in her sick bed if she knew what was going on. So, go and find your cousin. She's the only one out of all of you who I can honestly call a hunter. She has more fucking balls than the rest of my family put together.'

In shame, Benjamin lowered his shirt to cover his wrist.

* * *

It was late and the evening air made Ricky shiver. He sighed with disgust when Tatum said it was an old lady's house they were aiming to burgle. At thirteen years old, he was now of an age to know the difference between right and wrong.

The house had been carefully chosen because the sash windows were so old and rickety. Ricky watched as Tatum used his knife to break the lock. He knocked the pivot catch by inserting a knife between the two frames and dragged it along until it hit the lock and it broke open. Tatum lifted the window and nodded to Ricky to climb through. Just as Ricky swung his legs around and was sitting on the windowsill, a police siren sounded. Tatum let go of the top window and because the sash inside had rotted, it no longer held the window up. The frame came crashing down, releasing its glass pane and hitting Ricky squarely across his shoulders. As the separated glass sliced into his back, the pain was instant and took Ricky's breath away. Worse, Tatum didn't have time to lift the remains of the window carefully. Instead, he instinctively put his arms around Ricky's waist and dragged him out. Traumatized and gasping for breath, Ricky was suddenly launched into the back of the truck. Tatum must have used all his strength because Ricky wasn't small anymore. The shock crept into his bones and with the blood seeping through his shirt, he began to shake all over. The journey home seemed to last forever, and so by the time he reached the site, he was faint with pain and sick with fear.

Both Tatum and Tyrone had to help him into Jackie's caravan. It was so dark outside that Tatum hadn't seen the state of Ricky, nor the amount of blood on his clothes. But once inside the caravan, the bright lights showed the effects of the bungled break-in: there was claret all over his own shirt and arms.

Jackie was absolutely raging but not about the state of Ricky. She was swearing and shouting about the blood getting onto her carpet. But then, as Tatum removed his shirt, she gasped. 'Fuck me, Tatum. The boy needs stitches. How the hell can I take him to the hospital after last time?'

Ricky watched the pandemonium through watery eyes, as his mother, who he now saw as just Jackie, flapped around. Then, to his enormous relief, she told Tatum to fetch Mena. Mena was good to him; she would make him better.

If he hadn't been in so much distress, Ricky might have laughed at Jackie for being reprimanded by Mena. Viciously poking Jackie in the chest, Mena called her every name under the sun.

Gently, she laid him on the table and spoke with soft words. After carefully plucking the glass out with tweezers, she used glue to hold the deep cuts together.

Jericho, Mena's husband, then came barging into the van, knocking Jackie out of the way. ''Ere, Mena, give the boy me tablets. I can go a day without painkillers. It'll take the edge off the dear chavi.'

Gratefully, Ricky took the tablets and was out cold within minutes.

Chapter 20

After a few months staying with the Lanigans, Zara had looked for a property of her own. She found a farmhouse for sale, which was only twenty minutes' drive away, and quickly snapped it up. As a cash buyer, with no mortgage, there was no way anyone could trace her whereabouts. Its location was perfect: it afforded excellent views of the surrounding countryside and gave Zara early warning of visitors, be they friend or foe. The security shutters and doors, installed for her own protection, gave her peace of mind. She felt safe in the middle of nowhere in Ireland; it surely would be the last place anyone would expect to find her.

Her office was the room on the right of the house, opposite the living room. It had a window to the left side and one to the front. For security, she installed cameras covering the perimeter of the property, placing one facing the lane, so that she could spot anyone approaching. The lane was more of a dirt track, that ran for three hundred yards up to a minor road, which in turn led to a main road two miles further on. Other than the Lanigans and the postman, very few people knew where she lived.

She enjoyed the solitude and tranquillity, but she was not there to stargaze. Her new home was the hub of the business. And like her father, she was adept with technology and could run her affairs in Ireland without getting her hands dirty.

Davey hadn't quite let go of the reins, but he was slowly handing over his company to Neil and Jed, his youngest son.

Sipping her morning tea, Zara spotted a red BMW gliding along the lane. She smiled when she recognized the driver – Neil had obviously bought himself a flash new motor.

He stopped right outside and came bounding through the door, bigger than ever, wearing a tight T-shirt, a Dublin Hurricanes baseball cap and faded jeans. His hair had grown, the gentle waves now curled around his ears, and the summer sun had kissed his cheeks and given him a glow.

'You look pleased with yaself, Neil.'

She stood up to embrace him. 'Fancy a drink or . . .' She looked him up and down. 'Have you got a date?'

He kissed her cheek. 'How did yer guess?'

If she hadn't been so in love with Mike, she would have been drooling over Neil's strong Irish accent.

'The aftershave, the designer jeans, and the permanent smile on ya face, perhaps?' she replied, with a grin on her face.

He laughed and then blushed. 'Well, yeah, she's a real beauty and not a child either. She's my age, with long blonde hair and big blue eyes.'

'Blimey, you are smitten, if ya know the colour of her eyes.'

Like a teenager, his face looked young and excited.

He followed her to the kitchen where she put the kettle on. 'Coffee?'

He nodded. 'I think she's the one, yer know.'

Zara spun around to face him. 'Wow, it must be serious. How come you haven't mentioned her before?'

He shuffled from foot to foot. 'My last fair lady dumped me at the fecking altar and left me humiliated, so I keep my girlfriends private. Well, that is until now. She wants to get married. In fact, she proposed to me, so . . .' He delved into his back pocket and pulled out a small box. 'What do you think?'

She opened the lid and stared at the dazzling diamond. It was plain but clearly worth a mint.

'One lucky girl, is all I can say.' She handed back the box and her eyes fell to the floor. It was another reminder that she was alone and how she would have to wait another six years for Mike, when she would be older and less attractive. Mike may not even want her by then.

'Oh no, wait till yer meet her, Zara. I'm the lucky one.'

She squeezed his hand. 'Perhaps I'm biased.'

After that initial shaky start, the relationship between the Lanigans and herself had become stronger as each week passed, as they worked together to secure a thriving business all over London. Her knowledge of the underworld and the moneymakers was slowly but surely coming to fruition, and the proceeds were shared equally between herself and the Irish firm. Davey had put out the word that they'd instigated her death and were taking over her business. No one believed otherwise.

'So, when do we meet the future Mrs Lanigan then?'

He laughed again. 'Well, I was going to bring her to meet you yesterday, but she was unwell, so we turned back. She loves Ireland and said she could see herself living here. It was a shame because we'd almost reached the turning to your property when she was hit with a migraine.' He removed his cap and waved it under her nose. 'I'm taking her to see the Hurricanes play baseball in Dub—' He watched the blood disappear from Zara's face, as she stood there aghast.

'What's the matter?'

She took a deep breath. 'Sorry, Neil, it's nothing. I was just thinking about Mike, that's all,' she lied. Why would someone want to turn back so suddenly? She could have popped in, had a drink, and gone.

'Anyway, can you chase up Staffie? The shipment didn't arrive this morning. I checked the port. The ferries were on time and there was no weather disruption,' said Neil, wondering if perhaps he'd just misread Zara's expression.

But he hadn't. Her eyes were suddenly like a bush baby's, her heart in her mouth. 'Fuck! I know that shipment left the coast last night.'

Quickly, she hurried from the kitchen into the office and turned on the computer. Neil was not far behind her. 'What's going on, Zara?'

Neil registered her different expressions as her fingers flew across the keyboard. Scrolling through recent email messages, her face changed from confusion to exasperation. 'Something's fucking wrong. I'm now checking the tracker. I can follow all the vehicles transporting the cargo, so I can pinpoint where they are.'

'I didn't know you could do that.'

She waited for the tracker system to load up on the screen. 'I learned a lot from my father, and I should have been one step ahead. I guess this time I just took my eye off the ball. Fuck it!'

As the screen lit up, her heart beat like a pneumatic drill. With her head in her hands, she gasped, 'Oh no!'

'What, Zara? What am I looking at?'

She pointed to the four flashing lights and the map of London. 'The cargoes have been intercepted. Shit! The fucking police in London have them all . . . Look! That's their forensic headquarters.'

She snatched her phone and checked to see if there were any messages – nothing.

'I hope to God they haven't been nicked. I can't even call because the Filth will trace it. Phone your father and tell him to get the lads in London to swing by the lock-up. And it might be an idea to stay low and perhaps move out of your house. I have no idea how much they have on us.'

294

She ran her hands through her hair and tried to calm her thumping heartbeat.

Neil was mortified. 'Jesus wept. How the fuck did the police know? We were so careful.'

'Well, something's definitely gone tits up. Neil, get on the blower and let's sort this shit out.'

He didn't bother calling his father right away; instead, he spoke to Shamus, his cousin, who was in London, negotiating a deal with the Turks. The phone rang three times before Shamus answered.

'Shamus, get over to Staffie's and see if he and his men have been nicked, will yer?'

Listening to the conversation, Zara was shaking. There was a pause while Shamus spoke urgently to someone else.

'Right. Staffie, Willie and Lou have all been nicked. The old man, Arthur, escaped capture,' replied Shamus, out of breath.

'Get back to Ireland, Shamus, and pull the men out. Something's going down,' said Neil, taking control.

He turned to Zara whose face was as white as a pearl and her eyes filled with dread. 'We need to leave!'

She looked around the office. 'No, listen, Neil. You get going. I need to clear this lot up, just in case the police have my card marked – because we don't know what they know, and everything they need to lock us away for twenty years each is in this room. You go and let me clear up.'

He hesitated, not wanting to leave her behind, but he'd learned over the last few years that she was brilliant under pressure.

'Go, Neil, go!' she hollered, her nerves now completely rattled.

Acting on her demand, he tore away at full throttle.

She couldn't take the contents of the office with her, in case she was stopped, but it was almost painful not to, knowing the score. One of her father's sayings popped into her head: 'Knowledge will always have you one step ahead.'

She grabbed the notebooks containing all the contact details, the files with the accounts, and the specifics of all the restaurants, the owners, the dealers, and literally everything that would bring the whole business to its knees. She'd been converting everything onto a hard drive, so that she wouldn't find herself in this situation, but she'd obviously not done it fast enough. In a panic, she grabbed the paper files and threw them on the open fire. Setting the evidence alight, she ran back to the office and loaded her arms with more, frantically fuelling the fire.

Out of breath, she ripped her computer from the desk and placed it on the fire along with her phone and hard drives. Sweat dripped down her back from the temperature in the room. She couldn't think straight: her head was pounding, and the fumes from the burning plastic were making her gag. She opened the windows and the front door, to let the heat out while she tore around the house, searching for anything else that the police would find of interest. Her bedroom side tables and drawers were clean. She stopped, took a deep breath, and let out a heavy sigh. All done. All that remained was for her to leave, PDQ. Grabbing her gun from under her pillow, she flew back down the stairs and into the living room to find her car keys.

But in her mad mission to get out, she hadn't spotted the two cars that were hammering down the lane to the property. Stepping into the entrance hall, she suddenly clocked the door was wide open. As large as life and as ugly as ever, standing two feet away from her, was the man she detested the most, the only person on the planet who made her blood curdle and her skin crawl – Benjamin Segal.

They both glared at each other with eyes full of contempt. Zara noticed that Benjamin's hands were empty. For a split second, Zara felt she had the upper hand because her gun was tucked in the back of her trousers. She wasn't going to talk or give him a chance to manhandle her, as he'd done in the past. Whipping out the weapon, she held it in front of her, pointing it at his face. She didn't say a word but tried to gather her thoughts. Holding that gun gave her time to digest the last few minutes.

Then it dawned on her: his family had grassed up Staffie and the boys and had, no doubt, sussed that she was working with the Irish firm. But her mind had no time to dwell on recent events – it was the present she had to contend with, in the shape of this ugly bastard who was looking at her right now with a cocky sneer across his face. There was no expression of concern that a gun was pointing at him. Then she wondered if someone had broken in and removed her bullets. It was bizarre, and nigh on impossible. She was clearly paranoid. Yet the way he just stood there, confident and smug, put her on edge. Perhaps that was the plan; maybe Benjamin was shitting himself. But if he was, he was covering it well, with that annoying half-cocked grin that exposed his disgusting rusty railings. Except for a bird tweeting, there was silence. It was the same eerie stillness she always experienced when the snow fell late at night, like the calm before the storm.

The feeling was so uncomfortable, she had to make the first move. Clenching her jaw, she hissed, 'Get back!'

She stepped forward, forcing him to withdraw out of the front door.

'Put the gun down, Zara!' he demanded, his face showing a smug leer.

She took another step forward so she was standing at the threshold. This time, he retreated a little more. But he still didn't look unnerved.

There was no one around except Benjamin in his long brilliant-white shirt and black trousers. She could smell the sweat from his armpits as a soft breeze blew in her direction. It tainted the sweet aroma of the trailing honeysuckle around the front door entrance. His deep throaty chuckle destroyed the sound of the bees and tweeting birds. And his fat, ugly body distorted the view of the wildflowers in the meadow, gently swaying like a sea of colour.

As if her mind was going in slow motion, she watched the fiendish grin on his face expand. Suddenly, along with a whipping sound, came a sudden flash, like a windscreen wiper flicking across her view. She blinked as she felt a hard thump to her wrist. And then she saw his eyes; they were excited and alive with pleasure as a sudden gush of bright red blood shot up his gleaming white shirt and splattered his face.

She heard a heavy thud as an object hit the doorstep. Instantly, it made her look down. Her eyes were wide and terrified, and immediately her whole body convulsed in shock. *No!* Her severed hand was there on the quarry tiles, still gripping the gun. Staring in total and utter disbelief, as the blood spurted like jets, Zara felt no pain, only pure grief. The blood gushed relentlessly, and there was nothing she could do to stop it. The instant shock brought her to her knees while her eyes were focused on the devastating remains of her wrist. Like a thousand pricking needles, her whole body was alive with the utmost fear. Benjamin towered over her, cruelly kicking the severed hand and gun away like a piece of dog turd. She realized there was no sound; she had been shocked into deafness. Then, all at once, she heard a wail; it was coming from behind Benjamin.

'Noooo!'

Holding her arms as if she were cradling a baby, she snapped out of her state of disbelief and looked up to see her brother being held back by a man she didn't recognize. Ismail was screaming and trying to break free from the neck hold. Thrashing around red-faced and angry, he shrieked, 'Let me go, Griff, you bastard, you fucking bastard!'

Then she heard a spiteful, high-pitched woman's voice. 'You're gonna die, you fucking filthy Regan cocksucker bitch. I've been hunting you down for years.'

Zara glared at the attractive, blonde-haired woman. And in that surreal moment, she thought she recognized her.

'Let me fucking go!' screamed Ismail, who was still overpowered.

'Griff, take that poncey prick out of 'ere, will ya,' bellowed the woman. 'I've got more work to do with my samurai sword.' She held up a long, curved silver blade and kissed it.

As if someone had slapped her face, Zara's mind jolted into reality, as everything pieced together. The Segals and the Harmans were working together to bring the Regans down over a stupid belief. And there, just outside the house, being held down, was the back-stabbing traitor – her own fucking brother. Waves of dizziness swept through her body, the world closed in around her, and then, before she could move or say another word, she was unconscious.

The woman kicked Zara in the leg. 'Wake up, bitch. I want to hear your fucking screams, as I slice you to ribbons.'

Benjamin grabbed the enraged woman's arm and yanked her away.

'You shut ya mouth and do as I fucking say,' he growled in a deep voice. 'I need this house turned over. I want to know everything about her plans and her business.'

She shook him free. 'Okay. But then I want her for myself. And don't you ever fucking touch me like that again, ya great fat oaf.'

Ismail was still being held by Griff, Benjamin's brother-in-law. With his tear-stained face pushed onto the flagstones, Ismail was apoplectic with fury, seeing his sister's hand cut off. It broke his heart. His perfectionist attitude – almost OCD, in fact – extended to everything he could see or feel. Now his big sister had lost her hand. He felt almost sick in revulsion, at her and for her in equal measure, knowing his sister was anything but perfect and now she never would be.

There had never been any suggestion that they would kill her; the plan had only been to bring her back to London and make her sign over the properties, as a fair exchange for all the businesses that the Segals believed she'd taken from them. Seeing his sister in this state made him retch. Seconds later, he expelled the contents of his stomach onto the flagstones, partially coating Griff's arm.

Benjamin stepped over Zara, who was now slumped against the outside wall, the blood still oozing from her mutilated wrist. He dragged the woman who was still wielding the sword and took her with him to go upstairs and look for papers, phones, or anything that could yield vital information.

She shot him a look of annoyance. 'I'm fucking warning you, Benjamin. You manhandle me again, and you'll be the next candidate for my sword.'

While Benjamin searched the office, Zara briefly came to. Believing her life was slipping away, she wanted somehow to leave a message, a warning. With her remaining hand, she wrote in the thin layer of dust BENJAMIN SEGAL and underneath she etched HARMAN. With all her strength, she moved her leg to cover it.

Just as she was slipping from consciousness once again, Benjamin came marching through the doorway with his cousin on his heels, still gripping the bloodstained sword.

'Help me to get her inside. I want her alive for answers!'

The blonde woman was almost foaming at the mouth. She only wanted to kill Zara, and everyone linked to her.

Gripping both of Zara's arms, he hoisted her up.

He then laid her on the floor in front of the fire. She couldn't open her eyes, as they were so heavy, but she could hear everything – the crackling of the fire, the stomping of feet, and her brother's voice somewhere in the distance, pleading to be let free.

The woman's voice was hoarse. 'What the hell are you giving her *that* for?'

'I need this bitch alive, and if I don't stop the bleeding, I'll be left with a fucking corpse and no gain.'

Zara felt a sudden prick in her arm. Moments later, her body became heavy, and a warm, comforting feeling swirled around her head. She had been sedated.

Chapter 21

The sound of a ticking clock – tick-tock, tick-tock – pulled Zara from her deep slumber. The smell of disinfectant mixed with a recognizable musky odour made her blink and want to open her eyes. Yet her eyelids were so weighty. There was a sense of peace; maybe it was the smell or the gentle rhythmic sound of a grand-father clock. She was back at home in Izzy's old house, or perhaps it was a dream. Her fingers gently felt the soft bedsheets, but there was something not right. She was gripped by a terrifying sensation: with her right hand, she could move and feel brushed cotton, but why couldn't she move her left hand? Then, a cold chill entered the pit of her stomach. As she attempted to lift her arms, a horrific realization gripped her around the throat, trapping her breath. She was tied down. The surge of panic that ripped through her forced her eyes to open. The room was a blur, but when she turned her head to the side, there, up against the window, were the deep red velvet drapes. Then, when she lifted her head, her eyes focused on what was tying her to the bed, and she blinked furiously. 'No!' she screamed, as she saw the heavily bandaged wrist. There was no hand. The past came flooding back. Her breathing intensified and her whole body shook. Her eyes darted around the room, looking for someone. Her brother. He was the last person she remembered seeing, his face held down as he screamed. It was all coming back, piece by piece. Her home in Ireland, Benjamin, and that woman wielding the long sword.

Yet she couldn't understand why she was now in her father's house and tied to a bed with her handless wrist dressed.

She peered more closely and assumed that a doctor or surgeon must have attended to her because the dressing had clearly been done by a professional. Strangely, she experienced no pain, just a light-headed and sick feeling.

Seconds later, she heard the door being opened and instantly closed her eyes.

That voice made her stomach turn over. It was a dry, gritty sound that made her shudder. Benjamin!

'Don't you think by now she'll be well enough to speak? It's been a month.'

Shocked to the core, Zara wanted to open her eyes; however, something told her to keep them shut – to pretend she was asleep. Her inner survival mechanism was at work.

'Benjamin, I don't like this. I would prefer to give back all the money you've paid me and walk away. This doesn't sit right with me. And this house, it's like Izzy is watching me from the grave.'

'Palo, you've had the money, and I don't do fucking loans, so you will continue to do as I say.'

Zara knew precisely who Palo was. He was her father's doctor. He was a weak old man who had been struck off thirty years previously, yet the community still went to him for help rather than be put on a two-week waiting list to see their own doctor.

'Benjamin, she's not well enough for me to bring her around. We must keep her sedated until that wound has healed. I have another course of antibiotics. I'll feed them in her drip.'

There was a pause, making Zara wonder what was going on.

'Benjamin, I will continue to ensure that the girl is well and cared for, but you must leave me to it. I don't want you in the room again.'

'Since when do you give the orders?' growled Benjamin.

'There are many things, Benjamin, which I can turn away from, and not concern myself with, but there are certain times when my soul will override my fear and this is one of them.'

'Oh, shut up, you silly old man! Your job is to make her well. Tell me when she's ready to speak.'

'No! Benjamin, I will not be quiet. I don't like you hovering around or the way you look at her. It defies belief, and I won't allow it. I know what goes through your mind. It's disgusting. I will keep quiet about your plan. However, Benjamin, taking advantage of a woman under sedation, I will not keep quiet about. Do you understand me?'

It was the first time Zara had ever heard Palo raise his voice.

'You're going mad and blind, old man. Just get her better, I said!'

Zara listened as the door closed, and then she heard Palo's soft voice. 'I'm so sorry, child. Please forgive me.'

She felt the needle prick. Once again, she was unconscious.

* * *

One month later

Her eyes flickered, hearing her brother's voice. 'Zara, wake up,' he gently whispered.

His tone instilled an air of trust, but as soon as she opened her eyes wide, her vision was clear. Ismail was being held back by Guy. She was no longer in her father's bedroom. Her heart sank. Her body trembled. It was over: there was no escape.

Oh, Izzy, why did you have to play James Bond and build a secure underground room? She knew this room so well. Only Izzy, Ismail and herself had known about it. It was designed and built years previously, when he had been part of a more prominent firm. It wasn't a dark dungeon, far from it – Izzy would never have had anything as ugly as that in his home – and nor had he ever used it to hold anyone hostage. He turned it into a guest suite, as he called it. It consisted of a bedroom, bathroom, and a living room with solid wood cabinets, which contained books, games, an antique chess set and solitaire. There were no windows and no doors from which to escape. The only entrance into the area was a reinforced steel frame, with heavy-duty metal bars. He had been so smart and a real genius when it came to architecture. And such irony. If only he'd known that his invention would be used to hold his own daughter prisoner, he would have cut off his own hand. She closed her eyes again and pretended to be asleep.

'So now you are with us, Zara, it's only fitting that we share with you our plans because, my dear, they include you,' said Guy, as he shook her shoulder. 'Benjamin, untie her arms and sit her up. Like I told you before, Zara, your father wanted us to work together.'

She felt the ties being removed and Benjamin's heavy hand roughly pull her into a sitting position. Her body was weak, having lain in a bed for so long. Her only blessing was Palo, who had ensured that she was kept clean and moved constantly, so that she didn't suffer from bed sores or, worse, blood clots. However, being as weak as a kitten, she flopped all over the place. Even her eyes rolled around as if she were drunk.

Palo, who was standing behind Guy, stepped forward. 'You cannot just move her like that. She is very fragile. Her muscles will be like mush. She needs time to build up her strength. The drugs will have affected her brain, and so she will need time. You cannot just ask her questions and expect a lucid answer.' He hurried over, moving Benjamin out of the way. Looking directly into Zara's eyes, he winked. 'She may not ever really recover, you know. Patients kept sedated for so long can suffer brain damage.'

Zara heard the message loud and clear.

'Do you know where you are and what your name is?' he winked again.

With her head wobbling as though she were pissed, she slurred a wordless reply.

Guy and Benjamin were standing back, waiting for Palo to assess the situation.

'Do you know who this man is?' He turned and pointed to her brother, who was hunched up like a scared rat.

She allowed a dribble to run from her lips. Slowly, she shook her head.

'How many fingers am I holding up?' He showed two.

She lolled her head again and drooled once more.

Palo gently laid her back down. 'This process cannot be rushed, as you can see. Let's get her comfortable and give her some soup. She needs to build up her strength for her brain to heal. If it ever will, that is.'

Guy screeched, 'She lost her fucking hand! She didn't smash her bloody head.'

'She's been sedated for two months, so, therefore, the brain can suffer damage. If you remember, I didn't have the equipment needed to help her. It was your idea to keep everything that way. If she'd been in the hospital, the wrist would have healed in no time. You, Benjamin, may have saved her life by burning the wound, but you also caused a serious infection that has taken months to clear. And we cannot rule out that there could be severe consequences even if her brain does recover. So, please be gentle. She could still die.'

'Enough, Palo!' bellowed Guy.

When her feet first touched the floor, she realized just how weak she was; her legs wouldn't hold her up at all. She must have lost so much weight too because Palo and Ismail had no problem getting her into the bed; she was as light as a feather.

Just before they left, Ismail whispered in her ear, 'Not so big now, are you, dear sister?'

'Ismail!' screamed Benjamin. 'Get out, ya little jerk-off.'

She watched her brother scurry away like a pathetic rodent

after his cheese. She would never have imagined that her own flesh and blood would have allowed this sick, twisted game to go on. Her only option, she believed, was to play dumb and hope and pray that someone would find her. And it was her most fervent wish that the names in the dust weren't obliterated.

* * *

Mike left solitary confinement and was escorted by Eugene to the visiting room. The last visit from his father had knocked him sideways. The lock-up had been raided, the cars en route were confiscated, and the boys were in Brixton Prison awaiting trial. Neil had constantly tried to contact Zara. Receiving no response, he'd headed back to her house the very next morning only to find bloodstained floorboards and the remains of a computer in the open fire. He also discovered the name 'Harman' etched in the dust by the front door. There seemed to have been another name written there, but it appeared to have been disturbed by footprints, making it impossible to read.

Mike was heartbroken when he received a call from Neil Lanigan; his son dead, and now his one true love missing – probably murdered. He understood the saying, God pays back debts without money. None of it made any sense. Why, for example, would she leave a sign inscribed in the dirt? As far as he was aware, all the Harmans were dead. He racked his brains, night after night, until he fell into a tortured sleep.

The Lanigans had exhausted every avenue looking for her. They raided firms and interrogated everyone who had tried to take over Zara's manor, but they only found pathetic Jewish men who knew nothing. Davey now had most of the businesses run by his own men. But as to the whereabouts of Zara, they were hitting brick walls.

As Mike's name was called, he entered the visiting room, and for a second, he didn't know who he was looking for. Because although he'd spoken to Davey Lanigan on the phone many times, he'd never actually met him in person. The older man, smartly dressed in a navy-blue suit and a light-blue shirt, waved across at him. Mike could see the hardness in the man's eyes before he even had a chance to take a seat.

For his part, Davey was almost in awe of Mike: just his imposing size and manner deserved admiration. As soon as they shook hands, Davey could feel the strength in him. He hadn't met many like Mike.

'It's a shame, Mr Regan, that we meet under such . . . let's just say frustrating circumstances.'

Mike nodded. 'I won't let this go, you know. If there's another Harman left alive, I'm going to hunt him down, and I'll make a solemn promise to you now that he'll be ripped apart with my bare hands. They killed my son and now they have taken my . . .' He paused and gritted his teeth. 'My girl.'

'She loved you, Mr Regan. With all her heart, that woman adored you.'

'You talk as if she's dead.'

'I'm afraid I do. With me hand on me heart, I can swear to yer that I've done everything in my power to find her. No bastard knows a thing. This Segal family you mentioned on the phone were paid a visit. The son is one ugly pig. He cried like a baby and swore he loved her like a sister and wanted whoever had hurt her to pay with their lives. He even put up a hundred grand for any information regarding her whereabouts, or the name of the person behind it. It came to light that some of our business was once theirs, but they're nothing but a few idiots who dabbled in the big boys' game. So, I don't believe they're involved.'

'Did you find out who grassed my men?'

Davey shook his head. 'No, that's still a mystery, I'm afraid.'

Mike rubbed his face and sighed heavily. 'So, what now, Mr Lanigan?'

Davey clasped his large hands together. 'For now, we back off and leave well alone, carry on our business as usual, and, like everything in life, the truth will out.'

With his face screwed up, Mike glared. 'But what if they have her? What if she's hurt?'

Davey patted Mike's hand. 'See reason, Mr Regan. It's been six months now. If that blood at the property was hers, then we need to be realistic. She's probably dead.' He stared, hoping that his statement wouldn't have Mike flipping the table and going off on one.

'What about her brother, Ismail?'

Davey shook his head. 'He's just as concerned. The bloke's a proper nancy boy. He added another hundred grand as a reward, so it's like the skullcap and slipper brigade are all on the lookout for her too.' He straightened his jacket and leaned one arm on the table. 'Look, all I can promise is that whatever we profit from, I'll make sure your firm has its fair share. The minute I hear anything regarding Zara, you'll be the first to know.'

Mike was absorbing those words. 'I'm out in six years, if I don't do anything stupid to be put down the block again. I'll join you then, and I'll want some muscle. I'm going on the hunt to find who this Harman bloke is, because he sure isn't a fucking ghost. And I know Zara. She's no fool.'

'Mr Regan, no disrespect to her reputation, but what if the culprit left the name in the dust to throw us all off the scent?' Davey watched as Mike seemed to drift off to another world.

'No, I know she wrote that name because . . .' His thoughts went back to a time on the beach when they were soaking up the sun and she showed him her note, *Love me forever, Mikey Regan*, in the sand.

'She used her finger to scribble messages on my arm and make me guess what she'd written. It was a silly game but . . . it's what she did. So, I know she wrote that.'

'It's hard, Mr Regan, and losing your son as well, but I'll

make a promise that I'll not stop seeking out the truth, that I won't.'

* * *

For weeks, Zara was fed and handed tablets by Palo. He was often watched through the bars by her brother. She tried desperately hard to get her strength up, while still playing the brain-damaged victim. Her only ally was Palo, the old man with the compassionate smile. She never spoke a word but just did as he instructed. The exercises were painful to start with, but they were certainly strengthening her muscles. With his aid, she could stand and get to the bathroom, where at least she had a private moment, not overlooked by Ismail or the fat creep Benjamin.

The rattling of the metal door made her open her eyes. It was Palo, with a clean set of towels and a soft cotton tracksuit, which he placed on the chair beside the bed.

He walked into the bathroom, ran the bath taps, and returned with the same kind smile.

'A warm bath will ease your muscles. I have added some bath salts. Would you like me to help you or are you strong enough to walk unaided?'

Her eyes shot to the door and her shoulders relaxed. They were alone. She leaned closer. 'I can walk now, thank you so much. Palo, can you help me to get out of here?' she whispered in his ear, keeping one eye on the door.

He looked into her eyes and a sad expression darkened his face. 'I wish that I could. God help me, I wish. They have my home watched constantly, they will hurt my daughters. Just don't let on you can speak.'

'Why are they keeping me alive if they think I'm brain-damaged? I'm no use to them.'

He looked over his shoulder and leaned forward again. In a

conspiratorial aside, he whispered, 'Ismail has given his solicitor a letter saying that if he dies it will expose what they have already done to you, and to any potential harm coming your way. He wants to keep you alive. I think he feels very guilty for what he has done, as do I, Zara, as do I.'

'No, Palo, you have nothing to feel sorry or guilty for, but Ismail wants me alive to ease his conscience, not because he cares about me.'

'I know, Zara, I know.'

She smiled to herself. Ismail really was a weak man; her father was so right. She didn't know who she hated more: Ismail, Benjamin, or the blonde woman who cut off her hand and whose face now haunted her. It was over – there was no way she could break out. With only one hand, how the hell would she fight to get out? Her food was minimal, so her strength was weak. Racking her brains night after night, she tried to formulate a means of escape, but nothing came to mind – nothing that would work anyway.

'Is there anything you want? Because there is nothing I can do except tell them you need my care. I will try to find reasons to visit you as often as I can get away with.'

Zara wanted to hug the old man, but she couldn't risk anyone eyeballing her through the door. They would have her in an interrogation chair.

'Will they keep me locked away for good? Is that the plan?'

He nodded and his eyes filled up. 'I'm so sorry.'

'Oh, well,' she sighed in resignation. 'Do you think you could get me a television?'

His face lit up. 'Yes, I can use the excuse that it's for rehabilitation.'

Once Palo left, she gingerly walked to the bathroom. After struggling to remove her nightdress with her right hand, she stepped into the warm bath. It was her only solace. As she immersed herself, she had an overwhelming urge to take her own life. *What was the point of her existence now?* she thought. She looked at her bandaged stump and began to unravel the dressing. She hadn't seen what was underneath. Very carefully, she unwound the bandage until the last piece fell away. She didn't want to look at first, but then her eyes were drawn to her hideously scarred arm. Her heart sank. She was left without a hand and with the most horrific burn scars imaginable. What remained of her skin was black. She lay back in the bath and closed her eyes. She would have to put Mike out of her head. He wouldn't want her now. Those unsightly wounds made her feel sick, and she wouldn't ever want him to see them either. She sighed. What was she thinking? She was trapped, anyway. No one would ever find her. Izzy had made this basement escape-proof. Palo had his family to worry about. And because her bastard of a brother was so afraid of Guy, she would never talk him around. She was a prisoner, and unless she had a lucky break, this would be her home from now on. A tear trickled down her cheek and added to the bathwater.

That's how she saw herself – an insignificant drop in the ocean, with the world continuing around her, while she endured the confinement of this small suite with just herself for company. She knew she would eventually go insane.

'Aw, Dad, if you're looking down on me, I could really do with your help.'

PART FOUR

Chapter 22

2014, five years later

Waiting anxiously in the prison visiting room brought it home to Eric what he'd actually done. Looking around the cold, suffocating room, he wondered why on earth his brother would ever forgive him – Christ, he wouldn't have, if it had been the other way around.

As soon as Mike entered the room, Eric felt awkward and totally embarrassed. His brother looked rough, unshaven and dull-faced, the worst he'd ever seen him. Unexpectedly, Mike smiled and held out his arms. Eric held back the tears, but the emotion was written all over his face, as he rose from his chair and instantly hugged his brother.

'I'm so sorry, Mikey. Look, I know sorry doesn't cut it. I was scared but—'

Mike interrupted him. 'Eric, stop. I understand. It's okay, you know. It's all in the past. You didn't have to follow the business, you're your own free man, and maybe what we were doing wasn't right for you. I should have listened and not have taken the piss when you said you wanted to go straight. Admitting you were scared was the bravest thing you could have done. Anyway, it's all behind us now.' He took a deep breath and exhaled. 'You're my brother, my own flesh and blood. Ten years of being tortured, what with my son and then Zara, well, it puts things into perspective.'

Eric gave Mike a sheepish smile.

Mike noticed how big Eric had become. 'Spain is obviously treating you well. Are ya working out?'

'Yeah . . . Listen, Mikey. I've thought long and hard about things. At first, with you getting nicked, it killed me. I had to get away. Then, when Dad told me about Ricky, I just kept beating myself up. I blamed myself for taking on Travis. If I hadn't, Ricky wouldn't have been murdered. But, by then, it was too late to face you. What I'm really trying to say is, I felt so useless and guilty but . . .'

'Eric, it doesn't matter now—'

'Listen, Mikey, please let me finish, right? I did beat meself up, and I didn't tell anyone, but I came back, kept away from the usual haunts and the regular faces, and I tried to do some digging myself. I know the thought must have crossed your mind that it was me that grassed you up, after our fight.'

Mike sat back with his head tilted to the side. He noticed how his brother's speech was both more controlled and assertive – that had never been the case before. Mike put it down to the fact that, at long last, Eric had become his own person, stepping out from the subjugating effect of Mike's forceful personality. There was maturity there, and, yes, wisdom.

'Nah, Eric, never. We were annoyed, I grant ya, because you fucked off when I needed you most, but we never thought it was you that grassed. I don't know how much Dad told you, but we believe there's someone out there who was determined to have me and the boys put inside. Well, they fucking won. But, trust me, when I get out, I will hunt the bastards down and kill 'em. My boy and my poor Zara, I still think about them all the time. Yet Davey Lanigan and his son Neil have turned London upside down to find out what happened to her, and not a single fucking soul knows. So, trust me when I say I will be on the hunt as soon as I get out. Then, my dear brother, you can help me find who is responsible.'

'And, Bro, I will be holding her down while you rip her heart out.'

Like an electric shock, Mike jolted his head '*Her*? What do you mean . . . her?'

'I think I know who's behind it all.'

Eric bit his bottom lip. He could hear the sound of his own heartbeat. 'It's my ex.'

'Don't be daft. That silly slip of a girl, she's just like Jackie. She's all tits and extensions. Look, Eric, she may have fucked you off, but seriously—'

Again, Eric cut off Mike, and, surprisingly, he rolled up his long sleeve and shoved his right wrist under Mike's nose. 'Have you ever seen this before?'

Mike peered closely at what at first looked like a tattooed symbol before he realized it was simply drawn using a biro. 'What is it?'

Eric held his wrist there. 'Take a bleedin' good look. Do you recognize it at all?'

Mike looked at him in surprise and then studied the symbol, deep in thought. And then something hit him. 'Er . . . I think I do. Why?'

'Where, Mikey? Where did you see it?'

'It was in an old photo. It was part of Doris Harman's album. Funny, 'cos that photo bugged me, and I never knew why. It showed the Harman brothers and some other bloke who was only partially in the picture. He was baring his tattooed forearm. Eric, tell me, what is this all about?'

'Mikey, when Tracey came back from your gaff all scratched up, something strange happened. I hugged her and she went stiff. Now, Tracey was the sweetest girl, all feminine and cute, but she changed. She just shrugged me off and went upstairs to get cleaned up.'

Mike screwed his nose up. 'Eric, just 'cos she shrugged you off don't mean it's strange. Perhaps she was still fuming. Well, she definitely was when she left my house—'

'No, wait, let me finish. She was upstairs for ages, and when she returned to the living room with her bags packed, she really looked a different person. I remember her face and the way she stood there. For a moment, I was looking at someone else. She had no make-up on, her hair was tied back, and it was just the way she held herself. She was dressed in a tracksuit and trainers with her shoulders back. She looked through me, as if I was a piece of shit. Look, I know all this seems a bit mad, but I swear to you, I didn't recognize her. Then, when she spoke with this serious, deeper voice, I had to rub my eyes. It was this look on her face. Honestly, Mike, I was freaked out. She was cocky, but not like Jackie in one of her little tantrums. No, this was something else entirely. She looked like some weird psychopath. Her eyes were somehow mocking me, and she said, "I'm done here. It was nice knowing ya." Then she left.'

'Eric, she'd probably had enough. It was all a mess. What with Jackie pulling out her hair and me throwing her out of my house, she probably wanted to break all ties.'

'No, wait, listen, will ya. I never could get my head around it until a while ago. I was looking through some photos, and there she was with her arm around me. She always wore a tight bangle and never took the thing off. Anyway, when I looked closer at the photo, the bangle had moved up, and there was this tattoo on her right wrist. I copied the symbols, thinking she'd had some bloke's name removed by laser and hadn't finished the job properly. But it baffled me. I got a magnifying glass out and looked more closely and then I wrote down the symbols. Something made me do it. I guess some things just didn't add up about her. I remember something Dad once said. It was "Keep ya friends close and ya enemies closer." Anyway, I couldn't for the life of me work out who would have grassed you because there was only us that knew about the pit.'

Mike held up his hand. 'Nah, Eric, Zara's men knew too. They helped me to get rid of Scottie's body down that pit.'

'Mikey, Tracey was the spy. She knew where the pit was.'

Mike's face was full of thunder. 'You what?'

With his head lowered in shame, his voice a mere whisper, he replied, 'I was gonna marry her. I loved her, and ya know what it's like. Ya kinda show off a bit. Either that or it was pillow talk. She always seemed interested in me. And I know it sounds soft, but she was probably the only one that ever took an interest. Well, so I thought at the time. Little did I know, she was fucking bleeding me dry for information. I swear to God, I had no idea who she was.'

Mike frowned. 'So who is she, then? If she ain't fucking Tracey Man, the divvy blonde tart, who is she?'

'Mikey, think about it. Tracey *Man* . . . or could it really be Tracey *Har*man?'

Instantly, Mike went cold and goose bumps covered his skin. 'Harman. She's a fucking Harman!' His eyes nearly popped out of his head. 'That's the little blonde girl in Doris's album, sitting on Ronnie Harman's lap.' It took a few seconds to absorb it all before his mind went into overdrive. 'Carmella! Jesus, Eric, she's Carmella's daughter. Why didn't I think of it? They're not all fucking dead, then. Carmella and this Tracey are still alive. Zara scribbled a name in the dirt before she went missing. Harman. I thought it was another man, but it's not. It's Tracey's surname.'

Mike leaned back on his chair and sighed. 'But I still can't see how soppy Tracey could ever take down Zara. Tracey grassing me up for Scottie's murder is one thing, but, seriously, that tart wouldn't be able to take down Zara . . .' He gulped back the emotion in his throat. 'Not with the amount of blood left at the place. She must have had backing. I know Zara too well, and

Tracey wouldn't be powerful enough to take her on.' He suddenly cleared his throat and straightened up. 'What the fuck is really going on here? I get she may have grassed because – all said and done – we killed her family. But why hurt Zara? What the fuck does she have to do with it? And, as for the tattoo, I don't understand it.'

'Neither did I at first. But I spoke with Dad about the past because I knew he'd had a rift, years ago, with Frank. He said that he thought, back then, that the Harmans were part of something bigger. He had a big firm himself, and ya know Dad, he was clever, but he used some serious violence to fuck the Harmans off. I tell ya, Mikey, they were sly, and they did try hard to take out Dad's men, but they must have realized they were up against a force far bigger than themselves. So they backed off. Well, until now, that is.'

'It's just unbelievable that Frank's sons and Ronnie's daughter would want to carry on in their parents' shoes. Jesus, we're talking fucking decades ago.'

Eric gave a cheeky grin. 'Well, we did. Look at us, Mike. We're one big family; like father, like sons.'

Mike slowly nodded. 'Maybe, but still, what's this tattoo all about?'

'I dunno yet, but I'll try and find out. Maybe one of the lads has seen it before.'

'Okay, Eric, you see what you can find and keep me informed. I'll do some digging myself.'

Eric looked Mike squarely in the eyes. 'Do you forgive me, then?'

Mike nodded.

'Am I back with the firm?'

'You were never off it, Eric. You just had a break, that's all. Now go and get a tea and grab a serviette. I can't take anything back inside with me, but if you wet that paper and transfer that symbol onto my arm, no one can nick me.' He winked and then smiled.

Eric felt his heart beat faster; he'd missed his brother with all his heart and was well chuffed that Mike had forgiven him.

After a long and heartfelt hug, they said their goodbyes. Mike returned to the wing, with his cuffs rolled back so as not to smudge the barely discernible symbols. The officer assigned to the visits glanced down at Mike's arm. He had clocked Mike rubbing the wet tissue on his wrist. 'What's all that about then, Regan?' He nodded to Mike's new transferred symbols.

Mike grinned. 'It's an old family coat of arms. Looks good, don't it?'

The officer screwed up his nose as he peered at it.

'Uh, yeah, but that ain't your coat of arms though, is it?'

'What are ya on about?'

'Look at it. It's written in Hebrew.'

Stopping dead, Mike turned to the officer, lifting his wrist for the man to look closer. 'Ya what? Do you actually know what this means, then?'

The officer peered more closely and smiled. 'Yeah, I do, because, you see, I'm Jewish myself.'

Mike's eyes widened. 'Well, go on, then, mate. What does it say?'

The pale-faced young officer gravely replied, 'Hunter.'

Mike screwed his face up. 'Are you sure?'

He slowly nodded. 'Yes, I'm fluent in Hebrew.'

The inmate behind Mike tutted; he was itching to get back to his cell. The officer quickly moved them on.

* * *

Gloria was busy cleaning out the fridge when Eric came up behind her and made her jump. 'Aw, Gawd, Eric, I could've had a heart attack.'

He smiled at his mother's attempted look of annoyance, but she could never hold that look for very long.

'Put the kettle on, Eric. I'll call ya father in. He's just mowing the lawn. Why he won't get a gardener is beyond me.'

Eric knew why his father liked the peace and quiet. Gloria could talk the hind legs off a donkey.

Arthur turned off the mower and then stamped his feet to remove the grass before entering the kitchen. 'Hello, son, how did the visit go?'

Eric placed a mug of tea under his father's nose. 'Well, Dad, it couldn't have gone better. Why I've been so worried about how Mike would react to me after all these years, I'll never know. But I'm sure he's forgiven me. Anyway, I need to talk to you about something.' He gave his mother a look, hinting he wanted to discuss something privately with Arthur.

'Right, I've some laundry that needs sorting,' she replied, knowing it was business.

Once they were sitting in the dining room, Eric turned to his father and rolled up his sleeve. 'This tattoo. Have you seen it before?'

Arthur grabbed Eric's wrist and pulled it closer to his face. 'Yeah, something like that.' His face dropped. 'That was many years ago, though.'

'Who else had this tattoo?'

Arthur shook his head and stared off into space.

* * *

It was 1959 and he was ten years old. It was cold, but he was dressed in grey shorts and a holey pullover. He was running through the backstreets, from the Old Kent Road on his way to Bermondsey. The night was drawing in and the darkness descended suddenly. Charlie Ritz, Teddy Stafford and Big Lou Baker were on his heels. They were all laughing and running at the same time. Two Jewish lads, who were younger than Arthur, had also joined in the fun of knock down ginger.

Arthur had knocked at the door and turned to run, but a colossal giant of a man almost caught him. The man was furious, screaming and shouting at him. Arthur ran and was followed by the others until he was out of breath and his lungs burned from the cold. Behind them, they could hear the deep voice of the monster – as they saw him. But as young as they all were, they could run fast, and they did. As soon as they ran past the corner pub and into their street, they looked back, gasping for breath.

Arthur wondered where the two Jewish boys had gone. It was a shock to discover, two days later, that they'd both been killed with lethal blows to the head. Arthur and his friends were brought in for questioning because they'd been seen leaving the scene, but they were never charged.

When he reached the age of nineteen, Arthur was attacked in the middle of the night as he stepped off the bus. The attack was brutal and landed him in hospital with concussion, but he knew that the man who beat him had meant to kill him. It was the deathly whisper in his ear, saying, 'You and your firm will forever be paying for the murder of those two boys.' In among the pounding fists, he saw the tattoo on the man's wrist.

After that scary night, the lads wouldn't venture out anywhere alone. And it was the last time he mixed with the Jews again because he knew that the man who had attacked him was Jewish, and probably a relative of one of the dead boys.

He'd been unable to make sense of it then, and he'd not thought much about it since; that was, until now, when he saw the ink symbols on Eric's wrist.

The tattoo became a blurred memory, until one night, after Kenneth Keller was shot in the back, a note was shoved through his own letterbox. It had similar symbols. Underneath was written 'one down'. Teddy, Charlie and Big Lou all received a similar note.

Yet, as the years rolled by, it was viewed as a stupid threat. Arthur's biggest problem was the Harmans meddling in his business, squealing and grassing where they could – all of which was dealt with by Arthur's firm, swiftly and brutally, until the problem – or so it seemed – went away.

* * *

'Dad, this tattoo was on my ex, Tracey, but where have you seen it before?'

Gloria had overheard the conversation and couldn't help herself. She came into the dining room with her basket of wet laundry still in her arms. 'Let me see.'

Eric lifted his wrist and watched as her eyes widened. 'I know that tattoo. Carmella, that fucking snoopy bitch, had one on her right wrist too. I always thought what a bleeding ugly thing it was. I never asked her what it meant, though.'

Arthur was still recollecting the past. Without warning, he said, 'Glor, where are the old albums, love?'

She rolled her eyes, placed the basket on the carpet, and opened the large teak cabinet. 'There they are.'

Arthur glanced over her shoulder, and then, as she stepped aside, he pulled out the red album. Quickly, he flicked through the pages.

'Here it is. I kept that note. I dunno why. It just bothered me, I guess.' He placed the heavy album on the table and pointed to the faded note that had browned at the edges.

Eric looked at his wrist and then back at the note. It showed many differences, but the symbols were similar.

The phone rang, making all three of them jump. Gloria hurried over and answered it.

'Mum, put Eric on, if he's there.'

Gloria instantly recognized that her son had something urgent to say.

324

She called Eric to the phone. 'It's your brother.'

'Mikey?'

'Listen, I ain't got long. That tattoo means "The Hunter" in Hebrew. It's the same one I saw in old Mrs Harman's album. The more I look at it, the more I remember it. Do me a favour. Check out Ismail and ask him if he knows who else would have this tattoo. It's got to be linked, and he can read Hebrew. The little wanker's Jewish. He told Davey Lanigan that he would do anything to help find his sister.'

'Mikey, listen. Dad recognized the symbols too. It's a long story but it's to do with Kenny getting murdered and—'

He didn't finish. Arthur took the phone from him. 'Mikey, I have an idea what's going on. Do yourself a favour and keep your nose clean and stay out of trouble. I need you out on parole.'

'Dad, what the fuck's going on? . . . Dad?'

Arthur placed the phone down. 'Son, you and I have a little bit of business to settle.'

Eric was a kid again, with his father taking control. Just his firm deep voice was enough not to allow anyone to backchat, no matter how big they were.

'Hang on a minute.' Pulling out his phone, Eric connected it to the internet and started to look up the symbols. It wasn't easy because the Hebrew alphabet didn't translate simply into English. However, with a little patience, he finally worked it out. He translated the words "The Hunter" into Hebrew and *voila* – it matched the symbols on the tattoo. So Mike was right. Then he searched the ones that were on the note and put them together. His mouth went dry as he looked at those words: *We will hunt you down until you and your family are no more.*

He showed his father the screen. 'Look. That's what the note says, but why?'

Arthur said nothing and left the room before returning a few seconds later with his coat. 'This bullshit will end today. I thought this underhanded battle was dead and buried when the Harmans backed off, but I guess I was wrong. They've carried out this vendetta to destroy my family, and I will find out who's behind this, if it's the last damn thing I do.'

Gloria was open-mouthed. She hadn't seen or heard her husband talk that way for thirty years. The look in his eyes and the tone of his voice took her back to when he was a fighter, a respected and powerful man, with a firm that most wouldn't dare to cross. In some ways, she felt alive again, but the cautious side of her feared for his safety. 'Wait, Arthur,' she said, as she tugged his arm. 'What are you going to do?'

He softened his eyes and kissed her cheek. 'I'm going back to the beginning, starting with Ismail Ezra, Izzy's son. I have a way of getting answers, and you know me, Gloria. If they want a fucking war, then they'll have one.'

Eric was as shocked as his mother. He could now see how Mike took after his father. 'Wait! Dad, I'm coming with you. I let Mikey down once before but I ain't doing it again.'

Arthur looked his son up and down, and before he voiced any words of doubt he had about his son, he stopped. This was Eric's chance to show his worth. 'Okay. Let's get Teddy and Big Lou.'

Eric frowned. 'But they're . . .'

'Old? Yeah, I know, but trust me, son, they ain't stupid. And they're still dangerous, mark my words.'

Eric wasn't about to argue. He grabbed his coat and was about to follow his father out to the car.

'Wait!' called Gloria. As Eric turned to face his mother, she handed him a gun. 'Give this to your father. It's loaded.'

Eric grinned with amusement. His dear old mother was more involved in his father's antics than he'd ever realized.

As soon as Gloria heard them drive away, her heart was in her mouth.

She sat at the table and stared at the open page of the photo album, the threatening note. Why Arthur had kept it, she had absolutely no idea. She sniffed back her tears and flicked over the page. It was an old album consisting mainly of photos of Mike and Eric as little boys. Her eyes suddenly focused on a photo that she thought she had chucked out. It was of Carmella Harman, her sneaky home help. She had been mortified when they'd realized from Doris's photo album and the letter she'd left Arthur that her so-called trusted friend was a snoopy bitch. All those years of not knowing who'd been behind her Arthur's incarceration, and of course the murder of his mate Kenny and the supposed suicide of Monty – until now. Now, they knew different – Monty was murdered.

The photo showed Carmella holding Mike's hand. It was a summer's day, and Carmella had taken the boys from under Gloria's feet.

She pulled back the cellophane and removed the photo, but just as she was about to rip it to shreds, she noticed the unusual house and the little blonde-haired girl in the background. They were standing in the front garden. Gloria's eyes widened. It was Carmella's home. A big posh house too. How they'd never sussed that Carmella was a plant was beyond them. She'd never needed pin money – a few shillings for helping out – she must have been loaded. Gloria stared again, and then like a light bulb flicking on, she recognized the house. It was unusual, probably art deco. She'd only ever seen houses like this one in Dansōn Park, where she used to take the boys every so often. It was unmistakable, with the flat roof and 1920s windows. Her heart began to beat rapidly as she made a decision. She could be wrong, but what the hell did she have to lose?

Quickly, she grabbed her phone, her keys, and her secret weapon: a small handgun she'd found in the drawer years ago. It hadn't been on the property when the police raided the home. That was a bad time. It was just before Arthur was nicked and sent to prison for three years.

She brushed her hair, slapped on her lipstick, and put on some decent flat shoes, before sliding the gun down the back of her trousers and heading out of the door. It was still daylight – just. She knew exactly where she was going, so, without another thought, she tore away in her little BMW 1 Series – a birthday present from Arthur.

She pulled into Danson Road, close to the park, and slowly crawled along. She looked at the photo again and there, just across the street, was the house. It was the same except for the outside, where everything had been freshly painted and the garden all paved. She stared for a while and took a few deep breaths to calm her racing heart. 'Oh, Glor, don't be silly. The Harmans may have moved on years ago,' she said aloud.

Staring at the photo, her anger increased. All those years, the Harmans had held some grudge and tried to destroy her family's life, and now they'd succeeded. The thought of poor little Ricky, who'd left them without even a headstone to lay flowers at his grave, consumed her sense of rationality. The intense fury shot through her and nothing would stop her now if she came face-to-face with Carmella fucking Harman or her daughter, the bitch. Just as she was about to step out of her car, a black SUV pulled partially into the drive. Gloria was still raging. Out stepped a slim woman with mousy-coloured hair, dressed in a purple sports bra and black leggings, having clearly come from the gym. Gloria relaxed her shoulders. What was she thinking anyway? Of course, the Harmans would have moved on. This person was probably a professional who finished work and went to run a few miles on a treadmill. Then, suddenly, when the girl turned to the side to move the green bin that the dustbin men had left halfway across her drive, Gloria's heartbeat immediately went to fever pitch. It was *her*! Tracey. It was the trollop who had dated her son and who wore an evil tattoo that was apparently connected to the past. Just before she got out of the car, Gloria took a deep breath and tried to steady her mind. She was frantically trying to process what she could see now and relate it to her own past. She needed answers before she tore into the young woman.

Tracey put her key in the door, and Gloria watched as she turned the hallway light on. She bent down to pick up some letters and then closed the door. Right away, Gloria assumed that Tracey was alone.

The loud knock made Tracey jump. She wasn't expecting anyone; she'd only popped over to collect the mail and check on her dying mother.

As soon as she opened the door, her eyes widened in disbelief. Gloria Regan! She was the last person she would have expected on the doorstep. At first, Tracey was annoyed. Just the name Regan sent shivers down her spine. There was her mother upstairs in a bed, dying, her final and only wish being that the Regans were destroyed. Carmella never did recover from her twin brother's death. It haunted and taunted her so much that she became obsessed. Guy had made a solemn oath to his sister to avenge his brother's murder, and yet it was the Harmans who were being wiped out. She glared at Gloria; in her mind, she visualized wringing the woman's neck.

'Hello, Tracey. Can I come in?'

Tracey was taken aback. This was surreal. 'What do you want?'

'Oh, I thought we could have a little catch-up. It's been such a long time.'

Tracey curled her lip and smirked. 'Oh yeah, really?' She looked over Gloria's shoulders to see who else was about, but the woman was alone. Her mind then turned to revenge. Gloria would be easy pickings; she could kill the old dear and add another notch to her wrist. At least her mother would die with a huge smile on her face, and Uncle Guy would reward her highly.

'Why don't you come in,' she said with an engaging smile, as she stepped aside. 'We'll go into the lounge.'

Gloria hoped her jacket was thick enough to conceal the gun. She followed Tracey, clutching her bag, and gazed around the room. The lounge was unfashionable, with framed family photos adorning the walls, and there were more on the sideboard. The old cabinets were very 1970s and the fireplace was still the old electric type. Why Carmella kept it so outdated was a mystery.

Gloria turned to face Tracey. 'Just one word. Why?'

Tracey stood with her arms folded, planning how she could kill Gloria without leaving a mess. She had to admire her. Not just because even at her age she was still spritely and well dressed – she was wearing an emerald green jersey tunic and navy-blue trousers, her hair immaculately in place and make-up neat and very current – it was her body language that Tracey most admired.

Gloria knew something.

The tense silence was broken when a croaky voice from upstairs called down. 'Trace, is that you, love? Fetch me up a cup of tea. I need to take me tablets.'

Gloria raised her eyebrow. 'Your mother's sick, is she?'

Tracey nodded, still bemused by the woman.

'Well, you'd better not keep her waiting then, had you?'

Tracey stared, still trying to suss out what game Gloria was playing.

'She can wait. She won't be going anywhere. She's dying.'

'That's a shame,' replied Gloria, sarcastically.

Tracey returned the smirk.

Instantly, Gloria pointed to Tracey's arm. 'I want to see your tattoo. Show it to me.'

An uncomfortable feeling sent another shiver down Tracey's spine. What did this woman really know?

But what did it matter? She was already planning Gloria's demise.

She chuckled. 'It's none of your fucking business.'

Gloria calmly sat down on the cream, plastic-coated sofa with square orange cushions. 'Oh, but, Tracey, it is, ain't it? I mean, you were with my boy Eric just to get ya fucking great nose in *our* business. Your family murdered my dear little grandson and your lot had my Mikey locked up for twelve bloody years, so, sweetheart, it most certainly *is* my business. Now, considering you and yours had the front to carry out such atrocities, I can only assume you'll have the guts to tell me why.'

Tracey clasped her hands together, and with her forefinger, she rubbed her top lip. She removed the sweat band, revealing the tattoo and a notch carved into her wrist.

Gloria glared and her stomach churned. She assumed the notch was for Ricky. There and then, she wanted to whip out her gun and put a bullet right through the bitch's head.

'You know why, Gloria. You don't need me to tell you, but if you want all the fucking gory details, then that, dear lady, is what you will have,' replied Tracey, in an icy flat tone.

Close up now, Gloria could see that Tracey, with the blonde hair extensions and low-cut tops, toppling around in her Jimmy Choos, was now quite a muscular woman. With a deeper voice and no make-up, she looked almost manly.

'This is who you really are, ain't it?' Looking Tracey up and down, she went on, 'You ain't the dizzy dolly bird that wormed her way into my boy's life at all, are ya?'

With a deep chuckle escaping her lips, Tracey was getting a kick out of this visit. She thought, *What's the point in having secrets if the woman's going to die anyway?*

She decided she would goad the Regan woman with words before she wrung her neck.

'Dolly bird, huh? I'm far from a dolly bird, but I can act the part if I need to. Your son and Neil Lanigan, they love fake tits and blonde hair. Pathetic, both of them.'

Gloria had been told about Zara and the Lanigans. Her heart beat faster. Perhaps Tracey knew what had happened to Zara. At least she would be able to go back and tell Mike something. She knew he was suffering from a broken heart, what with Ricky and also Zara.

'I guess that notch represents the person ya killed, then? Would that be my grandson, or Teddy Stafford's brother, or even Zara ...?'

331

Tracey wasn't a fool. She knew what the old goat was up to.

So she laughed. 'Oh, Gloria, you have no idea, do you? Zara ain't dead, she's very much alive. But, hear this. I will be taking over, and Zara and Ismail, her puny waste of space of a brother, will be more notches on my tattoo. So, your darling son Mike will genuinely have another person to mourn. Anything to add to his suffering.'

It was Gloria's time to scoff. 'You don't think I believe that, do you? If Zara is alive, she would be hunting you down and burying you. I know about Zara. She's no silly bitch, unlike you.'

Tracey laughed even louder at Gloria's dig. 'Go on, Gloria, I know your game. I'm not stupid. Far from it, in fact. And the truth is, you can ask me whatever you like. Just don't try to wind me up to get your answers. Go on, try me.'

At that point, Gloria knew that Tracey wasn't planning on letting her leave this house alive; but then, Gloria wasn't exactly planning to walk away without killing Tracey. The Harmans had taken too much away from her, to be left with only a pot of Valium to turn to.

'Where's Zara? What have you done to her?'

Tracey took a seat and smirked. 'I cut her hand off, put her wrist in the fire, and then locked her in a basement under Izzy's house. She's a bit nutty now, not a danger to anyone. But Ismail, the little prick, insists on keeping her alive. I dunno, maybe he's getting some sick kick out of it. What else would you like to know? That is, before . . . Oh, never mind.'

'Where's my grandson buried and how did he . . .?' She couldn't bring herself to say the words.

Tracey's eyes lit up, watching the agony on Gloria's face and the resigned slump of her shoulders.

'That, Mrs Regan, I can't tell you, but I am sure his death was savage.'

In a sudden surge of fury, Gloria jumped up from her seat, the sneer and the mocking look too much to handle. This was her grandson she was talking about and Tracey's dismissive attitude sent her over the edge. She didn't even wait to point her gun; she whipped it from the back of her trousers, and, like an old pro, she released the safety catch and fired.

The bullet didn't hit Tracey in the head, it just missed her. But as Tracey went to launch herself at Gloria, the older woman cocked the gun again and fired – this time directly into Tracey's chest. Falling backwards, the look in her eyes was one of pure horror. The blood was instant. The gun may have been small, but it was no spud gun. Wheezing and gurgling, as Tracey tried to breathe, her body slumped to the floor, leaving Gloria stunned.

She had fired the gun and was now watching the woman slowly dying. Gloria's hands shook, and she stepped back, not taking her eyes away from her victim. 'You shouldn't have fucked with my family.' Tracey's head flopped forward and the gruesome sound of her gasping for breath stopped.

She was dead.

'Trace, have ya made me that tea, love?'

Having planned to kill the woman, Gloria was now stumped. What should she do now? She pulled her phone from her bag and called Eric. 'Son, where are you?'

'Mum, not now. I'll call ya when we're on our way home.' Eric assumed his mother was just fretting and was about to turn the phone off.

'Listen. Zara is in Izzy's house, locked in some basement or something.'

'What are you on about?'

'Just get over there quickly with ya father and the others. The poor girl's locked up in the house somewhere.'

There was a brief pause while Eric tried to absorb his mother's words. 'How d'ya know that?'

'Son, I haven't got time to explain. Hurry up, will ya?'

'Are you okay, Mum?'

'Yes, I'm fine, love. And one more thing. Please remember, you are doing this for your brother. Zara's his bird. She's all he has. I have to go. Call me when you find her.'

Eric bit his lip. He wasn't doing this for Mike; rather, he was going to rescue her hopefully for himself.

Chapter 23

Charlie Ritz rushed down the drive, still trying to put his jacket on. Eric was taken aback by the speed of the man. Willie was so much like his father Charlie, except the latter didn't have a huge scar down his face. And Willie was lanky, whereas Charlie was meaty. Lou, sometimes known affectionately as Big Lou, since he towered over his son Lou, had as much suaveness as a Portuguese pot-bellied pig. Still, no one would ever be brave enough to verbalize that notion. Once they were all seated, Arthur tore off.

'Now, lads, we have one shot at this. I have no idea who's in Izzy's house, but if the girl is locked up, then you can bet ya bottom dollar there will be someone guarding her,' said Arthur, taking his usual stance as the leader.

'All right, son. I've got me gun, a knife tucked in me boot, and me angina puffer.'

'And you, Lou?' asked Arthur.

'Yep, I've got me gun and me pepper spray.'

Eric had never seen them ready for a war. The way they carried themselves made it clear why they had gained a ruthless reputation.

'We need to get in there and grab the first skullcap and bring him to his knees. I want a shooter in his mouth and fucking answers. We may have been hunted for years, but I ain't having any of our families suffering the same. This ends today, once and for all. Anyone with a tattoo on their fucking wrist will get it from me, both fucking barrels.'

'Why didn't we bring Teddy?' asked Charlie.

'Because I reckon that what we uncover today will tell us who killed Monty, and he'll go ballistic. I want a controlled showdown.'

The sky was now loaded with dense clouds, the air was sticky, and soon a storm would be over them. As they turned into the drive that led up to Izzy's former house, a crash of thunder made Eric flinch. The others didn't even blink. A sudden eerie feeling came over him. In the distance, up the hill, with nothing around except fields and trees, the Georgian house, with its numerous tall chimneys, cast an imposing and somewhat daunting sight. Around the perimeter, it was equally dark and uninviting. Arthur turned the car's lights off and drove to within a short distance of the house.

'Only one car, Arthur,' said Lou, in his husky voice.

'What's on the number plate? Can ya see?'

Lou fiddled with his case for his glasses. 'Fucking eyes and hip. Jesus, I hate getting old.'

Eric struggled to see himself.

'It says I5MAL.'

'Ismail!' said Eric. 'So, her brother's there, then. The little fucking bastard, eh? If Mum's got this right, he must be in on it.'

Arthur was quick to jump in. 'Ya muvver's *always* right.'

'No sensor lights have come on,' commented Charlie.

Arthur stared at the monster of a house; it put him in mind of a vampire film he'd recently watched.

'It means we're too far away, so let's get out and walk on the grass and surround the house. Don't walk on the drive, in case the lights are pointed that way. Eric and Charlie, you creep around the back. Me and Lou will go to the front.'

As he'd thought, the sensor lights were pointing down the

drive. They walked to the side of the house and bent down as they crept past the windows. Nothing came on.

Lou held himself away from the door, against the wall, while Arthur knocked. With no glass in the door, whoever opened it wouldn't see who was there at first.

Izzy had installed cameras and floodlights, but since his death ten or more years ago, Ismail hadn't bothered to keep these in working order. Over time, various parts of the security system had failed, and his slapdash attitude had resulted in nothing being repaired.

Arthur banged hard and gripped his gun as he waited. A few minutes later, the door opened. It was Ismail, as he suspected. Once Ismail laid eyes on Arthur, he tried to close the heavy oak door, but with one hard kick, Arthur was through and into the hallway. Ismail had no time to run before he was snatched and pushed to the floor with a gun in his mouth.

'Who else is here?' demanded Arthur.

Ismail looked up at Arthur and then at Big Lou whose appearance made Ismail turn from white to grey. The man was colossal. The younger man's eyes almost bulged from their sockets. He tried to shake his head, but Arthur shoved the gun deeper down his throat. 'If you're lying, this fucker will decorate the hallway with your brains.'

'Lou, let the others in, will ya?'

Lou headed past Arthur towards the back of the house. Not really knowing where to go – he guessed the house had well over thirty rooms – he walked straight ahead until he came to another oak door on the left-hand side. The key was in the lock, and as he turned it, he saw a staircase leading to what appeared to be the basement. He turned around and there on the furthest wall was a set of French doors covered by red velvet curtains. Eric and Charlie were outside and eagerly came in.

They followed Lou back to the hallway where Arthur still had Ismail by the throat.

'Where's ya sister?' demanded Arthur.

Ismail was so terrified his legs shook as though he was having a seizure. Arthur took the gun out of Ismail's mouth. 'Where. Is. She?' he bellowed.

Ismail looked at the four men and knew he couldn't escape. He was alone this evening until ten thirty, when Benjamin and Guy were going to pay him a visit. So he guessed he would be tortured until then. What choice did he have but to tell them? But, more to the point, what could his sister tell them anyway? She was a dribbling, brain-damaged cabbage. 'She's . . . downstairs,' he gingerly replied.

Arthur grabbed his arm, almost wrenching it from its socket. 'Show me!'

Ismail took them to the side door that led downstairs; the others followed, eerily fascinated by the underground fortress. There in front of them was the metal prison door. But as they peered through the bars, all they could see was a warm, inviting room, with a red carpet, walnut cabinets, and a beautifully carved wooden bed. Arthur laid a mighty hand on Ismail's shoulders.

'Fucking open it!'

Fumbling in his pockets, Ismail pulled out the keys, and with unsteady hands, he turned the locks and stepped back.

All four men were completely stunned. Inside, sitting on a chair with a high back and dressed in a khaki brushed hoodie and matching cargo joggers was Zara. She was watching ITV's *News at Ten*, not even looking their way.

She didn't move until Arthur gently placed his hand on her bony shoulder.

Slowly, she turned her head. Then, as if she'd just come out of a trance, her eyes widened as they focused on the other men. Realizing that they were not connected to Guy at all, her gaze fixed on Eric. To her astonishment, her nightmare, which seemed to have lasted an eternity, was now at an end. Instantly, her body began to quiver, the relief so overwhelming.

Then she caught sight of her brother out of the corner of her eye. She gave him a look that he recognized – the one she'd used as a child when she'd fooled him into thinking he'd hurt her.

At that moment, he knew that for the last five years she had deliberately hoodwinked him again. His eyes looked for his only escape route.

Just as he was about to run, Zara screamed, 'Get him!' She knew she wouldn't be fast enough, but Charlie – who she could see clearly resembled Willie and was presumably his father – despite his advanced years, moved like a whippet. He lurched forward and caught Ismail by the hair, throwing him hard against the wall.

Arthur went to help her up. 'Are you okay, love? You're safe now, babe.'

With studied concentration, Zara's eyes focused on her brother.

Carefully, she rose from the chair and slowly walked towards the door.

Eric then spotted her wrist, and he gasped in horror. 'Jesus, what the fuck did they do to you?'

She didn't answer but stood over her brother, who was slumped on the floor. His big puppy-dog eyes, pleading with her, meant nothing.

'You evil fucking bastard. You taunted me every fucking day, you sick motherfucker!' Lifting her leg, she stamped down hard on his head.

Arthur didn't stop her at first. Far be it for him to do so. But then it dawned on him that he needed answers. 'No, wait, love, I want the fucking truth, and he's gonna give it to me.' He leaned down and gripped Ismail's wrist and then glared at the tattoo. 'Hunter, eh? Charlie, give me your knife. I'm ending this, once and for all.'

Ismail's eyes were wide, and he felt the bile rush to his throat. 'Oh, no, no, please don't cut me. Please!' he begged.

Then he looked at his sister, but he could see from the body language that there wouldn't be any sympathy from her. Instead, she grinned. 'Let me do it!'

'No!' said Eric. 'It's gruesome, love, and you're a lady. Let me get you out of here. Me dad's gonna make him talk.'

Zara looked at her own scarred wrist. 'Oh, believe me, I do gruesome. What answers do you want?'

Arthur shook his head. 'Love, don't you worry about it. Let Eric take you somewhere safe.'

'Give me the knife. Please!' she insisted.

Arthur couldn't argue with her. He understood that, after all this time, with her physical injuries and mental torture, he was in no position to deny her poetic justice. He handed the blade to her.

'No, please, I'll tell you everything!' shrieked Ismail.

Arthur eased Zara aside and glared down at Ismail, who was whimpering like an injured dog.

'Who else has that tattoo?'

'Oh, I can tell you *that*! Guy Segal and his fat fuck of a son,' said Zara.

'That tattoo has a meaning that's followed my family around like a bad smell for decades, and I want to know who's behind it and why!'

Zara let the knife fall out of her hand. 'Oh my God, it was you!' Her eyes shot from Arthur to Charlie and then to Lou. 'Do you remember back in the sixties when two Jewish boys were murdered?'

Arthur jolted his head and looked at Lou and then at Charlie. 'Jesus wept. So, all this really was about the murder of those two Jewish kids?'

Zara ran her hand through her hair and sighed. Ismail was visibly shrinking.

'That tattoo means "hunter". You, and the boys who were there that day, were hunted. An eye for an eye.'

'But that's fucking mad. We didn't kill them. We were only ten

340

years old.' He looked at the men who were staring at Zara in utter amazement.

Charlie banged the wall. 'All those years of being grassed up, bashed up, and wondering who the hell was behind it all, we still didn't have any answers as to fucking why. You mean to tell me that someone holds a grudge because they thought we killed two Jewish kids? Who the fuck were these boys anyway?'

An uncomfortable expression clouded Zara's face and she lowered her eyes. 'They were my father's little brother and Guy Segal's brother!'

Arthur's jaw dropped open. 'Your *father* was one of these so-called fucking hunters?'

It was Ismail who unexpectedly showed some courage. 'No. Izzy was a defector. He covered his tattoo. He was weak, not worthy of the ink.'

Lou gave Ismail a swift kick to his head. 'Shut up, you fucking lightweight prick.'

'When my father was just a teenager, he and Guy had a tattoo. I think it was just one of those things that kids did in those days. It would have looked cool. My father never went into great detail. He said he was ashamed and left it at that. I heard bits and pieces, but he was called a defector because he wouldn't join forces with Guy. I was betrothed to Benjamin as a baby because Guy and my father were close. Then they fell out, and a serious feud between them began. My dad drove the Segals out of the country. I was shocked to see Guy at my father's funeral . . .' She glared at Ismail. 'And worse, I now discover my own brother invited him.'

Arthur then turned to Ismail. 'Right, Lou. Let's tie this fucker up and gouge his eyes out!'

Arthur knew damn well that he wouldn't need to use Gestapo tactics to extract the truth out of Ismail. The man would roll over with a flick of the ear. Right on cue, he was proved correct.

'No, wait, I'll tell you what happened. Please, I beg you. Don't cut me.'

Charlie laughed. 'Nah, I wanna skewer his mince pies.'

Ismail screamed, 'Oh God, no, please!'

'You fucking sick bastard. Look at ya. You're so pathetic. Now, tell us the fucking truth!' Zara screamed.

As if he was reciting his early morning prayer, Ismail began exposing the truth. 'Dad said that he found out who had killed his brother. It was a man who lived down their street, but Guy Segal didn't believe him. They argued and fell out over it. It was his sister, Carmella, who wanted to bring you all down, one by one, and she married Ronnie Harman to help her do it . . . Look, please, that's all I know.'

'It was Tracey Harman who cut off my hand, wasn't it?' growled Zara. Her brother slowly nodded.

'But you have to believe me. That was never meant to happen. You were working for the enemy . . .' He paused. 'They wanted everything the Regans earned, as compensation for Guy's little brother's death. And . . .' He stopped and looked up at his sister with guilt written across his face. 'They wanted to take over Izzy's empire as compensation.'

'For what?' she shrieked.

'Because you . . . were not only fucking the enemy, you were working with him too.'

Zara let out a fake laugh. 'Oh my God, you lot are so *sick*. This was never about retribution for the murder of the boys. It was about jealousy and fucking greed. But my father must have seen right through Guy because, unlike you, Ismail, Izzy was a clever and fair man. But you! You're bloody stupid. The Regans' success ate away at Guy, and you, ya faggot, were sucked in by his pathetic pledge – your tattoo is pitiful. Why do you think Izzy hid his? I'll tell you why: because he grew up and learned the truth!' She glared at her brother and instantly wished him dead.

Suddenly, Ismail lost his little-boy look and showed some gumption. 'You're fucking wrong, Zara. You believe you know everything because Izzy put you on a pedestal, but these old men *did* kill those boys and Guy *is* a man of his word. He promised Carmella, who was close to him, unlike me and you, that he would . . .' He paused, as he slowly turned to face Arthur. 'He would destroy all of you, and your sons, and anyone else who got in the way.' His eyes then focused on Zara's scarred wrist, a smug look taking shape.

Without warning, Arthur cracked him hard around the face. 'And my grandson, an innocent kid. Where is he?'

Before Ismail could answer, a noise came from upstairs.

'Shhhh, there's someone coming,' said Lou.

Instantly, Arthur grabbed Ismail with his hand around his mouth and lifted him off the floor. 'Who's that?'

Zara answered. 'It's Guy and Benjamin, no doubt.'

They dragged Ismail behind the staircase, and Zara went back inside the room and acted as if she was a zombie again. Arthur pushed his gun against Ismail's head. Through gritted teeth, he whispered, 'If you say one word, I'll blow your fucking head off.'

Just as Zara expected, Guy and Benjamin opened the door and strolled down the staircase entirely unaware they were about to be ambushed.

'Ismail, where are you?' Benjamin called out.

The weight of the man caused the wooden stairs to bow . . . and creak.

No sooner had their feet touched the floor than Charlie and Lou appeared, holding guns in their hands and smirks on their faces. 'Well, well, well, if it ain't fucking Tweedledum and Tweedledee,' said Charlie.

Arthur emerged, holding Ismail. He clocked the fear on Guy Segal's face. But not only that, he recognized the man. Although he was much older, thinner and less upright, it was the same person who had nearly beaten him to death all those years ago when he'd stepped off the bus.

'What is this?' demanded Guy.

Arthur pushed Ismail towards Eric. 'Lock this cunt up, Eric.

343

And Mr Segal has just become the hunted! The tables have turned, and before I rip your head off, know this. I never killed those two kids. So you and your pathetic pact, with ya bravado tattoos, have wasted your whole life trying to bring us all down. But I think you knew that. You and the Harmans just used that as an excuse to get a firm together to take over my manor.'

He grabbed Guy's arm and glared at the tattoo. 'This should translate as "sly fuckers".'

Guy's mouth fell open; he'd worked out who they were, and, more to the point, what they would do. For a second, he took his eyes away from Arthur and glared at Zara, who had now joined them. She looked a different woman: clear-headed, eyes focused, and her mouth tight, not distorted and dribbling. With narrowed eyes and pursed lips, he hissed, 'I should have let you die!'

'No, Guy, you are so spineless that you got your kicks, along with your prat of a son, out of watching me. You thought I was damaged beyond repair, and in your sick, twisted minds you enjoyed having that power over me, a defenceless, mutilated woman.' Leaning on Arthur's arm, her chest heaving, she spat, 'You couldn't fight my father because he was stronger than you, and far cleverer and richer. You hated him, detested him, because it wasn't about the little boys who died, it was all about power. You and your son will never amount to anything because you never had it in you!'

'You ugly slag. Who cares? You're nothing now but a one-armed withered old bitch!' retorted Benjamin.

It was Eric who voiced his opinion. 'She may only have one arm, but unlike you, ya fucking monster, she'll have her freedom. And you and your father and everyone who wears that tattoo will be hunted down and taken out. But first, I'm gonna have you locked up.'

Arthur gripped his gun; he wanted nothing more than to put a bullet through Segal's head. Benjamin looked at the metal door and the rooms beyond, but his gaze was pulled back when Eric laughed.

'No, not down here. I'm calling the police. You'll know how it feels to serve time like my father and my brother have. You'll get to meet *real* men, because inside you can't hide who you really are. My brother knows enough inmates to make your life a misery. Everyone will know what you've done, and I hope you suffer.'

Even Arthur was shocked at Eric's idea. Grassing went against the grain – an unspoken rule – and yet Eric had a point. And in any case, since when did the Segals and Harmans play by the rules?

He smiled at his son. 'Yeah, call them. Fuck it. Zara, is it okay with you?'

She felt fragile, and it showed on her pale face. She nodded and almost collapsed, but Charlie managed to catch her in time.

The Segal family knew they could never get away with what they'd done. It was over, they knew.

'And, just so you know,' Eric said, 'when you do get released, if you ever do, then I'll come for you, and, mark my words, I will have that tattoo inked right across my back. I will be the hunter, and you,' he chuckled, 'will be the prey.'

Arthur and Charlie locked Ismail and the Segals inside the basement and waited for the police. Eric took Zara and Lou home.

* * *

Gloria was like a mother hen, fussing over Zara. It was very well received, since Zara had been living locked away for five long years with no hugs and no fuss except from Palo. He'd never held her, seeing that it was not his place to do so.

Plumping up the cushions and pushing a pouffe under Zara's feet, she wiped the woman's hair away from her face. 'Oh, my darling, I just can't believe it. Our Mikey's gonna go ballistic, but at least he has you back. He was distraught when you went missing. As you can imagine, we all thought the worst, but you're here now, and it won't be long before Mikey is home too and—'

'Mum, please give Zara a chance to breathe, will ya? Go and put the kettle on.'

Gloria apologized. 'Sorry, love. I'm just a bit overwhelmed. Anyway, I've left a message at the prison for Mikey to call. The only thing is, apparently, he's in transit. They're moving him to another jail, so I hope he gets the message.'

Zara looked down at her scars. 'It's good of you to help me like this, but . . .' she choked back a tear. 'He won't want me now. How can he? I'm . . .' It was hard to say the words. All she could do was stare at the remnants of her arm.

Gloria felt tears prick her eyes. 'Now then, you listen to me. Our Mikey loved you so much, and it knocked him sideways what with Ricky . . . and then you disappearing. He would love you, no matter what.'

'Mum, how did you know where Zara was?'

Gloria shrugged her shoulders. 'Listen, son, that doesn't matter now.'

Eric turned to face Zara. 'It's over now, love. They're all gone. Ismail and the Segals will be in prison, so you can stay here and get better and put some meat back on those bones.'

He felt a sudden sense of guilt. He'd wanted Zara for himself and even with her missing hand he would still have wanted her, so he knew it wouldn't put Mike off – after all, his brother had always loved her more than any other woman.

Zara blushed and then her thoughts turned to Tracey. 'They ain't all gone. Tracey is still out there somewhere, and I swear to God, when I find her, I will—'

'No need, babe, she's dead.' With that, Gloria swanned off to make the tea, leaving both Eric and Zara gobsmacked. Eric stared at the back of his mother and wondered if she meant that she had killed Tracey. Surely not?

Eric turned to Zara. 'How did you know Tracey was a Harman?'

Zara grinned. 'She was with Paris. I had a tip-off that Paris was seen in Blackheath. I caught up with them, and I assumed she was just a mate of hers. I beat them both, but then some bloke from the local Chinese called the police, so I had to run. But then, when she cut my . . . anyway, I recognized her and then I saw the tattoo. I just put two and two together. Still, it doesn't matter, now. They're all dead.' She frowned and pointed to the kitchen. 'But ya mum, though. I think that's more shocking. Ya don't think she killed her, do you?'

Eric chuckled. 'If she did, she ain't gonna tell us because my mum won't want us to worry.'

Zara gave a tired smile. 'I guess ya mum's a tough cookie.' She yawned.

Eric shook his head. 'Well, like they say, I guess behind every successful man there is a dangerous woman.'

He looked at Zara, who was now asleep, and tears filled his eyes. He felt so guilty and vowed never to abandon his brother again.

Chapter 24

The judge stared with beady eyes at Ricky. He had never come across a mute before. He wondered if it was a flaw in the gypsy gene pool.

'Richard Menaces, you have been found guilty on three counts of burglary, and so I sentence you to a year in prison.'

With no expression on his face indicating any emotion, Ricky stared back.

'Take him away!' ordered the judge.

Escorted by the court officer back down the stairs into the holding cells, Ricky nervously waited for the sweat box to take him to prison. It had finally happened; he was going down. The previous times in court he'd got away with a fine, then community service, followed by a suspended sentence. This time, it was not so easy. Sitting on the edge of the seat with his hands under his legs, he anxiously tapped his feet. He'd heard stories from the other lads on the site how tough it was inside, especially if you were a pretty boy. He didn't regard himself as pretty though, not when he looked in the mirror. No one ever referred to him as anything other than mouse, oaf or retard.

* * *

Tall for eighteen, he was also skinny and lanky. He'd never thought much about himself. He'd not had a normal childhood and had no education to speak of. That was down to his mother. She had made sure of that, especially after the incident in the hospital when the social services were called in.

He remembered it well, and at the time had hoped beyond hope that they would do as they said and take him away into foster care. He recalled the lovely lady, Elouise, with her soft voice and warm hands, as she stroked his hair away from his face. She'd given him a pen and paper and asked him to write down the answers to her questions, but he couldn't because he wasn't any good at spelling. He could only nod or shake his head. She'd asked so many questions. Did he go to school? Did Jackie often get drunk? Was the dog that bit him from their gypsy camp? He had thought about answering her honestly, but the fear of the consequences, if his mother found out, stopped him from doing so. So when the sweet lady asked if Jackie had ever hurt him, he shook his head.

* * *

His thoughts were interrupted when he heard the cocky, angry voice of Tyrone. 'Get yer fucking hands off me, you cunt.'

Tyrone's court case had been directly after his, and Ricky could only assume that he'd also received a prison sentence. Tatum had gone from using Ricky to climb through the windows, to pretending they were builders and robbing people blind. They were wanted by the Irish police, so they'd upped sticks and moved to England, to a site in Essex. Seth had another brother, who had bought a large plot of land and tarmacked most of it to withstand the caravans. Tatum, Tyrone and Ricky had been caught red-handed, because unlike in Ireland, the CCTV system was different. The estate they robbed had hidden cameras, and, unluckily for them, a detective also lived there.

Ricky couldn't speak, so Tatum made a statement that Ricky was the ringleader, the organizer. The judge, of course, didn't buy it, but because this wasn't their first offence, by any means, they were all sentenced to one year.

Ricky nervously waited and hoped that Tatum and Tyrone would be shipped to another prison, away from him. At least he was grateful that Tatum's other son Elijah hadn't been nicked as well, or he would have had three of them to contend with.

His life, already filled with shit luck, didn't end today. Travelling in the sweat box to Maidstone Prison, he kept his head down, but Tatum and Tyrone didn't. They chose to mouth off with their loud gobs. He wondered if the lip they gave did them any favours. Sure enough, it didn't. The officer pointed to the claustrophobic boxed area that Ricky was sitting in and then almost threw Tatum into his. A last dig of his baton made Tatum shut his mouth. He knew then that being mute wasn't such a bad thing.

''Ere, Mouse, are yer shitting it yet?' called out Tyrone.

Ricky was used to the jibes and the piss-taking and had only ever tried once to fight back. He'd ended up with not only Tyrone but also Elijah on his back. They blacked his eyes, split his lip, and tore his ear. He didn't cry but scurried away to the log at the edge of the woods.

The transport van came to a shuddering halt and the back door was opened. There, awaiting him, was Blair, Ricky's personal officer, dressed in a white short-sleeved shirt and black trousers with a dangling chain. He called out, 'Richard Menaces!'

Ricky nodded.

'You call me Gov. Got it?'

Ricky's eyes widened, and then the officer, who initially loaded him into the van, whispered in Blair's ear.

'Well, Menaces, you're gonna have to find a way to communicate . . .' He sighed. 'Okay, move on.'

Ricky trembled. The officer had the meanest eyes and there was not a jot of niceness about him. Still handcuffed, Ricky walked ahead, along the wire fence walkway, until he could go no further. Blair pressed a button and a loud buzzing sound went off. The toughened glass door slid open and Ricky was asked to walk ahead. Another official, a tall, slim man with a beard, guided him inside to a desk where three other officers stood. They handed him prison issues and ordered him to go into one of the side rooms where he had to strip, while one of the tall bearded officers checked him over. Then he was required to squat, although he had no idea what for, but he did it anyway. The officer then placed a mirror underneath him. Apparently satisfied, he then checked the inside of Ricky's mouth. The officer made him walk through a metal detector and then sent him into another side room to get dressed in his prison issues. Ricky hurriedly put on the grey tracksuit bottoms and pulled a drab grey T-shirt and then a lighter grey sweatshirt over his head. A plastic bag was then handed to him, which contained a few essentials.

As he waited by the next metal door, he saw Tatum and then Tyrone appear. Tatum was jumping about, acting cocky as usual, and Tyrone wasn't much better. They were also ordered to strip, at which Tatum made some comment about the officer being bent. Ricky looked away, determined to ignore them and keep his distance. He didn't want to be viewed as a pikey.

Blair pressed the buzzer by the wall and the heavy metal door slid open.

'Go in, Menaces!' he ordered.

As Ricky walked along the long corridor, he held his breath. The roughly plastered yellow walls were so cold-looking. On both sides of the corridor were metal doors painted in green gloss. A wrought-iron staircase led up to the next level. They moved forward, and Blair instructed him to climb the stairs. It was as if the prison was empty; there was not a sound to be heard except for the loud clanging of doors being shut. Once he reached the top, Blair unlocked a door and stepped aside.

'This is your cell. You're lucky, mate, 'cos you're on your own.'

Ricky smiled but his gesture was lost on the stony-faced screw, with his watchful eyes.

Once Ricky was alone, he shut the door and looked around. A metal bed, a plastic-coated mattress, and a chrome toilet took up most of the cell. At the end of the bed were sheets and a blanket. He placed his plastic bag on the small desk and his toothbrush on the shelf.

Just as he lay on the unmade bed with his hands under his head, he heard what sounded like a mass of men. Some were shouting, others laughing, and the cell doors were banging and clanging. He hadn't realized that while he was arriving and being shown to his cell, the men were in the exercise yard.

A voice he recognized was just outside his door. 'Oi, oi, Henry, boy!' called Tatum. Ricky remained in his cell. He could picture Tatum bouncing about and showing off.

'Cor, bruv, what yer doing 'ere?' asked Tatum.

The gruff voice replied, 'Same as you, Tat, no doubt. I got chored down in Dover. I upped sticks about two years ago, boy, and moved down ta Kent. On yer own, Tat?'

'Nah, Henry. I got me boy Tyrone. He got chored wiv me and ol' Jackie Menaces' boy, Richard, although he's a bit of a retard. He don't talk.'

Ricky strained to hear.

'Jackie Menaces?'

'Yeah, she's been back on the site for years now, bruv. She's a right dirty whore an' all. But ol' man Seth won't 'ave a bad word said about her.'

'Who's the boy, then? Is he Tiger's?'

Tatum laughed. 'Cor, mush, he could be anyone's. She likes to put it about. She reckons it's some bloke that'll kill her if he finds her. Me, I reckon it's all bullshit. Anyway, have yer seen Richard? He's a tall, lanky boy.'

'Nah, Tat. I've just come off the yard. You'll meet the lads.

They're cushty. There's me cousin Lexus, me nephew Kane, and a few others off the site who are in 'ere wiv me.'

'Nice one. Got any baccy?' asked Tatum, itching for a smoke.

'Fuck off, Tat. Smoke yer own. And listen, boy. Don't go getting in people's faces or throwing yer weight around. There are a few hard men in 'ere, who'll take yer 'ead clean off yer shoulders. Keep yer mooi down. They don't take too kindly to travelling boys in this nick. We've a bad name. Some pikeys have done over a load of oldies, and now they're tarring us all with the same brush, so slow down.'

Ricky could tell then that Tatum wouldn't be lording it over whoever this Henry was. He'd been well and truly put in his place.

'All right, bruv,' said Tatum, lowering his overexcited voice to a whisper.

'And don't call me bruv. It's a dead giveaway.'

Ricky got up from his bed and paced the floor, the words 'hard men' and 'pikeys' swirling around in his head. Surely, no one would know he was a traveller? He couldn't speak anyway. The noise outside was quietening down, and he wondered what was next. The officer had said that he would be put on a course to learn how the prison worked and what was expected, but he didn't say when. Suddenly, a buzzing sound like a fire alarm brought him out of his daydream. A deep, loud voice shouted, 'Lunchtime!'

Then there was another burst of activity. He could hear people walking and nattering. He remained where he was, too nervous to face the hordes of violent, scary nutters. Unexpectedly, his door opened, and there stood Blair, his personal officer, with that same stone-faced expression.

'Get ya tray and go to lunch, Menaces.'

Looking around for a tray, his hands were visibly shaking, and this was quickly noticed. 'In that bag!' Blair pointed.

Ricky quickly retrieved the tray and waited for instructions.

Surprisingly, a warm smile appeared on Blair's face. 'Come on, son, it ain't that bad. Just follow the others in the line and bring your lunch back to your cell. You'll get the hang of it.'

Ricky mouthed the words 'Thank you' and received a more generous smile from Blair. Immediately, Ricky felt his anxious mood lift.

Outside the cells on the landing were men of every shape, size and colour. They were all heading the same way, all walking with a swagger, with their shoulders back and their heads up.

As Ricky joined them, he received a few nods and some glares. Directly in front of him stood a man shorter than himself, with blond cropped hair and wide rounded shoulders. As the line moved towards the serving hatches, another line of inmates was walking back with their trays loaded. A heavyset black man with cornrow hair and a thick, jagged scar down his left cheek brushed past the blond man, but Ricky, who could spot an ant on a beach at twenty feet, noticed he passed him something. He wished he hadn't. For, as his eyes clocked the parcel changing hands, the big black man twigged that Ricky had spotted what he'd done. He stopped in his tracks, and his threatening eyes looked deep into Ricky's, as if to warn him. Ricky put his head down and shuffled forward, trying to slow his racing heartbeat. As he reached the serving hatch and held up his tray, a toothless greasy-looking inmate slapped a spoonful of mashed potatoes, a thin meat pie, and a portion of what looked like slushy cabbage on his plate, using his dirty hands to do so. Ricky moved on to the next hatch where he took a bottle of water. Keeping his head lowered again, he walked back to his cell. Although the food didn't look appetizing, he didn't care because he was used to Jackie's shit food at home. The only decent bit of grub he ever had was from any offerings Mena gave him. She often tried to fatten him up and would wander over to the log – his log – and hand him a pie or a fat meat roll wrapped in one of her tea towels.

Just as he'd finished his plate and swigged the bottle of water, there was a sharp knock at the door. He assumed it was his personal officer, or Tatum. He got to his feet and pulled open the door, only to find a strange face glaring at him. A short, fat black man, with blue eyes and gold teeth that were almost blinding, looked Ricky up and down and clocked the tatty trainers. Footwear can say a lot about a person: it was like looking through a window to a person's soul. He then studied Ricky's frightened grey eyes and smiled.

'What's ya name?' he asked, in a flat tone.

Ricky's eyes widened. He couldn't answer, so he quickly pointed to his mouth and shook his head.

'Someone cut ya tongue out?'

Ricky nodded.

The black man frowned, unsure if Ricky was serious.

'Dez wants a word, so follow me.' He didn't wait for a response but just walked out of the cell and along the wing to the end cell. Ricky followed, two paces behind.

Outside Dez's cell were two other black men. They watched with sneering eyes as Ricky approached. One sniggered and sucked on a roll-up and the other raised his chin in a threatening way.

'Go in,' said the blue-eyed man. Ricky hesitated at the doorway. Inside the cell was the big guy who had slyly handed the blond man the parcel. He was sitting at a desk on which stood a cup of coffee, a bar of chocolate, and a backgammon board. His shelf was loaded with books and trinkets and the walls were coated with pictures, photos and drawings. It was a far cry from his own bare cell.

Leaning back on his chair, he pulled a fat joint from behind his ear and flicked his head for Ricky to enter. 'Sit there,' he said, as he pointed to the chair opposite. Nodding to the fat man, the cell door was instantly closed, leaving just Ricky and Dez alone.

'What's ya name?' he asked.

Ricky expected him to have a Jamaican accent, but he didn't. He spoke more like a Londoner.

The nerves had got to Ricky and his legs began to tremble; there was something very ominous surrounding Dez. Ricky shook his head and again pointed to his mouth.

Dez leaned forward in a fast movement. 'Answer me!' he bellowed.

Ricky shrank back, his hands held up protectively in front of him. He could feel the sweat on his palms and the hairs on the back of his neck stand on end. He pointed to his mouth again and shook his head, before lowering his hands under the table and clenching them together.

Dez laughed as though he was coughing. 'Ya can't fucking rabbit, eh? Well, that's good, that's fucking good. So can you write?'

Ricky shook his head and lowered his eyes. Of course he could write a little, but he wasn't going to tell Dez that because it was a form of communication and he really didn't want to engage with the man. The atmosphere was loaded with intimidation and so he wanted to be out of there as quickly as possible.

'I bet you'd like a nice fresh pair of trainers, wouldn't ya?' Dez's voice softened.

Ricky didn't know what to say. His non-verbal skills boiled down to a nod, a shake of his head or a shrug. He went for the shrug. Then he wished he'd shaken his head.

'I'll sort you out a pair. Now, it's gonna be tough in 'ere. You're new, young, and with eyes like yours, you're bait. I can 'elp ya, though. Ya see, everything that goes on in this nick gets run by me. D'ya get me?'

Ricky didn't really understand but he nodded just the same.

'I know a few old men 'ere. They're dead ugly motherfuckers, and they'd love to get their hands on you. Those pretty eyes of yours and that innocent face, see, they could easily imagine you as a woman.' He gave a crooked, slimy grin and licked his lips. 'I know you wouldn't like that one little bit.'

Ricky understood precisely what Dez was on about. He didn't like the sneaky expression on the man's face.

'Wanna bar of chocolate?' He slid a Snickers bar across the backgammon board.

Ricky gripped both his hands tight. Accepting the chocolate would mean he was engaging in a deal of some sort. And by the threatening look on Dez's face, it wouldn't be in his own interests to do so.

'My offer is not acceptable?'

Ricky was now burning up with fear. He couldn't take the chocolate, but how could he refuse?

Just as he was about to place his hand over the Snickers bar, there was a knock at the door, along with a commotion outside.

Dez sat up straight as the door opened. A solid-looking white man, with giant hands and a scruffy beard, which coated half his face, stood in the doorway. 'Dez, mate, he's one of ours.'

Ricky recognized the deep voice as Henry's, although he hadn't met him face-to-face.

'You've got some fucking front, walking into my cell and telling me he's one of yours. Tell me, what the fuck did ya think I was doing? And, more to the point, are you suggesting there's a fucking divide?'

Henry shuffled nervously. 'Nay, Dez, I just thought you'd wanna know, is all. The boy's a retarded mute, a travelling boy, no use to anyone.'

Dez laughed. 'So why the fucking interest then, Henry?'

'We looks after our own. It's our way.'

Dez looked down at Ricky's trainers. 'Ya fucking scummy pikey. You expect me to believe that, do ya? Look at his feet.'

Henry cast his eyes down and then felt awkward because Dez was right. The boy had worn-out trainers that he wouldn't have given to his dog to chew.

'Now, fuck off, Henry, and make sure you and your scurvy lot keep their noses out of my business. There will be consequences, otherwise. D'ya get me?'

Henry gave a quick nod and left, pushing past Dez's lackey.

Ricky didn't know whether to follow Henry or stay where he was.

'That, there, is a good example of what goes on in 'ere. See, that Henry, he's a fucking wanker. He wants you to earn him money and what's he gonna do for you in return? Well, I'll tell you. Fuck all, that's what.' He clasped his hands together with his elbows on the table. 'Ya see, me, well, I'm not like the dog shit in here. If you do me a favour, I return it.'

Ricky was taking it all in. Any protection from the travellers was a short-lived notion. This man clearly called all the shots.

Without pushing Ricky too far and scaring the boy off, Dez smiled and said, 'Think about it. If you want protection, new trainers, decent food, and certain rights, then tomorrow, come and see me.' He looked down at Ricky's feet again. 'Size ten, I take it?'

Ricky quickly got up from his chair and hurried along the corridor. In a panic, he forgot which cell was his, and behind him, he could hear laughter. He knew his cell was somewhere near here. Then he saw the light that was covered by a wire cage; he knew his cell was next to that. However, he hadn't realized that there were more enclosed lights, and so with a dry mouth and his hands shaking, he opened the door of the cell he wrongly assumed was his.

Propped up on the bed, with a fag paper between his fingers, was a man who also had a scar down his face, which ran from his forehead to his chin. He was tall with a wild look in his eyes.

Ricky froze to the spot. *Oh my God, this place is full of monsters*, he thought. *I'm going to be eaten alive.*

The man stopped licking the fag paper. 'Lost, are ya, son?' His words were fast, but they had reasonable normality about them.

Ricky was now white and trembling. And he suddenly jumped, when the man with the long scar leaped up from his bed. 'Oi, I don't fucking bite. Christ, I might look like one ugly bastard, but you've no need to jump, fella.'

Ricky took a deep breath and wiped his brow.

'Fucking 'ell, lad, come in and take a seat, and before you think I'm a nonce or anything else, I ain't. Jesus, ya look traumatized.'

Ricky glanced behind him, closed the door quietly, and quickly slipped into the cell and sat down.

'I take it you've just arrived? Never been in prison before? It's hard, mate, eh? But listen, keep yaself to yaself. Don't get involved with anyone. That's my advice.'

At once, Ricky felt confident enough to look the man in the face; as he did, something stirred inside him. It was a feeling, a comforting sensation, yet he had no idea why.

'Me name's Willie. And what's yours, son?'

Ricky felt a sudden covering of goose bumps, as if someone had walked over his grave. He tilted his head to the side and tried to recall if he'd ever met the man before. However, although this inmate's style of talking stirred distant memories, they were so vague, he guessed he should attach little significance to them.

He pointed to his mouth and shook his head.

'What's that all about?' He frowned. 'Can't ya talk, mate?'

Ricky swallowed hard and sighed. He shook his head and gave a resigned expression.

Willie lit the end of his roll-up. 'Well, you're gonna be a fucking bundle of laughs.' And then he chuckled to himself. As he stood up, he ruffled the boy's hair. 'Wanna brew, mate?'

Ricky felt another odd sensation. No one had ruffled his head since he was a kid. At least that's what he thought he remembered.

He nodded and a gentle smile crept across his face, showing a hint of a dimple. Willie shook his head as if he was seeing things. That expression stabbed at his heartstrings. He turned away and pulled down two mugs from his shelf and popped a teabag in each. 'Wait there, lad. I'll get the hot water.'

Ricky felt the most comfortable he'd ever been since he'd arrived. Looking around the cell, he saw a few photos of a young lad around twelve years old, who looked a lot like Willie.

On the shelf there were books and toiletries, and under the bed, his shoes and trainers were neatly lined up alongside two plastic boxes. It wasn't like Dez's cell, but it was homelier than his own. Obviously, Willie had a family who sent stuff in. He wondered if Jackie would do the same, but then he thought, *Who am I kidding?* He would be lucky if she even came to visit. *No*, he thought, *make that unlucky*. If he ever saw her again, it would be a moment too soon.

Willie returned with two steaming mugs. 'There ya go, boy. Get ya laughing gear around that.' He sat on the bed and raised his mug. 'Cheers.'

Ricky grinned again and raised his mug. The warm liquid was like heaven. He hadn't tasted tea in a while and he found it so refreshing. His mouth had been dry since he was arrested. His anxious nerves had dried him right out.

'I don't, as a rule, get involved with new inmates. I keep meself to meself, most of the time, but – and I ain't being derogatory when I say this: ya look a bit like bait. Ya gotta be the youngest in 'ere. Are you on ya own?'

Ricky tilted his head to the side and rocked his hand back and forth, meaning 'so-so'.

Willie rubbed his bristles, contemplating how to word the next question. It was hard and a bit of a game, trying to ask a question that required a yes or no answer.

'Are there people in here ya know?'

Ricky nodded and curled his lip.

Willie laughed. 'I get it, mate. There are people in here ya know but you're not keen on?'

Ricky smiled and nodded.

'Are they family? The two new lairy little fuckers, Tit and Tat or whatever the fuck they're called?'

Ricky frowned at hearing their names and Willie had a pretty good idea why. He was not cut from the same cloth, that was clear. Willie wasn't sure why the gentle expression and open face were stirring feelings of protection in him, but, whatever the reason, he had the urge to take care of the boy.

He'd met Tatum and Tyrone when they'd arrived and wasn't keen on their bolshie attitude and self-assured ways. He'd laughed to himself, thinking how they would probably get the cockiness kicked out of them. They were banking on the support of Henry and a few other gypsies, but Henry didn't carry enough weight to protect them – not from the likes of Dez and his motley crew.

Ricky felt comfortable enough to try and communicate. He pointed to Willie and then ran a finger down his own face and shrugged.

Willie chuckled. 'How did I get this scar?'

Ricky nodded with a smile.

'Well, I used to carry this knife around. I called her "my girl". It's a diver's knife that I use in my line of work, see. Anyway, I got jumped by three old geezers, two in front of me, so I pulled me knife out and tore into one of them. I nearly took his arm off, but the sneaky bastard behind me grabbed the knife. The bastards used me own knife to cut me head in half.' He laughed and slapped his thigh.

Ricky's eyes widened.

'Oh, it wasn't that bad. I reckon it was the quack who stitched me up that fucked up. He must 'ave been pissed or something. He sewed me face like a patchwork quilt, the knob'ead.'

Ricky was still smiling and enjoying the way Willie spoke. It was different, yet so welcoming, compared to the gypsy chat.

Willie rambled on while Ricky listened. An hour or so had passed, when Willie sat up. ''Ere, fancy a game of pool? Me mates will be back from the gym. I'll introduce ya.'

Ricky nodded. He was feeling relaxed and safer with Willie by the minute, so he was more than eager to stay in his company.

They wandered along the wing and down the metal stairs to the ground floor. There were two pool tables and a few tables and chairs with chessboards and other games on them.

'This is the recreational area. The screws will put you on a course on Monday, no doubt, to tell you how it all works, but I can fill you in, mate. So, when the buzzer goes, it means lunch, or dinner, although the food's shit. We have exercise in the yard, where ya can get some fresh air, and we have a gym so ya can build up your muscles.' He pinched Ricky's arm and was surprised that under the baggy sweatshirt the boy had tight, solid biceps.

'I guess you already work out, eh?'

Ricky shook his head.

'No? Well, you'll have time in here, if ya want to.'

He looked Ricky up and down. 'I reckon you could build yaself into quite a lump, boy. What are ya? Eighteen?'

Ricky nodded.

Willie set up the pool balls and chalked the cues. 'Do you wanna break?'

Ricky shook his head; he'd never played pool before, although he'd watched it on his mother's television. So, carefully, he observed how Willie was going to use the cue, knowing he would have to do the same.

Willie placed it between his forefinger and thumb, and in one fluid movement, he hit the white ball that bounced the coloured balls. Two yellows went down the pockets. 'My shot again. I'm on yellows, you're on reds.'

He tried to pot a yellow close to the pocket but missed. Ricky then knew what he had to do and lined himself up just as Willie had done. The red ball expertly went into the far-right corner.

'Good shot!' laughed Willie. 'I bet you're a hustler, eh?'

Ricky gave him a cheeky grin and lined up the next shot. This was the most fun he'd probably ever had, and his anxiety about being in prison lifted.

He became so engrossed in this new fun game that he was oblivious to the other inmates surrounding them. A small group of black men were gathered around one of the tables, keeping a close eye on Ricky and Willie. Willie clocked them right away, and his eyes scanned the area for potential trouble. Henry was over by the other pool table with a couple of toothless gypsies.

As Ricky potted another red and lined himself up for his next shot, Willie chalked his own cue and clocked the unease between the gypsies and the black men. The latter were Dez's men, crafty and malicious inmates, who thought they ran the prison because they had control of the drugs, and ergo the power. The druggies were putty in their hands and would do anything Dez said, just to have their regular source of heroin.

Willie detested Dez, and the feeling was mutual. As far as possible, they kept away from each other, but Willie wasn't stupid, and if he had an afternoon nap, he would wedge his door shut with the rubber from an old trainer, to guard against the risk of being stabbed in his bed. He looked at Henry and tried to lip-read, but he wasn't completely au fait with the gypsy lingo. But their body language said a lot – they were on edge.

Unexpectedly, Tatum came bounding over, his whole demeanour leaving himself wide open. Being loud and animated did you no favours in prison; it was regarded as an opening to be challenged.

'Good shot, Richard!' he said, as he slapped Ricky hard on the back.

Willie noticed how Tatum's intervention had a devastating effect on the youngster's spirit. His shoulders slumped, and he observed the fear in the lad's eyes. It was so sad to see, and it pricked Willie's nerves.

'Oi, mate, d'ya mind? We're playing a game.'

Tatum held out his hand. 'All right, mush. Me name's Tatum. I'm his stepdad.'

'Oh yeah? More like a fucking monkey's uncle. I know who you are. We met earlier!'

Tatum lowered his hands; slipping them inside his tracksuit bottoms, he backed away. 'All right, mush. I was just being friendly.'

Willie looked back at Ricky. The downcast eyes and trembling hands told Willie that the lad knew Tatum and was terrified of him.

'I don't fucking do friendly!' spat Willie.

Ricky remained still and listened to the sudden silence, too afraid to look up. He knew how violent Tatum was; after all, he'd often been on the end of a quick punch to the ribs. A livener, Tatum called it. He'd witnessed Tatum bash a city slicker with a bat, nearly crushing the man's skull, during a robbery that had gone very wrong. Fortunately, they'd all managed to get away with that one. He was only ten at the time, but it was so shocking. He couldn't get the image out of his head of the poor man, dressed in a grey suit and holding his briefcase for protection, squirming around on the pavement. Tatum beat the screaming man with the bat so viciously that the blood from his head splattered everywhere, and a clump of hair matted with blood became stuck to the weapon. That violent act had terrified Ricky. From then on, he would do whatever Tatum said.

'No need to be like that, mate. I'm a stepdad to him,' said Tatum, as he turned and tapped Ricky on the arm. 'Ain't that right, boy?'

Still unable to look up, Ricky slowly nodded.

'See, mush! Anyway, Mouse, when you're done, I want yer to meet me cousins.'

Willie flicked his eyes from Ricky back to Tatum. He could easily sense that the boy was almost shitting himself and it angered him. This young lad was being wound right up, and all because of Tatum, the cocky twat, who had no clout. As for family, it didn't wash with Willie: no young lad should be scared of their father or stepfather. His own little boy wasn't scared of anybody, and that's the way it should be.

With his eyes narrowed, Willie watched Tatum walk back to Henry, who wasn't looking best pleased himself. The man suddenly grabbed Tatum by the collar and pulled him close, his face twisted in an angry snarl, as he whispered something in

Tatum's ear. Tatum looked back at Willie and suddenly put his head down, realizing he was being warned.

'Your shot, kiddo!' said Willie.

That word rang bells in Ricky's head; kiddo was a name that was like a warm blanket wrapped around him. He looked up and gave Willie a half-smile.

Willie knew then that the lad needed his help. He'd been bullied. Willie hated bullies.

After two more rounds of pool, Willie noticed another group of black guys who had appeared and were glaring over. The original four had increased to eight. Sitting at a table and surrounded by these foot soldiers was Dez. He had a clear view of Ricky.

Ricky, who was preparing his next shot, felt the atmosphere change. He looked up and followed Willie's eyeline. With quivering hands and his heart beating furiously, he held his breath. Willie was alone with just a snooker cue, and there like a pride of lions ready to attack him was Dez and his crew. Everything went very quiet as Willie and Dez held each other's stare. Ricky looked over at Tatum and Henry who were also watching the standoff.

'Got a problem, Dez?' shouted Willie, with a menacing growl in his voice.

The laugh that came from Dez's mouth was mocking. 'Yeah, as a matter of fact, prick, I do. That table is reserved for me from three o'clock onwards!'

Willie tapped his cue on the floor. 'Unless you're Her Majesty the Queen, then no one gets to reserve this table.' His voice changed from a dark tone to a sudden laugh that made Ricky jump. 'But then, again, ya fucking fudge packer, I reckon you are a fucking queen!'

At this point, some of the inmates hurried away. The gypsies remained, and the men surrounding Dez got to their feet, standing with their shoulders back and their legs apart, ready for a ruck.

Willie wasn't fazed at all. But Dez's wide, angry eyes shot to Ricky. 'Size ten, yeah?'

Ricky had no idea what that was supposed to mean, but Willie did. He held the cue like a bat. 'You dirty stinking wanker.'

Unexpectedly, Willie swung around and glared at Tatum. Taking five long, fast strides, he grabbed Tatum by his hair and dragged him over to the pool table. 'Ya want the boy as ya bitch, you have to go through this runt first. He's his ol' man. Ya know the rules.'

Tatum was trying to pull Willie's hands from his hair. 'Get off me!' he squealed.

Willie, however, didn't listen to Tatum – his eyes now back on Dez. 'The boy's fucking eighteen years. He ain't twenty-one. He's a boy, ya bastard!'

Dez laughed again. 'He's on the men's wing, so that makes him a fucking man!'

Willie let go of Tatum, who by now was in well over his head. His cocky stance and animated moves had disappeared, and he stood there looking sheepish. But Willie wasn't done with him yet.

'You, ya tit, asked for the kid to be on your wing 'cos he's family. Ain't that right?'

Tatum felt his face redden. He'd thought that by having Ricky on the wing with him he would have a gofer, or, if he felt inclined, he could sell him off to someone else – that someone being Dez. What he didn't bank on was any interference from a lump of a man by the name of Willie Ritz.

'Well, yeah. I wanted to take care of the boy, yer know. I wanted to see 'im all right.'

With one quick movement, Willie snatched Tatum by the back of his head and slammed his face onto the edge of the pool table, leaving the man stunned and nursing a bloody nose. Staggering back, with a look of horror, he mumbled, 'What the fuck was that for?'

''Cos, you're a cunt!'

Immediately, a screeching of chairs and mumbling of voices caught Ricky's attention. The men surrounding Dez were looking behind Ricky and Willie. Then, Ricky heard the deep husky voice of a man shouting, 'Oi, Ritzie! Got a spot of bother 'ave ya, mate?'

The voice was followed by another – a softer and more controlled one, from behind Ricky. ''Ere, son, give us the cue.'

Ricky glanced up to see a clean, smart-looking man who was shorter than Willie, with devilish eyes. He was roughly in his mid-forties, and despite his shorter size and stature, he wore the kind of confident expression that a Mafia don would wear. And then another man was suddenly by Willie's side, a stocky man with huge muscles, who put Ricky in mind of Popeye, or the Michelin Man. Bald and mean-looking, he resembled a pit bull, ready to go for the kill.

Dez looked uneasy and so did his followers. But he wasn't going to back down. Ricky was bemused because Willie and his friends were clearly outnumbered. But he could sense the clout that these three older men had, and yet, oddly, he wasn't afraid of them; in fact, he felt totally unafraid. And, if he'd had the courage, he would have stood by their side like a gladiator.

'I thought one scar on your fucking ugly boat was enough!' hollered the short muscly man.

Dez sized up each one. He sniggered and nodded. 'And you, Stafford, ain't the man for the job, are ya? It'll take a bigger fucker than you to take me down!'

Staffie looked at Lou and laughed. 'Lou, shall we tell him?'

Lou laughed along. 'Nah . . .' He nudged Willie's arm. 'What d'ya reckon, Willie? Shall we tell him?'

Dez was fuming. As far as he was concerned, he called the shots: he ran the drugs, the hooch and the phonecards. Men came and kissed his feet, if he asked them to. Yet Willie, Staffie and Lou were laughing at him – and worse, he had no idea why. Most inmates wouldn't have dared, but there was something about these guys, something dangerous. Usually keeping themselves to themselves, they worked out in the gym or played cards and generally kept a low profile. Dez was only too aware of their reputation and their power, though, especially when they united to form the dynamic trio.

Willie threw his head back and laughed as if he was hysterical, a sure sign he was either mad or on drugs. But Staffie and Lou knew that when Willie was in one of his insane moods, he was unstoppable, and, more often than not, they had to pick up the pieces.

'Nah, lads, let the fudge packer find out for himself.'

With intense anger, Dez jumped up, knocking a chair aside, and his jaw tightened. 'You're a dead man, Willie Ritz!' he spat, as he pushed his men aside.

'Well, I'm 'ere, ya prick, so come on, take me out.'

But Dez was now storming up the staircase, as Willie called after him, 'Nah, you ain't got the bollocks. You're a sneaky mother-fucker who only stabs people on the sly. Oh, and by the way, the boy's a size nine and he's wearing *my* trainers.'

The other men disbursed, leaving Tatum still nursing his bloody nose. Lou was shaking his head and Staffie was frowning. 'What the fuck was all that about?'

Willie nodded to Ricky. 'Me new little mate 'ere. Dez tried to buy him with trainers and that little shit of a man, his so-called father, sold him.'

Tatum edged his way back. 'No, yer got it wrong. Dez offered him protection. He said he'd look after him.'

Willie lunged forward, wanting to smash Tatum again, before Lou stopped him. 'No, Willie. Scum like that'll go screaming to the governor and you'll end up down the block,' came Lou's voice of reason. 'Leave him. Come on. Let's go.'

Before they had a chance to remove themselves, Officer Blair's voice echoed along the lower wing. 'Ritz, back to your cell!' His boots on the concrete floor sounded like a marching soldier. He was quickly joined by two other officers. Willie remained like a stone statue, still gripping his cue and glaring at Tatum.

Blair then grabbed Willie's arm. 'I said, go back to your cell!' He turned to Staffie and then Lou. 'And you two go as well!'

As if he had just snapped out of a trance, Willie blinked. Sneering at Tatum and shaking off Blair, he headed for the metal staircase.

Ricky's whole body vibrated with fear, too frightened to stay for fear of repercussions from Tatum. He quickly followed Willie up the staircase and along the wing. Willie stormed ahead, beside himself with fury, and as soon as he entered his cell, he slammed the door shut. Ricky stopped dead in his tracks, feeling awkward. He couldn't go into Willie's cell and he was nervous to go back down the staircase. He looked at the caged light, the next one on from Willie's cell, and poked his head gingerly inside. There, on the desk, was his plastic bag. This was his room. He shot inside and shut the door, leaning against it. The only way he could think of to jam it closed was to use his toothbrush. He retrieved it from the shelf, and then he rammed it under the door and yanked at the door handle to see if it had done the job. It fitted perfectly. At once, his shoulders relaxed, and as he sat on his bed, he managed to calm his pounding heart.

A few moments later, he heard a knock at the door. His body went rigid with fright. He held his breath. Another knock followed and still he wouldn't budge. He watched with his eyes on stalks as the door was forcefully pushed, but, thankfully, the toothbrush held it shut.

A low, threatening voice from the other side of the door said, 'Bad move. Dez ain't happy. He wants a word, and ya got 'til lights off to see him.'

Ricky was now shaking from head to toe: this was all such a nightmare. There was Dez and his mean-looking henchmen, and Tatum with his cruel scornful look that had implied 'Just you wait', and now Willie had shut the door on him. He tried to rationalize things and thought maybe Willie didn't know he had followed him up the stairs. The avalanche of worries consumed his thoughts until he heard another voice.

'Oi, what the fuck d'ya think you're doing? Get away from the kid. You make threats, and I'll make fucking promises.'

Ricky felt relief like never before. He had a big man backing his corner. It was madness; he'd not even done a thing wrong, he'd just kept his head down, and now, with not even a word because he couldn't speak, he felt a war was about to ensue.

Willie banged on the door. 'All right, Richard?'

Ricky leaped from his bed and pulled the toothbrush away from the door, allowing Willie to come inside.

'Sorry, matey. I had to go back to me cell before I did something I might regret. Good ol' Lou keeps me in check. He's that voice that sits on me shoulder and says "Don't do it."'

The fretful expression and hands clenched so tightly told Willie that the kid was a nervous wreck. 'Listen to me, yeah? I think I need to explain what went on down there, 'cos you look like you ain't got a clue.' He walked over to the chair and sat himself down. Ricky noticed how long his legs were.

'That 'orrible bastard Dez thinks he runs this nick. He was a Face at Wormwood Scrubs 'cos he had his two older brothers there with him. They're Yardies, and, to be fair, they are hard. Anyway, he lives off his brothers' reputation, so he has a load of arse-lickers running a business in 'ere. The scag heads do his running around for a bit o' gear, but – and this is the issue – that wanker likes boys. The younger and prettier, the better, and never of his own colour.' He stopped talking. Pulling out his tobacco pouch, he began making a roll-up. Then he eyed the boy, waiting for him to take it all in. He knew he wasn't retarded, just mute and scared. 'Now, Dez can offer you protection, and he will do so, all the while you're his bitch sucking his dick.'

Ricky suddenly went pale and his eyes widened like saucers.

'Yeah, I thought you'd be shocked. So, when he offered you

trainers, the minute you accepted them, he would call you his bitch. It's like a favour for a favour, but, in his case, a pair of fresh trainers means he can call that favour in every day of the poxy week.' He licked the fag paper and glued the edges to make a perfect roll-up. Looking it over, he grinned and then placed it between his lips, lighting the end and puffing furiously. 'I tell you what though, son. He couldn't have done that without running it past your ol' man, 'cos, believe it or not, there are rules inside, and you shouldn't by rights be on this wing. Ya need to be over twenty-one, but since you came in with ya father – or stepdad, whatever he is – he has the right to have you on his wing. The cunt gave Dez permission to have you working for him, whatever that meant.'

With a sudden reddening of his cheeks, Ricky was indignant.

Willie took another drag and sat up straight. 'I ain't in the habit of sticking me nose in people's beeswax, but I've got a son. Liam, he's called, and if he were inside, I'd make sure that he was looked after. See, that fella that looked like someone's shoved a tyre pump up his arse and blown him up to one hundred bar, that's Staffie. He's a good mate of mine and he's got a boy an' all. That other fella, the one that talks like a lawyer with narrow eyes, that's Lou Baker, another close pal. He's got twin boys, and so you can understand why we would look out for ya. Anyway, what I'm trying to say, without me mouth running away with me, is this. If you need our 'elp, you come and find us. And do yaself a favour. Try and stay in our vicinity. Come to the gym, eat with us, and just kinda hang around. That Dez won't fuck with ya then.'

He leaned back again and puffed on his roll-up. A comfortable silence put Ricky at total ease. He had taken a real liking to Willie. There was something so natural about him. It was a feeling he'd never had while living on the site with the travellers. He'd always considered himself an outsider who would never fit in. The way they talked and joked, it wasn't him at all. The quick Romany sayings and shady dealings made him cringe. He didn't belong and never would because he knew he came from another culture – he just didn't know what that was. Jackie had brainwashed him so much, he couldn't even remember his own real name.

He remembered his mother calling him Richard, among other names, like 'retard' and even 'goofy bastard', and Tatum and Tyrone calling him Mouse. His last name was Menaces, but he even doubted that to be true. His memory was vague, but he wondered if before moving to the gypsy site in Ireland he'd perhaps had a past.

The recollection from all those years ago of being sick and waking up in a small room with a bed, a wardrobe, a chest of drawers, and the distinctive smell of newness was somewhat unclear. It was hauntingly strange, and as he focused on his mother, even she appeared different. Her once-blonde hair was now jet black. She spoke differently, her words were faster, and there were some he didn't recognize. He would never forget the moment when he asked her why she was calling him Richard. "Cos that's ya fucking name, ya scabby little brat. Now, shut up with the questions. If you ask me one more time about ya father, then he'll end up locked away for a long time, or dead, so not another flaming word. Ya name's Richard Menaces, end of.' Whatever happened after that, he simply couldn't recall, except for the fact that whenever he was about to open his mouth to speak, no sound would come out.

As Ricky listened to his new idol, his eyes were distracted by the figure at the door. He nervously looked at the person who was standing there. Willie clocked the anxious expression on Ricky's face and followed his gaze. It was Tatum, with Tyrone just behind him.

Willie was like a rat on speed. He jumped to his feet and stood in Tatum's way. 'What the fuck do *you* want?'

Tatum was holding a pair of trainers. 'I got me boy some decent footwear.'

Tyrone, the image of his father, was there for backup, but the aggression plastered over Willie's face caused him to shrink his shoulders and lower his otherwise cocky gaze.

'Oh yeah? And where the fuck did those trainers miraculously appear from, eh? There's only one bloke in 'ere that keeps a stock of fresh Nikes and that's Dez!'

Tatum held the bright-white trainers like an offering. 'Nah, straight up, bruv. These were me boy Tyrone's, weren't they, mush?' He looked at Tyrone, who sheepishly nodded. 'Also, Richard's got a visit with his dear ol' muvver. I've arranged a VO on the gate. She worries, so if she sees the boy looking cushty, it'll ease her mind.'

Willie looked Tatum up and down. 'If you're lying, I promise you, you'll regret it!'

Tatum furiously shook his head. 'I swear down, it's the truth, bruv!'

Willie smirked. 'What's with the fucking straight up and swear down? What are ya, a fucking jack-in-the-box? I'll give the kid the trainers, but I promise you this. If they are from Dez, I'll shove them down ya throat without an anaesthetic. Got it?'

Tatum didn't move. He just smiled as Willie snatched them.

Chapter 25

When the buzzer went off again, it was morning. Ricky could hear men outside on the corridor walking and laughing. Willie knocked. 'Are you up, lad?'

Ricky was awake and pulled his tracksuit bottoms on to open the cell door. He smiled at Willie, who looked scruffy with his hair sticking up in all directions. 'Grab ya toiletries. I'll escort you to the showers.'

Ricky quickly did as he said, and as he turned to grab the towel hanging from the metal bedstead, Willie noted the scars on the boy's back. They were so horrendous that it made him shudder and gave him even more reason to look out for the kid.

'Sorry, son. I didn't mean to startle you, but those scars look nasty. I know there's no point in asking how ya got them. Ya can't speak.'

Ricky turned to face Willie. If only he could find his voice to tell him what had happened.

Then Willie realized that Ricky hadn't even tried on the trainers because the laces weren't tied up yet.

The shower cubicles were empty except for Staffie. He was lathering his bald head, much to the amusement of Willie, who teased him.

In their company, Ricky felt safe to get showered. Staffie handed him a bar of soap. 'All right?' he asked with genuine concern.

Ricky smiled and held up his thumb. Ricky was unaware of Staffie staring at him longer than he normally would.

After the shower and some breakfast, Ricky felt much better. It was the unknown that he was probably more afraid of. Once the routine was sussed out, he would become familiar with his surroundings. By twelve o'clock, he had enjoyed time with Willie and his friends, playing more pool and learning the art of poker. He wasn't looking over his shoulder anymore because he believed they had his back. The friendship that was beginning to blossom was like an answer to his prayers, and he was beginning to feel more at home in their company – certainly more than he'd ever done working with Tatum or living with his mother for that matter.

The card game was interrupted by Blair, who pointed towards Ricky with a cold stare.

'You're on a visit, so follow me. I'll take you over.' Ricky got up and followed as ordered, leaving his friends to carry on with the game.

'I dunno what it is about that kid, but . . .' Willie put down his cards, paused, and chuckled. 'I must be going soft in me old age.'

Staffie looked down at his pair of queens. 'It ain't that, Willie. I feel the same. Maybe it's 'cos the poor fucker can't talk.'

Lou slapped his last card down. 'That's four aces.'

Willie pushed him hard, nearly knocking him to the floor. 'Ya fucking did it again, ya cheat. Jesus, why I play with you, ya sneak, I don't know. Ya probably had that ace up ya sleeve before we even started.'

Lou laughed. 'Well, you should 'ave been keeping your eyes peeled . . . I like the kid. There's something about him, 'cos he don't come across like the other pikeys, does he?'

'Nah, he don't. Anyway, that bastard Dez is after him, and I for one ain't gonna let that 'appen. And there's another potential war on the horizon. Mike hates Dez with a fucking passion, and when he gets here, I can guarantee blood will be shed! He ain't gonna forgive him, and he certainly ain't forgotten that Dez burned all but one of his photos of Ricky. Mike doesn't know Dez is 'ere but he'll be fucking gunning for him.'

Staffie chuckled. 'Cor, I can't wait. It's gonna be like old times.'

But Lou had his serious face on. 'Mike's changed, you know. You saw him in the Scrubs. He's lost the fucking plot since Ricky . . .' He struggled to say the words. 'He ain't the same. He's angry and fucking dangerous.'

Staffie reshuffled the cards. 'Well, that may be so, but he's still our Mikey, and we can straighten him out and keep him on the right road to make sure he's granted parole.'

* * *

As Ricky embarked on another new experience – the visit – he felt a little lost. All his life, he'd been told what to do and where to be and had no way of arguing about it. So this part of prison life was actually quite comfortable. He waited with other prisoners for his name to be called. Once it was, he walked from the holding area into a room that looked remarkably like a canteen. It was noisy and busy, with women, men and children all excited to see their loved ones. There, on her own, like the queen of the gypsies, sat his mother. With her black hair piled high and her oversized gold looped earrings, she reminded him of a younger version of Bet Lynch from *Coronation Street*, one of his mother's favourite programmes. Her skintight, leopard print dress, and the overuse of the sunbed, epitomized the old saying 'mutton dressed as lamb'.

She saw him there, looking taller and much more confident than when he'd stood in the dock at court. He strolled over, sat down, leaned back and grinned. He didn't try to embrace his mother, and Jackie, for sure, wasn't going to change the habit of a lifetime and be mother of the year.

He looked over at the tuck shop area and then back at his mother, who tutted, 'All right. D'ya want tea and a cake or something?'

He gave a nod, followed by a satisfied smile. She couldn't hurt him anymore. She wouldn't raise her voice and call him names – this was too public. For once in his life, he felt he had the upper hand, and he wondered if that was perhaps because Willie's confidence was rubbing off on him. The pats on the back and the ruffling of his hair when he won at pool or cards had certainly boosted his spirits and made him feel liked and proud.

Jackie toddled back in shoes that were far too high. Not only did she have to steady the tray, but she had to balance on her heels as well. He looked around at some of the other women and noticed how respectable most of them looked – in comparison to Jackie. Dressed in jeans or over-the-knee dresses, they appeared mumsy, each hugging their son or husband with a softness in their eyes, all so different from Jackie. He had long gone past the stage of wanting a hug or a kind word; he knew neither would come from his mother.

She pushed the cake and tea towards him. 'There ya go, Richard, and 'ere are a couple of chocolate bars.' Her voice had changed again, seeming to be sweet, but it was a complete sham, and they both knew it.

'How's it going, son? Tatum looking after ya, is he?'

He wanted to laugh, but he didn't; instead, he glared before shaking his head. Jackie was visibly uncomfortable. That was when he knew there was something on her mind.

'It's tough at first, but trust me, boy, Tatum will make your life easier. Ya won't know it, but he will.'

With a raised eyebrow, Ricky gave his mother a smirk, as if to say 'Don't bullshit me.'

Slyly, she looked around the room and then leaned into him. 'Listen to me. In a minute, I'm gonna hand you something, and then, when the coast is clear, I'll give you a nod, and you'll quickly stick it up your arse. Don't make a big thing of it. Don't draw attention to yaself.' She scanned the room and then slid her fingers up into her loose bun and retrieved a small package. She made a fist on the table. 'Take this from me, and when I say so, wait for the nod.' Her eyes then turned to meet his, but she frowned when she saw him slowly shaking his head, still with a stupid smirk on his face.

'What's up with you, Richard?'

His grin turned to a full-on smile, and again he shook his head.

'What you saying? Ain't ya gonna take this gear from me?'

Another shake of his head left her flummoxed. Her son had never said 'no' in his life. If he had, she would have given him what for, but she couldn't whack him in here. Through gritted teeth, she growled, 'Ya better had take it, or when you get back in there,' she nodded to the door where he'd come from, 'Tatum will rip you a new fucking arsehole. He's trying to make life a fucking doddle for you, so just take the parcel and do as I say.'

Under normal circumstances, that tone would have had Ricky almost shitting himself, but not today. He picked up the tea, took a swig, and then he unwrapped the sealed fruit cake and ate a big bite. Jackie was seething and it showed: her oversized breasts heaved up and down whilst she tried to keep a lid on her temper. 'For fuck's sake, Richard. Hurry up and take the bleeding parcel, will ya? My liberty's on the line, if I get caught.'

With new-found pride, he just shrugged his shoulders and took another bite of his cake, enjoying both the taste and the frustrated expression on Jackie's face.

'If you don't take this parcel, ya do know that there'll be serious consequences for ya, don't ya? You'll start a flaming riot, and I'll tell Tatum it's your fault. I will, Richard. I'll fucking tell him.'

Much to her surprise and disgust, Ricky finished off the last of his cake, snatched the two chocolate bars, and then, with the other hand, he picked up the plastic cup and downed the rest of his tea.

'Oi! Where are ya going?' she asked, in a panic.

He blanked her, turned around, and walked towards the door where Officer Blair stood.

'All right, Menaces? Are you ending your visit?'

Ricky nodded and held up the chocolate as if to ask permission to take it through. Blair glanced over Ricky's shoulder to see Jackie, with a face like piss and vinegar, trying to shove something in her hair. He then guessed at what had probably just happened. He winked at Ricky. 'Yeah, go on, take them with you, but just don't tell the others.'

The boy had just earned Blair's respect; he didn't look like a druggy, and he didn't show off a shitty attitude either.

* * *

Willie, Lou and Staffie were all informed that the sweat box from the Scrubs had arrived. They couldn't wait for their mate to join them – it would be like old times. They hoped.

As soon as the metal door started to slide aside and Officer Harris appeared, Staffie's eyes lit up; he knew that Mike would be right behind the officer. And there, holding a big see-through plastic bag, was a monster of a man. He was bigger than ever, with arms the size of tree trunks and shoulders wide enough to carry a man on each. His cropped hair had greyed, which gave him a more urbane look, but his dove-grey eyes told another story. As he looked up, a half-smile spread across his face.

Willie and Staffie patted him on the back. 'Good to see ya, Mikey,' said Staffie, with tearful eyes. Willie was hopping about, very excited, and Lou held out his hands, which were roughly snatched as Mike pulled him close and hugged him. In turn, he embraced each man, rubbing Staffie's bald head and giving Willie a playful punch to the ribs.

'Right, lads. Let me get settled in and we can then have a good catch-up. I think we've a lot to talk about. Oh boy, are you lot gonna be shocked!'

Officer Harris stood back and allowed the interaction. If it had been anyone else, he would have marched Regan past his friends and taken him straight to his cell. But this guy was too big to argue with, and he had been polite enough at reception.

Mike's friends walked with him towards his new cell, and the crowd either nodded towards him or looked in the opposite direction; either way, his presence was felt, and the news spread faster than a dose of clap at an orgy.

* * *

The feeling that he had finally stood up to his mother was like having a weight lifted off his shoulders. At last, he could stand up for himself – and that was just the start. What could she actually do to him, anyway? The answer was, of course, nothing. As soon as he was back on his wing, Tatum and Tyrone came tearing along the corridor to his cell. But, this time, their imminent arrival didn't have him quaking in his shoes, as it would have done before. He ignored their calls and headed towards Willie's cell with the bars of chocolate – it was his gift to the man for helping him.

Tatum hollered even louder. 'Richard! Wait up!'

Ricky still ignored him and was now outside Willie's cell, although the big man wasn't inside. Ricky felt the nerves creep back in, because there, arrogantly swaggering towards him, was Dez. He was on the landing, and as he walked, his shoulders moved in line with his hips, like a robot.

'Tatum tells me you've a parcel with my name on it.'

Shaking his head, Ricky composed himself with his feet slightly apart; he now had to make a decision – to run or to fight. He'd never thrown a punch in his life, and the size of Dez told him that if he did so now he was unlikely to win.

Dez stepped forward, licking his lips. 'Oh no? I think you're telling porkies.'

Ricky was fixed to the spot, but his curiosity got the better of him when he heard loud cheers coming from downstairs. He managed to look down below and saw there was some kind of commotion. Dez also peered over the edge, but then quickly pulled his head back in shock. Grabbing Ricky by the collar of his sweatshirt, he dragged him along the landing into his own cell. After he'd slammed the door shut and kicked a rubber wedge underneath, he threw Ricky onto the bed and took a few large lungfuls of air.

'You, ya little faggot, you're gonna give me that parcel. Then, you're gonna round up my men. I promise you that you'll have my full protection. Ignore that ugly tramp Willie Ritz, 'cos believe me when I say there's gonna be a riot in 'ere, and you, sunshine, will be begging me for help.'

Ricky stared at Dez, taking in what the man was saying but thinking about what he'd seen downstairs. He'd only had a chance to see his friends and another big man, as they'd marched along the lower level, before Dez had hustled him away.

'I ain't got time to fuck about. Give me the gear!' he snapped, holding out his hand and clenching his jaw.

Ricky tried to get up from the bed but was instantly pushed back down again.

'I ain't fucking about, boy. Where's the gear?'

The harsh shove in the chest winded Ricky. It was a serious wake-up call. It made him realize that Dez was so much more powerful than him, and he could easily rip his head off. Accordingly, Ricky curled up against the wall into a shell shape. Dez was becoming incensed, and this was apparent when a heavy bang on the door made him yell back, 'Fuck off!'

The door banged again. 'Dez, it's me, Tatum. Has me boy got yer gear?' he asked, with a nervous gurgle in his throat, looking towards his son.

Ricky was pleading in his head for Tatum to keep on talking;

381

it was at least providing a much-needed distraction and possibly creating attention on the landing so that someone might come to his rescue.

Whoever that man was on the ground floor, it was making Dez agitated; his eyes were flicking around like he was watching a bluebottle flying across the cell. Seeing Dez hop around from foot to foot, as if he had hot coals in his shoes, Ricky also noticed the beads of sweat across the cokehead's brow. Thinking quickly, because Dez was about to erupt like a volcano, Ricky tried to come up with a plan.

'Dez, is there a problem?' called Tatum.

With that, Dez bellowed back, 'Ya fucking son won't hand it over. He has two fucking minutes, or I will cut the fucking gear out of him!'

What Ricky was unaware of was that Dez's source of drugs had dried up. And so the only hope of a good snort was the parcel being sent in by Jackie. Dez was so addicted that he couldn't go a day without cocaine.

* * *

Officer Harris led Mike to the top of the stairs, followed by Willie. The officer's job was to show him to his cell and watch him walk in, but he had a load of paperwork to do. 'Ritz, you can take Regan to the cell. It's the last door on the right.'

Willie was overjoyed: Mike would be on his landing, four doors along.

Mike nodded. The last cell along the wing was ideal; he could hear anyone coming down the corridor. Just as Willie looked ahead, he noticed Tatum and Tyrone talking to Dez through the man's cell door.

'Aw, fuck me, Mikey, you're only next to Dez Weller.'

Mike, for a moment, went rigid. He then turned to face Willie. 'That cunt's in this nick, is he?'

382

Willie nodded, but by the look on Mike's face, he regretted telling him. All the good humour and banter had suddenly disappeared. It was replaced with a look of pure unadulterated anger.

'Listen, Mikey, he's built himself an army. Bide ya time, mate. Don't go in blind. You know what a sly cunt he is.'

Mike wasn't listening, his breathing now heavy as he flared his nostrils to exhale.

Willie knew full well that the man Mike detested most was Dez. After the vicious fight they'd had years ago, Dez was left with a scar down his face. Whilst Mike was put into solitary confinement, Dez burned all but one of his enemy's son's photos. It was an unforgivable act. Willie assumed that after three years, Mike would have calmed down and would perhaps just give Dez a beating, but the expression on his face showed that Dez was a dead man.

'Listen, Mikey. Don't do anything. Not just yet, mate.'

Coming from Willie, this seemed quite out of character. He was the reckless one, not Mike, but times had changed.

Mike shoved the plastic bag into Willie's chest. ''Ere, hold this.'

Tatum turned and gasped, holding his breath. Stomping towards him was a huge man, who not only looked like a big silver gorilla from the zoo, but he appeared as though he'd just escaped from one.

Willie hurried after Mike, seeing that Tatum and Tyrone were still nervously hovering around.

He grabbed Mike's arm. 'Wait, Mikey. Something's going on.' Suddenly, the worry of Mike letting rip and getting shipped back out had switched to concern for the kid.

'Who's in there?' demanded Willie.

Tatum just stared in awe at Mike.

Before Tyrone could sneak away, Mike grabbed him. 'You two were asked a question!' came the deep gravelly voice. Tyrone shook all over, never having felt the hands of a real man, who could snap him in half as if he were a piece of kindling.

Willie had Tatum by the hair and was pulling his face an inch from his own. 'I said, who's in there?'

Tatum didn't know who he was more afraid of – Dez or Willie. He remained quiet, but Mike, sensing Willie's concern, decided to take over. He backhanded Tatum across the face, and although it wasn't a punch, more of a slap, Tatum still felt his jaw cracking.

'Willie asked who's behind the door. Now, if ya don't fucking tell me, I'll open it with your face!'

That threat was a given and Tatum looked at Willie in terror. 'Er . . . Richard.'

With that response, Willie punched Tatum hard in the ribs. He doubled over and collapsed on the floor.

Mike didn't care who this Richard was; all he wanted to do was to get in that cell and rip Dez's head off.

Willie banged on the door. 'You'd better let the boy out, or I swear to God, they'll need fucking tweezers to piece you back together, ya bastard!'

There was silence.

Inside the cell, Dez glared at Ricky, trying to plan his next move. All he could think was that he had something they wanted, and he would barter it because, right now, Mike Regan was somewhere inside the prison, and one of his best buddies, Willie Ritz, was outside that door creating a scene.

Little did he know that Mike was also outside and getting angrier by the second. Like the Incredible Hulk, his body was visibly inflating. It was all the adrenaline surging through his veins. He was pumping himself up ready to smash the door down.

Mike studied the quivering Tatum and the even more terrified Tyrone for a moment before saying, 'Do one!' The two gypsies didn't need telling twice: they hurried away like two frightened rats.

'Who's Richard?' asked Mike, now very concerned by the incensed look on Willie's face.

'He's just a kid, an eighteen-year-old that can't speak. Dez has tried to buy the poor fucker.'

384

Mike frowned. 'Why have you got involved?'

Willie was now in one of his insane moods. "Cos he's a good kid and Dez is a cunt.'

Those were good enough reasons as far as Mike was concerned.

* * *

Ricky felt relief that Willie was outside, and although he was trapped, with Dez pacing the floor, he knew that help would be on its way. He couldn't figure out how they would open the door, though. He would have to do it, somehow. Whilst Dez continued to pace and Ricky clocked the panic setting in, he focused on the door, his only means of escape.

Willie bellowed again. 'Let him out. If you've touched that boy, I swear to God . . .'

Suddenly, Dez jumped up onto the bed and reached for the ceiling light where he kept his knife. He tugged away at the cover. In that moment of distraction, Ricky threw himself off the bed and pulled the rubber from the floor. But Dez now had a knife in his hand, and a moment later he was holding the blade to Ricky's throat.

The door burst open. In rushed Willie, with Mike's giant figure taking up the whole doorway. Dez held Ricky against a metal cabinet. 'Touch me, and he gets it.'

Ricky was wide-eyed and motionless as he looked at Willie, silently pleading. Then his eyes flicked to the man in the doorway.

It was to be a life-changing moment he would always remember, but it was such a warm feeling, as if he was being wrapped in a soft duvet. Those powerful grey eyes and that broad chest, they were so familiar. He even recognized the scar on the back of the man's hands, the shape of his fingernails, and the small mole on his temple. But it wasn't the physical appearance that he felt a connection with, it was the soothing sensation, along with the intense feeling of safety that he projected.

'Fucking let that kid go!' growled the big man.

Ricky recognized that voice too. As deep and harsh as it was, it was like a harmonious lullaby.

Dez dug the knife deeper. 'Get away or I'll slice his throat.'

As if Ricky had woken up from a bad dream, he didn't feel scared one bit. On the contrary, he felt protected. How mad was that? Being held up with a weapon to his neck, knowing one false move could kill him, he remained transfixed on the big man. It was as if there was an invisible shield around him.

Mike was seething. He wanted so much to break Dez's neck, but he knew if he grabbed him, Dez was reckless enough to kill the kid. Mike was so intent on stopping Willie from making a silly mistake, he hadn't noticed the boy's face.

'All right, what d'ya want, Dez?' asked Willie through clenched teeth.

Dez turned to them. 'You keep that animal away from me and you can have the boy.'

Mike grinned. He had no intentions of letting Dez off so lightly. That was until his eyes met Ricky's, and he blinked. Was he going mad? He thought of the photos of his beautiful son that had been cruelly destroyed and burned by Dez, and the images washed through his mind like an old black-and-white film. All the memories he'd had of his boy – they'd gone. Until now. Was he seeing the eyes of his own son, or were the lost images embedded in his brain? The photos, this young man, and Dez, they all seemed to merge into a strange feeling that seemed to be playing tricks on his mind. Mike stared for a second and the atmosphere grew tense. Willie was watching the strange questioning expression on Mike's face.

But Mike was in a trance, staring. Then, as if nothing around him mattered, he rolled up his sleeve and looked at the tattoo that stretched the length of his forearm. RICKY MY BOY.

Ricky's teeth began to chatter in shock. His face turned a deathly white and his eyes grew increasingly wider. He knew that name, that term of endearment, and the tattoo. He'd once fingered the freshly inked skin and recalled the feeling of wonder and pride. Unexpectedly, tears filled his eyes and cascaded down his cheeks, and he felt powerless to stop them.

Mike knew then it was no mind-fuck. He witnessed the lovable expression of pure innocence and the unmistakable look that had always melted his heart. Held by that blade was his six-year-old. It was the little boy with the round pearl-grey eyes lined with black lashes, the long floppy fringe with that distinctive cowlick, the shoes on the wrong feet, and his school tie skewwhiff. He couldn't let Dez kill him, not now he had him back. Before he laid into Dez, he had to save his son. He was always a man of his word, but not today.

'Okay, Dez. Let the kid go and I'll back off,' said Mike, calmly.

Willie and Mike slowly stepped back, away from Dez.

'I have your word, Regan, that you will let bygones be bygones and forget about the photos, yeah?'

Mike looked at Ricky and smiled. He had to play it cool. 'Yeah, I'm a man of my word. Fuck the photos. Just let the kid go.' His voice, although cold, was not angry.

Looking from Willie to Mike, Dez tried to understand if they were serious, but their faces seemed calm and their words believable. He sighed with relief and removed the blade from Ricky and stepped back. Willie rushed forward. He yanked Ricky by the arm, pulling him to safety. It left Dez nervously holding the knife in front of him.

Mike pulled Ricky from Willie and gently guided him away from the cell. Staffie and Lou, who had gone back to their cells to get the hooch and snacks for their small welcoming party, had been informed of the trouble on the upper level. They hurried up the stairs, meeting Mike, Willie and Ricky in the corridor. Willie quickly ushered them all into his cell. There was just enough room, and then Mike shut the door.

Staffie sensed the strange atmosphere. Lou, though, was oblivious – he'd already sampled the hooch and was slightly pissed.

Ricky and Mike were face-to-face, and then the others watched as Mike performed a bizarre action. He lifted up the boy's hair and smiled at the heart-shaped birthmark. Ricky allowed the big man to do whatever he wanted because he was beginning to believe something he'd never even dared before.

Willie looked at Staffie, his eyes full, and he nodded. Staffie's lip quivered. 'Is he? Mike, is he?' He was desperate to know.

But it was Ricky who had the answers.

'Dad?'

Red-faced and teary-eyed, Mike grabbed the boy and hugged him, rocking him back and forth. The words were stuck in his throat, along with the emotional lump. But Ricky, for the first time in twelve years, had found his voice.

Lou suddenly caught up with events. 'What the fuck! Is he Ricky?'

Staffie was crying and laughing at the same time. Willie had his hands over his face, now sobbing like a baby.

'Yeah, yeah, it's our boy. It's him. I fucking knew it. I fucking knew he was special,' cried Staffie.

Mike was silent, still rocking, with his son's arms wrapped around his neck – just like he'd done when Ricky was six years old, on that day he'd sent him to Spain.

Suddenly, Willie realized that Ricky had spoken.

'Ricky, you can talk, mate. You can fucking speak!'

Mike let Ricky go and looked him over. 'Why couldn't ya speak, boy? What the fuck's happened to ya? We all thought you were dead.'

Ricky wiped his eyes. 'I, er . . . th-th-thought, you w-w-were dead too.'

'It's all right, son. Take ya time,' said Mike, as he wiped Ricky's tears away.

'Sh-she-she said, if I m-m-mentioned your name, you w-w-would end up in prison or d-d-die. I never did. I never spoke a word after that, even when Jackie told me you were dead.' He smiled and allowed more tears to plummet down his face. Willie stopped sobbing and tried to compose himself. It was such an enormous relief to all of them. The dark gloomy cloud that had surrounded Mike had now gone.

'Are you talking about your muvver?' asked Mike, slowly.

Ricky nodded and then he smiled. 'Yes.' He didn't have to nod or shake his head anymore; he had a voice. 'Yes, sh-she moved us to-to Ireland to live in-in a caravan next to Tatum and Ty-Tyrone.' He shot his eyes to the door. 'Tatum ain't me-me stepdad either. He's her bit on-on the side.'

Staffie jumped in. 'Did they treat ya well?'

'No-no, they were ev-evil, but it doesn't matter now, eh? I-I've got me dad, I've got me-me uncles, and I've got everything I pr-prayed for.'

Trying to control his temper, Mike had to change the conversation or he knew he would ruin this precious moment. But in the back of his mind, he was planning a bastard end for Tatum and Tyrone.

'Dez didn't touch ya, did he?' asked Willie, knowing only too well that Dez was a dirty sod who would have fucked the life out of Ricky, given half the chance.

'No, you got there just in time.' His stammer had subsided, and now he could speak fluently, he was surprised by how deep his voice actually was. His mother's threat had triggered a major psychological blockage that had stopped Ricky from speaking. The fear that his talking would result in harm to his father had stopped him from speaking altogether.

Chapter 26

The first order of the day was for Mike to get on the phone and break the news. He'd intended to call home as soon as he'd arrived because a note had been left at reception for him. He'd only been in transit for two days – from Wormwood Scrubs to Portsmouth, and then, finally, to Maidstone. What with all the excitement over Ricky, there just hadn't been time to square the circle.

Mike dialled the number and handed the phone to Ricky. Gloria saw that there was no caller ID and knew the call was from the prison.

'Mikey! Thank God you called. Didn't you get my message? Oh, never mind. Listen. Oh, hang on a minute. Arthur!' she screamed. 'Listen, son, we have some news. Ya father's just coming. Are you at Maidstone now with the boys? Right. Here he is. We've got something important to tell you.'

Ricky was smiling because his grandmother hadn't even realized it was him; he'd yet to open his mouth.

Mike rolled his eyes. He knew what his mother was like for not letting anyone get a word in edgeways.

'Nan.'

The line went silent.

'Nan, it's me. It's Ricky.'

Gloria suddenly took a seat as Arthur, now very puzzled by her expression, snatched the phone from her hand.

'Hello? Mikey?'

'No, Pops, it's me. Ricky.'

Again, there was silence. Mike took the phone from Ricky and winked. 'Dad, it's me. I've got Ricky, Dad. I've got him back. He ain't dead. He's here with me, right now . . .' Yet another silence followed.

'Dad?'

Mike smiled. He could hear his mother screaming with excitement in the background.

'Dad, I've had a VO put on the gate . . . Dad, are you there?' He then heard his father sobbing. That was a first: never in his life had he seen or heard his father cry.

'Son, I'm sorry. We're just a bit overwhelmed, but is our little lad really okay?'

'Aw, Dad, he's fucking handsome. He's my boy all right. I got him back. He ain't changed, apart from being a few feet taller,' laughed Mike, as he ruffled Ricky's hair. 'Just come up and meet him. He's missed his Pops and Nan.'

Gloria had obviously reclaimed the phone. 'Mikey, put him on. Just let me hear the baby's voice.'

Mike laughed. His mother always referred to Ricky as 'the baby'.

'Here, Ricky. Your nan wants to talk to you.'

Ricky took the phone. 'Nan, I'm here. It's me. I missed ya, all of ya, and I can't wait to see you.'

Gloria had calmed her screeching. 'Is it really you, my baby?'

Ricky giggled. 'I'll give ya a clue: You are my sunshine, my only sunshine,' he sang.

'Aw, Ricky. You remembered.'

'Nan, I sang it in my head every night before I fell asleep.'

Gloria was now in floods of tears. 'Aw, now look what you've made me do. I'm a right mess, but, my baby, I will be there this afternoon. Oh my God. I can't wait!'

'See you soon, Nan. I love you.'

'Aw, baby, I love you too.'

As Mike said his goodbyes, he suddenly thought about Gilly. 'Mum, pick Gilly up on the way, will you please?'

'Yes, darling, of course I will. Oh, and you'll also need another VO. That's why we phoned. Mikey, we found Zara. She's alive, son! She's alive! Eric and ya father rescued her. She's here, son, with us.'

Ricky watched as his father fell to his knees, a deep sob escaping his mouth. 'Oh my God! Is she okay? Can I speak to her?'

Gloria could just about make out his words, as they were trapped inside his cries of joy.

Zara took the phone. 'Mikey, I'm safe. Your father found me. I was locked away, but I'm okay. And . . . I love you, but, Mikey, listen.' She paused to brace herself. She had to tell him, warn him, before they met up, so he would have time to get his head around everything. 'You may not want me now. I'm different now . . . I'm . . .'

Mike heard Zara's voice falter and a sudden chill went up his spine. What had happened to her? His mind was now in a crazy place, and he went back to those darkest days in solitary confinement. It was a time when, free from the distractions of normal prison life, he would focus on those who mattered most in his life.

'What happened, babe? What do you mean?'

Gloria was now standing close to the phone with her arm around Zara's shoulders. 'Go on, babe, it's okay,' she urged.

'Mikey, I've lost one of my hands. The arm is badly scarred. Don't be alarmed, though, please. I just wanted you to know before the visit.'

'Oh no!' he cried out. 'Oh, my darling, what did they fucking do to you? Jesus Christ!'

'Mikey, please, I'm fine. Please don't worry about me. I'll come and see you this afternoon, and I would love to meet Ricky. I'm so pleased for you, Mikey. He was all you ever wanted, and you've got him back.'

There was a pause, before Mike said softly, 'Not only him, babe. You too.'

She was so overwhelmed with hearing his voice and those words – after all those years of being locked away and dreaming of him – that tears flowed in streams down her cheeks.

They said their emotional goodbyes and Mike placed his arm around Ricky's shoulders.

Ricky could feel his father trembling with shock and relief. 'Is she lovely, Dad?'

'Yeah, son. I know she ain't ya mother, but—'

'Dad, as far as I'm concerned, I don't have a mother. Not a proper one, at any rate. Jackie was never a mother to me, she was . . . Well, let's just say I never want to see her again.'

Mike listened and tears began to well up. His son was a gentle young man with a big heart, and now he wanted to know what he'd been through – what kind of a life he'd had.

Just as they were about to walk back to Mike's cell, Staffie came over with Crayford, his personal officer and the most senior person on the wing.

'Regan, Stafford's informed us of what's happened, so I've organized a double cell for you two . . . I'm sure you have a lot of catching up to do.'

He couldn't comprehend how the man must have coped for the last ten years, believing his son was dead.

Mike nodded. 'Nice one, Gov. Cheers, mate. And can I ask another favour? I've got VOs on the gate. Can I add another one?'

Crayford nodded. 'Yeah, no worries. I'll sort that out for you.' He looked Ricky over. 'You know, my son's your age.'

The minute Mike and Ricky were alone, Mike told him to stay in his sight and never to leave his side.

'Dad, I've no intention of doing anything else. I prayed every night for you to come and find me, and now you have! So, well, I ain't going anywhere.'

Mike felt ready to cry every time he looked into his son's eyes. All those years, all that pain, and now he had him back. Nevertheless, he wouldn't forget, and he wouldn't let it go. Eventually, he would hunt down Jackie and make her life a misery. But for now, he wouldn't taint the good feeling. Tyrone and Tatum could also wait. He wanted time to catch up and learn everything about his son. But the strange thing was, even though they'd been apart for so many years, they weren't strangers.

The news spread like wildfire and Tatum, Tyrone and Dez kept well away. Tatum was tempted to call Jackie to give her the heads-up, but he sensed that his every move was being watched.

Unexpectedly, once Ricky and Mike had gathered their things and moved into their new cell, Crayford arrived. 'Sorry to inter-rupt but you need to fill out the forms and meet your brief. I've slotted you in for this morning, so you'll be done by one' clock, in time for your visit.'

* * *

Willie stayed with Ricky while Mike was being briefed by his lawyer. The lads had strict instructions not to let Ricky out of their sight. Staffie, a regular gym user, offered to show Ricky the ropes. Willie followed, but he wasn't one for lifting weights. Lou joined them as well because he'd just had a row with his missus and wanted to vent his anger. The gym was basic: there were a few crash mats, two sets of weights, three punchbags and two treadmills.

'Go on then, son. Let's see what you're made of,' laughed Willie, as he patted Ricky's back.

Never having been inside a gym before, Ricky looked around, unsure what to try first.

Staffie, however, was gripping the heavy punchbag that hung from the wall. 'Over 'ere, Ricky. Give us a few right hooks.'

With a chuckle, Ricky hung his head, slightly embarrassed. 'I've never boxed.'

'Well, there's no time like the present. Give us all you've got, and if you're anything like ya father, this punchbag will be bouncing around the room.'

Ricky loved to hear them talk about his father. It made him so proud. Then he had a thought: he wanted to make his father proud as well. Standing with his legs slightly apart, he pulled his fist back and punched the bag. It moved Staffie half a step back but nothing major happened.

'Ricky, come on, lad. There's more in ya than that.'

Ricky grinned. The truth was he never knew what he had in him. He knew he could lift a fridge up into the air and onto a truck unaided. His thoughts flashed to that sad moment in his life. He remembered being so cold. It was the day before it snowed, and his fingers were like blocks of ice. He'd been passed a safe made from lead, which needed the combined strength of Tatum and Tyrone, and he'd very nearly dropped it. But with one fluid movement, he threw the safe into the back of the truck, only to find one of his fingers had twisted out of shape, and the pain ripped through him. When he showed Tatum his bent forefinger, Tatum grabbed it and tried to twist it back into position. He screamed out in pain and was cracked around the head for making a noise that could have had them captured.

Just as that memory diminished, there, in the doorway of the gym, stood Tatum, with his son behind him. Tatum didn't spot Ricky right away because he was partially hidden behind the huge punchbag.

Ricky's vision of the past and the sudden feeling that he wasn't afraid of Tatum or his son anymore pushed him to act. With his confidence at an all-time peak, he looked at Staffie and winked.

Glancing over at Tatum, Ricky whispered to Staffie, 'I have another punchbag, thank you.'

Willie was leaning against the wall, rolling a fag, when he spotted the two gypsies as they strolled in. Then he clocked the look on Ricky's face. As soon as Tatum saw Ricky, he turned to leave, followed by Tyrone, but Willie sidestepped and blocked the doorway.

'I don't want no trouble!' pleaded Tatum, with his hands up.

Tyrone was virtually shitting himself. He knew what he'd done to the boy. All those years of belittling him and bullying him were now coming home to roost, big style. He and his father were surrounded by real men, who would fuck them over in a New York minute. With his legs wobbling like tits on a belly dancer, he could feel his heart racing nineteen to the dozen.

Willie sniggered. 'No trouble, mate. Go on, you can use the gym. I'll tell ya what. Why don't you spar with young Ricky here? Ya know, show him how it's done, like.'

Tatum slowly turned to see the cocky look embedded on Ricky's face; it was not an expression he could ever recall seeing. Ricky was always the nervous skivvy, walking with his head down and his heavy mop of hair hiding his eyes. Not now, though; the kid was upright, with his shoulders back, sporting a daring look.

'Nah, nah, I'm all right, I was just gonna do a few press-ups.'

Willie grabbed his arm. 'Maybe ya didn't get my drift, did ya? The boy wants to spar, and so do you. Now fucking get over there.'

Tatum was forcefully shoved over to Ricky. Tyrone tried subtly to squeeze past Willie, but he had no chance. Willie snatched his hair. 'No, sunshine, you're gonna wait here, ya fucking little prick.'

Staffie and Lou stepped back ready because if Tatum landed a nasty punch then they'd poleaxe him. But it was written all over Ricky's face that he was going to give the gypsy a good pasting.

'Ahh, come on, Ricky, you ain't into fighting. I don't wanna hurt yer, boy . . .'

Tatum's arrogant words ripped through Ricky like a hot knife through butter. He took a deep breath, ready to make a move, but Tatum got in first with a blow to Ricky's stomach. Ricky bent over for a second, but instantly straightened up and grabbed Tatum by the hair and dragged him to the floor, where he pulled his fist back and gave the man two cheek-cracking blows. 'Take that, you bastard!' Then, jumping up, he pulled his leg back and kicked Tatum in the face so hard, he knocked him out cold. 'And that!'

Ricky went to launch into him again but was pulled away by Staffie. 'All right, tiger.'

The sight of Tyrone glaring with his mouth wide open spurred Ricky on. There was unfinished business to be done.

'And you, ya fucking pikey, you're next,' screamed Ricky, as he pulled away from Staffie and ran at Tyrone, ramming him into the wall. Fiercely pulling his head back, he head-butted Tyrone so hard that Tyrone's eyes instantly rolled back and he faltered. But Ricky wasn't finished. He pulled the lad upright with one hand and with the other he threw a rib-cracking punch that lifted Tyrone off his feet.

Astonishingly, Tyrone steadied himself and put up his fists; that was a bad move.

The older men watched in admiration as their young protégé proceeded to launch Tyrone into the air with an uppercut to the chin that would have made Amir Khan sit up and take notice. Now, Tyrone was out cold as well.

Staffie stood gobsmacked, Willie laughed, and Lou was rooted to the spot.

'Well, if he ain't Mikey's boy, then I don't know who is,' said Staffie, easing Ricky away.

'Catch ya breath, boy. Let's get you out of here. Those two scumbags'll no doubt grass.'

Willie spotted the officer who oversaw the gym; he was on his way down the corridor. 'Get Ricky outta here!' He looked over at a few men who were using the weights. 'They started it, yeah?'

There was a sea of nods; no one was going to argue over a few pikeys who weren't even liked.

Staffie and Lou hurried Ricky away. Willie stayed behind, as cool as a glass of iced tea. Johnstone, the senior officer, bowled into the gym and almost jumped when he saw Tatum out cold and Tyrone now recovering but groaning and holding his face. Johnstone looked at Willie. 'What the fuck happened?'

'Ahh, nothing, Gov. These two pikeys were having a row and it got heated so they bashed the fuck out of each other.'

Johnstone, an ex-army screw, frowned. 'Oh yeah? Really?'

'Ask them,' said Willie, pointing to a few of the onlookers.

Johnstone watched as they each in turn nodded. He rolled his eyes. 'Clear the gym and get back to your cells.'

Willie left with a smile on his face and pride in his heart. Ricky was a Regan, through and through.

* * *

The news reached Mike as soon as he returned to the wing. He tore along the landing to his cell to find his son and the lads talking over the event.

As soon as he stood in the doorway, he bellowed, 'I fucking told you lot to keep an eye out for me boy. Now I've just been told he's had a punch-up with Tit and Tat.'

Staffie was still grinning from ear-to-ear. 'Mikey, we didn't let him out of our sight. We were all there. Nobody would have hurt him. Anyway, ya boy's your fucking double. I reckon it would have taken the three of us to hold him back. He's like you, Mikey, just like you. The boy can fucking handle himself.'

Mike looked at the smile on his son's face. Ricky wasn't jumping up and down showing off; he sat there controlled and calm.

'It's okay, Dad. It's just something I needed to do. They deserved it. I didn't do it for no reason.'

Mike sat on the bed next to his son and ruffled his hair. He recognized there was quite a lot of himself in the boy. 'I know, son.'

* * *

By the afternoon, Ricky was excited and his true character, which had been constantly suppressed, was showing through. He laughed and had a smile that even his mother had never seen. After he brushed his hair and washed his face, he bounded down the landing behind Mike, ready to meet his grandparents.

Willie met them by the pool table and put his arm around Ricky. 'Now listen, boy, your nan will smother you in kisses and leave lippy all over ya face, so take it and smile. I wish I was a fly on the wall just to see their faces. They're gonna be so chuffed.'

Ricky grinned. 'I'll enjoy every one of 'em. I never thought I'd see any of you again. I've never had a hug or a kiss since the day Jackie took me away, so it's time for playing catch-up.'

A sudden sadness clouded Willie's face. It hit home that for most of his life Ricky had been deprived of the love that he'd had in such abundance in his early years.

He hugged the young lad and kissed the top of his head. 'Go on, then. Enjoy it, sunshine.'

* * *

As Mike and Ricky walked into the visiting room – as father and son – even they could not have predicted the welcome they were about to receive.

Ricky heard his grandmother shriek, 'He's 'ere!' She didn't care who heard or what anyone thought, as she jumped from her seat and almost threw herself at her grandson. Just as Willie had predicted, she plastered his face in kisses. 'Ahh, my baby, look at you.' She held him away to study him, the tears streaming down her face.

Arthur was by her side, awaiting his turn. He clutched Ricky's face, the tears beginning to form. 'Ahh, kiddo, you're just like ya old man when he was your age. I would've recognized you anywhere.'

Struggling to get up from her seat, Gilly gripped her walking stick. Gloria hurried back and helped her up. 'Go on, Gilly, give the boy a hug.'

Gilly was painfully thin and had shrunk into an old woman. It was a pitiful moment that made Ricky begin to cry. Very gently, he pulled her into his arms. 'Ahh, Nanny Gill, are you not well?'

Gilly couldn't speak. The lump in her throat was strangling her. She'd let herself go completely. After the news that they believed Ricky was dead, she'd given up caring for herself because she had nothing left to live for. Gloria and Arthur paid regular visits and had ensured her house was refurbished, as instructed by Mike, but she was so depressed she would forget to eat.

But Gilly's face instantly changed at seeing her grandson looking at her so affectionately. The truth be told, she'd expected to go to her Maker without ever seeing her adorable Ricky alive again.

'I'm well now, my boy. You've made me better just knowing you weren't d . . .' She choked, not able to say the words. 'Was ya mum good to ya, though?'

Ricky wanted to say, 'No, she was a bitch', but he saw the frailty and fear in Gilly's eyes and instead he just smiled. 'Yeah, Nan. I was fine. I just missed you lot.'

Mike knew then that his son was a special person; he cared for people.

As he glanced over his mother's shoulder, he saw Zara and Eric walking towards them. She was dressed in a long-sleeved black shirt and jeans. Right away, he saw that she was thin and her face was gaunt. To him, though, she was still the most beautiful woman alive.

He was determined not to cry, but the last two days had been so overwhelming, he couldn't hold it back. With his arms outstretched, he allowed Zara to fall into them. It felt so natural. 'Oh God, how I missed you,' he whispered.

'I missed you too, Mikey, so much. But you have to see my arm, before anything, because I completely understand if you can't bear to look – I can't even look at it myself.'

She tried to pull away, but he wasn't finished with the embrace. 'I don't care, Zara. I wasn't in love with your hand, you know. It was everything else.' Yet she had to be sure, and she knew when he saw the disfigurement, his expression would cement how he really felt.

She managed to release Mike's grip and then rolled up her sleeve. She was silent as he stared at the remains of what must have been a horrific ordeal. To her surprise and joy, he held her arm, brought it to his mouth and kissed it. She knew then that he meant it.

So many years inside, Mike had gone over and over the past. He'd realized that his biggest mistake was in marrying Jackie, when all the time he'd still been in love with Zara. He wasn't going to make another mistake. Although he wasn't yet divorced, he was determined to pop the question, regardless.

His voice cracked. 'Marry me, Zara. I love you, and I want you to be my wife. I don't have a ring, but when I get out of here, I want to get married.'

Gloria and Arthur were gripping each other's hands, waiting for her to say 'Yes'.

Zara turned her head to look at Mike's son, almost as if she was asking his permission. With his eyes round and excited, he nodded for her to say that all-important word.

'Of course, Mikey. You know I've wanted nothing more.'

Ricky jumped up and hugged her, and a strange emotion came over Zara.

They were a family.

Eric patted his brother's back. 'Congratulations.' And he meant it. He owed so much to Mike, after he'd dropped him like a hot brick when Mike had needed him the most. Nevertheless, hearing Mike's proposal to Zara still jarred him and he realized deep down, it was never to be. She was Mike's.

As Mike hugged his brother, he whispered, 'Thank you, Eric. You got her back for me.'

Eric lowered his head and forced a smile. In his heart, he had helped to get Zara back for himself. Trying to sound upbeat, he replied, 'It was her brother Ismail who had her locked up, and that Guy Segal and his son, the fat ugly cunt. But I promised I'd send them to you, Mikey. They're gonna be facing prison. They're all yours, Bro.'

'And Tracey?'

Eric looked over at his mother who was fussing over Ricky. 'Tracey's dead, Mikey. No one will ever hunt us again. It's over!'

'No, it's not over, Eric, trust me on that one. You watch what happens when I get out. Every Jew that worked for the Segals – every pikey that protected Jackie – I will fucking annihilate.'

Acknowledgements

Robert Wood for his patience and tireless editing, to make the book the best it can be.

Deryl Easton for all her sound advice.

My family for being there for me.

The NotRights book club for their wonderful support.

Nia Beynon for believing in me.

Turn the page for an extract from
Deceit by Kerry Barnes . . .

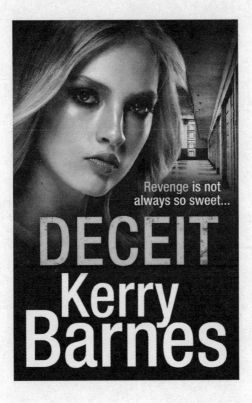

Revenge is not
always so sweet...

DECEIT
Kerry
Barnes

Prologue

With her eyes shut tight and the cover over her face, she held her breath and listened to the creaking, as the door to her bedroom slowly opened. She could smell his aftershave, that intoxicating smell that lingered after he would leave. A smell she had learned to detest. Each slow, deliberate footstep was like death itself creeping up on her. Small beads of sweat peppered her brow as she lay there, desperate for the nightmare to be over. Yet, as she felt the bed sink, she knew then it had only just begun. Another night of terror.

His slimy words and hot breath made her shudder, as he pulled back the covers and brushed his bristly chin against her cheek. She kept her eyes tightly closed and gripped the quilt in a vain attempt to prevent revealing her body that was barely covered by the thin nightdress she was wearing. She was conscious of her breasts. They had just started to develop, not big enough for a bra but not small enough for a vest. Still, she was aware that they were there, and so was he, as he ran his large calloused hands over her.

She winced and wanted to yell, but the fear of death was more frightening. He whispered those dark, cold words, 'Scream and you will die. No one will believe you; no one cares, but me. I love you, my little darling. No one will love you as much as me. Now, let me show you how much I love you.'

She pushed her head deeper into the pillow, unable to look at his ruddy face and those narrow, brown, lifeless eyes. Over and over in her mind, she said, 'Please go away, please go away.'

The wind banged the open window, and for a second, she was back in the room, and his heavy body, like a devouring octopus, lay across her. She fought to drift off to another place, deep into a storybook she'd once read, but the loud bang made her jump again.

As she tried to turn her tear-stained face to the side, she suddenly saw an eye, staring in through a partially opened door. She recognized those eyes, and begged and pleaded, with the terror on her face, for the person behind that door to rescue her. But that figure with its sorrowful look disappeared as quickly as it arrived and only intensified her fear. She was all alone, and she was powerless to prevent this and other sordid acts from continuing. Why? Because she was a child, and he was an adult . . . a monster.

Chapter 1

The cold wind ripped at her face and through her thick Ralph Lauren camel coat. Kara quickened her pace, cursing under her breath, 'Damn the fucking car.' She rarely swore in public, but this freezing cold morning, she felt like screaming obscenities. The bus stop was a short distance and rather than wait for the AA man, she headed off, determined not to be late for work.

Just as she reached the end of her close, she noticed a woman, the same one she'd seen staring at her in Tesco yesterday. Dressed in a long black coat and black gloves, the tall fair-haired lady grinned. Kara was about to say good morning when the woman curled her lip and smirked. Baffled by the odd interaction, Kara looked away. She put her head down and continued.

As she hurried along the main road that separated the private development from the council estate, she pulled her hat down below her ears to stop the wind biting and giving her an earache. The bus shot past her, and her heart sank. She felt like crying. First, the car wouldn't start, and now she'd missed the bus. She contemplated going home and calling in sick, but she'd had two days off last week with that excuse and it wasn't going down too well with her manager.

The only other option was to cut through the estate and catch another bus; they were more frequent from the other side. She had only ever done this twice before and both times had been a nightmare. On the first occasion, she was almost in the middle of a war between two families hurling bricks at each other, and on the second one, she was chased by a pit bull. Luckily, the owner managed to stop the dog in its tracks before it sunk its teeth into her. Even so, it frightened the life out of her.

She stopped at the kerb and faltered for a second before crossing the road. None of the winos would be out this early, the teenagers would still be asleep, and so she made a decision to go for it. Besides, she was frozen to the bone, and waiting another half an hour would really cause her to spin on her heels and return to the warmth of her home. She stepped off the pavement, making her way through the estate. It was so gloomy and dingy she felt as though she had entered a *Mad Max* film.

Why the council couldn't help these people by adding a play area or fixing the broken windows was beyond her. It saddened her to think that the poorer members of society were shoved into homes like these. It reminded her every day that they had nothing.

She passed the first block and was almost knocked down. A woman pushing a buggy wasn't looking where she was going because she had her neck craning over her shoulder, shouting up at the top maisonette, which was three storeys high. Kara looked at the baby in the buggy and smiled.

'You're a right no-good, a fucking wrong 'un, Billy Big Balls. I swear on me muvver's eyesight, you'll not fucking see me or the baby again, ya dirty cunt!' screamed the woman. Then, she turned to march on and glared at Kara, looking her up and down and making no bones about it. 'What are you fucking gawping at? Ya fucking snob!'

Kara was stunned. Before she could answer, the woman pushed past her, still shouting foul-mouthed insults. Glancing down at her expensive coat, long real leather boots, and Louis Vuitton handbag, she felt self-conscious and out of place. Again, she felt near to tears because she wasn't a snob.

She looked up at the man hanging over the balcony with a white vest and his arms covered in tattoos. 'Julie, get back 'ere, ya fucking stupid bitch. I ain't gone anywhere near ya fucking sister!'

'Go and fucking hug a landmine, ya rotten dirty scrot.'

Kara looked away and carried on ahead. The main road was now in sight, as she hurried her way through the rubbish, dirt and debris. Luckily, the bus arrived a minute or two later. The heat hit her, as she stepped on the bus and paid the driver. Instantly, the warm air made her nose run and her cheeks tingle. She got herself comfortable and waited for the driver to pull away.

But there was a hold-up. Kara looked out of the front window to see the mother with the buggy running down the road waving her hands to stop the vehicle. Kara smiled to herself. The woman had so much nerve to run down the middle of the road, swearing at the drivers of the two cars that hooted at her. The doors flew open and she hopped on, dragging the buggy behind her. 'Cheers, mate. Cor, it's fucking taters out there,' she said, out of breath.

The bus driver obviously knew who she was. 'Off back to ya muvver's, Julie?' he asked half-laughing.

Still struggling to find her purse, she replied, 'Yeah, that fat cunt has been sniffing around our Sharon again. I'm off up there to give her a fucking thump. Er, Tom, I think I've left me purse at home.'

Kara felt in her pocket for change, ready to offer the woman's fare, but the driver replied to the woman, 'Just get on, Julie.'

Kara watched as the skinny woman, dressed in a tight tracksuit and a body warmer, tugged the buggy and plonked herself onto the side seat. On the back of the buggy was a big bag that she dived into; she retrieved a dummy, sucked it clean, and stuffed it in the baby's mouth. Kara noticed the woman's hands were shaking and discerned the sores around her mouth. Her hair, tightly pulled back in a scruffy bun against her pale skin, did her no favours whatsoever. Two huge loop earrings dangled from her ears and a stud had been inserted through her eyebrow.

The woman noticed her staring and glared back. 'Do you know me or what? Ya keep staring, ya nosy prat!'

Kara looked away and stared out of the side window. Her intention wasn't to be nosy; she actually felt sorry for the girl.

As they approached the next stop, another young woman was waiting; she was so much like Julie, they could have been sisters. As soon as she hopped on, she plonked herself next to Julie. 'All right, Jue, where ya off to, then?'

Julie was searching through her tatty-looking fake Prada bag. 'Me muvver's, to see that skanky sister of mine. I found fat boy's phone with text messages on it, and I swear, it's her again. Well, she's gonna get it this time.'

The other girl was chewing gum and smiling at the baby. 'Jue, why don't ya just leave him? I mean, if it ain't ya sister, it's some other slag.'

Julie sighed and looked at her friend. 'Diane, where the fuck am I gonna go, eh? I can't live at me ol' gal's. My flat is all I 'ave, and that fat cunt won't get out. I wish he would get so pissed, he falls over the balcony and kills himself, or, I swear, one day, I'll give him a helping hand.'

Kara couldn't look at the girls; instead, she stared out of the window and listened to them talking about a world far removed from her own. She counted herself lucky that she had a job and money. Her life could have been so much worse. She had worked so hard though to get to where she was. Constantly studying – while everyone else her age was having fun enjoying parties, clubbing and sports – had been a huge personal commitment but a necessary one to have the options in life she both wanted and needed.

Fortunately for her, the next stop was just ahead. So, as soon as the bus came to a halt and the doors flung open, she jumped the two steps and instantly threw up, luckily missing her coat. *Where had the time gone?* she wondered. She should have waited for the AA man.

Eventually, she was through a security gate and inside her lab, ready to get to work. Her lab was the biggest in the building and situated at the end of the corridor; opposite was the office that her manager occupied. She knocked and entered, as she always did, but was surprised to see two men dressed in dark suits in the middle of a conversation with Professor Roger Luken.

'Ahh and here is Kara Bannon,' said Roger, swinging on his swivel chair that had almost worn down to the sponge cushioning. His ruddy complexion was stark against his pure white mop of thick hair. He was a fit-looking man for fifty-eight, and yet, with his white lab coat and red spotted bow tie, he did appear to be every bit the mad professor.

Kara smiled nervously, not aware of who the visitors were.

'Kara, this is Dr Chan and Professor Naughton. They flew in early this morning. They are here to discuss moving the research project over to Denmark. I have told them all about your work and they are eager to see the set-up.'

Nervously, she smiled again and her hands felt clammy. She wasn't used to working alongside strangers or being unprepared. Roger knew what she was like: she was meticulous, well planned and organized. Her boss must have known weeks ago. Under normal circumstances, he would have given her plenty of notice, but after the horrendous blunder she caused a few months ago, their relationship had changed. He wasn't so accommodating or friendly. She missed the banter and how he used to treat her with care and father-like kindness.

'Oh, I wasn't expecting . . . er . . . I mean, I haven't prepared.'

Roger waved his hand. 'Oh, don't be silly. They just want to see a dummy run. Besides, you will be leading the project in Denmark yourself.'

Kara raised her eyebrows and forgot herself. 'What do you

mean, Roger?' Her eyes darted from the visitors back to the professor.

It was Dr Chan who spoke up first. He could see how uncomfortable she was. 'It's lovely to meet you, Kara.' He put his hand out to shake hers. Flat and subdued, she returned the gesture.

'We think the assay that you have designed will fit in very well with our research and we would be honoured if you would work with my team to ensure we have the system operating at its maximum potential. There are always teething issues, and so it would save us time if you were to initiate the project.'

Kara tried to take it all in, but her sickness was back again, and the waves of nausea were washing over her and filling her with dread.

Roger firmly got up from his chair and turned to face the two men. 'Would you excuse us, gentlemen?' He guided Kara out of the room and into her lab. 'What's the matter with you? You look as if I have asked you to go to the gas chamber.'

Kara studied his concerned face and felt a twinge of guilt. She let out a weary sigh, as her eyes fell to the floor.

'I'm sorry, Roger, I didn't mean to appear so ungrateful. I just don't like surprises. You know me, Miss Fussy Pants.' She attempted to laugh it off.

For the first time, she saw the annoyance spread across his face. 'Kara, if you turn this down, then I am afraid you won't be able to continue with your research, including your own project.'

Those words were enough to wake her up and bring her back down to earth. 'Of course, I'm happy to go to Denmark and help set the project up. I was just shocked, that's all,' she replied, with forced cheerfulness.

Roger gave her a cold stare. 'Kara, you know how this works. You must be ready to work overseas at a minute's notice. These projects are not for us to run. You know they are designed here and used at the company's other sites. You are in a very privileged position. Many others would chew my right hand off to have the opportunities you've been given. Now, don't mess it up.' He shot her a warning glare that sent a shiver down her spine.

Kara was upset that he was teetering on being angry with her. She felt the burning vomit rising again, and without a word, she fled to the toilets and threw up. Ten minutes later, she returned to the lab to find Roger, with a pipette in his hand, already setting up the assay. He glanced over his shoulder with a look of disdain and she felt gutted to have disappointed him. The only thing she could do was put a smile on her face and take over.

'Right, where have we got to?' She squeezed past Roger and the two visiting researchers, before pulling on a pair of rubber gloves.

'I have just coated the bottles with T12 cells. Are you happy to take over?' He gave her a false smile.

Kara nodded and mouthed the word 'Sorry'.

By lunchtime, she felt exhausted and was glad Dr Chan and Professor Naughton were ready to head back to the airport. She much preferred to work alone. It was even harder making polite conversation with two strangers. She loved her job but liked peace and quiet to concentrate. Part of her work involved designing routine tests to identify various strains of viruses that may have mutated. She used tissue culture, a layer of human cells, to coat the flat-bottomed bottle, and then she added the viral samples, before further contaminating the bottle with various bacteria.

The results were promising, as they demonstrated whether the virus had the capability to infect the specific bacteria or attack the human cells. This determined the level of mutation. As the most senior bacteriologist in the team, with the exception of course of Professor Luken, it was also her job to test random samples of vaccine batches. Holding a position of great responsibility, she was also allowed to do her own research, which was funded by the company. It was a project that would hold her in high esteem among the top scientists.

The tearoom at the other end of the corridor was quiet. Most of the staff had gone to the main canteen. Kara pulled sandwiches from her bag and examined the limp cheese and bread, which had been made soggy by the overripe tomatoes. She threw them back into the box and pulled out an apple. Kara was startled by her mobile phone, which vibrated in her back pocket. She'd forgotten she'd had it on silent. As she struggled to answer it before it rang off, she didn't look at the number, assuming it was Justin, her boyfriend. 'Hello?' She tried to sound upbeat.

However, the voice that greeted her was anything but upbeat. In fact, it was chilling. 'Kara, Kara, perfect Kara, how's dearest Justin?' A cold, sickly chuckle ended the call.

The apple fell out of her hand and rolled under the table, as Kara stared at the number. The voice was unrecognizable but the call had come from her mother's phone.

Before she had a chance to call back, Roger popped his head around the door, and as soon as he saw her there alone, he came inside and sat opposite. 'So, what's going on, Kara? You have been offish for weeks now.'

Her face was blank. She seemed to be staring aimlessly.

'Kara, are you listening to me?' he growled.

His raised voice snapped her out of her daze. 'Weeks?' she mustered.

He ran a hand through his long wiry hair and nodded. 'Yes, Kara, weeks. You have messed up three tests. Luckily, I realized and corrected your mistakes before the results went out. And I haven't forgotten the serious cock-up with the pigbel drugs.'

She bowed her head in embarrassment. That really was a huge mistake and one she would never repeat.

'It's not like you. Usually, you are meticulous, and to be perfectly frank, you're faultless, but you cannot afford to mess up. These are safety class four bugs and you are trained in this area because you are so good at your job. If this keeps happening, Kara, you will have to go back to quality control.'

'I am really sorry. Look, I will go to Denmark and sort myself

416

out. I've just been feeling unwell. It's some dodgy virus I picked up from Papua New Guinea. When do I go?'

Roger stood up to leave. 'Tomorrow night. The flights are booked. A car will pick you up at seven o'clock, and you will be away for two weeks or longer, if need be.' His words were flat and not his usual endearing tone. Kara then heard him outside laughing with Sam James, the lab technician. Her heart sank. Roger usually laughed with her, but not today, and in fact not for a while now. She couldn't really blame him. It was her own fault – she was the one being distant. However, her pride wouldn't let her confide in him the reasons why she was not herself.

After making a cup of tea, she sat back on one of the mismatched chairs and sniffed away the tears that were ready to tumble down her face. The thought of going to Denmark for two weeks left her desolate. How could she sort things out with Justin if she was away in another country?

But there was also something else bothering her – that weird phone call. The only other person who ever answered her mother's phone was Lucille, the carer. But the caller's voice, although somewhat similar, had such an unearthly tone to it.

Continue Zara's thrilling story in
The Rules and *The Choice*

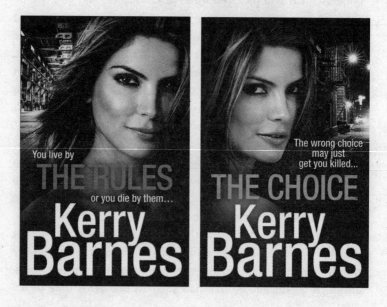